Kingdom Planet

The Final Kingdom

Kingdom Planet

The Final Kingdom

El Cid

Kingdom Planet

The Final Kingdom

This book is a work of fiction. Named locations are used fictitiously, and characters and incidents are the product of the author's imagination. Any resemblance to actual events or places or persons, living or dead, is entirely coincidental.

Published by
Lighthouse Christian Publishing
SAN 257-4330
5531 Dufferin Drive
Savage, Minnesota, 55378
United States of America

www.lighthousechristianpublishing.com

Other books by ElCid

The Big Lie - Publish America ISBN 978-1-4489-5137-6

Darkness Is Not Eternal - Publish America ISBN 978-1-63508-928-8

Chapter One
"DISCOVERY"

It was raining hard and the cold wind lashed at my face. As I stood there in the wee hours of the morning in a torrential downpour it didn't make a whole lot of sense, but in my emotional state, I really didn't care. There weren't any cars, trucks, buses or people moving - only the night creatures scurrying around trying to find shelter. The empty streets looked like a movie scene showing the aftermath of a town in the old West when all the cowboys had gone. There I was with my black Fedora pulled down low over my forehead and my trench coat collar pulled up high. I looked up at the tall gray office buildings that lined up like soldiers in formation creating an image of serenity and I thought to myself how ironic this appeared when just a short time ago there was anything but peace here. Why I continued to stand there getting soaked to the bone, when I came to my senses it all came together just how traumatized I was.

Standing there reflecting on the night's earlier events, my thoughts kept playing over and over in my mind like a scratched record. The thoughts seemed to project themselves onto the tall buildings as the rigid steel acted like a giant mirror reflecting them back to me. I don't know what's going to happen now, but whatever the outcome is going to be, the recent events I witnessed have provided a stark harbinger of future possibilities. As I vividly recall the night's events, the throbbing in my head grows worse and I struggle to remain standing. Slowly, I mentally walk backward in time trying to remember how I got here.

It was only a few months ago when everything seemed to be going along fine. I came to this city about two and a half years ago, almost to the day, having accepted employment at a prominent and highly touted international chemical company. Arriving here as a total stranger, with very little monetary resources at my disposal, I moved into a small apartment in the uptown section of the city. The neighborhood wasn't anything like the realtor's picture in his office. His verbal description painted a different picture also saying that this was the place to be if you're going to live uptown. I figured it would just be a temporary situation until I got myself settled in the new job, so I took it. Actually, for the rental price, the unit wasn't that bad although rather small. However, each morning when I stepped outside it was an adventure seeing what I might find roaming the streets.

Lenox Terrace was the name of the apartment complex and you could find characters here running the gamut from the sophisticated hustler to the poet laureate. Being raised in a small rural community just outside a metropolis in South Carolina, making the transition to big city life was challenging at first, but I managed to get the hang of it after a while. My growth however, was not without experiencing the games that people play here, especially when the street hustlers get wind of a country boy at large in the big city. I paid the price for my naiveté' more times than I care to set down in my memoirs, but it didn't take too long for me to discover that if I was going to survive here, even for the short time I intended to stay, I had better learn the way of the wise quickly.

I didn't have a problem meeting new people because I was always an outgoing sort and really kind of nosey. But now when I look back on my life, some of those that I met, I wish I had left them as strangers. This is not to say that everybody I encountered tried to take advantage of me, but the few who were bent on doing that, I discovered had the most diabolical schemes in their minds. There were a few people I got close enough to, to call friends but even with them I never got so close that we could share the things that were really embedded deep in my mind. One of those I could call a friend, was a cab driver I met at one of the social gatherings given by a neighbor in my building. If I had to give credit to anything here, I must pay tribute to the parties. From the first time I attended one at the invitation of someone I met at work, to the most recent one where I had this enlightening encounter, I always enjoyed the festivities. I learned more about people just being at those settings, than I had in the twenty-nine years of growing up in my South Carolina home.

Music at these parties was usually jamming and of course the latest of what everybody was dancing to was always on the turntables. Between what was being made available from the liquid refreshments to the quasi sugar to the refined plants being smoked, there were hardly any attendees who didn't get what they came for. As for me, I never got into partaking of the last two products but certainly became well accustomed to the variety of liquids that could elevate your psyche to the point where tomorrow never mattered. It was the result of one of my nights of heavily indulging myself with what had become my favorite beverage made by a gentleman whose first name was Jack, that I learned of the plot that was to take me into a world I never knew could even exist simultaneously with the one I knew. It was during a conversation with some co-workers that I found out more in this informal gathering than I did at any meeting I attended in the office. In the relatively short time I had worked there I had come to like the company and thought everything they did was great. Now hearing the things that were being said about the firm was really surprising.

At first I thought when the discussion turned to some things the company was doing, that here were some disgruntled employees who were venting their disappointments and frustrations and exaggerating the situation all because they weren't getting what they wanted. But when the talk started to center on a product that the company was developing specifically aimed at taking out a large segment of the national population, even though my mind wasn't entirely clear, the subject of the conversation began to resonate with me in a most interesting way. Still being relatively new with the company, I hesitated to offer my input on the matter because I knew there were a lot of things going on that I hadn't been exposed to. So I kept quiet and listened intently trying to gather all the information I could. The talk held my attention for a while, but as the night went on and the party got more intense, the topic's interest waned as other things caught my eye and grabbed my attention.

As the hour got late or actually early into the new morning and people were starting to disperse, just before I left to return to my own apartment, someone slipped a note in my pocket. I didn't discover it until I was home undressing and getting ready to retire for the night. When I looked at the note and who it was from with my weary eyes what it said didn't make sense so I tossed it on the night table and went to bed.

I awoke later that morning and my head was crying out for relief from what felt like a construction project going on inside. Jackhammers were pounding at full force. As I got up and stumbled into the bathroom to find my blue box with the plop, plop, fizz, fizz in it, I started to recall bits and pieces of last night's conversation. I picked up the note and looked at it again. This time when I read it began to make more sense than it did last night, but I still wasn't able to put it into any proper perspective. Slowly the talk and the words in the note started to come together. I poured some water and dropped the tabs in my glass waiting for the bubbles to clear then I sat down in the kitchen and reread the note again. What it was telling me was that in the position I held as a quality control manager assigned to new products, I should find out more about this new drug the company was starting to develop. I pondered the idea and decided that maybe I should check this out.

It was Sunday morning and I didn't have anywhere special to go but this note really started me thinking about some of the things I had seen recently in the office that I hadn't paid much attention to until now. Normally on a Sunday I would just fix myself a big breakfast and then lie around waiting for the day's sporting events to come on television. But today, the big breakfast was out, because my stomach wasn't ready for anything like that and probably wouldn't be until late afternoon. So, I decided to down a couple of pieces of burnt toast and some orange juice followed by a strong cup of black coffee and then hope for the best. The correlation that I was forming from the message in the note and the recent activities in the office was beginning to really peak my curiosity. Since it was part of my inquisitive nature anyway I thought I would wait for my self-medication to take effect and then go down to the office and do some investigating. This would be a good time, the golden opportunity because none of my colleagues I surmised would be there.

About an hour later, after returning to bed and listening to the Sunday morning news reports on the radio, I was beginning to feel like some relief was kicking in and my head was returning to some semblance of normalcy. I got up showered then dressed and made my way to the elevator. Living on the sixth floor in this building was always a gamble that the elevator would be there when you wanted it. And then, even if it happened to be stopped on your floor, the other part of the wager would be that it would move once you got in. I counted it as my lucky day when not only was it there when I got to it, but when I pressed the button to go to the first level it actually responded.

Maintenance here never seemed to have a very high priority for the super who I suspected was really also the owner that no one ever saw. He would always place the blame for things not getting fixed or done on this absentee landlord. Most of the tenants hardly complained anymore, especially those that had been living here for some length of time, because they knew that nothing was going to be done until it got done, so why bother voicing your dissatisfaction. In addition, most of them had outlived their original lease and were on month to month agreements so they were afraid to get to vocal or they would be out in a month or two. I sympathized with them because though this place was hardly the Taj Mahal, for the area I have to admit it was one of the better buildings.

I arrived at the lobby and made my way outside to witness the bright sunlight of this brand new day. As usual, the Sunday morning crowd moving around the streets consisted of the righteous churchgoers making their way to worship, the ones that called the streets home every day and were always out there, and then there were those who like myself were still recovering from the previous night's indiscretions. Many were walking either to the store to get some relief or to find someplace to begin the party all over again. I looked around for a taxi cab but was not surprised when I couldn't find one. Even during the week when you would think the drivers would know they could get a quick fare ferrying people from here to midtown, but there were few who came up here regularly. I was fortunate though to get a steady driver for during the week because I had met a cabbie named Alex at one of those parties who agreed to come and get me every morning. His rate was reasonable so we struck a deal and soon became friends. But being today was Sunday I didn't even bother to look for him or for the bus that ran only once an hour either.

Since no cabs were around, I started walking the three blocks to the subway entrance. I really hated the subway because I could never get used to walking down into this big hole in the ground and getting into an electrified steel box that was going to hurl me through some dark tunnels. As I descended the stairs I encountered the usual assortment of cave dwellers that were either content to just hang around the platforms seeking a handout or some others who were eyeing each entrant examining them to see whether this could be an easy prey. Even on a Sunday, it was no different. Occasionally, I would see a couple of police officers casually walking down there but the appearance of them was usually infrequent. My train arrived in just a matter of a few minutes and I stepped into the car and was on my way. After just a few stops, the A train brought me to the place where I would get off. Since it was Sunday, not many other riders were getting off with me but they were continuing on downtown or to that other borough on the far side of the bridge.

I got off walked down the platform and up the stairs back onto the street again to face the bright sunlight.

Reaching the top of the stairs coming out of the dark hole it was like I had entered into Oz compared to where I had just come from. The difference between the clean streets and the well maintained office buildings here as compared to the litter strewn roadways and the dilapidated units needing attention in my area, was like night and day. It always made me chuckle to think that the DPW (Department Public Works) only cleaned up between 34th and 110th streets; anything before or beyond that was on its own.

From the subway stop to my office building was just a short walk and the fact that there was no competition in getting there today made it an easy trek. Once inside I presented my credentials to the security officers maintaining weekend duties at the receptionist desk in the lobby and after a brief chat, I made my way to the first bank of elevators that would take me to the twenty-first floor. On the floor I walked down to the end of the hall where the main entrance was for the company. Although we occupied the whole floor and had several entry points, this one entrance was reserved for weekend workers. These were the people who were either trying to catch up what they didn't get done during the regular work week or for those who were having problems at home and this was the only place they could hide out for free. As for me, I was probably the only one there whose motive for coming in fell into neither category.

I walked through the large glass doors of the office suite and was met by the company's own security force who greeted me with a surprised look because I was not one of those who made it a habit coming in on a weekend.

"Good morning Mr. Powers how are you?" he said. "It must be something really important to bring you in here on a Sunday morning."

"Hello Dave, I'm fine thank you. Yeah, I'm working on a new project and I wanted to get a jump on it before the others got involved. You know what I mean."

"Yeah, I guess so. You want to jump the competition before they steal your thunder, right?"

"That's one way of putting it. Now sign me in please and let me get started."

"Okay, right away Mr. P."

He turned to his computer and punched in some information then gave me the nod to proceed down the hall. At the front of my office I looked at the sign on the door and beamed feeling a sense of pride. Even though I had been in this office a while now I was still basking in the feeling that I had arrived because here I was in the big city with an office that had my name on the door. There it was in bold letters, "Ronald L. Powers – QC Manager." To me the L in my name stood for "lots (of)" to go along with my last name even though the powers that I had here were extremely limited. I opened the door went in and sat at my desk to map out some strategy on how I was going to accomplish the spy mission I came here for. It was not like I had keys to everybody's office and on top of that I wasn't sure where to begin. After sitting there for several minutes, I decided that perhaps the one name that had been mentioned at the party would be a good place to start.

Reginald Codey was the name dropped at the party and his office was right near mine, so I thought that would be a good place to start. Reggie was the primary buyer for raw materials that the company used in making many of the drugs that we produced. His job was to find places that first of all had the goods and second willing to give the best deal. Often his investigative discoveries took him to other countries and he would be travelling for extended periods. However, when he returned he always went straight to the head man before debriefing anybody else. It never occurred to me until I heard his name at the party that what he did was anything out of the ordinary. But now as I thought about it and observed others who had similar functions, none of them went straight to the top before apprising his team of what he had.

I got up from my chair and eased my way over to his office and tried the door. To my surprise it was unlocked. Before entering, I looked around to see if anyone was watching then stepped inside. There was nothing unusual about the arrangement of his office nor was there anything that suggested wrong doing. His desk was neat and clean and all of the file drawers were closed. I felt a little silly at this point and started to turn around and leave when I noticed some papers crumpled up in the wastebasket. I figured since I was already inside why not be thorough so I picked up the papers and unraveled them. Scribbled on two sheets was something that appeared to be some type of code. The main portion of the body alluded to the purchase of something that was to be sent by air freight on an expedited shipment. On the second page there were the big bold letters "P.T.D.T. Y."

I folded the pages up and put them in my pocket. Since they were already in the garbage, I didn't think they would be missed. Not knowing whose office to visit next, I went back to mine to think. Once inside, I began to ruminate on just how information flowed around these offices. Then it dawned on me that there was rarely anything that was done, said or even mentioned that did not go through one of the ladies in the secretarial pool. So I made a beeline over to that area and starting snooping around. First I surveyed the in boxes for anything that appeared interesting, next I looked in waste baskets, and finally on top of file cabinets. Nothing stood out until I came to the desk of Kathryn O'Malley or Katie as she was known by the group. Tucked in the seam of her desk blotter was a document, a memo still in stenographic form but clearly indicated in bold letters in three places were the letters – P.T.D.T.Y.

After seeing that memo on the desk of the secretary to the Vice-President of Consumer Products, who also was my boss two steps removed, my curiosity was peaking and by this time my earlier medication was beginning to wear off. My headache was returning, so I decided to put away my Sherlock Holmes persona and return home. As I reversed my entry procedure and stopped at the security desk, I noticed the clock on the wall indicated it was now 3:00 O'clock. How quickly the time had passed and I didn't even realize it. The security officer said goodbye, signed me out and I headed toward the subway.

The next morning, Monday, I got up bright and early at my usual 6:00 O'clock hour. Although I wasn't due in the office until eight, I liked to have a casual breakfast, check out the news and relax a bit before heading out. Today was different. After what I saw in the office yesterday, so many thoughts were running through my mind it was difficult to relax. I took the scraps of paper I found in the office and the note given to me at the party and put them in my briefcase. Then I showered quickly, dressed and sat down to eat. At the office, I believed I might have more success in putting the pieces together. I finished breakfast, downed my second cup of coffee looked at the clock and walked out the door. I checked the time because I knew Alex would be pulling up just about now. He was always punctual and this I liked about him.

I walked out of my building into another bright sunny, but brisk, fall morning and looked for my ride. Sure enough like clockwork, I spotted him making his way through traffic headed my way. The car rolled to a stop in front of me.

"Hey mon, whaz happnin?" he said as I opened the door and got in.

Alex was a quiet guy from all that I knew about him. He was quiet in a way that was respectful but not rude. He had something about him that I liked even from the first day that we met, which was not too long ago. For the last three months he had been coming uptown to pick me up and deliver me to the business world. He never said much, but I knew we shared feelings just in exchanging the few words we did. It was like he would say something and I would be able to relate to it so much that I could almost finish any sentence he started. Although we bonded, we were different in a way that bound us together.

"How are you today my brother?" I said, talking to his face in the rear view mirror.

"Mon, dis rat race gittin tuffer eva day. Las week de boss mon pays me $350.00 dollas and I git a hunderd in tips. No mon can continue to live in dis city makin dat kine a dough. Sometime I feel like drive in up to the Chase Bank, make a big long term loan and run back to my island."

"Yeah, I know what you mean. Sometimes I feel like that too."

"You feel like dat? Naw mon, you can't feel like dat. You gotta nice job an you gwine somewhere. You jus needs ta stretch out and git outta that joint you stuffed in. Time soon you gonna wind up like the rest of dem folks dere stumbling through. How you manage to git dere anyway?"

"That's a long story and one day I'm going to tell it to you. But for right now let's just say that this is where I belong until I get a good hold on the handle that's going to pull me up out of there."

As we rode you could see the change in neighborhoods. The further we got toward midtown, the garbage and stench lightened and once again the streets got cleaner. The lighting got better and the air seemed to be purified from some invisible source that only worked in a small area of the city.

Alex pulled up in front of the tallest building on the block, known as Canon Enterprises where I worked. This was the Chemical Division. It was a normal corporation as corporations go, or so it was perceived to be from all outside appearances. The large glass revolving doors provided entrance into an inner world which so mocked the outside that upon first glance visitors all would agree that this is the way Corporate America should be. Only from the inside, the real inside, could anyone tell that what appeared to be happening was only a sham. The image just supports the old adage that things are not always as they appear to be.

When I first came to Canon I had been given the idea that this was the place to be employed. This was a place for someone like me to get started and rise to a place near the top of the corporate ladder. Little did I realize that the inner workings of this corporation had no plans for providing opportunities for me. The upper management network had other ideas about who joined the in-crowd and who didn't.

After Alex and I parted, I entered the building, checked in with the lobby security and started toward the elevators. When I reached my floor, I entered our office suites and greeted the regular receptionist.

"Good morning Lynn how are you today?"

The internal security officers were only there on weekends and after 6:00 PM weekdays.

"Good morning Ron, I'm fine thank you. Mr. Crandall would like to see you at 9:00 in his office."

Herbert Crandall was Director of Personnel, but I always suspected that he was into more than that.

I made my way down the hall to my office with still a half hour before meeting with Crandall. I opened my door and began to look around. Even though my door had been locked, it seems like someone had paid me a visit overnight. Things were not as I left them yesterday. I was very particular about how I left my office and where I put certain things when I finished. Someone had made a clumsy attempt at trying to arrange things as they found them but had not paid much attention to the little details. I never left pens out nor did I ever move the position of the pictures on my desk.

Then it occurred to me that someone who may have been at the party may think that I know more than I actually do about what the business was really all about. Things which I was discovering must be upsetting someone who could not afford to be exposed. But how could they know, when I was just finding out myself. I opened my desk and started to set-up for the day's business. With about fifteen minutes left before my meeting, I decided to grab a quick cup of coffee to settle my nerves which were beginning to twinge. Knowing about the search of my office and the upcoming chat with Crandall sent an eerie feeling through my body. It was the kind of feeling you see in the movies that says watch out Jack all's not in order.

At exactly 9:00 O'clock I stood at the threshold of Herbert Crandall's open door.

"Good morning Mr. Crandall how are you?"

"I'm good Ron, thanks for asking. Come on in and sit down, I'll be right with you."

He finished reading then turned to me.

"Listen I don't believe in a lot of small talk so I'll get right to the point on why I wanted to see you. I've been watching your work here for some time and I think you show promise for more responsibilities. I've decided there are some challenging opportunities in the company I believe you may be interested in. I see some abilities in you that I believe the organization may be able to utilize. Talent like your aggressive investigative nature can be a positive asset. I've discussed this with Mr. Jenkovitch and I would like to offer you an opportunity to get involved in some company research that will allow you to take full advantage of your skills. What I have is a chance which will give you maximum exposure and help you to advance. This is what you want isn't it?"

"Why yes of course Mr. Crandall, but I don't understand. I've only been here a relatively short time and until now my previous suggestions for improvements have been ignored."

"Ron, this is a large company and sometimes people go unnoticed. However, recently it was brought to my attention that you have a great deal of potential and deserve to be given a chance to explore more challenging tasks. Please consider my offer as a chance to do what I think is what you are looking for."

"I like the sound of that, but what did you have in mind for me?"

"There is a need for someone to get involved in our downtown production operation and find out why they are not producing as we expect them to. The production numbers there are not what they should be."

"You mean you want me to be a spy?"

"Well no, not exactly. I want you to go down there and observe the operation and report to me what is lacking and needs improvement."

"But what about Mr. Gilsenan, do I still report to him?"

"Yes. But as I said before I've discussed this with Mr. Jenkovitch so I don't think Larry Gilsenan will have any problem with it. However, I will advise him so he knows what you'll be doing."

"Mr. Crandall this sounds great. Will I have a free hand in the operation?"

"Except for reporting indirectly to me you will be totally in charge of your actions."

"Fine, I accept."

"Good! I think you'll work out well. There's just, one more thing Ron. I understand you have been doing some after hour research. I think with this new assignment you won't have time for that anymore, right?"

"Mr. Crandall I'll devote my full attention to the new assignment."

"Excellent, then we are agreed you will take this on and forget about your after hour research."

I left his office but his message really scared me. How could he know what I did here yesterday, assuming that the research he was talking about was that. Are there hidden cameras in here checking on the employees? My meeting with him almost confirmed what was being said at the party and now I knew I was on to something. There was something that the corporate powers didn't want me or anyone else to know. This was enough to really get me going.

I returned to my office and checked the phone messages. One was from Anthony Oliver which started me thinking again. Tony was one of the managers from the downtown plant where I would be going. I wondered why he would be calling me since I found out about the new assignment only a few minutes ago and he had never called before. I decided to return his call first.

"Tony. Ron Powers here, how you doin'?"

"I'm fine Ron. Thanks for returning my call. Say I heard you might be coming down here for a spell, is that right?"

"How did you know, I just found out myself?"

"Well you know how news like that travels. Is it true?"

"Yeah, I guess it is now since I just accepted the offer."

"That's great man, but I just want to clue you in on a couple of things before you get here officially - things like what's really going on."

"Things like what, Tony?"

"Well, it's kind of involved and I don't want to tell it to you over the telephone. Why don't we get together for lunch today and I can fill you in?"

"That sounds good to me. I need to come down there and have a look see at the place anyway."

"No! Don't meet me here. I'll meet you at the Peacock Palace on 8th Street. You know where it is?"

"Sure! I've been there once or twice. You sound a little edgy, anything wrong?"

"No! I'm okay but I just want to meet outside of this place. Some people here I don't see eye to eye with on a lot of things, if you know what I mean."

"Yeah, I truly understand. The Peacock is fine. About 12:30 okay?"

"Great! See you there then.

After I hung up, the voice in my head said you'd better be careful. Tony never called me before even though we had many occasions which could have prompted a call from him. His job at the plant was supervisor of assembly and production. Since my staff role at headquarters was quality control assurance dealing with methods and procedures, there were many times when we could have shared some ideas. Why was he calling now? Was he to be a future ally or was he trying to get to me early to steer me away from some of those same things I had just discovered.

I returned my other calls and then settled in to checking out the business of the day. The time moved quickly and it was 12:00 noon before I was really aware of it. The gong of the clock in the building tower that loudly announced the noon hour every day reminded me. Hearing that sound, I wrapped up what I was into and prepared to head downtown. I exited the lobby and walked onto the street to hail a cab. Cabs were frequent in this area and there was no problem getting one.

"The Peacock on 8th Street" I told the cabbie."

"Sure thing, chief" he responded.

He started the meter and we headed south. The same scene in reverse that I had seen that morning began to unveil itself. The deeper we got into the bowels of the downtown area the poorer the scenic view became. I often wondered why the company had chosen to build a plant in this section. After about a fifteen minute ride we arrived at the tavern. This was about the best place in the area for the local corporate types to gather. Even though it was not like a midtown watering hole, it wasn't bad. I paid the driver and got out.

As I started toward the place I noticed the streets were quieter than what I knew them to be at this time of day. The normal traffic jams and grid lock in the area weren't there and the people traffic wasn't there either. This gave me a strange feeling but I shook it off and said to myself, man get a hold. It was a little later than 12:30 so I walked through the front door and looked around for Tony. After a brief scan, I spotted him sitting at the bar and started that way. Tony was conversing with a woman who as I approached turned quickly got up and left. I said to Tony, "Wow man, did I scare her?"

"No man. She was at the end of her lunch and had to get back. How you doin'? I haven't seen you since the last quarterly product announcement."

"Yeah, but I've been keeping my eye on you guys though."

"Uh, huh that's what I hear. Why don't we go get a table and order? You want a cocktail or something?"

"Just a regular iced tea for me is fine."

He spoke to the barmaid then pointed to the tables and we headed over to the side area where they were and sat down. Tony sat facing the door and I had my back to it. The lighting in the place was kind of dim, I guess to give it some ambience. The waiter came over, took the order and headed toward the kitchen. Tony seemed a little nervous and I asked him what the matter was? He hesitated at first and then said:

"Do you know about Washington?"

I laughed at first then said "Yeah, it's the Capitol city where they make all those mistakes.

He laughed too relaxing a bit, and then said "I guess you don't know."

"I guess not." I repeated "What's Washington?"

"Washington is our code word for the government RFP (Request for Proposal) that we just responded to."

"What's the RFP for?"

"It's requesting a highly sophisticated drug product that wipes out people with their own chemistry."

"What? What's that all about?"

"Wait, there's something even stranger. I understand we were the only company to get the RFP."

Tony started to break the whole story to me when his face suddenly went pale as he looked toward the door. He started to get up when shots rang out. Pow! Pow! Pow! The force threw him backward about five feet to the floor. The blood spurted from the holes and he went down like a lead weight. I turned around to see if more was coming when I saw a short, stocky man quickly exit through the door jump into a waiting car and speed away. I turned back to Tony but there wasn't a thing anybody could do for him now. The crowd in the room panicked scrambling for cover and bedlam prevailed. I felt the shock beginning to run through my body. My knees weakened and my guts started to spill as I looked at the carcass of what was a man I was just talking to. I stumbled toward the lavatory and fell inside.

Moments later I heard the sound of sirens and then a commotion as the police rushed in the place pushing people around and asking questions of everyone still left. Not sure whether I should go out there or not, the decision was quickly made for me as two of them came in and threw me up against the wall. I was forced into the position and searched before I could offer any kind of statement. Even though I was dressed in the “Corporate Image” I was keenly aware that my blackness meant nothing to the cops about who I was. Up against the wall, I offered little resistance. They whirled me around after the search and at gunpoint demanded an explanation of who I was and who I was there with. In an attempt to satisfy their demands I started to speak, but still reeling from the shock of the recent event, my words wouldn’t come together and I began to babble like an idiot, not helping my cause much. Fortunately for me, a ranking officer came in and called off the troops before I was subjected to what I’m sure would have been a day to remember. I was walked back into the dining area and corralled with the rest of the witnesses and questioned further.

Most of the people who were still there were just as shocked as I was and the answers to the questions were just as idiotic. Considering that this was the case, the cops weeded out those that seemed least likely to be involved, based on what I had no clue, and released them. The few they determined may be suspect or have information not revealed yet, were detained and questioned even further. After about an hour we were all finally released and I hurried out of there.

I flagged a cab and headed back to my office. Once there, it was now about 4:30 PM and things were starting to wind down in the office for most for that day. However, when I walked into my office, I noticed that I had been paid another unexpected visit. This time there was no attempt to disguise the visit. Things were thrown around and left there. My chair had been knocked over and my pictures were on the floor. I ran out immediately and looked for Sally, my secretary to find out who had been there, but she was gone. I went back in to try to piece things together and come up with a clue as to what was going on, but found nothing to indicate anything. I picked up the phone and called Mr. Crandall to report what had happened with Tony only to learn that he had already been informed and was on his way to the downtown plant.

I was still assessing the damage to my office when someone appeared in my open door that I had never seen before.

"Mr. Powers?" the question came.

"Yes, I'm Powers who are you?"

"I'm Tango Hernandez from the downtown office. I heard that you were with Tony today."

I couldn't believe the news about all that just happened could move so quickly to involve so many people.

"Well Tango, are you a good guy or a bad guy?"

"I'm neither as far as you're concerned. But for your safety I'm here to see that you get all the protection you need."

"I need protection - protection from what?"

"Yes protection. You see I'm here to make sure that you as the last person to talk to Tony alive are not caught the same way as he was."

After hearing this statement, my mind again began to surge with pulses. I couldn't figure out where Hernandez was coming from. Who did he work for and was he for or against me really?

"I can tell by your reaction you're wondering why I'm really here. Let me assure you I'm only here to protect you. You see Tony was involved in some things you may not be aware of for the last few months and we have been watching him very closely."

Now the pounding in my head became even more violent and I stumbled toward my chair.

"Here let me help you."

He grabbed my arm and I felt as if a motorized vice had closed on it. Though he wasn't an exceptionally large man, his muscular structure gave the image of a Hercules. I accepted his help and eased into my chair. Once seated, I tried to regain my composure and talk with some sense.

"Tony and I were having lunch today to discuss my new assignment down there and that's all I know about anything. If he was involved in something out of the ordinary, I know nothing about it. That's it."

"Sure Mr. Powers. I have no problem with that. Please believe me I'm not here to do anything but help you."

Then the small powerful man started talking to me about an investigation being done on the downtown plant that has been going on for some months. The federal government had been alerted that chemical warfare being perpetrated by a gang of terrorists had infiltrated this country and were working out of our area. They suggested that a main faction of the gang had been hired by Canon and was using the corporate facilities to affect their mission. As he spoke, my mind was still reeling from what had taken place in the last few hours but a lot of what he said began to pull things together about what I had been finding out.

"Mr. Moto what do you want with me?"

"The name is Hernandez. Tango Hernandez and what I want from you is your cooperation in helping to coral this gang which may be the biggest boon to your career that you could imagine. These people are not here to help the corporation or anybody else. They are here to destroy you and eventually this country. I want you to become a part of this investigation and lead us to the insiders who are responsible for your friend's death and also for what may be a large threat to our society."

"What do you want me to do?"

"First I want your word that you are going to work with me and not against me in solving this affair. Second I want you to be available on 24 hours' notice, that is not leave town or disappear. There's no-one that can work from the inside better than you can and who has knowledge of the operations. Your help can be an asset in preventing what may be a major disaster in the making."

I agreed to help "Mr. Moto" mainly to get him out of my office now so I could go home. He acknowledged my pledge and left. I still didn't make a whole lot of sense out of the total picture but at this point I was exhausted. I thought about the afternoon again. Tony had just called me and got blown apart, but nothing I had uncovered before even implicated him in any wrong doings that the company was involved in. Then a thought occurred to me. I remembered that I had made a note to myself from my previous personal spy mission over the weekend. I looked in my special draw which housed a lot of notes that no-one but myself would consider important and pulled out a slip which showed that a large shipment of a raw herb called U3/G had been purchased by the company a couple of weeks ago. U3/G by itself was a harmless agent for relaxing anxieties or better known as a stress fighter. It never occurred to me that this element combined with another agent called COMED/5 could take the relaxation factor to a whole new level and to a point where the whole human system would be compromised. The ability to fight the slightest ingestion of even a mild strain of bacteria could be weakened.

Whether Tony was onto this mixing of the chemicals or whether this was even actually what was going on still wasn't clear and I was now at the point where my super large headache was preventing me from figuring out anything more. It was now about 6:00 PM and with my head reeling from the day's events I decided it was time for me to head back to my end of the city and try to relax. I tidied up my office, packed up the day's business tools put them away and headed home.

#######

Even though the hour was getting late and most of the workers had gone for the day, huddled around the big table in the conference room Herbert Crandall, Milton Jenkovitch (CEO), Leonard Jablonski (Dir. Of Plant Oprns), and Reginald Codey, who had just come back from his latest overseas trip closing new deals, sat talking. The automatic timer had already kicked into night mode dimming the corridor and common area lighting but the topic of conversation among these men made them oblivious to everything outside the conference room.

"Crandall, you told me you had everything under control" said Mr. Jenkovitch. "How the hell could this happen? His eminence will not be pleased when he finds out about your bumbling. This project is much too big a part of his master plan to have it compromised by mistakes."

"Milton, what happened was the result of one overly ambitious underling who thought he was doing the right thing. I've already taken steps to correct that situation."

"What do you mean correct it? Are you going to compound the error?"

"No. Believe me I can take care of it and nothing will harm the plan."

The discussion went on well into the late evening and as the anxiety level in the room began to mount from fear of what reprisal the one called his eminence might exact upon the group, each man was attempting to come up with a way to cover himself should he be called to be accountable. The murder of Anthony Oliver in broad daylight in a crowded place with many witnesses was not in any way shape or fashion what had been considered part of the project objective. Herbert Crandall's explanation to resolve the blunder was not registering as a positive solution with any of the table members. Milton Jenkovitch, as the CEO and highest ranking member present knew that he would be the first to be called, not Crandall, when the question of who was responsible came up before his superior. While he pressed Crandall for a more definitive explanation of how he intended to correct the error when the event had already happened, put Herb, as they referred to him, on such a defensive that the smooth talking executive actually began to stutter.

"Milton, I, I, I kn-know it so-sounds a little crazy but my solution is foolproof."

"Well dammit, let's hear it, and it better be good."

Herb Crandall went on to detail his solution to the group while each man took in what he had to say. Comments made at key points in his message were not endorsing his plan and it made him even more uncomfortable in getting agreement from the group that it was indeed foolproof. Finally when he concluded his mission strategy, almost in desperation for the lack of any other plan, they all agreed that what Herb was planning was what needed to be done. Each man, still not totally convinced that they were out of the woods, started to get up from the table to exit the conference room when a loud noise was heard just outside.

It sounded like a bomb had exploded. Already at high anxiety levels from all that had happened that day and from the tense discussion they had just concluded, the men scrambled out the door to see what was going on. When they stepped into the corridor they could see at the end of the hallway dark smoke emanating from the elevator banks. Fearing the worst, each man headed for the stairway running at his individual top speed. Mr. Jenkovitch being the elder in the group was having a difficult time keeping up with his younger subordinates and none of them was prone to help him. Breathing hard and a little dizzy he made it to the exit door and descended behind the rest of the group to the next lower level. They tried the entrance door to get in and see if an alternate bank of elevators was perhaps unaffected.

Alarms were going off and the sound of people rushing from inside could be heard even before they got the door open. As they entered the floor screams sounded as a group of workers who had been attending an organization meeting for another company in the building started running toward the elevator. The Canon group mixed in with them as they all attempted to get into a waiting elevator. Crammed into the single elevator car the group frantically pushed the street level button, but there was no response. "Obviously", Herb blurted out -"there are too many people in here. Somebody's going to have to get out." Not seeing any volunteers moving, he began to push some of them causing a melee to ensue. Mr. Jenkovitch who was behind Herb was having trouble maintaining his balance as the pushing and shoving surrounded him. Crandall was able to get a few people off and the door closed but the car still did not move.

Moments later a message came through from the intercom inside the car instructing everybody to get out. It was the night security crew advising everyone that a fire had indeed developed in the adjacent elevator shaft and the safety mechanism for all elevator service had triggered. Immediately the door opened again and the people who had been shoved out of the car along with others who had joined them were still there ready to engage those that had displaced them. Another scuffle broke out and it appeared that no one had sense enough to escape to the stairway exits. The battle didn't last long as it dawned on the contestants that they were preventing each other from getting out of a burning building. They disengaged each other and the race for the stairwells started. While bumping and shoving was rampant, a voice was heard near the end of the hallway yelling for them to walk and not panic. It was a security officer who had made his way up from the lobby to try and direct people out. He may as well have been talking to the walls because in the scramble to get down the stairs, no one paid him any attention. The mad rush to descend in leaps and bounds left the Canon group fighting for position as the much younger crowd from the lower floor got ahead of them. Poor Mr. Jenkovitch who was not in the best of health or condition, was hard pressed to keep up with the race and not be trampled. Clutching his chest as he moved he yelled out to Crandall to help him, but Herb just looked at him and kept going.

Finally, everybody in the stairwell was able to exit the building through the lobby emergency exit doors and onto the street. The fire apparatus was already on the scene and firemen were entering the building setting up to battle the fire. Although, no flames could be seen coming out of the elevator shafts, thick smoke was coming out.

Once on the street, Mr. Jenkovitch found Herb Crandall and told him that he wanted to see him in his office first thing in the morning, then left. Herb knew he was already having a bad day, but now his tomorrow was not looking to be too promising. Herb found Reggie Codey and said he wanted him to come and have a drink at the bar. Reggie, who reported to Herb was not in a position to refuse so the two of them started walking down the street to the local pub.

Manny's Place was a nearby watering hole that not too many of the corporate types frequented. The clientele there was made up of mostly the rough and tumble type who made a living off of the streets in various forms and fashions. When Herb and Reggie walked through the doors, several eyes immediately focused on them. Both men dressed in suits stood out from the rest of the crowd and even the bartender tried to steer them with his eyes and a nod of his head to a secluded corner of the room. Taking the hint, Herb grabbed Reggie's arm and guided him quickly out of the limelight toward the darkened corner. Luckily there was a small empty table and both men sat down. Minutes later a young scantily clad cocktail waitress came over and asked if the men wanted to order. Herb ordered a double scotch and soda while Reggie ordered a double gin and tonic.

As soon as the waitress left, Herb started talking. His words gushed out like a break in a main water line.

"Boy, the ole' man is really pissed at me. I've never seen him like that. You'd think I pulled the trigger on that Oliver guy myself, the way he acted at the meeting. If my plan doesn't work the way I laid it out, then I may as well resign and get out of the city. This is where I'm going to need your help."

"You need my help? What do you want me to do? The way you talked during the meeting it sounded as if you had everything all lined up."

"I do. But you are a key player in the line-up. Here's what I want you to do. Two days from now I want you to arrange another trip to that Rain Tree forest in Australia where you got that last shipment of our special product. You know the place I'm talking about. What's the name of the agency?"

"The Plant Place in Daintree Rainforest is what it's called, but you know how I hate going there. Its twenty miles into the middle of nowhere, the accommodations are lousy and they treat me like I'm one of their field hands."

"That's exactly why I want you to go there. I want you to take that idiot Brent with you and get him lost out there in the jungle."

"Are you talking about Brent Woodley from the assembly line down at the plant? I thought he was your number one henchman?"

"Yes, but I never thought he was a total imbecile. Oh I forgot you don't know. He took it upon himself to carry out the execution of Tony Oliver because I had said to him I suspected the man was getting too close to learning about P.T.D.T.Y. Tony was beginning to put the pieces together about the mixing of the chemicals and somehow he got hold of the RFP. Brent has to be disposed of before the authorities discover he was the shooter and with his mentality he would implicate all of us. You have to make him disappear."

"Just how do I arrange to take him on a trip with me when he has no qualifications and no experience at what I do? His boss is never going to release him."

"Don't worry about it, I'll handle that part. You just make the necessary contacts at Daintree and let them know you're coming, then arrange travel. I will have another purchase order prepared so that you have the proper cover to get going."

Herb Crandall and Reginald Codey sat there drinking and talking until the hour was getting late. Herb's nerves were settling down a bit as the alcohol became his pacifier, but still deep down inside he was worried about what was going to happen tomorrow when he faced Mr.

Jenkovitch. He really wasn't so much afraid of the wrath of the ole' man directly as he was of what might happen to him should his boss reveal his blunder to the adversary and the bigger boss learn of his role in what happened. The mere thought of a wrench being thrown into the wheels of the P.T.D.T.Y. project and throwing it off schedule because of one of his lackeys gave him great concern. The more he drank the more he talked about how much he felt like he would be the target of the one who he feared greatly. As the men sat talking, Herb started to twirl a signet ring on his right ring finger that had engraved in the red Jasper Stone the symbols triple sixes. The more he twirled, it seemed that the temperature in the room was heating up and the atmosphere was becoming smoky. Suddenly what sounded like a clap of thunder was heard and then all eyes were fixed on the entrance door as a tall mysterious figure appeared in the doorway.

CHAPTER TWO
"Encounter"

Brinnng! Brinnng! Brinnng! The old fashioned alarm clock sounded loudly awakening me from an almost catatonic like sleep. I only used it during the week because it was my motivator to get out of bed. As I struggled to open my eyes and lift my hand up to silence it, it seemed like consciousness was eluding me. Finally, mustering up enough energy I managed to locate and shut it off. I keep the old relic around first because it still works and second because nobody with even moderate hearing capability can ignore it. It's been handed down through generations in my family and somehow I ended up with it. I've been told there's a story that goes along with it about one of my greater grandmothers named Sulia who came to this city right after slavery ended and was given this clock as a gift. I never could get anyone in the family to tell me the whole story except that she was an exceptionally beautiful woman who had a child fathered by her former slave master. I am the lineage of that child. Other than that my only connection with her and the story, as far as I know, is this clock who people say has been blessed and that I should never let it go.

I'm not super religious or a big church going guy, but when I hear about things like what Tony was beginning to tell me, I wonder what is happening in this world. I can't believe a directive could come from within our own government requesting something as evil as this chemical agent - an agent that could destroy people using their own chemistry. I began to get myself together, get out of bed and start my day, but I couldn't help but rehash all that happened yesterday.

Going to the office today was promising to be very interesting, to say the least. My expectations of what to prepare for were scattered all over my brain. I knew that I was going to have to meet Mr. Crandall at some point because I was the last person to see Tony alive, but I had no idea how he was going to react to the situation. He has always impressed me, from the time I got here, as being a little strange, but how strange I was only beginning to find out.

I completed my morning routine and headed out the door to wait for Alex. As usual he was right on schedule and we were on our way.

"Good mornin' mon, you be good today?"

"Yeah Alex, I'm good. How are you?"

"Okay, I guess. Did ya hear `bout the fire las night?"

"No. What fire? When I got home last night I was so tired I got in bed and went out like a light. Where was the fire?"

"I think mon it was `round where you work at."

"Really? Can you turn the radio to the news and let's see if anything's on about it?"

"Sure thing mon."

Alex switched to a news station and almost as if on cue the reporter was talking about the midtown fire at Canon Enterprises last night. According to his report it didn't appear to be anything major, but what caught my attention was when he said the elevators had just recently been inspected and everything was in order.

Although he didn't say it, the implication was that there may be some suspicion about the cause. Now I know my meeting with Mr. Crandall was really going to be interesting.

Alex pulled up to my building and as I got out, I noticed that there was more than the usual police presence around it. There were even some news trucks and reporters milling around. Just out of curiosity, before going inside, I stopped one of them and asked what was going on.

"Excuse me, I work here. What's all the excitement about?"

"You say you work here?"

"Yes!"

"Would you mind being interviewed on camera?"

"Well that depends on what we're going to talk about."

"Sir you know there was a fire here last night don't you?"

"Yes, but I just learned about it."

"You don't happen to know of anyone who was working here last night do you?"

"No! Please tell me why you're asking?"

"We understand there were some problems in people getting out of the building and we would like to find out what happened."

At this point, it was beginning to sound like they were going on a witch hunt, so I politely cut off the conversation, excused myself and went inside. The buzz inside was as great as the activity outside. Even in the elevator people were whispering. It was difficult to actually decipher all that was being said, but from what I could tell it wasn't good. Now I was anxious to get to my office just to see what kind of messages were waiting for me.

Sally was on the phone so I just nodded my head in a greeting and walked into my office. I looked around carefully just to see whether I had another unexpected visitor, but all seemed to be as I left it. The message light on the phone was blinking as I expected so I sat down and started my review. The first two were routine status calls from some of my co-workers working with me on other projects so I skipped over them. But the third one was out of the ordinary and caused me to play it again.

"Mr. Powers, my name's Marsha Robinson. I'm a chemist at the downtown plant. You don't know me but I was the one talking with Tony when you came into the Peacock yesterday. I really need to talk with you soon. Please call me - my extension is 2342."

The message had a tone of some desperation, so I made a note to call her first when I finished my call review. There were four more calls, none which demanded my immediate attention. I was a bit surprised that there wasn't one from Crandall so I buzzed Sally on the intercom.

"Yes Mr. Powers."

"Sal please contact Mr. Crandall's secretary and find out if he's in today?"

"Sure Mr. Powers. I'll get right back to you."

"Thanks."

Before I returned Ms. Robinson's call I thought I'd better get me a cup of coffee and settle down. On my way to the snack area, I motioned to Sally that I was just going to get coffee and I would be right back. Since she was on the phone, she nodded in acknowledgement. In the snack area there were a few others standing around and talking. I could tell by the hushed tones that they must be discussing what everybody seemed to be buzzing about – the fire last night. I got my coffee and returned to my desk.

Just as I sat down the intercom buzzed. It was Sally letting me know that Crandall had not come in yet. This was somewhat surprising and I wondered if he was back at the downtown plant. Well, no matter, I said to myself and I started to call Ms. Robinson. Before I could dial, the phone rang and I picked it up.

"Good morning, Powers here – how can I help you?"

"Good morning Mr. Powers this is Tango Hernandez."

I thought to myself this is just what I need this early in the morning.

"Mr. Hernandez – what can I do for you?"

"Please call me Tango."

"Okay Tango, what's up?"

"Can you meet with me about 3:00 O'clock this afternoon, there's something I need to discuss with you?"

"Hold on let me check my schedule. I'll be free after 3:30 is that okay?"

"Yes that's fine."

"Where would you like to meet?"

"Mr. Powers I'll come to your office, if that's okay?"

"Of course Tango. I'm beginning to think you like it here."

"Not really, I just need to get out of here for awhile."

"Okay then I'll see you here at 3:30."

After we hung up the thought crossed my mind that maybe he was the one paying me the unannounced visits in my office, but I dismissed it. I buzzed Sally and advised her to put Mr. Hernandez on my calendar. About twenty minutes had ticked off the clock before I was able to call Ms. Robinson. The time was now almost 10:00 O'clock and I wondered if I was too late in getting back to her considering the urgent sound in her voice when she called. I dialed the number and waited. She didn't pick up and the call didn't go to her voice mail which was odd. I hung up waited a few minutes and redialed. This time, although she didn't answer, her voice mail message came on so I left a message telling her I tried to reach her and if she could call me between 12:30 and 1:00 I should be available.

So far today, with the exception of calls from Ms. Robinson and Mr. Hernandez nothing extraordinary has happened. I wondered what Tango needed to talk to me about but I was more anxious to speak with Marsha. Tony's death was still playing heavy on my mind and I couldn't dismiss the thought that he was onto something even greater and more revealing than what I had discovered. It was something so deep that it cost him his life. If this company was really producing a product so sinister how could they be doing it and no one know about it. No one that is except a few and that's what I was determined to find out. Maybe Marsha has some answers.

I returned my remaining calls and pursued the business of my other projects. Before I completely left to assume my new role downtown, I had to clean-up and resolve some outstanding issues here.

It's been said that time goes by quickly when you're enjoying yourself and having fun. Now whether this is a universal axiom or just a saying from some wizened old shrews I don't know, but when I looked at the clock on the wall and it read eleven-fifty I surmised that I must be having a real party. I had become so engrossed in my work that the passage of time was irrelevant. Hoping that Marsha received my message and was going to call me, I started wrapping up my final conclusions on the latest operational improvements at the plant that I was working on.

At twelve noon the gong in the tower sounded and I decided I'd better run down to the cafeteria and grab a sandwich or something and get back to wait for her call. I did so and was back in the office by twelve-twenty and settled into my chair. My dilemma now was whether to start eating my sandwich and have my mouth full when the phone rang or set the food aside until later and hope she was punctual. My stomach aided in my decision when the feed me message was sent to my brain and the corresponding abdominal sounds were heard. Not wanting to upset either, I opened the package and took a large bite.

As fate would have it, and it always seems to work that way, just as I was enjoying the taste of my Reuben, at twelve-thirty five the phone rang. Fortunately, I was able to finish chewing, swallow the mouthful and pick-up the receiver on the fourth ring before it rolled over to voice mail.

"Good afternoon Powers here, how can I help you?"

"Hello Mr. Powers this is Marsha. I'm glad I caught you. Listen I can't talk long now, but as I said in my message to you we really need to get together. Are you free after work today?"

"Hi Ms. Robinson, yes I can make myself free then. What time and where do you want to meet?"

"Do you know where the library at Colombia is?"

"You mean the school?"

"Yes, I'm a grad student there."

"I'm not exactly sure but I think I can find it."

"Well if you can meet me in a conference room in the science department at 6:00 O'clock I'll be there."

"Yeah sure I can do that. How will I know you?"

"Just ask the librarian at the desk for Mimi, that's what they know me by there. She'll direct you to the right room. I usually use the same one."

"Okay, I'll see you there."

"Good! Bye."

We hung up and I resumed eating. Somehow it seemed like I had met her before after we talked, even if briefly. I wondered if perhaps we had crossed paths at a meeting, a seminar or something but none came to mind. The tone of her voice now was much calmer than what she exhibited in her earlier voice message, so it appeared that she must have settled down.

My next thought was that of what happened to Mr. Crandall. I hesitated to try and check on his whereabouts again because it might present the wrong impression to his secretary. I figured if he wanted to see me, he knew where I was. So I turned my attention to what possibly could Hernandez want to talk to me about. It was funny, but every time I thought about him he reminded me of that Mr. Moto, the fictional Japanese secret agent from the `50's. I'm sure he would be thrilled to know that's how I perceived him.

As I sat there pondering "Mr. Moto", Sally poked her head in my open door and cautioned me that Mr. Jenkovitch was in the area and headed my way. I wondered why she didn't buzz me, then I saw the man quick stepping toward my office. She would not have been able to complete her message calling me before he was at her desk. Seconds later he burst into my office with a scowl on his face, pulled out a chair and sat down. I wasn't sure if his apparent rage was for me or not, but that was soon made clear.

"Mr. Powers have you seen or heard from Herb Crandall?"

I wasn't quite sure how to respond to him. Should I invent something to cover for my new quasi mentor or tell the truth?" I opted for the latter.

"No I'm sorry Mr. Jenkovitch, but I haven't seen nor heard from him since yesterday."

He pounded his fist on my desk and said "I told him I wanted to see him first thing this morning. Now where is he?"

I knew that his question was rhetorical, so I didn't attempt to answer.

"I know that he has created a special assignment for you. Have you started working on it yet?"

"No sir. I'm still wrapping up some unfinished business here, but I expect to start there next Monday."

"Good! I hope it goes well for you there."

His demeanor changed and he calmed down somewhat and I relaxed a bit too. He continued talking.

"You know the incident that happened to one of our plant managers is going to have a lot of people asking questions. You will probably have to field many of them. Has anyone made contact with you yet?"

Now I really wasn't sure how to answer him and my anxiety level went back up. Should I tell him about "Mr. Moto?" I decided until I knew more about where Hernandez was coming from and whose side was he on, I would not mention him.

"No sir, I have not been contacted yet. I do expect to be called by the police though."

"Yes I'm sure of that. Just remember when you talk to them or even the press you must protect the company image. Well I'll be going now. If you hear from Herb remind him he needs to see me."

"Yes sir, I'll do that."

He got up more relaxed than when he came in and nonchalantly walked out.

I couldn't imagine what Mr. Crandall could have done to anger the chief, but it must have happened last night. After he left it was now about two-thirty and I had one more piece of business I needed to attend to before receiving Tango Hernandez. I called down to the plant and asked to speak with Leonard Jablonski, the operations director. I wanted to let him know about the procedural changes my team had come up with that was going to affect his area of responsibility. Even though he had a representative from his staff working with us, I wanted to discuss the final outcome directly with him.

Fortunately, I got him on the first attempt and we talked at length regarding the issues. He wasn't entirely in agreement with all that was proposed, so we bantered the key points of contention for about a half hour before coming to an agreement that we could both live with. I made the necessary changes to the document and buzzed Sally to come in. Handing her the proposal with the revisions I asked her if she would type it up and have it ready for me tomorrow morning. She said okay and left.

I looked at the clock and it now read three-ten. Assuming that Hernandez was one of those people always punctual, not much time remained before he would be walking through my door. From the first time that he stepped into my office I was suspicious about exactly what it is that he does and now my suspicions were even more sensitized because no one that I talked to seemed to know anything about him. I was determined when he arrived to find out who he worked for and what his job is. As far as showing up in the company directory his name didn't appear under any organization heading and I'm sure he was not temporary personnel the way he was able to get into and out of this building.

My wait wasn't long because within minutes of the beginning of my reverie in walked "Mr. Moto." When I saw him I started to snicker which didn't sit well so he questioned what I thought was funny. I explained to him he reminded me of someone, without going into any great detail that used to always make me laugh. He responded by telling me his business here was no laughing matter and that I should keep my mind focused on what happened to my friend.

"Tony wasn't exactly my friend you know. If I hadn't accepted a new assignment at your location we probably would not have even been doing lunch that day. We were strictly co-workers and nothing more. But he did begin to confide in me something about what was going on in the plant. He never got the chance to finish his story."

I was saying this to try and elicit a response from Tango that might give me a clue about his role in the matter. Before asking him directly what he does, I hoped he would volunteer some information.

"Ron – may I call you that?"

"Sure Tango if it suits you."

"I would like to keep our relationship as informal as we can make it because I think we may be sharing a great deal of time together. The reason why I wanted to meet with you today is to go over something that was given to me by one of the chemists at the plant. It was a note that had the letters P.T.D.T.Y. prominently displayed on it and then some reference to a formula that was cut off but part of it referred to COMED/5. Now as the QC manager you might be able to shed some light on what exactly is that. And also where is the rest of the formula. What do you know about this?"

I was a little surprised at what he was asking me. How many people knew what those letters stood for and which chemist handed him the note. I didn't want to let on that I had seen the letters before so I pretended ignorance hoping he would elaborate a little more.

"Tango, not everything made down at that plant comes by my desk. In fact there are several products that I have nothing to do with from a QC perspective. Tell me which chemist gave you the note and what did he say when he handed it to you? Perhaps he knows what the rest of the formula is."

"The note was not handed to me but placed in my mail slot."

"How do you know then that it came from one of the chemists?"

"Because who else would be involved in formulas down there?"

"Tango would you mind if I ask you a question?"

"No not at all. Ask away. However, I don't promise to give you an answer."

"What exactly is it that you do and who do you report to? I looked up your name in the company directory both by organization and by individual name and nothing came up. Are you exempt from being in the database?"

"Ron, let's just say that I really don't work for your company but I have been implanted here as an undercover operative to search out, as I told you earlier, some bad guys who may be up to no good as far as the country is concerned."

"Oh then are you CIA, FBI, MIB?"

When I added the last category, even Tango had to laugh.

"Yes you may choose from either of the first two but eliminate the last one. I am not at liberty to disclose to you which one and who I report to within your company. It's confidential but let me assure you I can go straight to the top at any time I need to. Does that help clarify anything for you?"

"Yes it's now clear as mud and I understand completely"

Again Tango laughed and I was beginning to see a lighter side to him. Perhaps he was not as bad as he came off to be when we first met.

"Ron, perhaps I failed to impress upon you when I first came here the gravity of what may be going on at that plant. Now that your friend – I mean your co-worker has been eliminated, I'm sure that I'm on to something big there and I really need your help."

"Tango I'm willing to help you but I need to get some verification, other than your word about who you are and who you work for. As far as I know you could be telling me anything and I have no way to prove it."

"Short of showing you my ID, which I'm not about to, how do you suggest you confirm my identity?"

"I don't know, but if you want my help then you're going to have to figure that one out."

"Okay Mr. Powers have it your way. I will arrange to get you some proof without comprising my position. Before I leave though, are you sure you don't know anything about the letters I showed you or the missing part of the formula?"

"Mr. Hernandez, let's just leave it at when you can confirm who you are with me, then I may be able to help you more."

"Okay Ron, I'll be in touch soon."

He got up and walked out. I couldn't tell from his demeanor whether he was disappointed, angry or merely resigned to the fact that he had to come up with a convincer for me. We spent the better part of two hours talking in my office and when he left I realized that I was going to be hard pressed to get uptown and to the library to meet Marsha by 6:00 O'clock. In an unusual departure procedure for me, I just threw things in my desk as I scrambled to get out the door and hail a cab. Fortunately I was able to get one almost immediately and was on my way.

The cab driver knew the area where the school was but had no idea about where the library was located. He checked with his dispatcher and got the location but as it turned out we were within a couple of blocks but heading in the wrong direction. To turn around and get on the right street here was no easy task because of the one way streets and the traffic at this hour. I looked at my watch and it was already 6:15. I started to wonder whether Marsha would wait or leave because she thought I might not be coming.

It took another ten minutes for us to get rerouted and headed in the right direction, but we finally pulled up to the building. I paid the fare and jumped out. It was now almost 6:30 and I suspected I may have missed her. Climbing the stairs as quickly as I could I rushed inside and found my way to the science department. At the desk was seated a young man who appeared to perhaps be an undergraduate student.

"Hi, I'm looking for a grad student who goes by the name of Mimi, do you know her?"

"I'm sorry sir I don't know her but I just started here. Let me go ask someone else."

He got up and walked over to the computer tables where an older gray hair librarian was helping someone. From what I could observe, the older woman knew who I was looking for. She pointed to an area outside of the big room and the young man nodded his head and returned to the desk.

"Sir, she's in a study room upstairs – room 404. Do you know where the study rooms are?"

"No. Can you help me?"

"Yes. When you exit this room the way you came in turn right and take the elevator to the fourth floor. The study rooms are right down the hall."

"Thank you."

I almost ran out of there in an attempt to save some time getting to the floor. When I got to room 404 I looked in and saw two women and a man sitting at a small conference table. Trying to recreate the brief image I saw of Marsha as she hurried out of the Peacock I could only recall her very shapely legs which were now hidden by the table. Then I remembered that she had long dark red hair which I could now plainly see.

Boldly I pushed open the door and entered.

"Marsha is that you?"

The other two people turned and looked at me as if I had the wrong room. Then Marsha answered.

"Yes that's me. You must be Ron."

The others looked at Marsha apparently unaware that was her name. She politely asked them if she could have the room for a little while and she would explain later. The two got up and walked out and I stepped in and sat down.

"I'm sorry I just forgot to call you Mimi. Did I blow your cover?"

She laughed.

"No. No need to apologize it's just that they have never heard me called by my real name. I'm glad you were able to come I was beginning to suspect that you wouldn't. We have much to talk about."

"I tried to get here on time but I had a visitor from your location named Hernandez who took up a lot of my time."

"Hernandez. You mean Tango Hernandez?"

"Yes, do you know him?

"Yes. Even before the incident he's been in everybody's face asking a lot of strange questions."

"Do you know what his job is or who he reports to?"

"No. Nobody seems to know that."

"Yeah, I'm beginning to find that out. Anyway, he's why I was late."

"Okay no matter – you're here now. How much did Tony get to tell you about what's happening at the plant?"

"Not very much – he was just getting started when he was taken out abruptly. He did tell me about an RFP that the company is supposed to be working on that no other firm received. He said something about a new kind of stress reducer."

"Yeah, it's a stress reducer alright. It's one that will reduce you to a cadaver. But what else is so strange about it from what I can figure is that it's particularly targeted at the adolescent age group."

"What? This is getting weirder the more I hear about it."

"In addition to discovering the RFP, Tony had seen the secret production schedule for making this drug. It was to come out in tablet form that was to dissolve in water or any fruit drink. He was about to go to the authorities when he was murdered. He suspected he was in danger, that's why he reached out to you."

"Do you have the RFP or the production schedule?"

"No. Tony told me he hid it but didn't say where. We were talking about it at the Peacock when you came in and I had to leave."

"You have any idea where it might be?"

"Not a clue."

We continued to talk for about another fifteen minutes before Mimi felt like she was depriving her study team of valued time so we ended our conversation. We did promise to stay in touch. Neither one of us at this point had enough pieces of the puzzle to solve it anyway. I got up to leave as her fellow doctoral candidates, who were waiting anxiously by the door, walked back in. I politely excused myself and apologized for the interruption.

I left the library heading home with the thoughts about what I just learned racing through my head. Could it really be that my own company was involved in something so evil as what I was being led to understand? The more I focused on that thought the more I began to think about the people I was working for and around. This brought my mind back to Mr. Crandall.

#######

Herb Crandall and Reginald Codey sat mesmerized with their eyes focused on the mysterious figure in the doorway. Herb continued to twirl his signet ring and the room seemed to be getting hotter. The figure dressed in all black, including a black hat resembling that of a clergyman, started to move into the room. It was not as though he was walking but seemed to glide as he approached the table. Standing in front of the two men, he reached out his massive hand and touched Crandall on his shoulder. Herb shuddered for a minute then fell face down on the table. The mysterious figure then turned to Reggie and in a very raspy voice said “Let this be a warning to the both of you. The adversary is aware of your folly and he is not pleased. Should you jeopardize his plan again you and him will be destroyed. Do you understand?”

Reggie was shaking so badly he could hardly get the word out. He looked at the figure’s face but it was like looking at a wax dummy. It was devoid of any blemishes or telltale character marks but had the appearance of a chiseled statue. He finally managed to mouth the word yes and he slumped to the table.

The lights in the room suddenly went out briefly and when they came back on the figure was gone. Herb and Reggie however, were still lying face down on the table. The waitress who was standing nearby screamed and pointed to the two men. The bartender rushed over and examined them then hollered for someone to call 911. In a matter of minutes an ambulance and the police were on the scene. The two men were rolled out and taken to the nearby Memorial Hospital. The police began questioning the crowd about what happened but all they could get from them was a jumbled explanation of what they thought they saw. Totally frustrated at not being able to get enough information to make a full report that made sense, the police packed up and left.

When the police left the crowd started talking with each other trying to figure out what it was they actually saw. There were no two people who could corroborate the same version of the vision. Some said the figure was very tall, some said medium height, some said he was white, some black while others could offer no description at all. The bartender however offered and was thoroughly convinced that they just saw the devil.

At the hospital both men were admitted showing signs of severe trauma and a reaction to what the doctors believed was exposure to electrical shock. However, based on the report from the EMTs there were no electrical hazards in the area where the men were found. Baffled at how that could be the medical team performed a more in depth examination and discovered a large hand print dug into the shoulders of both men. Since the impression appeared to be that of a human hand the mystery remained regarding the electrical shock.

The hospital admittance staff unable to talk with either man was having difficulty in registering them. Identification found on both could not produce any family member or next of kin information. For both the only thing the staff could use to admit them was their Canon Enterprises corporate identification and business cards. The lead admissions clerk decided to use the telephone numbers on the business cards and call the office.

Although the men were brought in around 3:30 AM the call to Canon wasn't made until late morning that day. The call went in to the main switch board for some reason instead of going directly to the respective secretary's for each man. In that shuffle the message concerning the two men being hospitalized did not come to Mr. Jenkovitch's attention until very late afternoon. When his secretary received the word and informed him he wasn't quite sure how to react. He was still harboring his displeasure with Herb Crandall from the previous night's events.

"Hospital – he's in the hospital?" Milton yelled at his secretary.

"What on earth's the matter with him?"

"I don't know sir. That's all the information given to me."

"He'll do anything to keep away from me today. Jenn could you call the hospital, I guess he's in Memorial, and see what you can find out about him?"

"Yes sir, right away."

Jennifer Winston, Mr. Jenkovitch's secretary was a sharp and skillful worker. She was also keenly aware of the relationship between Herb Crandall, Reginald Codey, Leonard Jablonski, and her boss. She knew all about their clandestine after hour meetings and had often suspected that they weren't always discussing normal company business. Several times she had gone into the conference room the next morning after one of their meetings and discovered some odd items. In addition to quite a few slips of torn paper showing various coded entries she would often detect the smell of what she believed may have been incense burned. Of note she had on occasion seen the letters P.T.D.T.Y. on some of these scraps of paper. She never thought much about what it could mean.

She called the hospital and spoke to the head nurse in charge of the ICU where Herb and Reggie were recuperating. The nurse informed her that the two men had experienced some type of severe electrical shock and were being monitored for any heart rhythm irregularities. She went on to say they were in stable condition and expected to fully recover. Jennifer took note of all that the nurse told her and reported it to her boss.

"Severe shock huh? He probably stuck his finger in a light socket. Where did all this happen?"

"Sir I didn't get that, but it must have happened very early this morning according to the hospital nurse."

"Okay. Thanks Jenn that's all I need right now."

Jennifer turned around and walked out.

Milton sat back in his big chair contemplating what could have really happened. He knew that Herb was a bit out of sorts after the fire incident and the brief scuffle with the other tenants while exiting the building, but he didn't think that he was mentally unstable or anything. He kept trying to imagine how or where Herb could have been electrically shocked. While he was pondering the thought his phone rang. Normally he would have let Jennifer answer and wait for her referral, but this time for some reason his instinct made him pick it up.

"Hello this is Milton Jenkovitch."

There was a long pause and the silence was irritating for him.

Suddenly the line went dead and Milton angrily slammed his receiver down. A good five minutes passed and the phone rang again. Anxiously determined to vent his wrath on the next caller, Milton picked the phone up again.

"Hello who is this?"

"This is Tango Hernandez. Is that how you usually answer your calls?"

"No Tango, but someone just called a few minutes ago and hung up without speaking."

"Yes that can be irritating but perhaps it was a wrong number."

"Yeah I guess you could be right. Well what can I do for you?"

"I have a question for you."

"Okay ask."

"This morning I came across half of a document in one of your labs strewn on the floor and It had the letters - - D.T.Y. written on it. It appears like the first two letters had been smudged out intentionally. Do you know what they could have been and what does this stand for?"

Tango knew perfectly well what the first two letters were because he had seen it before, but he wanted to test Milton hoping he would divulge some needed information. Information he wasn't able to solicit from Ron Powers.

When Milton heard the reference to the letters, a chill ran down his spine and he hesitated before answering. Tango picked up on the long pause, but said nothing.

"Where did you say you found that paper?"

"It was in one of your labs. You know the one at the end of the corridor."

"Yes I know it but what were you doing in there. It's a restricted area."

"Mr. Jenkovitch let me remind you there's no area that's off limits to your Uncle Sam and right now I'm him. Please answer the question."

Milton was getting a little nervous. Not because Tango was asking a sensitive question but because he had a feeling that whatever happened to Herb and Reggie may have been the result of some punishment dispatched by the emissary. The very thought was making him cringe as he tried to formulate a response.

"Mr. Hernandez that lab is working on something for our government that is out of your department's jurisdiction. Now if I have to contact the mandating agency to talk to your superiors to keep you out of that lab I will do so. Do I make myself clear? Stay out of there."

"Milton, seems like I've struck a nerve there. What are you hiding?"

"I'm about to hang up. Is there anything else?"

"I guess not."

"That's fine. Just remember stay the hell out of that lab. Goodbye!"

Milton, even though he came across on the phone as sounding in control, was a nervous wreck. His thoughts immediately went to the idea suppose Tango claimed entry to the lab as a matter of national security. This could possibly supersede his restriction and blow the secrecy of the whole project. The dilemma playing out in his head was too much and was causing his system to react. His blood pressure was rising, his pulse was racing, he started sweating profusely and then - boom.

Chapter Three
"SCAPEGOAT"

It's been almost two weeks now since the Anthony Oliver incident and things are seemingly returning to normal operations both at the plant and headquarters of Canon Enterprises. The intensity of the police investigation has lessened and only a few people who were actually in the tavern at the time are still being interrogated. Herb Crandall and Reginald Codey have fully recovered and are back in their respective positions. Although back to work, each man has plainly embedded in his memory the encounter with the adversary. Herb was still fearful that until he took care of the cause of his problem he would still be subject to a repeat episode. He vowed to remedy the situation as soon as possible. Of course this meant dispatching Reggie to a foreign land so that it could be carried out. He called Reggie and set the plan in motion.

As for Mr. Jenkovitch, after his call that day from Mr. Hernandez, he allowed his own imagination to create such a possible scenario concerning the lab that it caused his own body chemistry to react in such a manner that it threw it out of balance. His blood pressure and heart rate elevated to such a level that the room started spinning he lost consciousness and slumped over his desk. By this time in the early evening most of the office workers had already departed for the day. However, fortunately for him Jennifer happened to be working late on a project he had given her a short time ago but she had not had a chance to complete it. Stumped by one of the statements he had included in the project overview, she went to his office to get clarification on what he really intended to say.

When she opened his office door she saw him lying on his desk breathing very shallow breaths and sweat pouring from his brow. Fearing the worst, thinking that he may have had a heart attack she went over to him and felt his pulse then called for security. The security officers hearing the complaint immediately dispatched the internal EMT's that were on staff for the building. Arriving in a matter of minutes they attended to Milton reviving him and moving him over to the big couch in his office. They wanted to take him to Memorial, but he resisted so strongly that they finally gave up and advised him to seek medical attention as soon as he could on his own because there may be some underlying problem. He acknowledged their advice and told them that all he needed was to lie there for a few more minutes and he would be fine. Reluctantly they gathered their gear and left.

"Mr. Jenkovitch, do you really feel alright?" Jennifer asked.

"Yes Jenn I'm getting there. I assume it was you that found me."

"Yes you were out cold and it scared me."

"Well I'll be okay. I'm just going to take a short nap here and then go home and really rest. Jenn, I want to thank you for your action I don't know what I'd do without you."

"That's alright. I was glad I came in when I did. The reason I came in was to ask you a question regarding this distribution project but now in light of things I'm sure it can wait until tomorrow. Do you want me to hang around a little while longer?"

"No Jenn, you've done enough good things for today. Go home and enjoy your evening."

Jennifer took another good look at her boss and decided that he seemed to be doing okay so she went out to her desk, packed up and went home. Even though he claimed to be okay Jennifer wondered what could have caused such a sudden collapse if it wasn't a heart attack. The EMT's didn't rule that out completely, but based on what they could determine that was not the cause.

#######

It had been sometime since I attended one of my building's house parties so when I received word one would be happening this Saturday I couldn't wait. The last few weeks have really been playing havoc with my psyche and my stress level. All of the things I was finding out about the company in such a short period of time on top of the murder that happened right in front of me was causing me some concern about my health. I tried to remain calm through it all but somehow each night when I got home I almost automatically rehashed the events of the day trying to piece together something that made sense. Not being any closer to discovering the glue that held this whole evil plot together was not helping. During this time I had several conversations with Mr. Hernandez and he has yet to provide me the proof he said he was going to give about who he was and who he worked for. So until I got that, my chats were very guarded on my part. I just didn't trust him.

When I found out that Mr. Crandall was in the hospital and that was the reason why he didn't meet with me that day, I was a little concerned. He didn't appear to have any physical or medical issues that I could determine, but in light of all that was happening now, anybody going down wouldn't surprise me - especially a man in his position. It was just a few days after he returned to work that he called me and asked if we could sit down and discuss how I was making out at the plant. I gladly accepted his invitation because I wanted to find out for myself what really happened to him. We scheduled a lunch meeting and he was going to come down to the plant where I was now officially stationed. Even though I still maintained my office at the headquarters building, I spent most of my time in a kind of makeshift residence at the plant.

He suggested we meet at the Peacock Palace because he wanted to get an idea of just where we were sitting when the incident happened. I had not been to the place since the incident and was a little reluctant to agree with him, but since he insisted I had to accommodate him. The time was set for 12:30 just as it was with Tony. That didn't help my nerves any either.

On the day Mr. Crandall and I were scheduled to have lunch, I called Marsha. I didn't want to refer to her as Mimi at work because I wasn't sure whether anyone else there did. I wanted to see if she had learned anything new that could help our inquiries. I learned that she had gone out of state to attend a product seminar and would not return until Friday. This was not unusual for the chemical staff to attend these functions, so I was not surprised. What did puzzle me was that these things were usually planned months in advance and I wondered why she hadn't mentioned she would be travelling. I couldn't dwell on the thought so I went through my day's routine and prepared to meet with Herb.

At 12:00 I stopped what I was doing and prepared to go to the tavern. Still feeling somewhat leery about the prospect of returning to the place where such a tragedy occurred my stomach was a bit jittery. I shook off the sensation by telling myself that unless I overcome this fear I will be apprehensive about going in there forever. With a new feeling of confidence I went down to the street got a cab and left. In just a few minutes I was there. The traffic pattern was as normal as I could ever remember it being and people were rushing about just as the business and visitor crowd would so often do. It was not like the day when I had that awful feeling that something wasn't right here.

I was a little early so I decided to go in and look around to see if anything had been changed. It was still just as dim as before and from my initial observation nothing had been rearranged. As I looked over the crowd I spotted some of my coworkers there, the same ones who had been there the day of the shooting, so apparently they had no problem in coming back either. My wait wasn't long when I saw Mr. Crandall come through the door and look around for me. I got his attention and waved him over to where I was so we could get a table.

"Hi Mr. Crandall how are you?" I said as we met and shook hands.

"I'm doing okay Ron, glad you could make it. Would you like a cocktail or something?"

"Just a regular iced tea for me is good."

He waived the waitress over and ordered the drinks as she handed us menus.

"How are things going in the plant? I hear you have been pretty busy inserting yourself into the operation. Have you come up with anything yet to bump up production?"

"Well sir, it's only been a few days but from what I have observed the production level may be low not because of any lack of methodology but some of that equipment is rather old. Pushing those antiques any harder could cause a bigger problem than low production - perhaps, no production."

"I know some of those pumps and filters are a bit old but not as old as all that. Besides most of our budget money now is being funneled into the new project in Lab 1. I don't think anything is going to change that."

"That brings up something else for me. When I tried to go into that lab I was denied entry. What do I need to get in?"

"Ron, please do not concern yourself with that lab. It is a particularly sensitive project and restricted access except to only a few people. I have trouble sometime getting in there myself."

He chuckled.

I got the message and resigned myself to not being able to go in through the front door, but I was determined to get in there. Having received such confirmation from him that something extraordinary was going on in there just elevated my curiosity and was leading me to believe that the answers to the questions Mimi and I have must lie there. While I was thinking about it the waitress came over and brought our drinks. She then took the food order and disappeared into the kitchen.

"So other than replacing all the equipment" he quipped, "What else do you see that could improve the overall operation?"

"Well sir, as I said it's still early yet and I haven't had much time to really study everything but I thought that piece of it would be a good beginning for improvement."

"Okay Ron. You keep at it I'm confident you'll come up with something. Now as far as the other activities we discussed, you haven't been doing any more of your after hour research have you?"

This question really bothered me, because now more than ever I was sure that there were hidden cameras in our headquarters office suites monitoring every move by the employees after 6:00 O'clock. Since I have no way of proving it, there wasn't much I could do or say about it, but I thought to myself if it's true then he should know that I haven't been doing any of that lately.

"No sir, I've been strictly devoting my time to the production project."

At that time the waitress came over and brought the food order. I must have been very hungry because I gobbled it down as if it was going to be my last meal. Mr. Crandall noticed my speed eating and commented asking whether I had a hot date waiting for me back at my office. I almost choked as I laughed, but I managed to respond and tell him I was just very hungry. We spent the next twenty minutes making essentially small talk about everything except the business. During that time I was finding out more about the man's personality. He opened up, almost inadvertently about his beliefs that there was a higher power that was guiding him and he was subject to obey his commands. I wasn't sure just how to understand what he was really saying but somehow I don't think he was referring to the same higher power that came to mind for me. The more he talked the more I was getting the feeling that he was deeply into some type of devil worship, but then he seemed to catch himself and abruptly cut off the conversation on that subject. He quickly looked at his watch and said:

"Wow look at the time. I've got to be getting back. Ron, it seems like you are on the right track so I'll give you some more time before we get together again. Remember one thing though, Lab 1 is not your responsibility."

He called the waitress over paid the check and said goodbye. The way he cut off speaking about his beliefs in the occult really got my attention. I suspected that he was strange, but now I was convinced that I should observe him even more closely and also keep my interaction with him at a respectful distance. During his whole discourse he did not seek any response from me nor did he allow for me to interject any of my thoughts regarding the subject. It was as if he was talking to someone other than me trying to declare his loyalty and pledge his devotion. It was a little disconcerting listening to him rant on, but what could I do this was his lunch meeting. In a way I was glad when he cut off the conversation and decided to leave. As he walked toward the door I watched him to see if there was anything different about him since the time when he came in. At this point I had to laugh to myself thinking: "Fool, what were you expecting to see?" After that I got my coat and returned to my office.

Once there I sat down and thought about the things Herb was telling me. I wondered could he be part of this evil drug scenario. He certainly would be in a position to have a key role. His relationship with the CEO and others in high offices would give him access to anything going on at Canon. As I thought more about it the fact that a product could be produced with only a few people knowing about it could only be concealed by those who have the power to do so. The ranking powers being in collusion to make this happen was truly a scary thought. But even more disconcerting was the idea that behind this collusion was something Herb was referring to during his soliloquy at lunch. Was there a greater power that was not only guiding him but also directing the actions of those who held offices in high places?

I reached for the phone because I wanted to share this new revelation with Mimi but then remembered she wouldn't be back until tomorrow. I didn't want to leave this new news as a message on either her phone here or at home, so I made a note to call her first thing in the morning. When I consider now how I was first introduced to all this intrigue, my previous disposition to dismiss most sayings that I hear at social gatherings regarding company business as just gossip has changed drastically. In fact as I recall the initial conversation, the groundwork that was laid to launch my investigation is now so firm that it's hard to believe the premise. Moreover, the initial source, the first revelator that I was exposed to, curiously has not been seen since that party - at least not by me.

The balance of my day was spent moving about within the plant viewing the various production lines with the hope that I would see something that could be improved. I still suspected that I was sent down here to keep me from discovering even, if only accidentally, something at the headquarters that the world was not supposed to know about – at least not yet. When I finished perusing the production area I just couldn't resist the opportunity to go upstairs and meander around the laboratories. Out of pure wishful thinking I hoped perhaps someone may have left the door to Lab 1 ajar and I could just walk in unannounced. The entry door had a push button combo lock on it and my hopes were that the last person to enter may not have closed the door completely. However, when I got there the wish died – the door was closed tight. I then took a deep breath thinking perhaps my nose might give me some hint as to what may be going on in there. This too was futile and not to be, so I kept moving back to my office.

#######

The phone rang.

"Hello this is Codey."

"Reggie, how are we coming with the arrangements?"

"Hello Herb. Well Houston we have a problem."

"What do you mean?"

"I had all the travel arrangements set but when I went to get the clearance to travel for Brent from his supervisor I was told he couldn't go."

"And why is that? I already talked with him and he said okay."

"Maybe when you talked to him, but now he said the police told Brent he couldn't leave the city."

"Oh, oh what's that all about?"

"From what I can understand the police are taking a closer look at him because of the holes in his statements. It seems that someone was able to identify a man hanging around the shooter's car. They have arrested him and he implicated Brent. They can't prove anything yet and they're not sure they believe him because he's a small time street hustler willing to finger anybody to save his hide. But anyway they want to question Brent some more."

"That's not good. Not good at all. That imbecile Brent will crumble under the slightest pressure and give up everybody and everything. We've got to do something quick."

"Yeah I agree but what? The police are watching him."

"I have to figure it out. I'll call you later before you leave for the day. Are you working late?"

"I wasn't planning on it, but I'll hang around if you want me to."

"Let's see what I come up with. Does the 'ole man know anything about this?"

"I don't think so but I'm sure it won't be a secret long."

"Of that I'm sure. Okay I'll talk with you later. Goodbye."

"Bye!"

Herb Crandall could feel his nerves beginning to unravel as he reached for his ring. He started twirling it. As he continued to twirl, the room was starting to heat up when his phone rang and he reached for it with his right hand.

"Hello Crandall here."

"Hello Mr. Crandall this is Brent Woodley from the plant. Listen I think I'm in some trouble and I need your help."

Herb feigned ignorance.

"What are you talking about?"

"You know that situation I took care of for you, well I think the police are suspecting me. What should I do?"

"Let's get something straight here. You didn't do anything for me. What you did, you did on your own. Now I'm going to try and help but you keep things clear on that issue."

"Okay, okay – now what?"

"Where are you now?"

"I'm still at the plant but about to get off."

"Alright go find a pay phone in the basement and call from that one in a half hour. I'll tell you what to do then."

"Okay Mr. Crandall I'll do that."

He hung up.

As soon as he hung up with Brent the wheels in Herb's mind starting turning. He sat back in his executive chair and folded his hands before his face as a diabolical scheme began formulating. How to make this man disappear was the question. Since sending him to a foreign country was out of the question now it must be done right here at home. He pondered the matter for several minutes and then it hit him. The idea he thought was so brilliant he couldn't fathom why it took him so long to think of it.

Brent loved skiing and ski accidents happen all the time. What could be a better way to dispose of his problem than to arrange one? It must be thorough and effective and the outcome must be sure. Now all he had to do was to cast the right players in his macabre production. Of course Reggie would have a key role, but in Herb's script for him he would not be the actual executioner. No one readily came to mind but Herb was not to be deterred in his mission.

Keenly aware that the half hour he gave Brent to call him back was approaching the mark,

Herb made up his mind that he would first set the stage by having Brent go to a site where the act could be performed. He would fill in the cast later. Knowing that Brent's movements were limited by his police restriction the place had to be not only conducive for a successful production, but it must be geographically compliant. There were no ski resorts within the city limits so Herb had to think of a way to circumvent the restriction. It didn't take long to come up with the idea that the most popular resorts in the area were just outside the limits. One in particular a place called Camelback would be an ideal venue.

At precisely 12:30 the phone rang.

"Hello Herb Crandall."

"Hi Mr. Crandall this is Brent. I'm calling just like you told me to."

"Yeah Brent hello again. Okay I've got it all worked out. You like to ski don't you?"

"Yes sir. I love to ski but what's that got to do with my situation?"

"Well I'm going to arrange for you to take off for a couple of days and go up to Camelback Lodge. You know where that is right?"

"Sure, I've been there lots of times."

"I plan to have you meet someone there who can resolve this whole matter for you.

Give me your home number and I'll call you later with the details."

"That sounds great Mr. Crandall. Do I have to pay for this?"

"No. Don't worry about a thing, I'll take care of it all."

"Okay here's my number."

Herb wrote the number down and said goodbye. Now that the plan was created and set in motion he just had to complete it by filling in the details. His next step was to get back to Reggie.

Ring, ring, ring.

"Hello this is Codey."

"Hey Reggie it's me again. I think I've got it all figured out. You know that ski resort we went to last year up there in the mountains?"

"You mean the Camelback Lodge?"

"Yeah that's the one. Well I think it will be a good place to make our problem go away."

"Really? What's the plan?"

"I don't have all the details in place yet but free up your weekend starting tomorrow. You're going to join our friend there at least through Saturday. I've already talked to him so he's all excited about going. We're going to have to smuggle him out of the city though. I figure we can do it from here. If he comes up here tomorrow morning you and he can quietly leave through the basement garage. Requisition a company car, I'll approve it, but use somewhere local as your destination. I'm going to make reservations now when we finish. The rest of the plan I'll finish tonight. I will call you at home around 9:00 O`clock and fill you in."

"Okay Herb I'll talk to you later."

Herb Crandall was sure now he had it almost all figured out. He believed that once he got home he would be able to put the missing pieces in place. As he prepared to leave office for the day he picked up his phone and called down to the garage to alert his driver he would be coming down soon. In his mind he was playing out the whole scenario of just how he was going to implement the resolution to the problem. His only fear was that if this attempt failed and Brent was pressured into exposing what he knew about P.T.D.T.Y., then what he experienced the night of the fire would be mild compared to what he could anticipate next time.

The ride home from the office took him on the scenic drive up along the East River to his luxury apartment on the Upper East Side. Upon arrival he thanked his driver as he usually did and gave instructions for what time he'd like to be picked-up in the morning. The driver acknowledged the instructions and got out to open the door. Herb enjoyed having reached this level of management where he benefitted from several company perks. On the outside it appeared that he was a man who had it all.

Once inside the building and in his apartment the façade of success came down. His first stop was to his well-stocked bar in which he prided himself in having only the best brand name beverages. Whenever he had invited guests over, which was not often, they were always impressed with his selections. Grabbing his favorite decanter which he kept filled with a top shelf brand he poured a double shot into his favorite large glass and enhanced it with just a splash of soda. Then he walked into the kitchen where he carefully placed the glass under the ice dispenser and allowed precisely two cubes to hit the bottom without causing an overflow. Now he was ready to sit in his comfortable lounger imbibe his quasi elixir and wait until the hunger monster seized him. His expectation was that during this time the missing pieces were sure to enter his mind.

Next to his lounger he kept a picture of his deceased wife and two daughters who were killed in a car accident about five years ago. Each night when he came home he would follow this routine and reflect on his life with them during a happier time. It was when Laura, his wife, was still with him that he was a true believer in God. Being raised for a period as an altar boy he had been given all the basics for adult life as a Christian. However, after the accident and his wife and daughters lay in the hospital clinging to life he prayed fervently daily petitioning for their full recovery. The period of angst grew longer and longer and it appeared like his prayers were not going to be answered. His anger mounted and his faith diminished until finally when he received word that they were gone, he could no longer restrain himself. He literally cursed God.

His time of mourning after the funeral seemed like it would never end. The bouts of depression alternating with brief episodes of manic elation were beginning to tear him apart until one day he happened upon news of a peculiar type of gathering which attracted his attention. Often he had heard one or two of his neighbors talking in the elevator about this enlightening meeting they had been to and how uplifted they felt at the end. At his lowest point he knew he had to get into something that could perhaps stabilize him. The next time he saw the neighbor he boldly asked how he could attend one of these meetings. The neighbor was more than happy to invite him.

At the appointed time Herb was picked up at his apartment and taken to a place in the city where he had never been before. It definitely wasn't on the east side but he wasn't quite sure about the west side either. After driving around for about twenty minutes the vehicle stopped in front of what appeared to be an abandoned warehouse on a dark street in a less than desirable area to him. He was having a hard time processing what kind of a meeting held here could possibly help him. When his host got out then opened the door and invited him to follow, he hesitated at first but decided to go ahead.

The duo entered the building through the front door. They were then immediately met by two people dressed in hooded monk type outfits. It was hard to tell whether they were man or woman or maybe one of each until one of them spoke. The voice was definitely a man's.

"Greetings Brother Michael - is this our new prospect?"

Being referred to as a prospect was not quite what Herb had imagined but he was too far in now to back out.

"Yes Brother Paul, are you ready?"

They started walking until they moved into a huge room totally lit by candlelight. A large crowd was in the center and the glow from the candles gave off a kind of eerie comforting feeling. Heavy aroma from burning incense was almost as intoxicating as his favorite scotch. Herb's host steered him to the center of the room and the gathering formed a circle around them. Slowly the crowd began to move in a counter clockwise direction while chanting something in a language that was unfamiliar. After a short period of chanting and circling, one end of the circle opened and a pathway was made leading up to a small stage.

On the stage stood a tall figure dressed from head to toe in a long black robe. In one hand he held a big talisman and in the other a long knife. Until the figure raised up his arms his gender identity was a mystery. When the sleeves of his robe fell back exposing his muscular arms, the question about gender was answered. As Herb's host moved toward the stage with him in tow, the chanting grew louder and more intense. Suddenly the tall man dropped his arms and the chanting stopped. From the side entrance another figure also dressed in black robe walked in leading a goat tethered to a rope. The docile animal was led to a spot center stage and held there until someone from the crowd came and placed a large pail under its head. Then the two figures in black seized the goat and the one with the knife slit its throat while the other caught the flowing blood in the bucket.

The silence was broken as the chanting began again. The tall man turned to the rear wall with the bucket in hand and began speaking to a figure projected on the wall. He raised the pail high above his head and chanted fervently petitioning the beast to accept his sacrifice and appear before them to anoint the new prospect. The chanting again intensified until at the height of the fever pitch a loud clap of thunder was heard and the beast appeared in front of the projected image.

Herb could hardly believe what he was seeing and then the beast transformed himself into the figure of a human male and extended his hand. Not knowing exactly what to do Herb felt compelled to extend his hand also. The beast grabbed his hand and squeezed while shaking it. Herb felt such a sensation of peace and serenity he was in awe of what he had just witnessed. Then the beast spoke.

"If you will subject yourself and worship me, then this shall be your reward. Serve me and you shall have joy and comfort for as long as you are mine."

Herb had not felt such peace since before the death of his family. Tears welled up in his eyes as he lowered himself and kneeled before the beast. Then the beast beckoned the tall man to bring the bucket. The beast dipped his hand into it and spread the blood across Herb's forehead. With the other hand he touched Herb's shoulder and chanted. At the end of the ritual Herb was told to rise and join the circle for he had been accepted and was now one of them. When the ceremony concluded at night's end, he was given a signet ring emblazoned with the number 666 in the stone and told this was his pacifier. And as long as he served his master obediently, whenever he needed comforting he was to embrace it.

His reverie ended and Herb returned to the present moment. Just as he predicted the answers were now available. Within his gathering were many worshippers who were of questionable character. Amongst them was one in particular who Herb knew was very skilled at what he needed to have done. Only a phone call away he was confident that this person would be happy to help a brother out and incur the indebtedness of someone in Herb's position. He got up and went to his den to find his book of numbers. Right near the front of the book was the name and telephone number of the man he sought. He dialed the number and waited.

"Hello you have reached a number that is currently not in service please try your call again later" was the message that came on. However, before Herb could hang up another voice followed.

"Just kidding if you're looking for Ivan he's not here right now - at the sound of the beep leave your message and he'll get back to you soon."

That's the kind of person this character was - a real joker and Herb knew it. He had served time in several different correctional facilities over the years and developed a real warped sense of humor. In one of them he had been recruited to serve the beast. Now it was time for Herb to utilize his particular skills. Having no choice but to wait for the return call, Herb decided to appease the hunger monster that was now demanding his attention. He went into the kitchen took out one of his favorite TV dinners and threw it in the microwave.

About an hour later the phone rang.

"Hello this is Crandall."

"This is the voice of your conscious reminding you of your sins - repent, repent, repent."

"Okay Ivan knock it off. I've got something I need you to do."

"Yeah what is it top dog?"

"I have a problem with someone who I need to make disappear right away."

"No not you top dog."

"Come on Ivan this is serious."

"Alright enlighten me. What's the deal?"

"A man named Brent Woodley who works for me is in a position to cause me a major problem – even our adversary."

"Man how did that happen?"

"No time to explain now. Here's what I want you to do. I've arranged for him to go with Reggie Codey, you know Reggie, up to the Camelback Lodge tomorrow morning. You know where that is right?"

"Yeah I've been there."

"Well I want you to meet Reggie there at 10:00 AM and he'll introduce you. Sometime over the next two days make him go away."

"Just like that huh? You know what I used to get for that?"

"No but I'm sure we can work out something."

"After this you're going to owe me big time you know that. I'm going to need some advance cash."

"How much?"

"Let Reggie bring five large with him when he comes and I'll solve your problem Saturday morning. This guy does ski don't he?"

"Yes. He'll be no problem getting on the slopes."

"Okay. Consider it done. Small bills brother, remember I like small bills."

"No bigger than a fifty, is that okay?"

"That will do."

They hung up and Herb paused for a minute to recompose himself before calling Reggie. Even though he knew Ivan for a few months and had seen him regularly at the ritual meetings he had never prevailed upon him before for his services. He wondered whether he was trading in one problem for possibly an even bigger one. In any event whatever the outcome he knew he had to take care of the Woodley issue first. Herb picked up the phone and dialed Reggie's home number.

"Hello."

"Hey Reggie, this is Crandall how you doing?"

"I'm okay boss I've been waiting for your call."

"Yeah well I just finished finalizing the plan. You know Ivan from the gathering?"

"Yeah I think so why?"

"Well he's going to do the job. You're going to take Brent with you and meet him at the lodge at 10:00 AM. I will have an envelope for you to give him. Pick it up from my office around 7:00 AM I'll be there."

"Alright boss. See you tomorrow."

"Goodnight."

Herb hung up and then called Brent Woodley.

"Hi you got Brent."

"Hello Brent this is Mr. Crandall."

"Yeah I've been waitin' for you."

"Are you alone?"

"Yeah why you ask?"

"No reason just wanted to give only you the details for tomorrow morning. You're going to meet with Reggie Codey at 7:30 AM in the basement garage. Have your bags with you. You two are going to drive up to the lodge together."

"Are you coming up?"

"No I don't think so. You go and have fun. Don't worry about anything."

"Okay Mr. Crandall. Thank you."

"Goodbye Brent."

Friday morning came and Brent in his small apartment was all excited as he packed for his free excursion. In his mind he convinced himself that Herb Crandall was doing him a favor in return for what he believed was a service he had done for him. Even though it was told to him that what he did was not for Mr. Crandall, he was not accepting it. Brent was not part of the gathering nor was he a prime member of the group. How he came to be included in the P.T.D.T.Y. scenario was only because the power group needed an inside person who knew how to run the production line for the secret product. His being given key information about the project was never intended by the majority of the power group, but at Herb's insistence it was done. Herb's intention was to recruit Brent as his new prospect for the gathering.

Packed and ready Brent called for a taxi then went downstairs. Only a few minutes went by before one rolled up at his door and he got in. At Canon Enterprises with bags in hand he made his way to the basement garage. He was early so he decided to sit down at the front gate and wait for Reggie. The attendant spotted him and asked what he was doing. Brent explained that he was an employee and wanted to wait there for his co-worker. The attendant moved him inside to a special waiting area.

Reggie entered the garage a short time later in his own car and parked. He saw Brent in the waiting area and told him he had to go upstairs and pick up something but he would be right back. Brent acknowledged him. Fifteen minutes later Reggie came down and got his bags from his car. Then they both went over to the motor pool where a reserved company car waited. Reggie completed the sign out process and they exited the building on their way to the mountains.

When they arrived at the lodge and pulled up to the visitor's center Reggie told Brent to wait in the car while he checked in. Brent thought this a little strange but he was so excited and anxious to get to the slopes he dismissed it. Inside Reggie looked around for Ivan but didn't see him. It was well after 10:00 O'clock so he began to wonder whether there had been a miscommunication about the time. Believing Ivan must be around somewhere he decided to go ahead and check in. The registration had already been taken care of by Mr. Crandall so it was just a matter of picking up the keys. Herb had reserved a two bedroom villa for Reggie and Brent in the name of Baron Adams so that there would be no record of anyone's true identity. Even the credit information used was bogus. Ivan made his own bogus reservation.

After he received the keys Reggie decided to look around for Ivan. He was aware that Ivan loved practical jokes so he prepared himself for anything that might happen. He went by the restaurant and sure enough there was Ivan casually having breakfast. Not surprised at this Reggie went in and sat down at his table.

"I thought we were supposed to meet in the lobby."

"Yeah that was at ten. It ain't ten now is it? You got something for me?"

Reggie was a little taken back by Ivan's remarks so he stared at him for a moment trying to determine what his attitude was. Then he reached in his coat pocket.

"This what you're looking for?" he said as he pulled out a thick envelope.

When Ivan went to reach for it, Reggie pulled back.

"Listen son you don't want to mess with me so hand it over."

Reggie gave it to him. Ivan opened it and started flipping through the bills.

"Looks okay. Have our boy out on the Conderoga Trail by 8:00 O'clock tomorrow morning and then leave him to me."

"Don't you even want to meet him so you know who he is?"

"Yeah! When I'm finished eating. Don't rush me."

Ivan continued eating his meal oblivious to Reggie staring at him. When he finally finished he wiped his mouth and said: "Leave the tip" and got up. Reggie sat there hesitating but then reached in his pocket and left a small tip. The two men then walked out to the car to meet Brent.

"Brent I want you to meet somebody."

Brent opened the car door and got out.

"This is the man Mr. Crandall told you he wanted you to meet. Ivan this is Brent - Brent meet Ivan."

"I'm so glad to meet you sir. I hear you're going to help me."

"Yeah that's right. I'm going to take real good care of you. Now why don't we all go change and then take a ride on the slopes?"

"That sounds great. Reggie we all checked in?"

"Yes Brent we're in villa 2036. I believe it's right over there. Okay Ivan we'll meet you at the lift in about twenty minutes."

"Fine, see you there."

The group separated and went to their respective rooms. Brent was pumped, he couldn't stop talking. He was continually praising Herb Crandall for how good he was setting him up. Reggie had a hard time restraining himself from laughing as they went inside their villa. It didn't take very long for both men to change and head over to the ski shop for Reggie to get his equipment.

Brent had his own so he just advised Reggie on what to get. At almost twenty minutes on the mark they were at the lift and Ivan was there waiting. Ivan watched Brent carefully observing all of his mannerisms and moves. He was figuring out just how to carry out his mission most efficiently.

At the top of the main trail the trio dismounted the lift. Brent not waiting for the others rushed over to the trail and started down. Ivan not wanting to lose sight of him pushed hard after him. Reggie in no rush took his time and when he got to the hill his companions were gone. Ivan had to use all of his skills to catch up with Brent who was ahead of him. Ivan was very focused trying to determine just what level of expertise Brent had. By the time they reached the bottom of their first run Ivan had it all figured out. When asked by Brent if he was going again, Ivan declined and said he was going to his room because he had to do something. Reggie came down a short time later and agreed to go again with Brent.

After a full day of skiing and having fun Brent asked Reggie back in the villa about Ivan. Since he hadn't seen him again after the morning meeting, he was curious about how he was going to help him. He asked Reggie how well he knew him and what did he do. He questioned why if the man was going to help him he didn't even talk to him. Reggie replied that the man was very good at what he does and he would be in contact soon. No sooner had he said that when the phone rang.

"Hello this is 2036" Reggie answered.

"Hey this is Ivan. I want you guys to meet me down in the town at a little restaurant called the Mountain Top on Astor Place right off of Main Street."

"What time?"

"7:00 O'clock. Be on time."

"Okay, okay we'll be there."

Ivan just hung up - no goodbye.

"Wow that guy is really weird" Reggie said.

"And he's gonna' help me?" Brent responded.

"You heard the conversation right? He wants us to meet him downtown at seven. I guess we're having dinner there."

"Might it be something else?"

"With that guy I really don't know."

It was now almost six and the pair figured they had at least a half-hour to kill before going out so they sat around and watched TV. The news came on and the lead reporter referred to a statement by the police indicating they had narrowed their search down to a single suspect in the recent murder of a Canon Enterprises employee at a local downtown restaurant. He further stated that they were now searching for that suspect to place him in custody. When Brent heard the report he nervously asked Reggie "You think they mean me?"

"I don't know but it doesn't sound good. Let's hope Ivan is as good as he thinks he is."

"Yeah, I sure hope so or I may have to stay here."

Reggie didn't say it but he thought – "You don't know how right you are."

At six-thirty the two men readied themselves to go meet Ivan. Brent was very familiar with the town and knew about many of the eating establishments but he had to admit he had never been to or even heard of this place. They rode around for some time trying to find it and Reggie knowing Ivan was a stickler about time was worried that if they arrived too late he would pull one of his pranks. Fortunately Brent had an idea where Astor Place was and he directed Reggie to turn onto the street at the right time. They arrived at the place with time to spare.

Mountain Top was right in the middle of the block sandwiched between an antique shop and a year `round ice cream parlor. It was a small quaint operation with table seating for about twenty patrons. It had a cozy set up with subdued but adequate lighting ideally suited for quiet conversation. It touted Italian American cuisine as their specialty on the menu and Reggie thought this seemed to be out of character for Ivan. As expected when they walked in the door Ivan was already seated at a table staring at the door. He spotted the duo and waived them over. Before they could even get comfortable in their seats Ivan spoke.

"Have you heard the news?"

"What news you talking about?" Reggie responded.

"About the murder case involving your company. The police have a suspect they're looking for. Maybe it's you" and he looked right at Brent.

His words sent chills down Brent's spine and he thought about whether this man was really going to help him.

"I just thought I'd let you know in case you didn't. Anyway let's order."

He changed the subject as quickly as he brought it up. Reggie continued to think – "How weird is this guy." Ivan waived the waitress over and they all ordered. After that initial question Ivan had nothing else to say. Reggie attempted to break the silence with some small talk but Ivan put his finger to his lips indicating – hush. Reggie stopped talking and just looked at him. Brent was totally at a loss about what was going on so he just sat there. Finally after several minutes Ivan spoke.

"I needed to meditate for a moment because I was receiving a message from the adversary."

When Brent heard him say that he freaked. "This is the man whose gonna' help me." Reggie grabbed his shoulder to settle him but Brent was very unsettled. Then Ivan said:

"Calm down son you're in good hands" and he smiled.

Reggie was at a loss for what to say next. The timing of the food order delivery couldn't have occurred more appropriately for the situation. As the waitress began setting the plates down in front of each man, Ivan continued to smile while both Reggie and Brent looked perplexed. Without any hesitation Ivan dug into his meal. Both table mates observed him for a minute trying to fathom what he was all about but drew a blank, so they dug in also.

For the balance of the dinner not much was said as each man was reluctant to talk. Several awkward minutes went by even after they were finished dining. It was Reggie who broke the ice.

"Ivan you invited us here. Did you want to talk about something?"

"Oh no man, I just didn't wanna' eat by myself. Now that we're all finished we can go home."

"Okay but who's paying the tab?" Reggie asked.

"This one's on me - even the tip. I'll see you guys tomorrow on the hill at 8:00 AM right?"

When Reggie heard Ivan was paying, he almost yanked Brent right out of his chair.

"Yeah right Ivan - 8:00 O'clock is fine."

Brent was still staring at Ivan when Reggie starting guiding him toward the door. Ivan just sat there with his odd smile and stared back.

When they got home Brent let it all out.

"That guy is nuts. He can't help me. He's the one that needs help. He needs a shrink."

"Alright calm down, calm down. I told you he's good at what he does so tomorrow you should find out. Now go to bed and get some sleep."

"Yeah okay - but you're right about him, he is really weird."

Chapter Four
"Dark Shadows"

Friday's at Canon Enterprises to me are usually pretty much laid back and easy going. At least that's the way it is at headquarters. Since I've been at the plant I'm finding it to be quite different. With production schedules to meet and constant pressure from the board of directors for the labs to continually come up with new products, the scene here is definitely not the same. The laid back attitude is absent for sure. Push, push, push seems to be the motto for the operation.

I tried calling Mimi again but still her recorded message came on. Nothing in it indicated what time she would be returning so I figured I'd make another attempt later this afternoon. My schedule today isn't extremely challenging so I decided to get some overdue paperwork out of the way. As I worked, one thing kept coming across my mind. I've been hearing that the police have narrowed their focus down to one or two people in their investigation. I don't have any names but the rumor mill has it that both are from the production lines. Wondering who it might be stimulates my curiosity. I'm just beginning to know the line people here but I would be hard pressed to pull one out of a line up. They all look like regular hardworking blue collar citizens. I know I couldn't even begin to suspect anybody, so I put the thought out of my head.

As the work day drew to a close and my excitement mounted in anticipation of tomorrow's shindig, I reluctantly allowed my last thought's to move to Tango Hernandez. It's been almost a week since he's tried to contact me. I wondered now, since the police have two people of interest in sight whether he had taken me off his radar screen. I hoped it was true, but my sense of reality said it probably wasn't. He just hadn't got back around to me. Besides he still had not provided me with a convincer about who he was so maybe that's why the avoidance. Whatever the reason for his absence was fine with me.

I wrapped up my final tasks, painstakingly put away my business tools and headed for the exit. The closer I got to street level the more the ready for the weekend feeling took over my psyche. Riding home in a cab was not like coming in to work. Since Alex only picked me up in the mornings conversing with a different driver nightly was just not the same. Tonight however was different. The driver who picked me up this time was very talkative especially when he noticed the building that I was coming out of. He asked what I thought about the news report concerning the suspect police are looking for in that Canon murder case. I had not heard the news report so I questioned him to give me more on what he heard. He responded by telling me that the police were down to one person and they were on the verge of taking him in.

This news didn't exactly put a damper on my spirits regarding the weekend but it sure got me thinking about who the one suspect could be. As I reviewed once again in my head the people from the production lines, still no one stood out as even a possible suspect. If it was true that one of them is really responsible for murdering Tony then he must have had a really good reason for doing so. If he or she was so involved in the secret drug scenario why would he choose to commit murder in the middle of the day in some crowded public place? That part didn't make much sense to me, because from all that I was discovering about what may be going on inside the Canon upper management it seems that the power group would have a more sophisticated way to make Tony disappear.

As the scenery changed and we approached my neck of the city the driver concluded his news reporting by telling me that he didn't know much about what they made at Canon but he wondered whether the killing of that employee had anything to do with any of the products they made. For the driver to say that it sparked a new line of thinking for me. I believe he was referring to possible espionage within the pharmaceutical industry but on the other hand could he have been thinking something else? Could there be among the public's thinking that something was amiss at Canon Enterprises? I started to question him about what he really meant, but then we arrived at my stop and I settled my fare and got out.

The Friday night festivities around my apartment complex were already beginning to heat up when I made my way into the building. For some reason the street hostesses were out a little earlier than usual but then I remembered it was the beginning of the month and the government checks had already been distributed so the Johns were on the prowl. I made my way up to my apartment and settled in hoping to catch some of the news that the cabbie was referring to. I poured myself a glass of Mr. Daniel's brew and plopped down in front of the TV. As the intoxicating beverage entered my system I could feel myself relaxing while the nightly news came on. The reporter corroborated what the cab driver was saying and the mystery about who it could be intensified for me. Could it be someone that I have spoken to or even worked briefly with? Refusing to acknowledge even the possibility, I dismissed the thought and went in the kitchen to prepare dinner for myself before watching a DVD movie then going to bed.

#######

On Saturday morning during ski season the slopes at Camelback were usually packed with many visitors. Reggie and Brent got up bright and early anticipating another fun day. It was bright and sunny and even the wind was calm. Both men decided to forego any breakfast saying they would eat after their first run. They grabbed their gear and headed toward the lift. Even though it was only 7:30 Reggie decided that he was going to get there not just on time but ahead of Ivan. This time he was right. They arrived at the lift and there was no Ivan in sight. Then Reggie thought - could Ivan have already been here and gone up? His thought was corrected almost immediately when he saw Ivan making his way toward the lift.

"Good morning men, how are you?" Ivan said with an extremely happy tone.

Both men hesitated before answering trying to figure out what mood was Ivan in today.

"We're good" Reggie answered.

"Great! Shall we go?"

They boarded the lift and headed up the mountain. At the top just as they did yesterday Brent jumped off first and pushed toward the hill. This time however, Ivan didn't give him a big head start. He jumped off right after and pushed behind him. He did turn around for a moment though and motioned to Reggie for him not to follow. Reggie got the message and took the next lift down.

Brent hit the hill with a hard push off stroke and went sailing down. Ivan right behind him doubled his effort and stayed close. A number of skiers had bunched together in front of them neglecting the guidelines for the trail. However, when Brent exerted himself he moved out in front of the pack. Ivan did the same. They were about half way down when Ivan veered out to the right then suddenly turned sharply back headed toward Brent. They were now well ahead of the pack. As Ivan pushed harder to gain speed, it appeared that he had more than a ski pole in his right hand. As he approached Brent at full speed Brent saw him but couldn't believe what was happening. He tried to maneuver to avoid the collision but it was too late. BAM! He was hit.

Not only was he hit with such force that it sent him tumbling head over heels, but at the moment of impact the object that Ivan had in his hand, a hypodermic needle filled with curare, was jabbed into Brent's neck. Brent continued to tumble down the hill for several yards before coming to rest on a gentle portion of the slope just off the main trail. From the position that he ended up in it was clear that his head and neck suffered severe trauma. Ivan who had aimed his hit so skillfully that he suffered just a minor bruise to his shoulder, skied down the slope at full speed after the tumbling body. When he got to Brent he quickly searched his pockets to remove his wallet and any remaining identification he had on him. Not wasting any time Ivan pushed off again in a cross country direction to the other side of the slope then completed his downhill run to the bottom.

By this time the pack caught up with the body lying on the hill. Although they saw the man tumbling no one had witnessed the collision nor did anyone see Ivan skiing away. Quickly one of the skiers alerted the ski patrol who arrived on the scene very quickly, but not in time to be able to do anything for Brent. Short time later paramedics also arrived and removed the body. Brent was taken to the local hospital and placed in the morgue. The medical team diligently searched the body for any identification but found none so Brent was entered into the files as "John Doe" - DOA – cause of death apparent broken neck. No further examination was made at this time and the file would be reopened on Monday.

Ivan checked out of the lodge via the video checkout system in his villa and was on his way home within minutes of having completed his mission. He was careful not to leave traces of him ever having been there, especially regarding his true identity. Reggie left a short time later after returning his gear to the ski shop and was also careful to remove any possible links to the real him or anything that Brent may have left behind . Once he crossed over the border heading into the city he called Ivan on his mobile phone. The phone rang several times but there was no answer and no voice mail message. Reggie wondered whether he had called the right number so he found a place to pull over and he carefully checked the number. He had dialed correctly but when he tried again the result was just the same. Now he was concerned. Where did Ivan go and was he sure that everything went as according to plan? Not being able to come up with an answer he got back on the road.

#######

Saturday morning found me enjoying the extra time in bed with no loud alarm clock going off and no urgency to get up. Even though I was fully awake I lay there steering up at the ceiling reflecting once again on what I heard last night on the news. I figured it would be just a matter of a short time before they caught the man they're seeking but again I couldn't help wondering who it might be. I turned on the radio expecting to hear an update on the issue, but this morning's news was dominated by turmoil in several foreign countries. Even when the local news did come up there was nothing about the search. In a way I wasn't surprised because if the person at the plant heard the news like everybody else he or she was probably in hiding, at least until Monday.

I got up and looked out the window at the bright sunny day and decided it would be a good time to do the errands I had been putting off during the week. After completing my usual morning routine including breakfast, I dressed and went out.

I love Saturday mornings here especially when there's a beautiful day. The difference between the sights at night and those in the early morning daylight hours is like seeing a cleaned up nightclub the morning after the party's over. This is not to say that a miraculous clean up occurs overnight here, but it's just exhilarating to walk the streets in the morning and breathe in the fresh air.

My first stop was at the cleaners to pick up my shirts. Next I was off to the shoe shop to get my resoled shoes. I really needed to visit the supermarket next but not having a car or a cart there was no way I could carry everything at once so I returned home. When I first came to the city I was told I wouldn't need a car and so far I've managed pretty well but every so often I wonder whether I should get one. Conveniently all the businesses that I need are located within walking distance except for the market and that was driving me to consider a car.

I knew I had to go back out to the supermarket because my cupboard was getting bare, but right now I wanted to check in on the news again to see what the status was on the police hunt. It was still early but I flipped on the TV and zeroed in on an all-news channel. I sat there through a whole segment until the news reports began repeating. Nothing at all was said about the hunt - not even that it was continuing. I thought this was a little strange since yesterday it was getting a lot of attention. Then I started to wonder if something had happened that the police were not yet ready to provide details on. Anyway, I shut it off and went to the market.

The rest of the day I spent cleaning the apartment and watching college football. I purposely refrained from turning on the news because at this point I was gearing up to enjoy the party tonight and didn't want anything on my mind that could dampen my spirit. It's been awhile since I attended one of these parties and my plan was to meet someone new and perhaps lead up to a lucky night for me. I busied myself with the chores until around six o'clock when my stomach told me it was time to eat something. Not too far from here is a small but very clean soul food place that serves the best smothered chops and greens I have ever had - even in my southern home town. Since I knew I would be doing some drinking tonight, I thought it best to put a good foundation in my system to mitigate the long term effects of the alcohol.

After gorging myself on a delicious home cooked southern style meal, I returned home to relax before party time. It was now about 7:30 and I wasn't planning to go out until much later so I thought I'd take a nap. The urge to check in on the news before doing so was still nagging at me but I resisted the temptation. For some reason I had the feeling that tonight was going to be a very special night and I wasn't going to let anything spoil it.

#######

Not sure what to do next, Reggie just drove around for a while. When he got home late Saturday afternoon he was about to panic not being able to reach Ivan to debrief on the mission. He immediately went to his home phone and dialed again. The result was the same - no Ivan. Now Reggie was shaking. Suppose things went wrong and Brent survived. He would be able to expose the hit man and ultimately tie him into the conspiracy. Sweat started to accumulate on his brow as he tried to figure out what to do next. He didn't want to contact Mr. Crandall on a Saturday unless he absolutely had to, but right now he was giving that idea some serious thought.

He took his bags threw them on the bed then went in the living room and turned on the TV to see what the latest news was. The highlights for the hour were still focused on overseas turmoil. He watched and waited for the local news then finally a report came on about the ski accident at Camelback Lodge. His attention level rose as he turned up the sound.

"Earlier today around 9:00 at the popular Camelback Lodge a young man believed to be in his mid-twenties had a horrific skiing accident. Witnesses say he must have lost his balance and went tumbling head first down the hill. Reports from the local hospital say that he suffered a broken neck and was D.O.A. - dead on arrival. At this time his identity is still unknown. Further reports state that he also suffered severe facial lacerations and contortions that may make picture identification virtually improbable. Now in other news ...."

When Reggie heard the report his pressure must have dropped fifteen degrees as he relaxed and leaned back on his sofa. His fear of exposure subsided and he turned his attention back to Ivan. He knew Ivan was weird but he didn't think he would become unreachable after such an important task was to be accomplished. He made a mental note that come Monday he was going to lay it all out for Herb about Ivan's behavior. He also thought about the next gathering. He was going to make it his focus to try and observe him more closely.

As he got more comfortable and relaxed after his trying ordeal of uncertainty, he wanted to cleanse himself of the guilt trip that was beginning to envelop him. He went in the bathroom and ran a tub full of hot water hoping this might abate his anxiety. While soaking in the soothing water he reflected on how it was that he became involved in this whole sordid adventure. Unlike Herb Crandall he was not drawn into the gathering as a reaction to a very painful family experience, but it was something that happened in college. During his college days he was fascinated by a group who always seemed to be on top of things. One day he decided to approach one of them and start up a conversation. He was amazed at how this student who was only in his second year was so much in control. Initially the young man hesitated to confide his secret with Reggie out of fear that he might be exposed. However, after a while as they became friends, the young man invited Reggie to a meeting.

Deep in the mountains of West Virginia one moonlit night his new friend came to his dorm room and got him. Reggie was a little surprised because there was no previous indication that this was going to happen. But when the young man explained that he had been laying the groundwork for the group to accept a new convert and tonight they were ready, Reggie couldn't refuse. He wanted to have the same kind of control that the young man appeared to have. They rode for some time in a car driven by an older man who was dressed in all black. Reggie heard the student refer to him only as Zoan.

Not much was said during the ride but Reggie was getting excited anticipating some type of fraternity like initiation. When the car veered off the main highway onto some back roads the street lights became almost non-existent. The road, in the darkness led up to an old mansion set far back and surrounded by an iron fence. They passed through the front gate and drove around a circular driveway up to the front door. Once inside they walked down a long dimly lit hallway which led into a large back room where about twenty people were assembled. They were all dressed wholly in black and each one holding a candle.

Zoan and the young man led Reggie into the group center and told him to kneel and face the front. The group was making a humming sound that sent a tingling sensation through Reggie's body. He wasn't sure what was going to happen next but when the group leader came forward and placed his hand on his shoulder, the tingling turned to shivers. He felt as if an electric probe had been applied to his body and an exhilarating feeling consumed him. No words were spoken, but the humming grew louder and more intense until finally it suddenly stopped.

The figure that stood before him lifted up Reggie's head and asked "Do you want to belong?"

Reggie responded with a very feeble yes. The figure repeated the question louder this time. Reggie answered with an equal increase in volume "Yes, Yes."

"Hold out your right hand palm up."

Reggie willingly complied with the command. Then from seemingly out of nowhere a sharp knife was produced and a swift shallow stroke was made across Reggie's palm drawing a small amount of blood. When the blood was drawn the figure clasped Reggie's hand in his and swore an oath.

"By the power of the adversary vested in me I bind you to the fold and commit your spirit to him."

Reggie felt like the weight of the world had been lifted off of his shoulder and he just wanted to sleep a peaceful sleep. He must have gone to sleep or something because all he could remember after that was waking up the next day in his dorm room bed with only a small scar across his right hand. From that time on he felt like he had been elevated to a new level of confidence and became a devoted follower of the gathering. It was through that group that he was able to land his position at Canon Enterprises and introduced to his new branch of the gathering.

Herb Crandall was also following the news that Saturday afternoon. He too was anxious to know the result of his production. When he heard the report that it was successful and his scheme had materialized as envisioned, he felt an ironic sense of achievement. His perception of Ivan as the right man for the job was validated but he was still leery about whether he had traded one old problem for a new one possibly more devastating than the first. His confidence increased that his position in the overall master plan of the adversary would be solidified. Basking in this new feeling of having pleased the emissary he spent the balance of the day enjoying the peace he felt when twirling his ring for brief periods.

#######

When I arrived at the party it was already in full swing. It was no surprise that the place was packed and the music had people up and dancing. I greeted the host who had become a good friend and eased my way through the crowd over to the bar. As I walked through I recognized many of the faces who usually came out for this. Some of them were as usual from Canon. What I didn't see, so far, was the person who dropped the note in my pocket that got me started in the whole Canon intrigue.

The bar had several king size bottles of an assortment of liquors and chasers and there was no shortage of anything. In the air was that distinct aroma from the burning of that herbal weed so popular at parties. I grabbed a large cup and poured myself a double portion of my favorite beverage mixed with my favorite chaser then began to circulate. Moving cautiously trying not to spill my drink I looked for a place to sit down for a minute. However, before I could do so a woman grabbed my arm and pulled me onto the dance floor. I had seen her before at one of these affairs but couldn't remember her name or who she was. It really didn't matter because she probably didn't remember mine either. The main thing was that we came to party and so we did.

When the music stopped I went in search of the drink I had set down on a lamp table but of course it was gone. At these parties after a while it was no unusual occurrence for someone to pick up a drink they hadn't poured. I wasn't upset in the least so I just went back to the bar and got another one. It was then that I looked over in the corner of the room and saw a most attractive young lady standing talking to another woman. From this distance and in the subdued lighting I could see she was fine but to what degree I needed to get a closer look. As I started moving in her direction I was careful not only to protect my drink from spilling, but I wanted to also avoid being dragged onto the dance floor.

As I moved closer I really felt like this could indeed be my lucky night. Her facial features became more distinctly visible but it was the covering on her head that made me realize who this was. In the lighting from where I was before I couldn't make out clearly the dark red hair, but now closer to her I saw it was beautiful and so was she. It was Marsha - Mimi.

When it dawned on me who this was I stopped for a moment. I was having difficulty processing that this was the same woman who I saw in the library dressed in rather bland student like attire. Now my eyes were feasting on the short tight leather skirt that accentuated her beautiful legs. Then my eyes moved up toward her face, but not bypassing the leather jacket and tight sweater that exposed just enough cleavage to make the viewer eager to see more. Her golden brown complexion and almost perfect features highlighted by make-up that could have been the work of a professional gave me pause to hesitate before speaking lest I stutter or babble. I was so glad when she spoke first.

"Hi Ron how are you? I didn't see you come in."

"Oh I'm good. You know I've been trying to reach you."

"Yes I figured you might be. I got in very late yesterday afternoon and was sure you had already left the office so I didn't try to call you. Why didn't you leave me a message? Oh excuse me do you know Linda? She's an accountant in the office at the plant."

"No I don't think we've met. I'm glad to meet you."

"Linda is responsible for me being here. When I got in yesterday she had a message waiting for me on my home phone saying I had to come to this party. Being that I needed a stress break I agreed with her and here I am. What were you trying to reach me about?"

"I have some new news about Tony's incident and that drug thing, but I certainly don't want to tell you about it now. We came here to party so let's do it. Linda I'm coming back for you."

I grabbed Mimi's arm and led her to the dance floor.

We were having such a great time dancing and laughing the night just seemed to fly by. It was obvious that I was not the only man in the house competing for Mimi's attention. Linda, who was also a looker, was not being ignored either. I did notice however that many of the potential suitors were bringing drinks whenever they came over. What did surprise me was that Mimi, as well as her friend, was drinking several of them. By the wee hours in the morning as the party was beginning to wind down and the upbeat jams got slower and more sensual, I made it a point to stay close to Mimi. Now whether it was the alcohol or something else I don't know but she hung on to me also. The other suitors got the message and backed off.

I held her close as we danced and it appeared things were going well, but as the hour grew late I noticed a change in her. As she attempted to talk her speech was slurred and her eyes were becoming glassy. I knew then it was time for her to leave. I looked around for Linda but she had already been claimed and was heading for the door. I managed to catch up with her and we talked for just a moment. She was also like Mimi.

"Linda how did you and Mimi get here?" I asked.

"We took a cab, why are you asking?"

"Aren't you going home together?"

She smiled a sly smile and said "She's a big girl now why don't you take her home?"

With that said she and her male friend went out the door.

Quickly I went to find Mimi. She had taken a seat on the edge of one of the couches and was beginning to nod. I sat down beside her and starting talking.

"Mimi, Mimi it's time to go. Where do you live?"

She straightened up long enough to whisper in my ear the address. I asked where her over coat was. Fortunately she remembered. I was glad that she had maintained custody of her purse. I went and got her coat and bid the host goodnight commending him for another fabulous affair. He acknowledged me while looking at her and smiling. I knew it was cold outside but I didn't bring a coat because the party was in my building so I had to decide whether to take her to my place to get my coat or just tough it out and take her home.

As we stood outside the apartment door she was insisting she wanted to go home now so the decision was made for me. I knew there wouldn't be a taxi anywhere around here now so I did what I had to do. I called Alex. After several rings he finally picked up.

"Hello, dis betta be good."

"Alex this is Ron I'm really sorry to call you at this hour but I need your help."

"What it is mon?"

"I need you to come and get me and take me somewhere."

"You mean now?"

"Yeah Alex now, I need you now."

"Where are you?"

"I'll be in the lobby of my building when you get here."

"Alright, alright mon I be there soon."

He hung up and I walked Mimi, who was hanging onto my arm to keep from falling, to the elevator. We reached the lobby and I sat her down while we waited. I tried talking to her but I could see now she was drifting into another world. My memory is not that great for remembering names and addresses when people first tell me, but when she whispered her address earlier it stuck because it was in an area which I wouldn't have guessed she lived. It was the Upper East Side.

Alex pulled up in front of my building about twenty minutes after I called him. I could tell he wasn't thrilled about having to get up in the wee hours of the morning but I knew I had no choice. Mimi and I walked out and got in.

"Where we goin' mon?" he said in a less than amicable tone.

"103 East 86th Street."

"East 86th Street - who you know live there?"

"This young lady lives there."

Alex turned around to get a good look at her and then he asked: "She okay?"

"Yeah she's alright - just needs to sleep. Listen man I'm sorry about all this, I owe you big time."

"Only for you brother, only for you."

He drove off and we sat in silence until he reached the posh apartment building. I thanked Alex one more time and gave him a good tip then lifted Mimi out of the car. She was able to walk although rather wobbly, into the building when the doorman recognized her.

"Excuse me sir, is she alright?"

"Yes she's fine I just need to get her upstairs."

"And may I ask who you are sir?"

At this time Mimi lifted up her head enough to look straight at the doorman.

"Bradley he's okay - he's my good friend, now goodnight" she slurred her words but he got the message and retreated to his station. I helped her to the elevator and asked what floor. She didn't answer but reached out and pushed the button for the 23rd floor. When we got to the door of her apartment she fumbled a minute for the keys but soon the door was opened and we were inside.

What struck me the most as soon as we walked in was the view of the magnificent city lights at night, even from the hallway looking through the large living room picture window. The apartment was laid out in high quality furnishings amidst a modern décor. She smiled as I was admiring the view then grabbed my hand and led me into the extra-large bedroom where she stopped, turned around, put her arms around me and kissed me hard. This was not exactly the way I envisioned my night and a real test of will power was taking place within me. I gently repulsed her. Obviously she was burning with desire for some action which under other circumstances I would have been more than happy to oblige her, but right now in her current state she couldn't really know whether it was the alcohol or something else that was in control. When I resisted she stepped back went over to the bed sat on it for a minute looking strangely at me then fell backward closed her eyes and went out.

It was rather awkward now trying to determine what I should do next. I didn't want to just leave her like this alone, but on the other hand did I have the right to do what I was thinking? I opted to be the golden knight and play the hero as I carefully undressed her and put her to bed. It was impossible for me to know what she might have been thinking but the smile on her face as she slept was like that of a small child in bed on Christmas Eve anticipating tomorrow. I meticulously folded and hung her clothes in the huge closet then took a seat on the divan. Before closing my own eyes to sleep, I looked at her once again to firmly etch this beautiful vision in my mind. Then I turned off the light.

The next morning when I opened my eyes she was already awake but just lying there looking at me. She wasn't angry or anything she just looked at me saying nothing. I wasn't sure just what to say so I waited to see what would come next. Finally she spoke.

"Did I make a complete fool of myself last night, because I sure don't remember?"

I was relieved to hear that she was in a somewhat jovial mood so I responded likewise.

"No but you sure had a good time."

"Why are you sitting over there, did we do anything naughty?"

I smiled and answered "No - I didn't have the heart to take advantage."

"Well Diogenes I found him for you" she said playfully.

"Diogenes. Who is Diogenes?"

"Oh he was just someone who spent his whole life looking for an honest man. I guess he didn't know about you."

"Well if he found me I'm not so sure he would have been pleased if he knew what was going through my mind."

She laughed and said "Better luck next time. Please hand me my robe. Not that I'm being modest since you have already seen all that I have to offer but please hand it to me anyway."

I got up to get the robe and almost stumbled because my head was spinning from last night's indiscretion. She took the robe and got up with her front to me allowing me to briefly view one more time before putting it on what I missed.

"You must have had just as much as I did. Don't fret I have just the thing for both of us."

She went into the kitchen and starting making something. A few minutes later she came back with a glass and handed it to me.

"Here drink this, you'll feel better."

She was right. In just a matter of a few minutes it was like I had not had anything to drink at all.

"Wow, what is this? You ought to patent it."

"It's a chemist's secret and not yet ready for prime time. But maybe one day once I get that piece of paper with the PhD. on it then I will pursue that thought."

"By the way what will they call you when you get it - Dr. Mimi?"

"I don't care what they call me as long as the doctor is in front of it. Now if you don't mind I'm going to take a shower and dress. Would you like to watch?"

I didn't know whether she was joking or what until she said: "Just kidding. Please wait in the living room."

I had not seen this persona before and was a little surprised but happy to know she had a fun side even when sober. Once she left and entered the bathroom, I got up and took a look around. Everything in the place was of a quality that I didn't think could be afforded by a chemist working at Canon. My curious mind went to work trying to figure out how she was doing it. While I was perusing I came across a large picture in the living room of a man in uniform along with a young boy. I had seen something in the bedroom that I didn't pay much attention to before but now it was registering. The picture in the bedroom had not only the man and boy in it, but she was standing next to him with the boy in front. It was not hard to figure out then that this must be her husband. The uniform was that of a Port Authority Police Captain.

When she came out I casually asked her about the man. As she sat down at her dressing table to comb her hair she lowered her head before answering.

"He was my husband, the love of my life - killed in a stupid incident three years ago by the negligence of one of the Port Authority's eager beaver rookies. All that you see here is the result of their paying for his mistake. I am receiving and will be until my son is through college a very large annuity. The money is great but it can't come to bed at night and certainly doesn't help my loneliness.

You caught me last night in one of those moments when I was really missing him. Sorry about that."

"I'm sorry I asked I didn't know."

"It's okay I live with it by trying to be mother and father to my son and immersing myself in my work and my studies. But if you want to help me, my son needs someone like you he can look up to. Are you available?"

Again I couldn't determine whether she was kidding or not but I answered anyway.

"Do you come along with the job?"

She laughed then answered: "Without question."

She finished with her hair then asked me to return to the living room so she could dress. When she came out she looked stunning again. She asked what I would like for breakfast and I thought - all this and she cooks too. We had the traditional full breakfast and enjoyed the light conversation about last night. While we talked and ate I couldn't take my eyes off of her.

"Please stop staring at me, I'm getting embarrassed."

"I'm sorry but I can't help myself. You are just so naturally beautiful."

I finished eating and told her she's all cleaned up but I need to go home and do the same. Realizing now that I hadn't said anything about what I found out on the job, I asked her if we could have lunch or dinner today so we could talk about it. She declined saying: "No not today because I have to go to church and pick-up my son." I was about to volunteer to go with her but then I knew that wasn't quite my thing so I said maybe we can do lunch tomorrow. She said okay. Just as I was heading out the door she stopped me.

"You know I must go to church because my father is the pastor and he expects me there every Sunday. My son will be there with my sister and her kids. That's who he's with right now."

"You're a preacher's kid?"

"Yes I'm a PK why do you seem so surprised - because of last night?"

"I don't know I just guess you're full of surprises. Well I will have to go with you sometime but not today."

We both laughed and I left.

##########

Marsha's father, the Reverend Doctor Edward Stanton Devereaux was the pastor of a large church in Englewood Cliffs, NJ. He was well known both throughout the state and internationally for his platform of preaching the gospel emphasizing the coming Kingdom Of God. Several TV shows and even a cameo appearance in a movie were to his credits. His church, Holy Trinity Church of God, had been founded by him and a group of young clergymen from within the state several years ago and was still growing. Having come up from New Orleans, Louisiana in the early 90's he was seeking a place to establish a church where he could espouse what he believed to be the true mission of Jesus Christ.

During his years in New Orleans he had become thoroughly disenchanted with the Catholic Church and his parish. From childhood he was raised in the tradition of Catholicism and was fine with it until he reached college. After receiving his call to the ministry and matriculating at Xavier University where his studies led him to dig deeper into his own beliefs, he discovered something about his religious upbringing that confused him. As he delved more and more into the history of his professed faith he was finding more conflicting information about the tradition as practiced and that which the Bible taught.

Stanton was the second oldest boy in a family of three boys and two girls. Creole by heritage, both his father and mother were devout Catholics who never challenged the tradition. When he announced to them his calling, they were ecstatic thinking he was on the road to becoming a priest. It was in his sophomore year at the university while researching a church history project in the library that he discovered the relationship between the Catholic Church and the Holy Roman Empire. This enlightening discovery shook his core foundation. Further investigation led him to read about Nazi Germany and the church's complicity in their practices. At first he didn't want to accept it, however researching the subject thoroughly he was finally convinced that he could not be a part of this.

His first thought was to run to Melinda, his campus sweetheart, and reveal his discovery. Melinda, also of Creole heritage, was one of the lovely co-eds at Xavier who had captured Stanton's heart from the first time he saw her as a first year student. Within that first year and over the summer they became very close and he would confide in her all that was in his heart or on his mind. Running to her now with his news was no surprise for her, except that she was also Catholic and not quite ready to believe him. He promised to provide her with evidence of what he read which he did a short time later.

Both of them as young students dependent on their parents support knew that by telling them what they found out it could jeopardize their college future. They were confused about what to do. Stanton loved Melinda and wanted to marry her but he knew if he left school this could never be. The only jobs that he ever held were those of working in and around the nightclubs doing menial tasks but collecting decent tips. But now since he had been called he was determined to finish his degree and see where God would lead him. They both continued their studies keeping hidden within them what he had discovered to appease their parents.

After graduation, him with a theology degree and her with a Biology degree and a teaching certificate, they decided to get married no matter what may come their way. Melinda was anxious to tell her mother about their plans but Stanton cautioned her to wait until he at least had a job. His persistence and diligence in scouring the job market quickly landed him an entry level management position in a major telecommunications company in the city. He was to start in the Human Resources Department. The hiring manager was impressed with his grades and when he saw that his discipline was theology he believed he should be able to work well with and manage people. Melinda also had no difficulty in finding work. She was going to teach science at one of the city's middle schools but she would not start until August and it was now only May.

With Stanton at least having a job they made the announcement to both parents. Melinda's family was excited and happy for them, but Stanton's was somewhat distant in their response. They were still hoping he was going into the priesthood. It took weeks before they accepted the fact that their number two son was going to marry Melinda, but when they did they gave blessings. The wedding was planned for one year later in June.

At this point Stanton still had not discussed his desire to abandon the Catholic tradition with his parents. They were aware that he had not been attending mass with them for some time but whenever they asked him why not, his response was always that his studies kept him tied up. Since he was maintaining a high grade point average, they didn't question him further. Having made his decision almost two full years ago, Stanton started investigating other faiths and religions to see what would be right for him to exercise his calling. His interest was drawn to the Baptist denomination and that's what he chose.

A short time after Stanton started working for the telephone company and getting settled into his new function, he felt compelled to find a Baptist church through which he could begin to minister. Browsing through the telephone directory and yellow pages was not giving him the feeling that any one listing he saw was the one for him. Getting a little frustrated and disappointed in his search he called Melinda and asked her what she thought. Her reply was so intuitive that he was embarrassed for not having thought of it himself.

She said: "You want to find a place to do God's work, why don't you ask Him where He wants you to do it." He immediately discarded the phone book and began to pray for God's guidance in the matter.

Four days past, five went by and finally in the middle of the sixth that happened to be a Friday when he was at work having lunch with some of his colleagues the answer came. Somehow the conversation had turned to religion and the role of the church in modern society. His associates were not aware that he was an aspiring minister, but one of them turned to him and asked what he thought the role should be. His answer was so profound that the man asking the question was amazed. He then asked him another question more pertinent to a specific church. When Stanton again responded astutely the man wanted to know what his background was. Stanton complied and told him of his training and his desires. It so happened that the man was a deacon in a fairly new Baptist church on the outskirts of the city that was growing at a rapid pace and was looking for an assistant pastor. When Stanton heard this a chill ran down his spine as he felt his prayer being answered.

Arrangements were made to have Stanton meet with the current pastor the next day – Saturday afternoon. The pastor, Reverend Cleophus Joyner, had relocated to New Orleans a little over a year ago from Newark, NJ and was in the process of building up his congregation. During the interview Stanton was enamored of the preacher's credentials and his professed work with the gangs during the riots. His espoused platform of preaching the real message of Jesus Christ and the

Kingdom of God was just what Stanton wanted and had been looking for. They bonded. Rev. Joyner was equally impressed by Stanton's desire to minister and profess what the Bible really teaches.

It was agreed after just that one interview that Stanton was his choice to be an assistant pastor. Now all he needed was to appear before the deacon board to be confirmed. The date was set for next Thursday evening at 6:00 O'clock. Stanton left the clergy's office eager to run and tell Melinda but more so he felt a sense of accomplishment in that he was now on the road to fulfilling his desire.

Stanton and Melinda as they usually did on a Saturday night went out for dinner and then to a movie. Over dinner he was so excited about his new opportunity he could hardly speak slowly enough to get all his words out so that she could understand. Melinda sharing his joy was also excited and looking forward to being the wife of a minister. Their joy for the evening however was somewhat diminished by what they saw happening just outside the theater as they made their way toward it.

During this period in many cities across the country there was major discontent among the people. Factions were squaring off against one another in support of or in opposition to the Vietnam War, racial oppression or some other unrelated cause. In front of the movie house were two groups confronting each other waving signs, banners and holding sticks. In the distance the sound of sirens approaching pierced the serene night air upsetting what was otherwise a calm evening. In a matter of minutes several police cars and a paddy wagon were on the scene dispatching a small army of uniformed police officers. As they exited their vehicles and took up positions in front of the theater and in between the two groups, the bullhorn held by the leader barked commands to the crowd.

"This is an unlawful assembly. Put down your signs, disperse and go home."

The crowd paid no attention to the orders but continued to walk around in a disorderly fashion shouting vulgar epithets at each opposing faction and the police.

"You have been warned. If you do not cease and desist immediately you will be arrested" the sergeant hollered again through his public address horn.

Once again the crowd was unresponsive.

Stanton and Melinda had stopped their approach far enough away to be safely outside of the melee but close enough to see and hear all that was taking place.

"Do you see that?" Stanton said.

"Yes, but I can't believe it" she replied. "I knew these things were happening in a lot of places but I didn't think it would happen here."

"Let's get a little closer so we can really hear what's going on."

"No, my love we don't need to move a step closer. Don't you see all those policeman over there? You want to get arrested with the crowd?"

"No of course not but I would like to know what's behind all this. If I'm going to be a good minister I need to understand what drives people to act this way."

"All in good time, all in good time my dear. I don't think that tonight is the night you need to start your ministry and possibly end your career all in one effort."

When she said that Stanton had to laugh as he realized that her voice of reason as usual was right on point.

The police were becoming more agitated as the crowd continued to disobey their demands to disperse. The lines had been drawn and the police were forming their riot formation. It appeared that the confrontation between the law and the citizens was about to escalate. To complicate matters more, the early show had just finished and people inside the theater were coming out. As they passed through the exit doors and saw all the commotion going on many were frightened and confused. Not knowing whether to return inside or continue trying to get to their cars several of them who were in front just stopped. Patrons behind them unable to see what was going on in front of the first line became anxious at the delay in getting out of the building and began to push their way forward. Now there was friction both inside the theater and outside of the building. The police could see what was happening but were indecisive about what their next move should be. Should they continue to contend with the crowd that was in front of them or should they separate their ranks and deal in part with the problem behind them.

It was an interesting dilemma. So far no one had been hurt in the melee but as tempers began to flare the mood of the crowd was getting intense. The patrons in the theater were pushing and shoving each other to exit the building while the crowd outside were generally hostile toward the police and each other.

"This is your final warning" said the sergeant.

As he was barking his final threat another police car showed up on the scene. This time a lieutenant and the captain got out and took over the command.

"People you have been warned, there will be no further warnings. If you do not disperse immediately then these police officers will start making arrests," came the words from the captain.

"Sir, I don't think we have the means to arrest all of these people" said the sergeant to the lieutenant.

"I have no intention of trying to arrest them all but we need to get control of this situation now before it becomes dangerous. How are we on tear gas?"

"We have an ample supply. Do you want to start it?"

"On my orders toss a few cans into the center of the crowd but wait for my command."

"Listen people we do not want to get anybody hurt but if you don't obey our orders than you will be responsible for whatever happens."

"Two, four, six, eight we will not cooperate. Two, four, six, eight, we will not cooperate," came the reply from the crowd.

"Okay sergeant you can toss the cans."

With that instruction given several cans of CN tear gas were launched into the middle of the crowd then a big cloud of white smoke erupted. Gasping and coughing ensued immediately as people on the street started inhaling the fumes. Right after that the running started as the crowd began to take off in all directions. Signs were thrown into the air, sticks were hurled toward the police and general mayhem broke out.

"I can't believe this is really happening here" Stanton said. "My God what could possibly be behind all of this?"

"Come on dear let's get out of here. Come on let's leave here now."

Melinda started pulling on his arm insisting that they head in the direction opposite the mayhem. Stanton couldn't turn his eyes away from what was going on. He wanted to see just what was going to happen next. She kept tugging and tugging as he resisted. Finally she was able to get him to start moving away from the excitement.

The people inside the theater finally were able to get the first line to move into the open space outside. By this time the air all around the area was filled with tear gas fumes. As they entered the smoke they too began to cough and gasp. The small group of officers who had separated from the main body tried to contain them and direct them into an area off to the side, but as the movement to get out of the theater increased the people ran into and through the officers knocking some of them to the ground. Seeing what was happening to their fellow officers the main body of patrolmen moved toward the theater patrons.

"Stop, stop before we shoot" said the words from one officer's mouth.

By this time there was no stopping the patrons or the crowd. Bedlam was at its height. Even the older people who were part of the group inside the theater were scrambling to find a place of safety but there was none. It was as if what had been intended at the start to be a peaceful protest had suddenly turned into mimicry of the Vietnam War brought home to New Orleans.

The intensity of the skirmish heated to such a point that all sides were afraid for their lives. The police were caught in the middle of a fracas that they were not in control of. The patrons and the crowd were the subjects of something which they could not have imagined at the beginning of their evening. Things were getting so heated that it was hard to imagine that this was taking place in the middle of a so called civilized modern day city. As the tension built up and tempers flared on all sides control was completely lost and then it happened.

Chapter Five
"Hearts Afire"

As the seasons change, spring into summer, summer into fall and fall becomes winter so do the hearts of men. But unlike the seasonal change which has a rhythm dictated by the supreme conductor the hearts of men change erratically. An old adage says that the very young are innocent and pure in heart, but the heart is malleable and as they age it is subject to corruption. As the young grow older and become leaders the purity of heart becomes suspect. There are times when a leader will command obedience and the followers will obey, then there are times when the hearts of the followers will not be subject to any directive. Who can know what really controls the heart?

The adversary's plan has been conceived and delivered to those who must carry it out. Through artfully deceptive schemes a following of committed hearts have been induced to volunteer. With promises of peace, prosperity and power, the evil one has caused those who have pledged their allegiance to him to forfeit their God given spirit. By aligning with a source they do not fully understand, for them, the die has been cast.

At Canon Enterprises Herbert Crandall (Director of Human Resources), Reginald Codey (Product Development Manager), Milton Jenkovitch (CEO), Leonard Jablonski (Director of Plant Operations), and Brent Woodley (Line Supervisor), comprise the volunteer group who are the purveyors for P.T.D.T.Y. Of course Brent has been eliminated from the group in an effort to maintain integrity, such as it is. The time is fast approaching when the plan calls for implementation. The pieces are all in place except for a replacement for Brent. There are several candidates who are knowledgeable about how to operate the line, but none are part of the gathering. The question now for the group is two-fold. First, is how much information should be provided to the selected candidate about the secret product and second should he be converted for the sake of security. An after-hours meeting has been called and all must come. Attendance is mandatory. The time to meet is 6:00 PM and the place is the conference room outside of Mr. Jenkovitch's office. Jennifer has been notified and she will be setting it up.

Leonard Jablonski was at the first meeting when Herb Crandall told the group about his strategy to correct the problem caused by Brent Woodley. No one from that meeting however, was alerted to the change in plans that Herb had to make because of police interference. As far as Lenny knew, the original action had been executed and all was in order. Finding a replacement for Brent in the grand operational scheme he didn't think should be a problem. His concern was the need for having this big meeting to discuss it.

Milton Jenkovitch was also, as were the rest of the group except Reggie, not aware of any change in the original plan. His reason for calling the meeting was not just to talk about Brent's replacement but to consult with the adversary about the start-up schedule. According to the RFP, code name "Washington" the target date for having the product ready for distribution was just a few weeks away. The lab development was almost complete, the initial marketing plan and vendors were ready, the production schedule had been created but what was needed finally was the emissary's assurance. He wanted assurance that the Washington contact was one of his, that the RFP was only Canon's and that it would be fully funded.

As for Herb Crandall, he was anxiously looking forward to this meeting even though he knew he had not told the others about the plan change. He was confident that since the result was as forecast, he would still be considered a hero should the change become known. In his mind he was sure the adversary would be pleased. The overall success of the project was now just a matter of timing and he would be a significant contributor. How the group would be rewarded in the end was something he had dreamed about since he first joined. For him peace, prosperity and power were sure to come.

These were the key players in the devil's orchestra and until now just like the Saber Dance Symphony all the pieces were in harmony. It wouldn't be until three days later the fact that Brent Woodley was missing would disrupt the harmonic flow.

#######

I arrived at the plant early today hoping to hear whether anyone had been taken into custody. So far the only one unaccounted for is a line supervisor named Brent Woodley, who I hadn't met. I'm told he was usually in very early, well before his line workers, but not today. Right now no one seems unduly concerned because there were other capable supervisors here to cover for him. However, my curious mind picked up on the absence and I began to inquire. He had not called in sick nor was he scheduled for any vacation. But since everyone else went about their daily routines undisturbed, I decided to do as the Romans do when in Rome - I went to work.

The temporary office I was given here was nothing like my headquarters set-up. It was much smaller with very little space for file cabinets. But most importantly it did have an adequate size desk, a telephone and a modern computer. When I got back to my desk from nosing around in production my message light was on, so I sat down and started my review. There were four and all of them routine check-ins from my headquarters staff except for the last one. This one was from Tango. I was a little surprised because I hadn't heard from him for weeks.

His message was short and right to the point. He wanted to meet with me again but this time he wanted to go to the Peacock Palace. I couldn't imagine why it was he wanted to meet me there. I was sure he had already checked the place out. Anyway I returned his call and agreed to meet with him. The time was set for 1:00 PM. It was now just about 10:30 AM so I had a lot of time before then. Whenever I heard from him it always started me wondering exactly what it was that he was charged to do other than what he told me. He still hadn't provided me with anything that could convince me of his legitimate function. Even though I asked several people both here and at headquarters, no one could explain who he really was or what he was supposed to be doing. It was as if he just showed up one day and started grilling everybody he came across. After a while no one got excited about it, they just accepted the fact that he was doing what they assumed he was supposed to do.

After I finished my daily routine tasks I wanted to try and talk to Mimi before meeting with Tango. Rather than call her I thought I would walk over to the lab area and see if she was free. I really wanted to see her anyway. Once there I had to peek in each one of the five labs because I didn't know which one she was assigned to. There was only one that I knew she wouldn't be in - Lab 1. In my third peeking effort I looked through the entrance door window and saw her at a lab table by the window. She had returned to her very bland looking appearance which made me shake my head. In her loose fitting white lab coat and her hair pulled up under a cap, unless you knew, you wouldn't believe this was the same woman I took home Saturday night.

I wasn't sure whether to go in or not, so I just stood at the window hoping she might feel me staring at her. Call it whatever you want ESP, strong vibrations, faith or just blind luck it worked. She stopped what she was doing and looked toward the door. At first she just nodded but when I beckoned for her to come over she looked around then she did.

"Hi how are you?"

"I'm just great thank you. Do you have school tonight?"

"No, I have nothing on Monday's. Why?"

"Remember I told you I have some news to update you with."

"I remember but I have to go home today right after work. I don't have anyone to pick up Jerry."

"Jerry's your son right?"

"Yes. His real name's Jeremiah but we call him Jerry."

"Okay I'll try you again tomorrow."

"No wait, I have a class tomorrow. Why don't you come on over tonight and we can talk then. I'll fix you dinner and you can meet Jerry."

"You make a good offer. I can't refuse that dinner thing. I'm in. What time should I get there?"

"Six-thirty would be good. That's about what time we usually eat anyway."

"Sounds good to me, I'll see you then. Will I have a problem with Bradley?"

"Bradley. How do you know Bradley?"

"I guess you don't remember but when I brought you home he wasn't going to let me in. But you straightened him out about who I was."

She laughed.

"Wow I really must have been out of it - won't be doing that again. I must apologize to him because he's really a great doorman and he always looks out for me. No he won't be a problem, just ask for Mrs. Robinson, not Mimi, in 23G at the reception desk when you walk in."

I turned around and went back to my office.

That afternoon when I arrived at the Peacock there was no sign of Tango. It was about ten after and I was sure we had agreed to meet at 1:00 PM so I found a table and waited. By twenty minutes after and there still was no sign of him I thought I'd better call my office to see if he left a message. There was nothing from him. I didn't have his number with me so I decided since I was here and the food is pretty good to go ahead and order lunch. For some reason the lunch crowd was unusually light today and I wondered if there was something that I had missed.

After several minutes my order came and the place was beginning to fill as more patrons came in. This made me a little more comfortable but there was still no Tango among them. By the time I finished eating it was after 2:00 and still no show for Hernandez. I couldn't continue to wait especially having no idea what happened so I returned to the office. When I got there the message light was on and I hoped there would be one from him. Sure enough he was the third caller.

"Ron, this is Tango. Listen I do apologize for missing our lunch appointment but I received an urgent call this morning summoning me to return to Washington post haste so I had to leave right away. I'll try to call you sometime tomorrow morning and fill you in on why I wanted to meet with you at the Peacock. Talk to you then, goodbye."

Although I was glad to receive the message and to know that nothing had happened to him, the urgency in his voice started me thinking again about Washington's connection with what was going on here. Ever since my exposure through Tony that day at lunch about the R.F.P. code named "Washington" I've been attempting to put together what department in the government issued the proposal. Since neither Mimi nor I have seen the actual document and no one else outside of the group seems to know anything about it, identifying a department is practically impossible.

The fact that Tango was called back at this time made me even more suspicious of him and what his role is in the whole sordid plot. Was he a good guy or a bad one kept going through my mind. When he first came to my office at Headquarters he said he was there to help and protect me. Protect me from what, he never fully explained except as it was related to Tony's demise and he didn't want that happening to me. But right now he would have a hard time convincing me that he didn't have anything to do with that incident.

I wasn't going to be able to piece together anything more about that until I talked to him tomorrow so I put it out of my mind. There were still some more things I had to attend to before shutting down for the day so I returned all my calls and took care of them. One of them was going back down to production to see if anything new had occurred since this morning. Nothing seemed to be out of the ordinary operations and things were running as smoothly as they normally would. It was like the change in line supervision was a routine occurrence. Satisfied that I wasn't going to learn anymore here today I went back to my office and put away my tools. My focus turned now to seeing Mimi tonight and finding out whether her cooking was good at more than just making breakfasts.

#######

"Jenn is everything ready for tonight?"

"Yes Mr. Jenkovitch it's all set up" she answered through the intercom.

"Did the package I'm expecting come yet?"

"It did and I put it in the conference room just where you told me to."

"Very good. Listen there will be no need for you to stay here tonight during this meeting. It's a very special one and once we get started the door will be locked so we're not disturbed. Okay?"

"Sure Mr. Jenkovitch. Will it be alright if I leave a little early?"

"That's fine Jenn, just let me know when you're going."

"Yes I'll do that."

Milton Jenkovitch, as the CEO knew that the overall responsibility for the success of the project was in his hands. Since he first became aware of the leak that was discovered by Anthony Oliver and the resulting action by one of Herb Crandall's people to plug it up, he wanted to go over the top to assure that everything was still moving along according to plan. His efforts to make sure that his superior would be pleased at the progress were valiant. The one thing that was totally beyond his control was the role that the Washington bureau contact would play in the matter. Tonight he was going to implore the adversary to reveal to him and the group who the contact was. His need for assurance that that part of the deal was being covered was great. Milton had to be very careful how he broached the issue so as not to appear that he lacked confidence, or more precisely, lacked faith in the emissary's ability to control the contact.

As he sat at his desk rehearsing in his mind how he was going to make his appeal, the fact that he had not had a debriefing from Herb Crandall on the solution to his problem was making him uncomfortable. Milton was aware that the police were closing in on someone from his plant so he was anxious to have Herb confirm that their activity would not lead to anything detrimental to the project. He buzzed Jennifer on the intercom.

"Jenn would you give Herb Crandall's secretary a call and tell her I'd like to see him in my office in an hour?"

"Right away Mr. Jenkovitch."

About ten minutes later Jennifer called Milton to let him know that Mr. Crandall would be there at 3:00 O'clock as requested.

In Herb Crandall's office he was still enjoying his high looking forward to tonight's meeting until the call from Milton came. All the air in his balloon suddenly escaped as he pondered why his boss was summoning him now. Was this just a routine conference in preparation for the meeting or was there something more that he should be concerned about? Immediately what came to mind was the change in plans on how to dispose of Brent Woodley. Should he have told Milton right after that weekend? Didn't Milton see the news report that the deed was done? But then again how would Milton know they were talking about Brent? These were the questions running through Herb's mind. Was he going to be put on the hot seat for not revealing the plan change? Now more than ever he realized that life's elevator can not only take you to the penthouse, but it also goes to the basement.

Right or wrong his only option now was to explain fully why he had to change his strategy. He would be sure to emphasize that the method was not as important as the result – and the result was good. He believed he could appease Milton with his explanation, but now he wasn't so sure about the adversary. There was still some time left before he would see Milton so he went to get some coffee - all the while twirling his ring as he walked.

At precisely 3:00 O'clock herb was at Jennifer's desk asking her to let Milton know he was there. Jennifer buzzed him and he responded saying Herb could come in. At the door Herb still hesitated before going inside.

"Come on in Herb, come on in and sit down."

"Thanks Milton. You wanted to see me?"

"Yes, just give me a minute here."

Milton was just finishing signing some papers and he wanted to get it done.

"Okay that's done. Now how are things going?"

Herb was immediately on the defensive. He wasn't sure whether Milton was looking for something specific like the plan or was he referring to things in general, so he chose to respond to the general.

"Things are going great. Everything is in order."

"That little problem we had is it solved now?"

"Yes sir, it's all taken care of."

"Can I tell the emissary that without fear of wincing?"

"Sure! I tell you everything is good. We're right on target."

"What about the police, I understand they're still nosing around?"

"Not to worry, they don't have anything now."

"You're sure."

"Absolutely!"

"Good, then we should have a great ceremony tonight. That's all I needed. You got questions for me?"

"No, I'm good. I'll see you later then."

#######

Before going over to Mimi's I decided to pick-up something for the occasion. I figured a bottle of good wine would be fine for us but what do you get a young boy who you know absolutely nothing about. Getting the wine was no problem, but when I went into a big time toy store there were so many choices my confusion escalated. It would have been helpful when I asked the salesperson for assistance if I had a clue about what the kid might be into. After some brief bantering, the young man came up with a suggestion that sounded failsafe to me so I bought it. It was a remote controlled fire truck with flashing lights, siren, reverse – the whole nine yards. I figured what little boy wouldn't want something like that where he could remotely race through the house and drive his mother crazy.

When I arrived at the beautifully accentuated lobby of her building I had to laugh to myself at how I could have missed all this the first time there. But then I remembered between the potential confrontation with the doorman and trying to attend to her needs, I wasn't exactly paying much attention to the décor. I went over to the reception desk and as advised asked for Mrs. Robinson in 23G. The woman behind the desk was very friendly and politely asked for my name. She then called Mimi on the intercom and announced me. After receiving the okay she pointed me to the elevator and said I could go up.

Once on the floor I noticed something else I didn't before. The hallway was extremely quiet. Either there was no one else home on the floor or the apartment walls were so thick they suppressed all interior noise. Whatever the reason it was impressive. At her door I hesitated for a moment before ringing the bell. Not because of her but I wanted to make a good first impression for the kid. So I gathered myself and pressed the button. She opened the door and invited me in – no kid with her. Once again she had that stunning look even though she was moderately dressed in a conservative lounge outfit.

"Come on in. Let me take your coat. Jerry – Jerry come here and meet Mr. Powers."

It was not like he rushed from his room to greet me, but it was more like the command dragged him out from his activities. From his appearance I would have guessed he was around nine or even ten but I learned later he was only seven. He was tall for his age and well built, not skinny. He approached me with some reservation and extended his hand as I'm sure he had been instructed to do. I received it and shook his hand.

"Hello Jerry I'm glad to meet you. How are you?"

"Hi, I'm okay."

"Here I brought you something. And Mimi here's something for you too."

"Thank you. Mommy can I go back and play now?"

"Yes, but why don't you show Mr. Powers your room. Maybe he would like to play a game with you."

"Sounds good to me, okay with you Jerry?"

Surprisingly he perked right up at that.

"Yeah great! Come on lets go."

He grabbed my hand with unusual strength and started pulling me toward his room. Before we left I heard her say "You didn't have to do that you know, I mean the presents."

I just looked back, winked and smiled.

Obviously he was happy to have someone to play with – even if it was an adult. When I entered his room it was vividly clear what he liked. All over his walls were posters of his favorite basketball heroes. Even on one end wall was an adjustable basket set-up with two soft basketballs underneath. In addition his toy collection far exceeded that of the average youngster. Even though he seemed to be appreciative of my gift, as I looked around and saw other remote controlled vehicles, I was confident by the weekend mine would be lost in a corner.

Jerry guided me over to a toy Hoops Basketball game that was like a small bowling alley but with a basketball net where the pins would be. It had a timer on it and the objective was to make as many baskets shooting from the end of the set-up as you could within 1 minute. The one who had the most baskets in 5 minutes won the game. He challenged me to a game and it was really fun.

I won't mention here how badly this youngster outscored me, but it was painfully obvious he had been practicing - and he was just good.

Just as I was about to seek revenge, being down 3 games to 0, by starting another round, the call from the kitchen came and playtime was over. I learned quite a bit about him in the short time we played together. Not only was he knowledgeable about the real NBA basketball but he knew about a lot of other things as well. I was impressed with his intelligence.

"Come on you guys I'm waiting" the call came again with more urgency this time.

We put the balls down and headed to the dining area. It was not really a dining room but a cleverly designed spacious eating area right off the kitchen. We sat down at the table on each side leaving the head of the table vacant. It was obvious, but I don't believe intentional, that seat was still reserved for he who sat at the head once. When we were all seated Mimi asked If I wanted to say the blessing. I was a little embarrassed and had to decline saying I was not really into doing that. She said she understood and went on and said grace. I looked at Jerry to see his reaction but there was no expression indicating anything.

The meal was exceedingly good, more than I expected. It validated my perception of her cooking skills. The salmon had a sauce that delighted my taste buds and I had to ask her about it. She explained it was from an old Cajun recipe that her grandmother had taught her. Needless to say everything else with the meal was more than satisfactory. I couldn't resist the temptation to ask "Does this kid eat like this every day?" The answer was an emphatic no but as you can see looking at him, he's not starving. We both laughed.

All through the rest of dinner the conversation was light and playful including Jerry in all phases. The more he spoke the more I was impressed with how much he had been exposed to. It was very clear that his father had spent a great deal of time with him, but it was also obvious that his preacher grandfather had a heavy influence. At one point he even asked me why I didn't say the blessing. Fortunately I was bailed out by Mimi and didn't have to answer, but it stayed on my mind.

When we finished eating and Mimi asked Jerry if he had finished his homework, I couldn't help thinking how much homework could he have? So I asked her. She told me he was seven going on eight in a couple of months and the private school he attended believed strongly in getting their students acclimated to doing homework and even research early. What more could I say, that explained a lot. Jerry left the table and went back to his room. Then I started to tell her what I learned at Canon while she was gone.

"While you were away I had lunch with Herb Crandall, you know the Human Resources Director."

"Yes I know him - what happened?"

"Well during the meal he went off into this thing about some greater power pulling his strings. At first I thought he was kidding or about to go into a religious God thing, but he went totally in the opposite direction. I'm convinced he's a devil worshipper and not the only one at Canon. He kept on talking about it like I wasn't even there, but he caught himself and cut it short."

"You believe that has something to do with Anthony's murder?"

"No, not just that. When I told him I needed to get into Lab 1 as part of my project, he almost had a breakdown. I was outright forbidden to go in there. Something strange is going on in there - I just know it."

"Yeah I know you're right about that. I can't get in there either. The chemists who work in there are hardly ever seen outside of the lab so you can't talk to them."

"We have to figure out a way of getting in there. I believe a lot of the answers we need lie there."

"I agree, but that lab is like Ft. Knox. How can we get in?"

"I'm still working on that part, when I got it figured out I'll let you know. The devil worship part is really what's bothering me. What about that?"

"You need to talk with my father and my sister about that."

"I can understand talking to your father, but how does your sister fit in?"

"She teaches Sociology at the State University in Jersey and she is deep into occult studies. I'm sure she could help and she would love to find out something like that is going on inside Canon Enterprises. As a matter of fact her doctoral dissertation was on World Religions and The Occult."

"Is she a doctor?"

"Yes a PhD and so is my father. It runs in the family."

"And you think they would take time to talk to me about it?"

"Sure, I can set it up."

"How?"

"Every other Friday we all get together for family dinner at my father's house. I'll just tell my mother I'm bringing a guest. She'll love that."

"Wow am I family?"

"Oh no, for that you have to first file an application and then my father must approve it."

We both laughed.

"Seriously, you think it would be okay to discuss this at your family dinner?"

"Well of course not during the meal but afterward when we all sit around and talk about the world's problems this could be a great discussion topic. Midge will eat it up."

"Who's Midge?"

"Oh that's my sister Marilyn who we call Midge."

"Do you all have nicknames?"

"Yes and if you come there often enough you'll have one too."

"Okay I'd love to talk with them. When's the next dinner scheduled?"

"It's this Friday. What's on your schedule?"

"Absolutely nothing. This could be the highlight of my week. Should I rent a car?"

"Why would you do that?"

"Well how are we going to Jersey - catch the train?"

"No. I have a car. It's downstairs in the garage."

"As I said before you are full of surprises."

It was a little after 9:00 when Mimi went and put Jerry to bed. But before that he surprised when he asked me if I was coming back. I really felt a genuine connection to this young man. There was something about him that was just so pure and innocent that the tragic incident leaving him fatherless at such a young age just served to emphasize the unfairness of life. After that for the next few hours we sat around sipping the wine and talking about the strange things happening at Canon.

Mimi has been working at the company much longer than me but she revealed never before had she seen a lab completely closed off to other chemists other than the ones assigned there. Whatever was going on in Lab 1 had to be so sensitive that only the Federal Government could mandate such secrecy. She even recalled noticing a change in Herb Crandall who was the one that hired her. It was as if a whole new personality suddenly took him over after the deaths of his wife and daughters. She couldn't understand it but she definitely noticed.

It was after 11:00 before we paid any attention to the time. The wine was mellow, the conversation engaging and the company enjoyable but we both knew tomorrow was another work day. So I reluctantly got up from a most comfortable sofa and said goodnight. She got my coat and walked me to the door. Before leaving I thanked her for the fabulous dinner and a most pleasant evening, but when I tried to kiss her she turned away. I looked surprised but then she said.

"I like you but I don't want to rush things. I'm not quite ready for this yet and I hope you understand. The other night was just my submission to the alcohol and loneliness. Tonight I'm in control."

I smiled and said: "I do understand and I won't push it. Goodnight."

#######

Around 4:30 Jennifer walked by Milton's office. The door was open so she stuck her head in.

"Mr. Jenkovitch I'm going to leave now if it's alright?"

"Sure Jenn, but before you go would you check the conference room one more time? Make sure the door is closed when you finish."

"Will do. Have a good meeting!"

"Thank you Jenn - goodnight."

Jennifer went to the conference room and made sure as she had been instructed that the strange package was placed at the head of the table and that all the expected attendee chairs had a tablet and an ashtray in front of them. She always thought this strange but that was what he wanted. After her last check she closed the door and left for the day.

At exactly 5:15 Milton Jenkovitch stepped out of his office and looked around to see who was still on the floor. As expected all of the employees had gone. He took a casual stroll through the area and even checked the men's lavatory. Then he hollered into the ladies room just to make sure. Confidant that he was alone he went into the conference room and began preparing for the ritual. First he went to the end of the long conference table and found the package Jennifer left for him. After examining it to make sure she had not opened it, he tore off the wrappings and looked inside. All of the things he ordered seemed to be there so he started taking them out. There were candles, candle holders, incense and a talisman. He carefully removed the items and set the pentacle down in front of what would be considered the head of the table. Then he placed a candle in its holder in front of each chair and dropped a tab of incense in each respective ash tray. Satisfied he had covered everything he took a seat and waited for the others.

At about ten minutes before the hour the group started filing in. First to arrive was Herb Crandall with an excited and happy expression on his face. Next came in Leonard Jablonski who still didn't see the need for this meeting. He was not aware of Milton's agenda and thought it was just going to be about choosing a successor for Brent. But when he stepped into the room and saw the setup he knew right away it would be about much more. One by one the others arrived including two new members who had been recently added to the group.

Except for the two newcomers, no one was surprised to see Mr. Jenkovitch not sitting at the end of the table but in the first chair at the right hand side. The head chair was reserved for the special guest. Milton greeted each attendee as they walked in and asked if they were prepared to have a good session. No one dared answer in the negative. After the last devotee was seated Milton instructed the group to light their candles and ignite their incense. In a matter of minutes the incense aroma filled the room and with the lights turned off candlelight was the only illumination. Milton began his presentation by standing up with his arms lifted high above his head but looking down at the floor.

"Satan, O Satan supreme prince of darkness and ruler of this world we who are your followers worship you. On this night we once again humble ourselves before you and invite your presence here. We beseech you by the powers you have already granted to us to make yourself visible before our eyes and take your exalted seat at the special place held open for you."

When he finished speaking he sat down and folded his hands in front on the table and waited for a response. The wait was short before an extreme gush of air out of nowhere blew out the candles and the room went completely dark. The silence was like dead air in a vacuum as they collectively waited to exhale. To them the wait was like an eternity passing even though in reality it was less than a minute. As mysteriously as the candle flames were extinguished they self-ignited and the room once again glowed.

In the midst of the amber glow the head chair was no longer vacant but now occupied by an imposing figure of a man dressed in black. His black suit, white shirt and red tie confirmed the image of his power. Except for his inordinately long finger nails and blazing red eyes his appearance was like that of a funeral parlor director. All seated at the table fixated on the presence waiting for it to speak.

"My children, my subjects why have you summoned me here tonight?" came the words from the evil one's mouth.

From the very first day that Milton Jenkovitch had become aware that an RFP had been received by the Research and Development department and subsequently handed over to Leonard Jablonski in operations involving a product that was extremely unusual, he knew that it had to be more than just an ordinary request. When he examined it closely and determined that if his company was to produce this drug it could have a devastating effect on not only the community but possibly the nation, he knew that he was going to need help from sources greater than what he controlled to get away with it. As a high ranking member of the gathering he was confident that if the proposal was being sent to Canon as part of a plot from the master who they served to begin his final conquest of all humanity, then he would have everything he needed at his disposal. However, since the time of the RFP receipt he had not had a vision, received any personal vibrations, nor anything that would lift his spirit concerning the validity of the document as being from the adversary.

He had allowed the laboratory staff, marketing people and even operations to begin product development because he felt that when the time was right he would receive the confirmation he needed. As the time for actually getting the drug into distribution was fast approaching according to the RFP, he was beginning to feel very uneasy about who in Washington was the issuer. To complicate matters he was getting more and more concerned about the investigative activities of Tango Hernandez who had suddenly appeared on the scene without any prior announcement. In addition, even though he was aware of the early after hour research being conducted by Ron Powers and had been advised by Herb Crandall that it was no longer an issue, he was not absolutely certain it was true. All of these things in concert were making life uneasy for him to continue to move forward. As a result of his discomfort, he wanted to be reassured that all was in order and he especially wanted to be in contact with the main character at the Washington Bureau.

"O exalted one please forgive my impetuousness but as you know the time is coming soon when your plan must be completed and implemented. Until now there has been no confirmation from Washington that this RFP is indeed your plan and not coming from someone inside there. I have been directing funding from other projects to fund the development of the drug called for, but I need to be able to justify those expenses to the Board of Directors who I report to at the next board meeting in one week. I need, no this group needs to know that our spending is just and the RFP will cover all of our development costs. That is why we need you here" these were the words spoken by Mr. Jenkovitch.

There was a long pause as the imposing figure at the head of table just looked around the room at all of the attendees. Staring each one in the eye he seemed to be testing the loyalty of his subjects. The tension in the room was growing rapidly as each member once again held his breath waiting for the response. Finally after several long minutes the answer was issued.

"Are all of you questioning my methods or have you completely lost your collective minds? I selected each one of you at this table to become part of the beginning of the greatest conquest in all of earth's history. For your efforts when it is done you shall enjoy the power and prosperity that you hunger for. But you must be patient and do not challenge or question me or my methods. There are many things which you do not understand nor do you at this time have the capacity to absorb the knowledge. The time will come, as long as you continue to serve me, when you will achieve goals which you cannot begin to imagine. When I have overcome He who continues to stand in my way, then through me all that I promise shall be yours. Serve me and be rewarded, betray me and you will die. The choice is yours."

As they sat there stunned by the vehement diatribe of the speaker each member felt the fear within them penetrating right down to the very essence of their being. Cold shivers of trepidation shook each one until the adversary raised his hand and suddenly an unbelievable atmosphere of calm came over the entire room. Then each one settled down and recalled the peaceful feeling he had when he first became a convert. Even though the question posed by Milton had not been answered, it was like the whole room had been changed to Shangri-La and it no longer mattered. Milton like the others was caught up in the mystical hypnotic aura, but deep inside he knew he needed his question answered. Caught between enjoying this moment of serenity and inviting the wrath of the one providing the peace, Milton was fighting an internal battle. The dilemma for him was clear. If he chose to accept the calm as the adversary's devious way of avoiding an answer, then he would be no closer to knowing his funding status. On the other hand if he repeated the question would it be perceived as a challenge and he would risk being punished. He had no valid way of balancing the weight of the two sides on his decision scale so he looked around the table to see whether anyone else shared in his quandary.

Herb Crandall caught his eye and even though he could sense the anxiety emanating from his manager, there wasn't much he could do in the way of support. He oscillated between looking at Milton and the adversary to see if either was about to engage the other. It was a tense moment even in the eye of the storm. Herb wondered if the others were sensing the same vibrations Milton was giving off or were they content basking in the artificial peace. He didn't have to wait long before he watched Milton do the unthinkable.

Mr. Jenkovitch rose from his seat and walked to the opposite far end of the table. Whether he believed placing some wide space between him and the adversary would be helpful was unclear to everybody in the room. In any event, he positioned himself behind the chair of one of the new group members and launched his appeal. With his arms raised and widespread like a mother hen's wings covering her brood he began.

"These are your children O mighty one who serve you with a dedicated heart. We live to worship you and do your bidding. You have sanctioned me to lead them and

I will obey your commands, but for me to continue in that role I need the answer to my question."

As soon as he said his last word, once again a sudden gust of wind engulfed the room blowing out all the candles. Darkness permeated the room and the sound of silence accompanied it.

Chapter Six
"Links"

In Washington it was the beginning of another beautiful late fall day. The morning sun was shining brightly and the moderately cold air was moving but not brisk. The usual frenetic pace of the citizens as they moved about performing their daily routines was a clear indicator that things were seemingly normal. That is normal to the untrained eye. But to anyone who was really perceptive, something going on here was not right. Hovering in the air was a strange sense of the something is about to happen feeling that no one can ever really explain how it comes or even why.

Deep down inside the bowels of one of the federal buildings sat Tango Hernandez along with two other men huddled around a small desk. They were in an untitled office hidden amongst the several adjacent offices labeled Department of This and Department of That. This office was a clandestine meeting place for the trio. It was here that Tango had been summoned by his superior. News that a secret document pertaining to Canon Enterprises had surfaced and the need for a thorough investigation was being discussed.

Months ago one of the agents associated with Tango's organization had accidentally overheard a conversation at a table in the building's cafeteria. The talk centered on a biochemical agent that would help their boss become master of the world. At first the agent thought the group was just joking but when they began discussing a master plan and named Canon Enterprises as a major cog in the wheel of that plan, he took it seriously and listened more closely. It seems that someone high up in the Human Services Department was behind the whole thing.

Although the agent didn't get a name he heard enough to know it was someone here in this building. When Tango was first dispatched to Canon he was to search, under the cover of a federal DEP agent, for any connection the company might have with the overheard conversation. His task was also to determine just how serious was the threat of this supposed lunatic who wanted to be master of the world.

At this moment the trio was going over the strategy to identify and arrest the high ranking D.H.S. officials. From the sparse information they had including the document linking Canon to the plot, it was very difficult to pinpoint the culprit without exposing the whole plot and inviting major scrutiny from other governmental entities. The challenge for them was to get their targets and not cause a panic in the city and possibly the nation.

Tango was explaining to his colleagues all that he had discovered since being at the Canon plant site. He especially focused on the lab where he found the partial document alluding to a chemical formula and some coded letters. His reference to the conversation he had with Milton Jenkovitch in which he was warned to stay out of that lab didn't sit well with Tango's partners. They quickly reminded him that he had the backing of whomever he needed in order to complete his investigation. Tango acknowledged the power backing but urged them to focus on the problem at the source which is in this location before sending him back to Canon. They all agreed.

In another part of the building up on the 14th floor there was another meeting going on at this time. This one also had three attendees but clearly they were discussing the same topic but from a very different perspective. These were D.H.S. officials including the top manager and two of his subordinates. The focus of their discussion was not how to thwart the activities going on at Canon Enterprises, but to insure that the P.T.D.T.Y. project got carried out. Theodore Messinger, the department head was reviewing with his colleagues the importance of the success of the project as part of the master plan. The secrecy of their involvement was critical. He was aware that some other agencies were questioning his budget but he was sure that he would be able to continue with the subterfuge. Specifically the questions centered on funds that were not aligned properly with other agency expenditures in his department.

He was very adept at manipulating entries so that what was shown on the balance sheets was not actually the expensed item. His skills were even more proficient at being able to create an R.F.P. for something his department would fund without the knowledge of the rest of the department. Theo, like Milton had been hand-picked by Satan for this job. His greed and hunger for power made him an ideal candidate and when the time came for him to be converted his confrontation and dialogues with the evil one made him an easy sell.

The R.F.P. had been created per the specifications given to him directly during a gathering ceremony of his local branch of worshippers. There was to be no doubt as to its ingredients or its purpose. The formula to develop the actual product was to be left up to the chosen pharmaceutical entity. The name of the chosen producer was given to him in a dream nights after the ritual, but it was so vivid he had no problem remembering. Canon Enterprises was the name of the selectee. The R.F.P. was prepared and the diabolical plan was set in motion.

#######

After the candles blew out in the conference room and it became pitch dark the temperature dropped rapidly and severely. Moments later instead of the candles reigniting as before, the lights came on and the attendees could see the smoke from their breath because of the cold. The imposing figure that formerly occupied the head chair was gone. Milton, somewhat paralyzed from fear, managed to instruct everybody to get out immediately as he rose to exit himself. Before leaving his position he noticed a piece of paper in front of him that was not there previously. He grabbed it and continued heading toward the door right behind the group.

As he watched the others scrambling toward the elevator to get out of the area not knowing what was going to happen next, he elected to go back to his office. Once inside he composed himself and read the note. The message printed on the note appeared as if it had been burned into the paper yet without consuming it. He had no doubt who it was from and again fear rose up inside of him. With trembling hands he held up the note and read it.

"You will never again challenge me in front of my followers. Be warned if you do it will be your end. I have chosen to give you an answer to your question this time only because of them. Tomorrow you will receive a telephone call from Washington that will provide you with what you seek. Question me no more after that but carry out your mission."

Milton dropped the note as his arms fell to his side and he leaned back in his chair exhausted. The hour was late but he knew he had to go back into the conference room to see whether it was okay or he would have some heavy explaining to do in the morning. Cautiously he tiptoed into the room and looked around. The temperature had returned to the normal setting so he quickly started to collect the ritual items and placed them in the box. What he failed to notice however was the talisman that had fallen to the floor and under the table. Satisfied he had removed all evidence of the meeting he turned off the lights and went home.

The following day at Canon headquarters Jennifer came in to work early as she normally would. Milton would not be in until later that morning. After setting up her desk and getting her morning coffee she went to the conference room to see if it was okay for the next scheduled meeting. While casually walking around the room she happened to spot the talisman on the floor under the conference table. She picked it up and examined it. The markings on the piece were not strange to her because she had seen them before but never on a trinket like this. Her first thought was to turn it over to her boss, but as she examined it more closely the numbers 666 engraved in the center caused her to have a second thought. On previous occasions she had come across odd items and curious smells after these meetings but she never paid much attention to it until now.

She had often heard some of her co-workers talking about some of the strange things they believed were going on at Canon. Until now she had dismissed it as just gossip. Now she was curious and wanted to find out more. Who should she approach about it was the question. Since she didn't have anything with her to carry it out in and she didn't want anyone to see her with it, she carefully hid it in the conference room credenza. She would come back and get it later. Her next step as she returned to her desk was to figure out who she should turn to. No one immediately came to mind, but then she remembered some time ago overhearing her boss talking to Herb Crandall about some employee nosing around in the offices after hours. She wondered if that employee could possibly have any idea about this. She spent several minutes trying to recall the employee's name, but without success. Feeling a little frustrated she gave up on the idea and went about her daily routine.

Even though she busied herself doing her normal work she couldn't get the talisman out of her head nor could she let go of the idea that the nosy employee might know something. So she interrupted her normal activity and revisited the thought about who he could be. Then the idea came to her that since he reported to Mr. Crandall, if she looked in the database for his people perhaps seeing a name would trigger her recollection. She diligently searched his organization staffing list but nothing there helped her remember anything. Once again feeling a little frustrated but determined she tried to recall more of the manager's conversation. Finally it came to her that during that discussion Mr. Crandall had proposed the idea of offering the nosy employee a position away from headquarters. She also remembered the man was not one of Crandall's people but worked for Larry Gilsenan and Crandall would have to talk to him before making any formal offer.

Now she redirected her search to the Gilsenan organization. About a third of the way down the list the name Ronald L. Powers – QC Manager came up and for her the light came on. This was it he was the one they talked about. She wrote down his extension on her note pad and decided to call him later. First she had to think about what she would say. She wanted to be sure not to give away anything before she confirmed he was the right one. How would she begin? What would be the reason for her to be calling him? These were the questions she had to answer to herself before calling him.

Ron came in at his usual time expecting this to be just another day. The only thing he was anticipating was a call from Tango which he figured may or may not happen. As was his new routine since being at the plant, he would set up shop for the day then go straight to production. After grabbing his morning coffee he made his way to the lines. Things were humming along at the normal operational pace. Under the guidance and supervision of the fill-in line supervisor no one seemed to be missing Brent Woodley. Ron was still puzzled that for the second day no one had even inquired about why he was missing.

He checked in and talked with some of the line workers asking their opinions on how they thought the operation could be improved. Not surprising no-one had any suggestions. They all were just content to continue doing what they do and look for the next paycheck. Ron moved around from station to station and finally ended his tour at the area that was being retooled and set-up in anticipation of a new product coming out. He was curious that he had not been given any specs on this new product, even though he suspected what it might be.

Satisfied that he had covered all stations and there was nothing new to improve or add to his reporting, he went back to his office. Each passing day he was beginning to wonder how much longer he would be on this assignment. He had not been able to come up with anything that could improve production except replacing some of the equipment and he had already reported that idea. So when they would meet again would his report be any different and what would Crandall say? He still suspected that getting him out of the headquarters office was just a way for them to keep him from investigating what he had learned at the party. He felt strongly about it, but there was nothing he could do but play along.

Meanwhile he was picking up bits and pieces of information that were getting him closer to understanding what was happening at Canon behind the obvious scenes. When he walked in his office he saw the message light flashing so he started reviewing them. He was expecting Tango but the first caller wasn't him.

"Hello Mr. Powers this is Jennifer Winston, Mr. Jenkovitch's secretary. When you have an opportunity would you return my call? Thank you."

A call from the CEO's secretary got my attention quick. Either I'm in big trouble or perhaps a promotion is in the works. I couldn't convince myself that the latter was the case so I knew I'd better return that call pronto. I dialed the number and waited.

"Hello this is Jennifer, how may I help you?"

"Jennifer this is Ron Powers you called me?"

"Yes Mr. Powers thanks for returning my call so promptly. There's something I want to talk to you about but I'd rather not do it over the phone. What time do you go to lunch?"

"This sounds serious, am I in some kind of trouble?"

"Oh, no it has nothing to do with Mr. Jenkovitch. Well, not as far as you're concerned anyway. No I just need to get your input on something that I think you may know about."

"Okay, I usually go around 1:00 but I'm flexible. What works for you?"

"I usually go at 12:00 so I'm back by 1:00 when he usually has appointments."

"Alright 12:00 is fine, where would you like to go?"

"I don't think we should meet in the cafeteria here because I don't know who knows you, but just about everybody knows me. I don't want anyone trying to create something."

"Yes I know exactly what you mean. So where then?"

"There's a little deli right around the corner on W. 46th St. called the Sandwich Mart. Do you know where it is?"

"As a matter of fact I do, I've been there a few times but I didn't think they had any place to sit down and eat."

"That's true most people don't, but if you go all the way to the back there's a door that opens to a nice cozy eating area with tables. I don't know why the owner keeps it so secret but as I said it is a cozy little hideaway."

"Okay, I'll meet you there at 12:00. How will I know you?"

"I am brown skin with long black hair and I will be wearing a tan top coat. I'll try to get the first table as soon as you come in the door so look there first."

"Good, I'll see you then."

"Okay. Goodbye."

Now things were really getting interesting. The CEO's secretary wanting to meet with me, what could that be about? I filed away the thought and continued reviewing messages. The second one was Tango and he just said he'd try me again this afternoon. In a way I was sorry I missed his call because in his last message when he said he had been called to Washington immediately, I figured something very important must have happened. Whether he was going to share that with me or not could be anybody's guess but I figured when we finally talked I'd try to get it out of him.

It was still early before my lunch date so I decided to sort out all the pieces I had of the Canon enigma and perhaps come up with a reason why Jennifer wanted to see me. I knew that Herb Crandall was deeply involved in whatever was the reason for murdering Tony, but until now I couldn't place Mr. Jenkovitch in the puzzle. Maybe he was part of the conspiracy too. I had no way of knowing how high the culpability went. Moreover I wondered if he too could be one of the devil's disciples. The more I thought about it the more I was convinced that he had to be included with them or the cover up couldn't possibly be so effective.

Except for my conclusion about the CEO's involvement, I still didn't see how Jennifer could be in the mix. Could she be one of them also? I had a difficult time believing that but then again anything's possible, especially around here. Of all the pieces that I could put together there was nothing to even slightly point to her. Then I thought maybe she like some others had seen or heard something regarding the incident and just wanted to share it. Why pick me? All kinds of questions were running through my mind but I knew the only way they would be answered was when we met.

Around eleven-thirty I caught a cab hoping I could get there by our rendezvous time. Right at twelve o'clock we pulled up in front of the deli and I walked in. As many times as I had been in here, it was strange that I never noticed the door in the back. Maybe it was because I was always in a hurry and just wanted to get my sandwich and return to the office. This time I went all the way to the back and found the door. I could see why most people missed it. It appeared like a door to a stock room or an employee area so who would have guessed where it led. I opened the door and just like she said there was a nice well laid out cozy room with ten tables- five on each side. As I looked around there were several people eating and talking but no one matching the description she gave me. One table in the back corner was empty so I headed for it. Before I could even sit down the door opened and in walked the person looking like what she described so I waved her over. She saw me.

"Mr. Powers?"

"Yeah, I'm Powers, but please call me Ron. We don't need to be so formal here."

"Okay, I'm Jennifer. You know there's no service back here you have to go and get your food."

"Fine, let's go."

She then suggested we leave our coats to hold the table. I hesitated at first, but when she said there was only one way out and we could see everyone coming and going I agreed we left the room, went back in the deli and ordered. There was a pretty large crowd so it took some time to get our order. While we waited I tried to engage her in some small talk but she seemed rather cold. I got the message and shut up. As soon as we got back in the dining room her climate changed and she became very talkative.

"You may have thought I was being rude to you out there but as I told you earlier a lot of people at Canon know who I am and I don't trust any of them. Everybody knows about this place and some of them may have been out there that I didn't see. In here I can see everybody so I know who's here. I'm sorry if I offended you."

"No you didn't exactly, but I was curious because you called me and then I find you didn't want to talk. I thought that to be a little strange. Anyway we're here now so what's on your mind?"

"Before I tell you that, I need to ask you something."

"Sure go right ahead."

"Some time ago I overheard my boss and Herb Crandall from personnel talking about somebody doing some after hour research that was making them very nervous. Was that you?"

"Now before I answer that, it stays here right?"

"Yes of course. I just need to know that before I share with you what I have."

"Okay then, I'm your guy. They were talking about me."

"Good!"

She then started talking about the talisman she found this morning and all the other times she had found odd items and funny smells in the conference room after these meetings. She also mentioned the gossip she heard from other secretaries that she before now had just considered as just that. When she finished telling me all she heard and saw I knew now this intrigue was even greater than I suspected. In return I shared with her the things I had found and also heard. Together we came to the same conclusion - there was an evil plot unfolding at Canon Enterprises.

I asked her if she knew Marsha Robinson, a chemist at the plant. When she said she didn't I told her what Marsha and I were doing to unravel this mystery and asked if she would like to join with us? She said definitely yes. Then I told her about Marsha's sister and the dinner I was going to on Friday. I asked her if I could borrow the talisman to let Marsha's sister look at it. She agreed and told me to meet her after work right back here and she would give it to me. It was settled, I would meet her after work and she became part of our team. We finished eating and went back to work.

It was about 1:30 when I got back to my desk. No sooner had I walked in the door when the phone rang. It was Tango.

"Hello Ron Powers here."

"Ron this is Tango how are you?"

"I'm fine. Are you back in town?"

"No, I'm still in D.C. – will probably be here a couple more days. Listen I'm glad I caught you, you seem to be quite busy."

"Yeah you know how that goes, I'm learning new things every day."

"It's funny you should say that because so am I. The reason I had to leave so abruptly the other day is because of something that was found here that involves Canon. I've learned that there is something here connected to that partial paper I found in the lab there. One of the agents here found the top half of an R.F.P. that lists Canon as the only addressee. What's called for in the document, even though many details are missing and must be contained in the other half, is the development of some type of drug that will specifically affect adolescents. It just goes to substantiate what I told you before about a plot underway in the city. When I get back, which should be on Friday, I want to sit down with you and go over everything. There must be a link between this and Anthony Oliver's murder. In the meantime I'm going to ask you to think hard about what he was telling you at lunch that day. Will you do that?"

"Yes of course Tango I'll try to help, but remember you never did prove to me who you really are."

"On Friday, in light of everything that's happened lately, I think I can gain your trust. I'll call you Thursday afternoon and see what time we can meet on Friday."

"Okay that's fine just don't plan on meeting very late on Friday because I have a dinner engagement."

"Alright we'll work around that. Talk to you later."

"Right! Goodbye."

After we hung up it was very clear that there actually exists an R.F.P. for a special drug. I just wished there was a little more time I could have spent with Tony. Maybe he would have told me where he hid the documents. One way or another, things were starting to come together and the vision of the puzzle is not as nebulous as it once was. Perhaps after meeting with Tango and then with Marsha's father and sister, the clarity needed for a final solution may even come closer.

When Milton Jenkovitch came in the office it was about 9:30 AM. He stopped by Jennifer's desk to check with her for anything that might need his attention. She looked at him and it was obvious he didn't have such a good night. At first she thought he may have had another episode of what happened to him before, but when she asked if he was alright he quickly answered yes and went into his office. From his outward appearance Jennifer wondered whether something happened at the meeting last night, but she knew better than to ask him.

Milton rushed in and sat down at his desk still feeling the lingering emotions from his experience at the meeting. Even though he had several cocktails at home, the relief he sought eluded him. So now in addition to his anguish he also was experiencing the after effects of his imbibing. He recalled the note that said he was to expect a telephone call today so not knowing what time it might be he tried to steady himself and be ready to receive it.

Throughout the Canon Enterprises floor of the building all those who were present at last night's meeting were still feeling the after-shock of what happened. Caught between fears and clinging to abject commitment to something they believed would bring them great rewards, the fear side of the equation was causing concern. After seeing last night the other side of the one they chose to follow, the glitter of the perceived gold diminished severely. But they all knew that their signed contract would not be terminated by the holder in their favor, so they continued with the mission.

For all those who were not at the meeting there was a lighter side of activity. All day long there was a buzz circulating around the offices and cubicles that Canon along with two other major corporations was going to be sponsoring a youth basketball league for the city. Many of the employees had heard the rumor even outside of the Canon community. For most of them it was exciting to think that their company was going to be part of doing something positive for the city's young people. The talk was even saying that their CEO had proposed the idea to the Mayor and City Council which made them feel even better about the firm. How sad they would be if they only knew his motive.

When Jennifer heard the buzz she too was excited but she was more reservedly enthusiastic knowing what she knew about Mr. Jenkovitch. She was a little puzzled though because she had not heard any of the upper managers talking about it and nothing had come across her desk like it usually would for something this big. Curious about the buzz she wanted to ask her boss regarding its validity but decided not to just in case she wasn't even supposed to know. If he wanted her to know she was sure he would inform her. Instead of asking Milton she decided to call Ron and ask him if he knew about it. Several attempts were made but she was unable to get him so she left a message to call her.

Milton sat in his office behind a closed door since the time he came in. It was starting to get late and Jennifer was getting concerned because he hadn't even come out for lunch. His early instructions to her were that he was expecting an important call from Washington and he didn't want to be disturbed. She knew that the call he was waiting for did not happen so she wondered whether to check on him and see if she should bring him something to eat. At first she was going to try him on the intercom but then said I'd better go see if he's okay. Just as she got up the phone rang and she could see it was his line on her call director. Normally she would intercept his calls on the third ring but this time she let it go to see if he would pick up.

"Hello - Canon Enterprises" he said.

"Hello this call is for Mr. Jenkovitch are you him?" came the female response from the other end.

"Yes you got him what can I do for you?"

"Please stand by while I transfer your call."

There was a long pause then finally a man's voice came on.

"Mr. Jenkovitch my name is Theodore Messinger Director of Human Services in Washington. How are you?"

Milton hesitated a minute to compose himself before answering.

"Yes Mr. Messinger I'm fine thank you for asking. How can I help you?"

"I believe I need to help you. You received an RFP from my department some time ago and we are in receipt of your proposal. I just wanted to follow up and see what the status is."

Milton became a little hesitant wondering whether the emissary had contacted this man and if so what did he tell him? Could this call be a coincidence or is the man following instructions? If he was following instructions why didn't he know what the status is? Caught between not being sure if this is the call he had been advised about or really just a mere coincidence, Milton became suspicious and acted cagey.

"Sir, I am concerned about the funding for the project and would like to know where that stands since we have already begun the development work?"

"Did you not receive the approval letter explaining the project details including the funding schedule?"

"No I didn't. When was it sent?"

"Hold a minute let me check. It was sent about two weeks ago to your attention at the address we have on file."

"Well I haven't seen it but you said the proposal was approved. Will it be fully funded?"

"Mr. Jenkovitch all I can tell you over the phone is that it was approved. Please find the letter for the full details. If you can't locate it please contact my assistant Miss LePore at (202) 555-6000 ext. 234 and she'll see about getting you a copy."

"Okay good. Thank you Mr. Messinger, I'm glad you called."

"Yes so am I. Goodbye."

After he hung up Milton still wasn't sure whether this was the call or not, but no matter now because he had an answer even though it didn't come the way he expected. His job now was to find the letter. He pressed the intercom button.

"Jenn can you come in here a minute please?"

"Be right there."

"The call I was expecting just came in and I've been informed that a letter from the Human Services Department in Washington was sent to my attention about two weeks ago. Do you remember seeing anything like that?"

"No Mr. Jenkovitch not right off but I'll go check the log and see."

"Please do that right away, it's important."

"Will do, is that all?"

"That's it for now. Thank you."

Jennifer left his office and began checking the files. No more than ten minutes later she pressed the IC button.

"Mr. Jenkovitch I found the letter information, it was logged in on Wednesday October 25th at 3:30PM. I remember now giving it to you with a few others. That was the same day you got sick. Okay?"

"Yes Jenn now I remember. Thanks again."

Milton started recalling what happened. That was the day he had received the call from Tango Hernandez that upset him severely. He had taken the letters Jennifer gave him and put them in the bottom drawer of his desk to read later. But after talking with Hernandez he was in no condition to read anything. When he returned to work after his episode he didn't remember the letters or where he put them. Even now he wasn't sure but he started checking his desk drawers. In the bottom drawer on the right hand side where he kept his miscellaneous items he opened it and there it was. He had banded the stack of four letters.

He quickly took out the package and ran through it. Right in the middle was the letter he sought and he opened it. Scanning it searching for the part he was most anxious to read his anxiety was abated when he saw the statement that told him the project would be fully funded payable in two segments. He didn't even bother to read the rest of the letter but put it down and breathed a sigh of relief. It didn't matter anymore whether the emissary had directed the call, what did matter was he had his answer. However, what lingered in his mind beyond that was the fact that he had challenged the adversary.

Before leaving for the day Jennifer called Ron one more time.

"Hello this is Ron."

"Hi Ron this is Jennifer did you get my message?"

"No I just this minute walked in from a meeting. What's up?"

"I wanted to know if you heard about the new youth basketball league Canon is sponsoring?"

"You know that's interesting because it was one of the items talked about in my meeting. How did you hear about it?"

"A few people here have mentioned it to me but I haven't seen anything official. Is it?"

"Well yes and no. My understanding is that Canon is not the official sponsor but is partnering with the VCS drug store chain that is taking the lead. The third partner in the deal is the Sherington Hotel chain and together they will merge and support the PCAL league that's already operating. I think it's a great idea but I wonder why Canon is doing it."

"I thought it strange too but maybe it's good for the public image."

"You may be right. Anyway whatever the reason it looks like it's going to happen. Anything else you need?"

"No I just wanted to confirm the story. There are so many rumors floating around here. You have a goodnight."

"Yeah I'll try and you too. Bye."

When I finished talking with Jennifer I started thinking about Canon's focus on the young. Was there some connection between this new youth league support and the mystery drug aimed at them? Why that target? Nothing I could imagine gave me any sense of justification or any rationale for it. At one point I thought the pieces were beginning to fit together and I could almost see the big picture, but now with this new announcement another piece was added that I couldn't place.

On the third day of Brent Woodley's strange absence finally someone besides me started asking a question. After the meeting at which Leonard Jablonski thought a replacement for Brent was going to be discussed and no decision had been made, he knew now it was going to be up to him. First he had to ascertain and confirm the status of his employee. When I came in that morning he was already in production questioning some of the line workers asking if they had seen or heard from Brent. No one could help him. His next step was to check the personnel files to see who his emergency contact person was. In my mind I wondered why it took him so long and now he was acting with a sense of urgency. Had something happened I was unaware of?

Just out of curiosity I went by Leonard's office to see what he had learned. In case he questioned my interest I was going to tell him that Brent was the next person on my list to interview as part of my assignment. To my surprise he didn't ask but instead volunteered to tell me he spoke to a sister of Brent's and she said she was the only close relative left in his family. He added that she had filed a missing persons report with the police and they were investigating.

From earlier conversations with Tango I knew the police were already looking for Brent as a prime suspect in Tony's murder case so I wondered how long it would take them to connect the missing person report filed by his sister. When we talked Leonard Jablonski didn't seem at all upset or rattled that his lead production supervisor was missing for three days. He seemed to be more concerned that the fill in person was an apparent devout Christian woman. The plan to have Brent run the line for the new product could never have her do it because she might discover what the product could do.

The complications that were beginning to manifest in Leonard's life were causing him to question how much Milton was in control of the overall project. He also questioned the stability of Herbert Crandall, who he blamed for his being in the position he's in now. To Leonard if Herbert had not presented the impression to Brent that he was on a fast track to upper management then he wouldn't have acted so impulsively causing this whole problem.

I watched Leonard seemingly fall apart today as he tried to come up with a reason to dismiss the fill in woman who was doing a good job running the line. He couldn't just remove her without cause yet the time was getting close when he would have to put someone in charge of the new line and he knew it couldn't be her. Desperate for a way out, he called Herbert and pleaded for help. His expectation was that Crandall would commiserate and provide a personnel process that could solve his problem.

He reached Herbert and explained his plight but was surprised at the response. Crandall told him he couldn't help from a personnel perspective but he would put him in touch with someone who may be able to help him for a fee. When Leonard heard that he asked if this was the same solution he used for his problem. Crandall answered yes and Jablonski hung up.

Leonard was obviously very disappointed in the outcome of his call to who he believed was an ally. Now that time was becoming a major factor in getting the new line ready to run on the day that start-up was scheduled, he was in a quandary as to how to resolve the problem. If he allowed the back-up supervisor to become the permanent replacement then he would run the risk of her discovering the secret and if he passed over her and selected someone else she would probably file a grievance with the union. He certainly didn't want the union to launch an investigation and uncover the real reason. If that happened he knew neither Crandall nor even Jenkovitch would support him and have to confront the adversary again.

By lunchtime Leonard, having arrived at no easy way out, was almost at the point of taking Herbert up on his offer. Even though he was already having a bad day matters worsened when he received a telephone call from a Detective Sergeant Callahan at police headquarters asking him to attend a meeting tonight. It seems that new witnesses had come forward regarding the Oliver case and the detective just wanted to talk with Leonard as Brent's supervisor about it. Leonard started having mixed emotions about attending the meeting. On one hand could there be a possible solution here or would the hole he was in just get deeper? He tried to think positive thoughts and envisioned all the rewards coming that were promised to him.

#######

At police headquarters in the Pocono Mountains Detective Mike Casio was nearing the end of his tour for the day. As he sat at his desk he looked over the list of cold case files. Right at the top was one that he had seen before but never had the time to get into. Now that he had just wrapped up a case he thought would be a good time to revisit this one. This was the case of the ski accident at Camelback Lodge a few weeks ago. Originally it was filed as an accident but when the autopsy report turned up a large fresh amount of the drug curare in the victim's system, the status was changed to suspicion of murder. However, it remained a cold case because the victim's face was so badly damaged it was unidentifiable. After the big success with his last case Detective Casio was feeling ambitious so he decided to pull the whole file and read it. When he got the records and returned to his desk he was surprised at how thick it had gotten since he last looked at it. Undaunted by the file size but a little weary from the day's activities, he decided he might do better by reading it again first thing in the morning.

Since the time of the ski accident no one was actively searching for Brent Woodley except his sister and the police. But even his sister didn't file the missing person report right away because she knew her brother had a habit of not keeping in touch with her for long periods. Now that the report was filed and it went out over the police network covering four states, she was hoping he might turn up or someone with knowledge of his whereabouts would contact her.

As for the City Police Department the day they went to the plant to take Brent into custody and were told he was not there they were faced with a dead end trail. Surveillance of his apartment and his local hangout places revealed nothing useable. With nothing else to go on they too made it a cold case file.

From that time until now Herb Crandall, Reginald Codey and Ivan were confident that they had solved the group's problem. Ivan had been paid, Reggie had been complemented and set-up for a salary increase and Herb was just feeling good about the whole thing. They had never met nor even heard of Detective Mike Casio whose reputation for dogged tenacity and persistence in solving cases had gained him the nickname "Fido". He was known for getting his teeth into a case and not letting go until it was done.

The correlation between what was happening in the mountains and the activities in the city regarding both the Oliver and Woodley cases was about to merge as if someone or something was directing the process. Like a life size jig saw puzzle it may first appear to be unfathomable, but when all the pieces are located and brought together and the matches are made – how gratifying is the accomplishment.

Leonard Jablonski left work still feeling a sense of trepidation and anxiety not knowing what was going to happen. Having to meet with the police was not something he had planned on or even remotely thought about. He was asked to come in at 6:00 O'clock so he had about an hour to fill before that. His first thought was to stop in one of the local bars and have something to calm his nerves, but when he reflected on who he was meeting with, walking in there with the smell of alcohol on his breath wasn't such a good idea. So he decided to get something to eat instead.

Inside the small Chinese Restaurant he ordered a light dinner. While waiting for his order he was able to see a television and the news was on. News reports for the last few days were being dominated by talk of escalating tension in some European and Mid-Eastern countries and how a rising diplomat was being positioned to deal with it. Leonard sat there thinking how ironic it would be if war broke out over there before Canon could finish their product and get it into that marketplace.

By the time he finished eating it was just about right for him to head over to the precinct. He hailed a taxi and within minutes arrived there. Once inside he asked at the receiving desk for Detective Callahan. The desk officer called the sergeant and advised he had a visitor then directed Leonard upstairs to the second floor where the offices were. When he got up there Detective

Callahan was waiting in the hallway and greeted him. Then he guided him to a small conference room where two other people were sitting. Detective Callahan introduced the group to each other and then started the session.

"Thanks for coming folks I really appreciate you taking the time and coming down here especially on such short notice. I invited you here because we think we finally have a break in a case I know you have heard about and we need your help."

Besides Leonard Jablonski the two other people were employees of the Peacock Palace where the Oliver incident occurred. They had been called down because the new witnesses had identified them as being outside smoking when the getaway car sped away. It was reported that they must have seen the shooter and also who was driving the vehicle.

"Mr. Porter and Miss Malu according to the eyewitness statement you were both outside of the restaurant that day when the incident occurred. Is that right?"

"Yes we were just having a break" said David Porter.

"Did you see the gunman enter the getaway vehicle and speed away?"

"I saw a medium height kind of stocky man run out of the building and get into the car in front of the place but I don't know if he was the gunman or not."

"Yeah that's what I saw too" echoed Diana Malu.

"If you saw him again would you be able to recognize him?"

"I don't know it happened so fast" responded David and again Diana echoed him.

"If I show you some pictures do you think it might stimulate your recollection?"

"Possibly."

Sergeant Callahan left the room and went over to a file cabinet in another room and took out a book of mug pictures of former criminals. Minutes later he placed the book in front of the couple and asked them to go through the pictures and see if anyone looks like someone they may have seen that day. The couple started reviewing the mug shots but after spending several minutes flipping through the pages neither one of them could say that any one of the people shown in the book looked like the man who ran out of the restaurant that day.

"Okay. That's alright. Now what about the driver of the car, did you see him?"

"Yes, the car was sitting there for a while. But it wasn't a him, it was a her" David said.

"Can you describe her?"

"I think so. If I remember right she was --------------."

David went on to provide a description of the woman driving the car and it was corroborated by Diana. Detective Callahan thanked the couple again and told them they were finished and could leave. After they were gone he turned back to Leonard.

"You heard all that right?"

"Yes but you know I wasn't at the restaurant that day."

"Right we know that but the man we're looking for we have been informed works for you. His name is Brent Woodley. Isn't he one of your workers?"

"Yes."

"We can't seem to locate him. Do you know where he is?"

"I'm afraid I can't help you there, he's been absent."

"Well no matter, we'll find him. Now you also heard the description given for the driver. The two eyewitnesses who came in earlier this week described her as someone who might also work at your plant because she comes to the restaurant regularly. I knew it was a female driver when I said he to Mr. Porter and Miss Malu but I wanted to see if they would pick up on that. Sure enough they did and it agreed with the other eyewitnesses. From the description you heard does it fit anyone at the plant you know?"

Leonard couldn't believe what he was hearing because the couple's description so closely matched his fill in supervisor's looks that he couldn't resist the temptation surging through his brain. In his mind he was thinking here is my opportunity to solve my problem and not have to do it the Crandall way. So he went on to provide details to the detective and gave up the supervisor. When Detective Callahan told Leonard he would be visiting the plant tomorrow to pick her up, it seemed like a heavy weight had been lifted off of his shoulders. The detective thanked him again for coming and for his cooperation and said he was finished. Leonard Jablonski got up from his chair and walked out of the precinct knowing he had exercised one his master's diplomacy skills - he lied. As he hit the street a big broad sinister smile came across his face and he went home happy.

Chapter Seven
"Perceptions"

In the beginning was the Word, and the Word was with God, and the Word was God.
The same was in the beginning with God.
All things were made by him; and without him was not anything made that was made.
In him was life; and the life was the light of men.
And the light shineth in darkness; and the darkness comprehended
it not. (John 1:1-5)

It was Wednesday night around 7:00 O'clock when Reverend Devereaux sat in his home study reviewing the scriptures as he prepared for his upcoming Sunday sermon. He had been in prayer the last few days asking God for guidance on what he should be telling his congregation especially in light of all the recent turmoil that had been happening abroad and also at home. In his spirit he felt burdened by a lack of clear direction for where he was to lead his flock in their understanding of world events and the Kingdom of God. For weeks he had been watching and listening to news reports about potential wars and escalating strife between major European powers. Even here at home he had been observing incidents that suggested surging lawlessness among the so called civilized people.

When the divine answer came and he was inspired to look closely at the first chapter of John it seemed that as many times as he had read it before he had never received the message that he was getting now. It was becoming clear the Lord wanted him to embark on a spiritual journey that would take him into a realm of understanding prior to now he did not have. His experience had not prepared him for such as was to happen in the next few hours. The journey was to cover the next four weeks and he would delve into the real message that Jesus Christ while he walked the earth in the flesh came to deliver. The final segment in his four sermon message would be one that his flock would receive the true intent of God's purpose for creating the earth.

As he reflected on the scripture penned by St. John and incidents that were happening daily in the news it reminded him of a time long ago when he was still in Louisiana. He recalled a night when he and Melinda were still dating and they would spend Saturday nights going to dinner and then see a movie. This one night which clearly stayed in his mind was a sort of harbinger of things to come. He momentarily drifted back in time and the mental picture was almost as if it was happening again.

He and Melinda on this Saturday night went out for dinner and then to a movie. They were celebrating his first appointment as a minister. Their joy for the evening however was spoiled by what they saw happening just outside the theater they were going to.

At this time many cities across the country were having skirmishes among the people. Factions were squaring off against one another in support of or in opposition to the Vietnam War, racial oppression or some other unrelated cause. In front of the movie house were two groups in confrontation. Approaching sirens pierced the night air upsetting what was otherwise a calm evening. In minutes several police cars arrived dispatching a small army of uniformed policemen. They exited their vehicles positioned themselves in front of the theater and in between the two groups. The bullhorn held by the leader barked commands to the crowd.

"This is an unlawful assembly. Put down your signs, disperse and go home."

The crowd paid no attention to the orders but continued to walk around disorderly.

"You have been warned. If you do not cease and desist immediately you will be arrested" the sergeant hollered again.

Once again the crowd was unresponsive.

Stanton and Melinda stopped their approach far enough away to be safely outside of the melee but close enough to see and hear all that was taking place.

"Do you see that?" he said.

"Yes, but I can't believe it. I knew these things were happening in a lot of places but I didn't think it would happen here."

"Let's get a little closer."

"No, we don't need to move any closer. Don't you see the police over there? You want to get arrested with the crowd?"

"No of course not but I want to know what's behind all this. If I'm going to be a good minister I need to understand what drives people to act this way."

"All in good time. I don't think tonight is the night you need to start your ministry and possibly end your career all in one effort."

Stanton laughed as he realized her voice of reason as usual was right on point.

The police got more agitated as the crowd continued to disobey. The lines had been drawn and the police were forming a riot formation. It appeared the confrontation between the law and the citizens was about to escalate. To complicate matters, the early show had just finished and people inside the theater were coming out. As they passed through the exit doors and saw all the commotion going on, many were frightened and confused. Not knowing whether to stay inside or continue trying to get to their cars several of them who were in front just stopped. Patrons behind them unable to see what was going on in front of the first line became anxious at the delay in getting out of the building and began to push their way forward. Now there was friction both inside the theater and outside of the building. The police could see what was happening but were indecisive about what their next move should be. Should they continue to contend with the crowd that was in front of them or should they separate their ranks and deal in part with the problem behind them.

It was an interesting dilemma. So far no one had been hurt but as tempers began to flare the mood of the crowd got intense. Patrons in the theater were pushing and shoving each other to exit the building while the crowd outside were generally hostile toward the police and each other.

"This is your final warning" said the sergeant.

As he was barking his final threat another police car showed up on the scene. This time a lieutenant and the captain got out and took over the command.

"People you have been warned, there will be no further warnings. If you do not disperse immediately then we will make arrests" came the words from the captain. How are we on tear gas?"

"We have an ample supply sir. Do you want to start it?"

"On my orders toss a few cans into the center of the crowd but wait for my command."

"Listen people we don't want anybody hurt but if you will not obey our orders than you will be responsible for whatever happens."

"Two, four, six, eight we will not cooperate. Two, four, six, eight, we will not cooperate" the crowd replied.

"Okay sergeant toss the cans."

Several cans of CN tear gas were launched into the middle of the crowd then a big cloud of white smoke erupted. Gasping and coughing ensued immediately as people on the street started inhaling the fumes. Right after that the running started as the crowd began to take off in all directions. Signs were thrown into the air, sticks were hurled toward the police and general mayhem broke out.

"I can't believe this is really happening here" Stanton said. "My God what could possibly be behind all of this?"

"Come on let's get out of here now."

Melinda started pulling on his arm insisting that they head in the direction opposite the mayhem. Stanton couldn't turn his eyes away from what was going on. He wanted to see what was going to happen next. She kept tugging and tugging as he resisted. Finally she was able to get him to start moving away from the excitement.

The people inside the theater finally were able to get the first line to move into the open space outside. By this time the air all around the area was filled with tear gas fumes. As they entered the smoke they too began to cough and gasp. The small group of officers who had separated from the main body tried to contain them and direct them into an area off to the side, but as the movement to get out of the theater increased the people ran into and through the officers knocking some of them to the ground. Seeing what was happening to their fellow officers the main body of patrolmen moved toward the theater patrons.

"Stop, stop before we shoot" said one officer.

By this time there was no stopping the patrons or the crowd. Bedlam was at its height. Even the older people who were part of the group inside the theater were scrambling to find a place of safety but there was none. It was as if what had been intended at the start to be a peaceful protest had suddenly turned into mimicry of the Vietnam War brought home to New Orleans.

The intensity of the skirmish heated to such a point that all sides were afraid for their lives. The police were caught in the middle of a fracas that they were not in control of. The patrons and the crowd were the subjects of something they couldn't have imagined at the beginning of their evening. Things were getting so heated that it was hard to perceive this was taking place in the middle of a so called civilized modern day city. As the tension built up and tempers flared on all sides, control was completely lost and then it happened.

One shot rang out then another, then another and before long a number of bullets were flying through the air. The policemen were just shooting in every direction and the crowd was running for their lives. Many fell as they attempted to flee. Blood and guts spewed everywhere and for a while it appeared as if it would not end. No one saw this coming and none could have thought this would be how they would end up. There was no rationale as to why the first shot was fired but it was learned later that one over-zealous officer decided he had enough and wanted to do something to end it. The people were panicked and the cops were too. The tension led up to the final outcome which was death. Death in such numbers that the next day's headlines would have a field day in describing what happened. The numbers in the end were eleven dead and sixteen wounded.

Ambulances were heard rushing to the scene and in minutes they were carting the dead and wounded away. Satan the devil was having a ball watching this unfold and finally Stanton had the answer to why this was all happening. He carried this memory with him even until now as he was preparing his initial sermon for the series.

He opened his eyes from his reverie and tried to refocus on the task at hand. A bit strained from his recollection, he decided to take a short break and get something to snack on. Melinda met him when he got into the kitchen and reminded him that Mimi was bringing a young man to dinner with her on Friday.

"Good! It's about time she got her nose out of those books for a while and started having a life again. Who is this guy anyway, do we know anything about him?"

"Well she said he's a high level manager at the headquarters where she works and she believes you'll like him."

"Now why would she say that when I haven't even met him?"

"Because remember she's your child and she knows you."

He laughed then said: "Yes you're right how could I forget that."

Stanton opened the refrigerator took out a cup of yogurt and a juice then sat down and ate. After his short break he returned to the study and resumed his preparation.

While he was in the spirit thoughts began to flow so quickly he was having a difficult time writing as fast as he was being inspired. He was directed to go back in his Bible and revisit Genesis, Leviticus and Deuteronomy to get the right perspective on what his message should entail. As he did so a new enlightenment came to him and he was amazed at this new revelation within an old text. He spent the rest of the evening pouring over his new notes and absorbing the new found truth.

#######

When Leonard Jablonski came to work on Thursday morning there was a new spring in his step and his face was still smiling. To him his troubles had been abated and he could now get on with making the right choice for a new supervisor. It was just a matter of time before Maria the fill-in would be escorted from the building by the police and the problem would be solved. He started making plans for just how he would set up the new line to meet the early production demand on startup day. Before she even left the building Leonard had called his new prospect into his office to discuss the position.

Down in production the operation was functioning smoothly once again under Maria's direction. Her subordinates truly liked her and performed well. No one could have guessed what was about to happen within the next hour, especially to her. The whole plant was certainly aware of what had happened to Anthony Oliver and some were even privy to information regarding Brent Woodley as a suspect. But none knew anything about what Leonard Jablonski did yesterday.

It was shortly after 11:00 O'clock when the commotion started in the reception area of the plant. Several police officers entered the building demanding to see the head person. The receptionist was trying to explain to them that Mr. Davidson, the Vice-President in charge of the site, was on an international conference call and could not be interrupted. The police were not taking no for an answer and insisted she assist them or be held accountable for her actions. They told her that they were there to make an arrest and it was going to be done one way or the other. Confused and intimidated she wasn't sure exactly what to do so she dialed Leonard's extension.

"Yes this is Leonard."

"Mr. Jablonski, this is the lobby reception desk, the police are down here looking for Mr. Davidson. I told them he's on an important conference call and I can't interrupt him but they won't listen. What should I do?"

"Okay Beth don't panic I'll be right down."

Leonard excused himself from his prospective supervisor and literally ran to the elevator. He was excited and feeling the rush of things happening in his favor. When he got to the lobby the police had calmed down somewhat but were anxious to carry out their mission. Leonard talked with the sergeant who showed him the warrant for Maria's arrest. Leonard then escorted them to the production area and pointed her out.

"Are you Maria Sanchez?"

"Yes why you ask?"

"We have a warrant for your arrest. Please come with us."

"Arrest, arrest for what? I did nothing."

The police explained the charge to her, read the Miranda rights then walked her out of the building.

Leonard was having a hard time pretending to be bewildered at what just happened. Inside he was bursting with joy. For those employees in the area who could see what happened, genuine bewilderment showed on all of their faces. Leonard immediately took charge and directed them to report back to their work areas. He watched them vacate the lobby and then went smiling back to his office to finish with his new business.

By the time he reached his office the word had already spread around the plant about what happened. The employees who were witness to the police action wasted no time in informing their co-workers. When word got to Ron he was appalled because he had not only met the woman but had interviewed her. He found her to be an upstanding, righteous person and he refused to believe that she had anything to do with what she was being accused of. Quickly he made his way down to Leonard's office to inquire about his version of what happened. Leonard was still in session with his new supervisor and did not acknowledge Ron's request through Leonard's secretary, to see him. Ron advised the secretary that he would come back later but very soon.

Ron's next move was to go to the labs to see if Marsha could be interrupted. When he got there he learned that she was at the headquarters building in mid-town attending a meeting. He didn't know whether she had heard about what happened but then he realized since she was away from the plant, how could she. The news about Maria had circulated throughout the plant and everybody was talking about how they believed she had been set-up. The more Ron listened to the buzz the more he agreed with the talk and started thinking about who would gain anything by committing such an act. His conclusion immediately pointed to Mr. Jablonski.

How many of the top managers were involved in the plot he had no way of determining, but as more strange things keep occurring it all seems to center around the same key people. He went back to his office and looked again at some notes he started making a short while ago when he and Marsha were comparing ideas. The same people seem to come up whenever he thought about a particular incident or event. His assessment of the reason for the murder plot and cover up always linked Herb Crandall, Reggie Codey, Milton Jenkovitch and now Leonard Jablonski. He was convinced of the motive but was still unsure about what the real objective of the new drug was. The fact that it was designed to affect only the adolescent population was still an enigma and he was becoming more suspicious about why Canon was getting into the sponsorship of a youth basketball league. What was the connection?

As he was pondering the matter his phone rang and it was Herb Crandall calling.

"Hello Ron Powers here."

"Hello Ron, Herb Crandall how are you?"

"Hi Mr. Crandall I'm fine how are you?"

"Oh I guess I'm doing okay. Listen I just wanted to check in with you and see how things are going down there. Is everything alright?"

"To be honest with you sir, I haven't come up with anything new to improve production since we last met but I'm still working hard on it. There's been a lot of things happening around here making it difficult to maintain focus."

"Things like what?"

"Well take today for example. The police came and arrested the fill-in supervisor for the main production line. She was covering for Brent Woodley and I thought she was doing an excellent job. I couldn't imagine she would be involved in anything, much less what I heard they are accusing her of doing."

"Oh really? Just what is she being accused of doing?"

"The unofficial word here is that she was the driver of the getaway car that supposedly Brent Woodley used to make his escape."

When Herb heard that he had to pause a minute to gather himself before answering. He had not heard this story and it came as a big surprise to him but he knew that this had to be the work of Leonard. Was this his way of resolving the problem he had called about?

"What on earth is going on down there? First there's a big incident and now people are being hauled out under arrest. Did you see it happen?"

"No sir I wasn't actually there but I received my information from some reliable sources."

"I'm coming down there this afternoon. I want to talk with Leonard Jablonski. Are you going to be around, I'd like to see you after that?"

"What time do you think you're going to come? I have just one telephone meeting with my staff back there at 3:00 O'clock that I can either cut short or postpone if I have to."

"Yes why don't you postpone it please because that's about the time I should be finishing up with Leonard and then I'll come to your office."

"Fine I'll do that. See you then."

Herb Crandall got off the phone with Ron and then immediately called Mr. Jablonski.

"Hello Jablonski speaking what can I do for you?"

"Leonard this is Herb have you lost your mind? I just heard from Ron Powers about one of your people being arrested and taken out of the plant today. Is that true?"

"Yes it is. I had to do something to get her out of the way so that the project would not be jeopardized on startup day. The solution you offered was not in my eyes the best way to handle it."

"At least my way there would have been no slip ups. Now you have put all of us in a position to be exposed. Did you ever consider the fact that she will have an airtight alibi for her whereabouts at the time of the incident?"

"Of course I have Herb but that really doesn't matter. By the time they go through processing her and going through and substantiating her alibi, I will have put my guy in the position and the reason for doing so will be rock solid. No union could question my decision based on even her being suspected of doing what the police claim."

"You got it all figured out huh? For your sake I do hope it works out that way. Listen I want to come down there at 2:00 O'clock today and discuss some details about that and the project. Are you available it's important?"

"Yes I will be here."

"Good because there is another thing we need to see about and that's Ron Powers. I sent him down there to get him off the case here but I see that has only made things worse as far as his being nosy and getting into our business."

"Yes I agree. I think he's becoming a real threat to the project. Do you have something in mind for him?"

"We'll see. Let's discuss it when I get there."

#######

Back at police headquarters in the Pocono Mountains Mike Casio had finished reviewing the growing file on the now revised ski accident case at Camelback Lodge. His sense of curiosity had led him to check out some reports that had come in that day on missing persons. Strangely one report led him to examine it more closely and there seemed to be a tie in to the case in front of him. The description of the missing person in the report seemed to fit the description of the body that was still in the morgue at the hospital. Even though the picture of the person shown in the missing persons report was an older one and he knew that the face of the cadaver in the morgue could not be repaired enough to make a good match, there was something deep inside of him that was telling him there was a connection. He took the M.P. report and made arrangements to visit the hospital once again to look at the victim.

Upon arrival there he was escorted down to the morgue and the body pulled out for his examination. When he looked at it this time he noticed something that he had not seen before. There was a strange mark on his right hand. At first glance it looked like some kind of symbol for a club or fraternity or something but when he examined it more closely he saw that it was the mark of the beast from the book of Revelations in the Bible. How could he not have seen this before? Beginning with that he began to look at other features of the body and compared them to the description in the M.P. report. He also asked the medical staff questions about blood type, DNA mapping etc. After a short while he concluded that this was indeed the person satisfying the M.P. report.

He went back to his office and contacted Detective Callahan of the C.P.D. and advised him of his findings. Sergeant Callahan thanked him immensely and told him he was looking forward to receiving the written report. Between the two astute police officers it appeared that some progress was about to be made in solving the case of the missing Brent Woodley. However, it was not going to be that easy because there were other dimensions that would interfere. In the time that it was going to take Mike Casio to get the report down to Sergeant Callahan many things were going to take place. First was the problem of verifying who the killer was in the Oliver case; and second who would be responsible for taking charge of the investigation. Each officer wanted to receive credit for solving such a headline grabbing case and each wanted exclusive honors for doing so. Even within the law enforcement community there was enough mendacity to go around more than once.

Now more and more the pieces of the puzzle, as Ron Powers put it were beginning to really come together. As for Ron, though he was not privy to what was going on at this moment, he could sense even from where he was that something was happening and it was big. In his office after talking to Herb Crandall he felt some strange inner vibrations that were telling him there were some forces working with him he wasn't even aware he had inside. His association with Marsha had given him a slight sense that there was more to him than he realized, but he had yet to discover who he really was. This would not be revealed to him until he met her father.

#######

At 2:00 O'clock exactly Herb Crandall walked into Leonard Jablonski's office and sat down.

"So you think you have the bases all covered do you?" Herb said even before saying hello.

"Damn right I do. I've thought it out completely and unlike your solution to the group's problem which you think has no room for error, mine is going to work. As I told you on the phone, by the time the police get finished going through all of their procedures, I will have closed the gap on filling my supervisor position and the line will be ready to run come start up day. I've already selected my new man and he has agreed to accept the role. He's not one of us yet, but I believe we can convert him if we need to. That doesn't really matter because I sense in him the same greed and lust for power that attracted all of the rest of us to the fold. He will work out quite nicely for the purpose that we need him for."

"I'm glad to see you're so confidant in your scheme. I just hope for your sake, and I guess for ours too that it doesn't blow up in your face. Now we need to talk about the other issue I came down here for – Ron Powers."

"Are you going to make him disappear like you did with Brent?"

"No, I don't think that's the answer for this problem. Besides I think he's too clever to fall for a trap like Brent did. No we've got to find a way to deal with him by making him want to disappear on his own."

"Okay - and just how do we do that?"

"When I sent him down to work in the plant I enticed him with an offer of taking a position that would provide him with greater exposure to upper management. Exposure that could help him move up in the ranks more quickly. You know he jumped at the offer. What I'm thinking may sound a little farfetched to you but I think if we get him to come to one of our gatherings, we might just be able to swing him over to our side."

"You're kidding right? I don't see in him any sign of leaning in our direction."

"Not just yet but I believe given the right encouragement it could happen."

"What will you promise him now, Milt's job?"

"No not quite that high but what I can do is create a position that would give him enough of a boost so he'll forget about the things he doing. The trap will be that he has to attend one of our meetings and let the adversary work on him. I'll bet that will do the trick. Money and power, he wants that just like the rest of us."

"You know that may not be such a bad idea after all. When will you approach him?"

"Actually I can do it today. I'm scheduled to meet with him right after I leave you so let's lay the foundation and see what we can build on it. I'll let you know how it turns out."

"I'll say one thing for you Herb you've got a lot of chutzpa. I wouldn't have even dreamed of doing that."

Herb left Leonard's office and checked the time. It was now about fifteen minutes to three. That would give him just enough time to go down to the cafeteria and get a light snack. Since he had skipped lunch he was starting to feel the effects of a diminished sugar level and he wanted to have his best sales game ready when he talked with Ron. After scoffing down his sugar booster he made his way back up to the office levels and headed toward Ron's. At the door he stopped and peered in before entering. Ron was there but he was on the phone, he spotted Herb and beckoned him in. He motioned for him to have a seat and then whispered that he would be off in a minute.

"Mr. Crandall how good it is to see you" Ron said playfully.

"I see you're in a good mood today Ron. Things must be going well for you. What's this I hear about the police coming here and taking people out?"

"Right! As I was telling you over the phone they arrested Maria Sanchez the temporary supervisor filling in for Brent Woodley. They say that she was the one driving the car that was used for his escape. I can't believe they have anything positive that could substantiate that charge, but in any event she's out of here."

"What do you think about it?"

"From the little bit that I know about her having interviewed her briefly as part of my assignment here , there's no way anybody could convince me that she would do such a thing. She just doesn't seem like the type of person to become mixed up in what took place that day. I'm sure she'll be cleared just as soon as some witnesses come forward to verify where she was at the time of the incident."

"Yes, I have heard that too. It's a shame it had to happen to her, just when she was, as I understand it, ready to assume the supervisor position permanently."

"That was kind of ironic. It looks like someone set her up to keep her from getting that job. Anyway now Leonard Jablonski will have to find a new candidate for the job. I don't think he wanted her for it to begin with, I don't know why."

"Well enough about that. I've already spoken to Leonard on that issue and now I want to discuss you and your future. How do you honestly feel about the assignment you're working on here?"

"Honestly?"

"Yes feel free to answer truthfully."

"Well Mr. Crandall after I made my original assessment about what could be improved here, I kept on looking and talking to the workers on the lines but I haven't found anything else besides an equipment change that would make any difference in the operation. I see the engineers are setting up an area that looks like a completely new line ready to start. Perhaps some of the current products could be shifted over there. I think that would help a lot. Is that right?"

"Yes there will be a new line operating there and you will see the partitions going up soon because that operation has already been dedicated to the product. As I believe you already know, we have a government mandate for a special product and that will be the line for it. You did know about that didn't you?"

Herb was now trying to assess how much Ron really knew about the new drug.

"I had heard something about it but not anything verifiable. Why wasn't I included with any product announcements?"

"It was only given to a few people because that's what was called for by the specs. You needn't concern yourself with that you will not be involved. Now please answer my question about the assignment here."

"Yes as I was saying, I looked around at everything I could and there's nothing short of new equipment that could make any difference. My staying here longer is not going to change that."

"When we talked the last time, I was getting the impression that you might be hitting a wall but I wanted to allow you time to see if it was really there. Now I'm convinced that we need to move you somewhere else. I've been thinking about placing you in a different role back at the headquarters. This time it wouldn't be an assignment headed for a dead end but something you could really sink your teeth in. What do you think about that? "

"I wouldn't mind returning to my office back at headquarters, but what kind of an assignment do you have in mind this time?"

"I don't want to give you too many details now, but I would like to invite you to an offsite meeting next Friday evening where you will meet some people and learn about what could be possible for you in the near future. You'll even see some of your co-workers from right here and headquarters there. You don't have to answer right now, but I need to know at least by Tuesday so I can set things up for you there. How's that - are you on board?"

"It sounds interesting but let me think about it. I will get back to you before Tuesday. If I don't accept this assignment will I go back to my QC position?"

"Yes sure if that's what you want. But I think after you attend this meeting, you won't want to return to that. Okay then it's settled, I'll expect to hear from you on Monday then."

Mr. Crandall extended his hand and Ron shook it then he left. When Ron grasped his hand he noticed the signet ring with the symbols inscribed in the stone but he could not make them out clearly without being too obvious. After Herb walked out Ron thought about what was said regarding the new offer and having to go to some special meeting outside of the company to learn about it. Somehow it felt uncomfortable and he didn't think this was the way an offer should be made, but then again he reflected on how top managers made decisions affecting business issues at lunches, on golf courses, even in the men's room so he dismissed his suspicion.

#######

Reverend Devereaux was so absorbed in examining the scriptures he had been directed to that he was almost overwhelmed at what he was seeing. The thoughts that were coming to him were deeply inspired. He knew he couldn't begin to preach to his congregation all that he was seeing in this one sermon but he would have to spread it out over the course of the four weeks. But right now he had to start thinking about just how to start it and give them enough so they would want to return each consecutive week to hear the next installment.

Then he went back to the book of Genesis and looked at the first line. After that he went to the Book of St. John and looked at the first line there. In comparing the two he saw clearly that the "In the beginning" statement in John actually preceded the Genesis thought. The Word who later became Jesus Christ was at the time of creation with God and therefore was the actual creator of the earth. When he delved even further into the reason for earth's creation he discovered that it was to be a place where God could begin his family. Before the creation of man in His own image God had dispatched Lucifer the highest ranking angel in the heavens to the planet to develop it and make it a model place for the whole universe. When Lucifer rebelled, usurped his powers and even threatened to challenge God for His supreme position, Lucifer was defeated and one-third of the heavenly angels were cast out of heaven with him. The planet after that became barren until the first sentence in Genesis when it was recreated.

Based on this new insight, Reverend Devereaux felt he had to make the people understand clearly that the roots from which all mankind came from was indeed that of the first Adam but he wanted them to also know the reason why Adam was created. When Lucifer failed in his mission, God wanted to begin again but could only trust in a being that had his character and innate truth inside him so he created a being from the very earth and placed in him His spirit and likeness in His own image. All of the angels had been created as immortal beings but the first man was created with a mortal soul and God's innate character that he had to learn to properly use. Man was also given free will through which he could choose to be obedient or not.

Over a period of six days God recreated the earth and placed in it all the things that the first man would ever need to fulfill the purpose for which he was made. Even before he was made, a verdant garden was in place, birds flew in the air, fish and mammals swam the seas and every living creature that walked or crawled about would be subject to him was created. Man was given the ideal opportunity to live a life resplendent with all that nature would provide and it was to be his forever. When God looked at all He had created and saw that it was good, he had compassion for Adam and saw that he was alone. So out of Adam's body a rib was taken and was used to create a companion for Adam who was called Eve.

After Lucifer's fall from grace and he was cast down to the planet he became the nemesis of God - the adversary called Satan the devil. He too was in the garden where both Adam and Eve had been created. His plan from the very beginning of man's creation was to defeat God's plan for Adam and Eve to prosper and fulfill the purpose for which they were made. His beguiling ways and deceitful methods which he had developed prior to his fall were now being honed in a manner which he would apply all of his skills to inflict the greatest challenge to the early man. Using his ability to assume any form he chooses he took on that of a serpent and placed himself in the garden nearest his target.

Among all the trees that God had placed in the garden that bore fruit which were good for the body, for nourishment there were also two outstanding trees. One was the tree of life and the other was the tree of the knowledge of good and evil. As part of his first test of obedience to determine whether man would be able to fulfill his purpose, God issued instructions to Adam telling him that he shall not eat of the tree of the knowledge of good and evil. The penalty for doing so would surely be death. The instruction was not given to Eve but to Adam and the serpent chose to prey upon Eve to execute his plan. Eve was confronted and through the wiles of the devil was convinced that to eat from the forbidden tree would not cause death but would awaken in both her and her husband a new insight into living and be like God. Eve, convinced that it was not wrong to do so did eat an apple from the tree. When she did not die immediately she chose to entice her husband to eat of it also. The first act of disobedience had been committed and the future of the species called man had been set in place.

When God discovered that both Adam and Eve had disobeyed his instructions he banished them from the Garden of Eden and set them on a course that would affect all men for the next six-thousand years. Only through His compassion was the first couple not given the penalty of immediate death for their actions but they were also not permitted to escape without being subject to some corrective measures. For Adam hard work and difficult toil would be his challenge to get the earth to yield substance to allow him to survive. For Eve she would bring forth offspring by enduring severe pain and anguish. As for the serpent, for his role in causing the couple to sin, he would be cursed to forever crawl on his belly and eat the dust of the earth. And so it was established that the relationship between man and the devil from this beginning was as enemies. Satan knew that the only way he could prevail in defeating God's plan for man's future was to destroy his creation.

Reverend Devereaux upon internalizing this divinely inspired message was now ready to put it into the form of a sermon. He wanted to be very careful that he would not inundate his flock with more information than they could handle in this first part of the series. How should he begin with so much to cover was his concern? He tried to place himself in the seat of the listener and view the sermon from that perspective but it was not giving him the right incentive. Whenever he had to prepare a difficult sermon in the past he would always refer to his expert listener and rely on her sage advice. Although she was not the liturgical scholar, he had learned through all the years of their marriage and her watching and listening to him in the pulpit that she not only had the sensitivity to know when people would stop listening to him but she was always helpful in getting the point he needed to deliver over in the right way.

He put his pen down and once again got up and headed toward the kitchen. However, this time she was not there but had retired to another part of the house in which she enjoyed watching television. He didn't want to disturb her enjoyment of one of her favorite programs but he knew that if he was to finish preparing the sermon tonight which was his plan, he would need to get her input. So he eased his way into the family room and sat down beside her.

"Did you get finished?" she said.

"No and that's why I'm in here."

"Oh do you need Ms. Winfrey's advice?"

He laughed hard and then said: "No not hers but I do need yours."

"Okay should I turn the TV off or can we talk over it?"

"I believe we can work around it because for what I need when I tell you what it is, that program won't matter. You know when I told you before that God has been placing something very heavy on my heart and I need to relay it to our congregation, well just now in my study I have been given some very profound revelations and I'm not sure how to begin to deliver it to the people in a sermon."

"Stanton you have always been able to come up with a stirring sermon and get the message you received across to the people why are you perplexed now?"

"Honey I don't know but it seems like what I'm being challenged to deliver this time is so profound that it's going to take at least four weeks to complete the task. It has to do with something you know I've always been concerned with and have tried to make people understand in the past, but now with all that's going on in the world it appears the time is really drawing near when it is absolutely necessary the people understand that these are indeed the last days spoken of in the Bible. The coming Kingdom Of God is not as far away as most people want to believe and the message must be all about that."

"You've spoken about that before what's so different about it now?"

"Before I was never able to see it so clearly from the beginning as I have just now seen it. I've been given a new insight into this whole idea of why the earth was created and why man was even brought into being. God has a divine plan for the future of man even with all his faults and shortcomings. From the very beginning when Adam chose to disobey, God should have ended the program right there but he chose not to and gave him a second chance. I realize now that God has been giving us second chances for so long that the time has come when even his patience is exhausted. When you look around and see all of the things that man is doing to his fellow man and the evil perpetrated on one another, you must begin to see that this is the height of inhumanity. Also, when you observe all of the natural calamities and disasters that are taking place in increasingly shorter spaces of time for each occurrence, the message must be clear who's doing it. My dilemma is how to get that over to them without being overwhelming right from the start. That's where you come in."

"Oh - you want me to deliver it for you? I can you know if that's what you want."

Her answer really made him laugh and he became more relaxed as he usually would after talking with her about whatever was heavy on his mind. The real answer for him was not there yet but in just talking with her he had gained a new sense of encouragement. He felt reenergized and ready to go back and tackle the sermon preparation.

#######

At the close of the business day Ron left his office and decided to walk by Marsha's lab to see if she was there. When he arrived there he bumped into one of her co-workers coming out of the lab. The man knew the two of them had some kind of relationship going from seeing them together a few times before but he wasn't exactly sure to what extent. So he casually mentioned he was an associate of Marsha's and was concerned about some things he saw which didn't appear to be above board going on in the other labs. Ron stopped his exit and engaged the man in conversation to try and determine what he knew about any of the things he was also concerned about.

"You say you work with Marsha?"

"Yes we are assigned to the same project and I talk to her quite a bit. But it's not our lab that I'm concerned about."

"No? What lab are we talking about then?"

"Its Lab 1 right at the end of the corridor. The technicians going in and out of there are very clandestine and secretive. They don't even talk to the rest of us who are certified chemists just like they are. Whenever I have tried to get something out of any of them, the answer is always the same from each – this is a top secret project and they are not at liberty to discuss their work. It just seems so weird they are the only ones who know anything about what's going on in there. I think they're up to no good if you ask me."

"Do you know how you can get into that lab?"

"Are you kidding? It would take a high level clearance and a bulldozer to enter there."

"Yeah, that's the legal way. What about a midnight entry?"

"No way, I understand the lab has extra precautionary devices connected to it to ensure no illegal entry. I know what Marsha's concern is – the same as mine, but what's yours?"

"I don't know if you know or not, but I was the one that was having lunch with Anthony Oliver at the Peacock Palace when he was killed. You know about that don't you?"

"Sure, everybody here knows about that."

"Well during lunch that day he was beginning to tell me about a lot of strange things that Canon was getting involved in that, as you say were not above board. One of them was the development and production of a new drug aimed specifically at the adolescent population."

"What's so strange about that? We develop products for that market all the time."

"None that will destroy them using their own biological chemistry I don't believe."

"That's fantastic you got that from Mr. Oliver?"

"Yes and since that time I've learned a great deal more to substantiate his story. I think there is a conspiracy taking place within the highest ranks of the company and they are trying to get the drug to market in the near future without any of us knowing about it until it's already out there."

"Are you doing anything to try and stop it? I know you are a Quality Control manager."

"I can't do anything until I have some proof and right now I have nothing that I can use."

"Is there anything I can do to help?"

"Yes as a matter of fact there is. Get me into that lab."

"You don't know what you're asking. I could get fired for even trying to do that. Moreover, if knowledge of what's going on in that lab got Mr. Oliver killed, I don't want to end up the same way."

"I understand but right now that's the way you could help the most. If you're genuinely concerned about what's really going on in this company and for the lives of maybe thousands or more of our young people then that's what needs to be done and soon."

"Well when you put it like that there is one possible way to get in there undetected but I don't know if it could even work."

"Man if there's even the slightest way to get in there it has to be tried. It's that important."

After a short pause in our conversation while the man continued to think about the prospects and the risks he finally conceded that the prevention of such an outcome was worth more than the risk of discovery. He then introduced himself as Martin Siegel a senior chemist in Marsha's lab and began to lay out his plan to get into Lab 1. At first it sounded to me to be like something out of one of those James Bond action movies but when I really thought more about what he was saying it didn't seem so farfetched. What he was describing was a plan to enter the lab through one of the ventilation tunnels that ran through all of the labs. It could be easily accessed by entering into an opening in his lab and following the right link in the tunnel to the opening in Lab 1. The only thing he couldn't be sure of was whether there wouldn't be some kind of lock on the screen in that lab.

We decided to carry out the plan even without the knowledge of whether it could be successful or not. By eight O'clock tonight all of the day time personnel should be out of the building and only the night guards present. I knew from having stayed late in the building a few times that there were only three night guards who patrolled the site like clockwork on regularly scheduled intervals. It was not difficult to determine the pattern they used because they did it the same way every night.

I told Martin this and he agreed to meet with me in my office at seven O'clock. There was only one problem with our plan. After six when the guards took over access to the building the only way to be admitted was to be signed in and documented. If the plan was to be successful there could be no record of our having come back to the office after hours. I thought for a good while about how to circumvent having to go through the main entrance and the receptionist station and came up with what I considered risky but a possible means. There were three rear door exits in the plant that were equipped with a fire alarm device that would trigger an alarm once the door was opened. I believed if we could figure out a way to disable the alarm device then we could leave the door ajar before we left the plant now. Martin was not too enthusiastic about my plan but he was willing to look at the door since we had no other alternative.

When we got to the door that was closest to my office I traced the wiring for the device back to a panel that was not too far from the door itself. Surprisingly a lock was on the panel but it wasn't closed. When I opened the panel door there was no indication which wire was the one for that door. Martin who was standing beside me looked at me and I looked back at him with an expression saying okay what now? Neither one of us was any expert electrician. So the thought of disabling all of the wires was out of the question. Then it occurred to me that it was still early and the night guards had not come on duty yet. If Martin was to open the door and close it quickly, even though the alarm would sound for a minute, I was sure none of the day time people would pay it much attention. Once that was done, I would be able to see which wire fed it because of the LED next to the terminal. Martin agreed and went to open the door. Just as planned the LED lit up and my decision was made. I disconnected the wire and closed the panel then Martin and I opened the door just to be sure it was disabled and left the building.

At home I couldn't help thinking about what we were about to do, but it seemed that this was the only way I could really discover what was needed. At just before seven when I arrived back at the plant fortunately it was dark on that side of the street and no one was around. I got there before Martin but he came shortly after. The door was still slightly ajar just as we left it so we eased it open the rest of the way and sneaked inside. Getting up to the lab level without being discovered was easy because we were in between the guard rounds. Once inside Martin's lab he led me over to where the vent was and unscrewed the covering screen. When I looked at what he did, I asked him how we were going to unscrew the covering when we got to the other lab. He laughed and then showed me a kind of magnet that he said would work fine for the job as long as that screen is set up the same way as this one. I entrusted the task to him and we both climbed in the vent and started to navigate the tunnel. Since his lab was just a short distance from Lab 1 the crawl took only a few minutes and we came to the vent. Just as he said he maneuvered the magnet so that he was able to dislodge the screws on the other side.

Everything seemed to be going along fine and we were about to enter Lab 1. From all that I could see in the semi-darkness there were a lot of cages with an assortment of animals. There were more lab tables in there than what I recalled seeing in Marsha's lab and there were beakers and vials everywhere. Even Martin commented on how differently this lab was set up than his. Just as we opened the vent screen and started to move into the room a loud noise was heard coming from something that was sitting on a table facing the screen. After the noise then came a bright flash and loud ticking and we both saw something moving toward us from out of a corner.

Chapter Eight
"New Insight"

Around the city this time of year most people are getting into a festive mood anticipating the upcoming holidays. The normal hustle and bustle of the locals shopping and foreign visitors gawking at the height and magnificence of the tall buildings and department store window displays are even more intensified. Wherever you look there is a sight that gives you the feeling something good is coming. This was all true now except in the case of Detective Sergeant Callahan who at this moment was experiencing anything but the something good feeling.

It was early Friday morning and Sergeant Callahan was sitting in his Captain's office being taken to task for making an arrest that had become a big issue for the department. Not only had it backfired to the degree that it reached the Mayor's desk, but it had also caused a major backlash from a certain segment of the city's minority population. As it turned out after Maria Sanchez's arrest at her place of business and in front of several of her co-workers when a number of people came forward to witness her whereabouts at the time she was accused of being at the scene of the crime, the fact that her story of innocence was corroborated by so many made the CPD look very foolish. It was embarrassing for the department to first have made the false arrest, but in addition, to have detained her in the lock-up for over forty-eight hours before the witnesses were allowed to enter their testimony, just added further insult to the situation.

The Captain was laying into Callahan who prior to this was one of his star officers. His fury was being fueled by the fact that the Mayor had called him and read the news headline telling the whole story. The primary issue for the Mayor was not so much the misguided apprehension, but the lawsuit that was almost sure to follow. His words to the Captain were in no uncertain terms that there was going to be a heavy price for his department to pay should the suit actually be filed. The Mayor was insisting that all of the details on how the screw-up occurred be on his desk by lunchtime today.

"Callahan you're usually pretty thorough with this type of stuff. What the hell happened here?"

"Sir I interviewed several witnesses from the plant where she worked and all of them described her as the driver of the getaway vehicle. Even her supervisor corroborated her description. None of them had any doubts about what they saw. We used this as our basis for the arrest. You know as well as I do that the public was clamoring for a resolution to this Oliver case and up until now we had nothing."

"Yeah, yeah I know that, but now we have an even bigger problem. Have you spoken to her since she was released?"

"No Captain she won't return my calls and I'm sure as hell not going by her house to force the issue."

"Well we have to do something or this whole thing is going to blow up bigger than what it is now. Do you think she's getting an attorney?"

"Don't know Cap, but I'll try to find out."

"Okay Callahan see what you can do. Make any kind of peace offering you can within reason and I'll try to honor it. Now get started."

"Yes sir, I'm on it."

At the plant when Maria came into work she reported to production just as she normally would and found the new supervisor running the operation. He was surprised to see her and didn't know what to say. He felt badly after talking with her for just a few minutes because he had not been told the whole story about why he got the job. He suggested she go talk to Mr. Jablonski right away and maybe he could straighten things out. He really didn't want to give up his new promotion, but he also didn't want to be in the center of what he suspected was going to get ugly.

Leonard Jablonski was not aware that Maria had been released and he was going about his usual routine. When she appeared at his secretary's desk requesting to see him he saw her and became very unsettled. He didn't know that many of her co-workers after hearing about her arrest had gone down to the precinct and demanded her release. Since it had been two days ago when she was removed from the building he assumed that she was too embarrassed to return to the plant. He had no way of knowing that it was her union representative who not only was among those who went down to the stationhouse but it was he who strongly advised returning to work immediately.

As he peered through his partially opened door, he could see that his secretary was getting ready to call him.

He immediately picked up his phone and pretended to dial a call. When he picked up the receiver his secretary could see that his line light went on and she hesitated dialing the intercom. She told Maria he was on the phone and asked her to have a seat and she would try again in a few minutes. Leonard was trying to stall as long as he could to give himself time to figure out just what he was going to tell her when he did let her in. He couldn't tell her the truth and he didn't have a feasible lie ready that would be sufficient.

After several minutes of just holding the receiver off the hook and pretending to be on a call, he decided he would just face her and say that because of her being arrested he had no choice but to assign her duties to someone else. Of course this was partially true, but he was well versed in telling half-truths because of his association with the master deceiver. He hung up his phone and almost immediately the intercom rang. His secretary advised him that Maria was waiting to see him and asked whether she should send her in. He again paused momentarily, then said "yes send her in."

Maria opened the door and slowly walked into the office. Leonard sat there behind his large desk with a broad smile on his face and pretended he was glad to see her. His facetious smile belied his true sentiments and the greeting was rather awkward and clumsy. Maria observed him carefully and had no trouble picking up on the rouse so she was very careful how she spoke.

"Maria how good it is to see you again. I didn't know you were home."

"You didn't bother to try and find out either did you, Mr. Jablonski?"

"Well I thought your union people would handle it. They did, didn't they?"

"Yes they did but you could have come to the station to see about me too. Who is that working in my spot?"

"Well Maria you know we are getting ready to start up that new line exactly one week from Monday and I didn't know what was going to happen to you so I had to put somebody in your place to start training. Unfortunately, I had to give him the job permanently so it would work out okay. But don't worry I have something else for you. Are you cleared of everything?"

"Yes. It was all a big mistake and they apologized a lot when they let me go. But anyway that's over, so what's this something else you have for me?"

"I can't give you all the details right now, but why don't you go down there and work with him until I have it all worked out."

"Work with him or for him?"

When Maria said that in the tone she used, Leonard knew it was not going to be easy for him to put her in a lesser position even though he thought he had worked out a feasible story for his union defense of his decision. He started to stammer slightly when he tried to explain to her that she would be working for him, but only for a short time until he could make the other arrangements.

"So that's the way it's going to be huh? Okay I know what I need to do now."

Maria made her last statement turned around and stormed out of his office. Leonard wasn't sure whether he should feel relieved at her leaving or should he have major concerns about what it was she was going to do. The one thing still uppermost in his mind though was he had a man in place ready to start the new project who was going to be obedient. He would worry about her antics as they surfaced.

However, it was not too long after she left his office Leonard got nervous thinking about what she was going to do so he went to production to see what was going on. The new supervisor greeted him and asked if he had spoken to Maria. He answered yes and told him that she was going to be working for him for a little while. Leonard looked around and was a bit surprised that she didn't come back to the area. Now he wondered just where she went. He walked around to see if she might be talking to any of the other workers but when he didn't see her anywhere he went back to his office. What was running through his mind was whether she was capable of sabotaging the project in any way. In light of the way she left his office he felt she might be capable of doing anything. Now he had to prepare for another possible snag in his plan.

On the way back to his office he met Ron in the elevator and for a minute his thinking shifted from Maria to what Herb had said about something needing to be done with him. Ron greeted him with a smile and they briefly exchanged sarcastic pleasantries while skillfully disguising their contempt for each other. Leonard asked Ron what he had been up to lately and the reply was startling. Ron told him that he had discovered something very interesting about the company's new product line and he was investigating the intended use. Leonard immediately started thinking about just how much had he discovered and what did he really know. The time for the new product's production release was so close none of the insider group could afford to have it exposed prematurely.

"And what is it you've discovered Mr. Powers?"

"Well Mr. Jablonski I think I've hit upon a new drug now in development that's not exactly in compliance with the standards the company expounds."

"Oh really and just what does that mean?"

"I'm afraid I can't tell you that right now but stick around and keep your ears open. You will be hearing about it real soon."

The elevator arrived at Ron's floor and he got out leaving Leonard in a quandary about what to do next. He was sure from just this brief encounter that Ron was onto something the group needed to discuss. And just as Herb said before, the time for Ron's disappearance was now. It should be done either by the above board method Herb proposed or by the other method that Herb could also propose. Leonard got back to his office and immediately got Herb on the phone.

"You know who I just had an interesting conversation with?"

"No, please enlighten me."

"It was our favorite conversation subject - that Ron Powers guy. He was telling me he had just discovered something interesting about a new product being developed. From the way it sounded it seems like he is really onto what's going on. We only have one more week before this thing goes out the door. Can we afford to have him get in the way?"

"Are you sure he wasn't just baiting you into revealing something he was fishing for?"

"I don't think so. He seemed to be very confident he knew something that would be of interest to me. I didn't tell him anything but he implied I would be hearing something from him very soon. What do you think he meant?"

"Again I think he was just trying to get something out of you. We already know he suspects something but I don't believe he has anything solid to go on. Nevertheless, I have already set the stage for him to attend our next gathering and expose him to the emissary. After that he should not be a problem anymore."

Ron left the elevator and went to his office. He was delighted that the seed of concern planted in Leonard's mind seemed to have reached fertile ground. Even though Leonard tried to hide it, Ron could tell from his expression he had piqued his curiosity. Aside from that, Ron thought about what happened last night during his late night excursion into lab 1.

He and Martin Siegel, a chemist from the lab where Marsha worked, had found a way to breech the security and successfully enter lab 1. Once inside they found some very strange items. But before they were able to get to that point, when they first exited the vent a bright flash went off and then a loud ticking sound was heard. The two men were startled for a moment, but Ron encouraged his accomplice not to panic as they searched around the room for the source of both light and sound. They moved toward the ticking sound first and discovered a turntable connected to a timer that apparently had been scheduled to begin turning just as they were entering the room. The turntable held several vials that Martin presumed were scheduled to start mixing at the timer's preset mark. While the vials were spinning, they saw something out of a corner in the room approaching them, but when they looked more closely, it was just the shadow of the guard in the hallway making his rounds.

The duo then turned their attention to what caused the flash. Since it didn't go off again they had nothing more to go on but to guess where it came from. They examined the turntable mechanism to see if there was something else connected to it that might have flashed, but found nothing. As they looked around the dimly lit room Martin commented that not only was the layout different than any of the other labs, but also the animals in it were mostly counterparts to the human species. There were also several vials in the refrigerator that contained something totally unfamiliar to him. Not wanting to spend too much time roaming about the room, especially when they had no idea whether there were any hidden traps, Ron suggested taking one of the vials from the refrigerator and getting out quickly before the guard comes back on his return route. Martin lifted one of the vials, made sure that it was not leaking and placed it in a thermal container from off of one of the tables. The two men then reattached the vent screen with the screws that had fallen on the floor.

They walked over to the door of the lab and Ron looked out first to ensure that the guard wasn't headed in their direction. Next he examined the door carefully to make sure that there was no alarm to be triggered from the inside then he opened it slowly and they quietly entered the hallway and exited the building through the same door they sneaked in.

Martin still had the vial containing the unknown specimen but after they exited the building he told Ron that it couldn't be analyzed in his lab for fear of him being discovered. The question now was where could he take it to do the analysis? There was only one other possible solution. At the university, Marsha had access to all of the labs and with the modern equipment in each of them performing the type of examination needed would be easy. Martin told Ron this and suggested he ask Marsha to help. Ron was confident she would want to help because now they had something concrete to go on.

The next day Ron couldn't wait to share the discovery and after he finished his morning routine he went down to the lab area to find her. This time when he got there he found her talking to Martin. From the door he couldn't tell whether he was filling her in on what they did or something else but he knew that as excited as Martin was after they left lab 1 he wouldn't have been surprised if he had already told her everything. The lab door was slightly opened but Ron hesitated walking in because he wasn't sure whether there was some restriction to lab personnel only. Fortunately, Martin spotted him and turned Marsha to look also. She left him walked over to the door and went out to greet Ron.

"I hear you've been very busy lately" she said smiling.

"Yeah, I guess Martin has already told you what we found. Did he also tell you that we need your help now?"

"Yes he did and I have to be very careful about how I go about doing that type of research in the school's laboratory. There are many procedural protocols for doing experiments, especially if a science professor hasn't sanctioned them. I believe I know a way to get around them though, but I need some time to set it up. Where is the vial now?"

"I think Martin has it at home but we better ask him to be sure. Is it alright if I go in your lab?"

"Sure this is not lab 1. But why are you asking me since you've already breeched a secure lab anyway? Come on just put on that lab coat and follow me."

I walked behind her as she led the way over to Martin. The other chemists didn't even pay me much attention so I guess non-chemists coming in there was not a strange occurrence. When we got to him he had already guessed what we were coming to ask him. He jumped right in explaining that the vial was in a safe refrigerated spot in his home lab but he wasn't sure at what temperature he should keep the sample. He didn't have time to check the setting in lab 1. Moreover, he said that they should do an analysis quickly because he was afraid of losing the integrity of the sample. Marsha heartily agreed and told him how she planned to help with that, but her next scheduled lab study was not until next Wednesday. They conferred with each other for a few minutes and reasoned that if the sample was being developed to affect the human metabolic system then it should be kept at the temperature they agreed upon. At least, they surmised, this should preserve it for the few days they needed.

It was settled. Martin would keep the vial and monitor it while in his possession until Wednesday when he would release it to her to do the analysis. Martin left us and went back to doing his regular work. I turned to Marsha and asked how much risk was she going to incur by compromising the protocols of her school? She reassured me that she had no intention of jeopardizing pursuit of her degree when she was so close to getting it. The plan she had in mind was in a strict sense not in keeping with the rules, but it was not so devious as to warrant her dismissal from the program should she get caught. Although she didn't go into any great detail for me about just exactly what she was going to do, the confidence she displayed in being able to execute our plan gave me the feeling she knew what she was doing. After she said that, I felt assured she would get it done and we were finally going to have something solid and revealing to solve the mystery.

Before I left her lab I asked if we were still on for dinner tonight at her parent's house. She replied indeed we were and we'd better not be late getting there so I would make a good first impression on her father. I asked what time should I meet her and she replied to be at her place no later than 6:00 O'clock. She said she'd be ready to go and that would give us just enough time to drive and be there by 7:00 PM. I thought about my scheduled meeting this afternoon with Tango, who had a propensity for wanting to have lengthy conversations, and was trying to figure out how to shorten our visit. But I also knew that he had something important he wanted to share with me, so how brief could I make it and still allow him to do his thing in his fashion.

When the time rolled around for Tango to be walking into my office I was hoping he wasn't going to be too late. Actually, I selfishly was thinking that he might even make a last minute call and tell me that he had been unexpectedly detained in Washington and we would have to reschedule. There were so many things on my mind I wanted to talk with Marsha's father and sister about that giving Tango my full attention was going to be difficult at best. Unless he had something really dynamite to engage me, I was planning to just agree with whatever he had to tell me and then suggest that if possible we continue at another time.

As it turned out he was at my office door almost exactly the time we had scheduled to meet. As usual he didn't wait for an invite but strolled in and sat down as if he were the company CEO.

"Ron, good to see you ole` buddy" he said cheerfully.

I wasn't quite sure what was prompting his jovial mood but I was ready to play along if it was going to expedite the conclusion of our get together.

"Well you seem to be in an extremely good mood. Everything must have gone well with your visit back to Washington."

"You might say that. Things are beginning to come together more quickly than we anticipated and I'm finding out more each day about what's happening here. As I told you earlier, I found a document in your lab 1 that has some very leading information on it. Even though it's not complete enough to be certain about what it totally means, my associates have uncovered some more detail about who in D.C. may also be involved. I think now I can share with you what we know and hope that you will share with me what you've found out lately."

"You know that all sounds good and I promised to help you, but there is still one thing that we haven't crossed the bridge on."

"Oh yes of course. You want to know who I am. I've checked with my superiors and now I can reveal to you who I am and who I'm working for. You see when I first met you after the Oliver murder, I wasn't sure whether you might be involved with it or not. But now from all of the pieces of information I and my colleagues have gathered I have removed you from my list of possible suspects. I am a CIA agent who was sent here even before that incident to investigate the possibility of some terrorists plotting to use chemical agents to infect large portions of the population in major cities. However, what we're finding out now is that, the part about the chemical agent use is true, but the portion of the population that we were first alerted to is not holding up. We have also discovered that the directions for the plot are not coming from anyone here in the city, but from some high level officials working right under our noses in

Washington. Steps are being taken right now to apprehend those individuals, but my task at this point is to pin down just what chemical agents are going to be used and specifically on who. Does that help you?"

"I suspected you might be one of those guys but pardon me for still being somewhat leery. Can you show me some identification now?"

"Gladly, Mr. Powers. Take a look at this."

He reached in his jacket inside pocket and pulled out what looked like a passport but it was his CIA ID along with a gold badge. I looked closely at the picture and except for some difference in what could be the fact that it was not a recent picture, it was definitely him.

"Okay Mr. Hernandez I'm convinced now where do we go from here?"

"As I said I've told you where we are with what we know, now it's your turn. I still have the feeling that you are in some danger here and I was sincere about wanting to protect you, but you've got to tell me everything you've uncovered so I can do that."

"Before I do that Tango, there's just one more thing I need to know. Do you believe the devil is real?"

"Well I think it's possible but, why do you ask?"

"Because some of the things I'm finding out are leading me to some conclusions that there is more working here than normal everyday occurrences. I have a strong feeling that we are fighting against some powers that are more than human. You know something like some spiritual powers."

"What makes you say that?"

"Well for one thing a few weeks ago I had lunch with one of the executives that I am temporarily assigned to and during lunch he went off on a tirade about him serving some higher authority. At first I thought he was getting religious on me and was referring to God, but then he went on to allude to another master and I know he wasn't talking about my God. Then there was another thing. You might know Jennifer, Mr. Jenkovitch's secretary; she found a trinket in his conference room after a late night meeting and she found some markings on it that were definitely occult. She told me that there was a group of those high level managers who have meetings like that frequently and almost always when she would come in the next day to see if the room was ready for the next group, she would find either some strange bits of paper with weird symbols on it or experience some strange smells. "

"This trinket you referred to do you have it?"

"Yes I do, but I can't give it to you because I promised I would return it to her right after I had it looked at by some experts I believe know more about that type of thing than I do. I'm meeting with them tonight. That's the dinner meeting, I told you about. After tonight I believe I'll know more about what it means and how it may have something to do with everything that's going on at Canon. On Monday, I'll tell Jennifer that you would like to look at it and then it will be up to her."

"Okay Ron, that sounds like a plan. But when you talk to Ms. Jennifer, please don't share with her my true identity. It's not for public knowledge right now. And also please emphasize to her that I really need to be able to possess that item for a few days. Be forceful if you must, but keep in mind I can legally call for it if necessary as part of my investigation."

"I don't think that will be necessary. You see she's part of my team and I think we are all looking for the same things - first a solution to who killed Tony and why and second what kind of insidious plot is underway here."

"Fine Ron I hope that's the case. Why don't we plan on meeting again Monday afternoon and update each other. Meanwhile, I have to meet with your CEO again. It seems that he also has something I need to look at."

"Okay Tango - Monday it is. Why don't we say 3:00 O'clock that usually works for me."

"Good, that works for me too."

Tango left my office and I was happy to see by the clock that it had not turned into a marathon meeting like I was afraid of. It was almost quarter to five and that gave me just enough time to wrap up some of the things I was working on get home in time to change and go meet Marsha. Before I left the office I made a quick note for myself not to forget where I put the talisman I got from Jennifer. I had hid it outside of my apartment just in case there really was something weird about it.

When I got to my apartment building the usual Friday night circus was already performing and I had to make my way around the three rings to get home. In my haste I didn't notice that in the lobby there were some new faces that didn't seem to belong there. It was hard to determine who actually belonged there on a Friday night but this time the crowd had some faces that definitely were out of place, even for here. It was not until I had changed and came down to retrieve my package containing the talisman from the storage room that I saw something very interesting. A man whom I had not seen here before was gesturing to me to come over and talk with him. I knew that I didn't have much time if I was going to make it to Marsha's place by 6:00 but the man was gesturing so hard that it seemed urgent. I walked over cautiously and greeted him. When I got closer there was a glow surrounding him that caught my attention because I had never seen anything like this coming from a person. Before I could say anything the man spoke.

"Do not be alarmed by what you think you see in my appearance, but you must listen to what I have to tell you for it will affect your future and those you care for. I have been sent here to warn you about some events that will be taking place very soon and the outcome of those events will depend on the choices you make. Be diligent in your search for answers regarding the evil that is present in your workplace, but also be careful with whom you share your knowledge. Tonight you will hear words of wisdom from a man who is a true prophet of God and he will give you what you need to continue your search for the truth. Do not be afraid to ask him hard questions for he is equipped to answer correctly. Go now and know that there is something in your possession that has been given to you as a blessing, treasure it for one day it will serve you well."

I wanted to ask the man just what he was talking about, but when he said go now it was almost as if he was dismissing me and I strangely felt the need to leave.

Realizing that I was running out of time if I was going to stay on schedule, I left quickly and headed out the door. However, before I hit the street I turned around to get another look at him so I would remember his face, but a shiver ran down my spine because in that short a span of time he was no longer there.

I had called Alex before I left my office and told him I would need a ride just about this time so I was confident my ride would be outside waiting for me. Sure enough he was there just like I knew he would be. I got in and told him we were going to that posh place again on the East Side where he took me before. He joked about me moving on up like the TV sitcom and we both laughed as he made his way through the Friday night traffic. In a matter of minutes I was at her building and scrambling to get to her place on time. I paid Alex and told him I would not need him to get home. He gave me a big grin and said goodnight. I knew what he was thinking but I didn't acknowledge anything.

Inside the lobby I went to the receptionist desk and as before announced that I was there to see Mrs. Robinson. Bradford was not in sight so I assumed that he was either off or attending to some other duties. I received the okay to go up and caught the first elevator available. On the floor again the extreme quietness still seemed to be very strange but now I guessed this is the way it always is. I got to her door and rang the bell. Jerry opened it and grabbed my hand and pulled me in. He was glad to see me and asked why I hadn't come back before now. I was glad to see him too, but I didn't have a good answer so I just said I'm sorry. Marsha hollered out from the back that she would be ready in a minute and for me to make myself comfortable. Jerry started to usher me to his room, but I told him I didn't think we had time to start another game. He said he just wanted to show me something and kept tugging me toward the room.

Once inside he pointed to a large signed poster of one of his favorite NBA basketball players that he had received from the grandfather that we were going to see tonight. He was excited about it and excitedly told me that his grandfather knew everybody. I didn't realize it at this time, but I later learned he wasn't far from being right. Marsha came out and called for us to come on before we would be late so we left the apartment and headed back to the elevator.

In the elevator Marsha pushed the button for the garage and unlike the elevator in my building the response was swift and the ride was smooth. Arriving at the garage level we got out and walked over to where her assigned space was. I wasn't a bit surprised having seen her apartment and heard the story about her settlement that parked in her space was a late model white BMW 725i. I did all I could to hide my wowed expression but she looked at me and just smiled and winked as she opened the doors. Jerry got in the back and buckled up while I took the front passenger seat. Marsha said she would let me drive but since we were kind of cramped for time she had better do it.

We pulled out of the garage and headed toward the bridge to Jersey. On the Jersey side it wasn't long before I saw signs directing us to Englewood Cliffs. Shortly after that we pulled up in front of a large stately colonial nestled in a cul-de-sac with five other houses. About half way around the semi-circle she turned into a driveway and we got out. Jerry didn't wait for us to get out but ran up to the front door and rang the bell. As we followed close behind, I saw the door opened by another young man who couldn't have been too much older than Jerry. He grabbed Jerry and playfully pulled him inside with both of them laughing loudly. Coming to the door right after that was a tall tan and beautiful lady who looked so much like Marsha I knew right away that it was her sister. Except for the lack of red hair the other features were like that of a set of identical twins.

Marsha went up hugged and kissed at her then introduced me. She said she was delighted to meet me and welcomed me in. I told her I was happy to meet her also and had heard a lot about her. She looked at her sister smiled and said I hope she didn't overdo it. I then told her I was very anxious to talk with her about some things I think she would be interested in. She responded by telling me that Mimi had briefed her a little on what it was so after dinner she looked forward to that conversation also. We walked down a short but stately hallway that was lined with pictures of some very famous civil rights figures. Many of them were autographed. I couldn't help but notice that in some of them there was a man other than the famous celebrity, who I suspected had to be her father.

As we turned to enter the living room the man I saw in the pictures greeted us. He was about six-feet four and although the mixed gray hair had claimed much of his head, he stilled maintained the stature of a solidly built middle-aged man. He extended his hand and I quickly took it with both of mine as I let him know that it was a real honor and pleasure to meet him. We shook hands and he invited us all to sit down for a little while until the call would come from the kitchen for us to go in to eat. Looking at her father and sister I could see the strong Creole heritage present in all of them. Her father was a handsome man, but I couldn't wait to see her mother because for the girls to have such beauty it must have come from her.

We were just beginning to have a pleasant conversation about our trip coming over when the call came from the kitchen for us to go to the dining room and sit down. I looked at Marsha for my queue as to where I should sit and with her eyes she directed me to sit at the right hand of her father who of course sat at the head of the table. Marilyn looked at me then at Marsha and smiled an approving smile as she sat on the other side next to her two children. Just before Mrs. Devereaux came in to start serving, Marilyn announced to me that in this house she was called Midge and Marsha was Mimi and then she introduced her children with their nicknames. After that she said to us her father is Dad but I should call him Doc and her mother is Mom to them but to me she is mother Devereaux because that's how his congregation addresses her. I got the message and looked at him for some guidance but all he did was nod his head in agreement with what she said.

When Mother Devereaux, came in with the final dishes, I had a chance to look at her closely. Even in the autumn of her years she was still a stunning naturally beautiful woman who had maintained a well-defined figure. A woman of medium height she moved with such grace it was a joy to watch. It was very clear now where the girls got their looks. Both daughters had been blessed with the best of both parent's genes. She set the dishes down then took her seat at the opposite end of the table. After Mimi introduced Ron to Mom, Doc then took over and assumed his leadership position. He told everybody to take the hand of the person sitting next to them and then he blessed the food. It was not an exceptionally long prayer as I would have expected from the head of a church, but it was rather short and right to the point.

As we ate it was easy for me to see just where Mimi learned her culinary skills. The food was delicious and appealing to the eye in its presentation. I looked at Midge, having learned that she was divorced and said to myself it must have been something else to have caused her separation because if she cooked like this as her mother and Mimi did, I couldn't see any man in his right mind leaving her. The conversation during the meal was light and stayed away from topics that Doc knew we were sure to discuss later. Surprisingly even the children took part in what would normally be adult talk. Doc encouraged this and said unless they are allowed to express themselves early in life, then they would grow up shy and afraid to speak their mind. I wasn't sure that I agreed with him on this, but I didn't dare voice my opinion at this point.

After the meal and being offered a choice of a variety of desserts, I felt like I had been to a five star hotel in the city. We all got up from the table and Doc instructed the children to go to the playroom that was downstairs in their finished basement. Then he walked ahead of the sisters and me to the large family area that was also downstairs but away from the playroom. Mother Devereaux went to the kitchen but told us she would be coming down shortly. As we passed by the playroom I looked in and saw what would be the envy of any young person and even some adults. It was equipped with video game consoles connected to a television, the same basketball shooting game that Jerry had in his apartment and a small pool table. It was obvious that the Reverend Doctor Devereaux was doing quite well for himself and he doted on his grandchildren.

When we got to the family area it was set up with a long couch, a loveseat and two recliners all positioned around a radio/TV/turntable combo that was enclosed in an elegant piece of furniture. Midge took what appeared to be her normal seat in one of the recliners, while Doc gravitated toward the other deeper cushioned recliner leaving the couch and loveseat available. I wasn't sure whether I should sit on the couch and leave the loveseat for Mimi or be bold and sit with her on the loveseat. The decision was made for me when Mimi took my hand and led me to the loveseat.

"Mr. Powers Mimi tells me that you work at Canon Enterprises with her. How do you like it there?" her father started the conversation.

"Yes sir I do and please call me Ron. I thought until recently that I liked the company very much but now I'm not so sure."

"What do you mean until recently?"

"Well I don't know how much Mimi has told you but I've been finding out a lot of things that are going on within the infrastructure of the operation that are just not right. Mimi and I have discovered that there is even evidence of a new drug they are developing that will harm a lot of young people if it's allowed to get to market."

"Yes she has mentioned something about that. Ron, do you believe in God?"

The question kind of caught me by surprise and I almost stammered with my answer. I knew at some point he would probable ask me that but I just wasn't expecting it right now.

"Yes I do but I have to admit I haven't been going to church too much for quite a while. Why did you ask me that?"

"Because what I'm about to tell you will make you want to change your life style very quickly. Mimi has grown up in a house where we study the Bible and are followers of Jesus Christ. She has been exposed to the fact that the world is about to change very dramatically in the next several years. Whether she has chosen to share this with you I don't know, but let me assure you that the things both of you are finding out on your job are just a sign that things are beginning to happen right now that have already been predicted a long time ago.

Doc was really starting to peek my interest and as I looked at Midge she was smiling because she knew where he was about to go.

"Ron I want you to come to my church this Sunday because I'm going to begin preaching on a subject that's going to take me at least four weeks to get the message across to my congregation. It involves what I'm going to give you a slight preview of right now. I'm not going to go into a great deal of detail because I don't want to scare you but you must understand that the next few years of all of our lives are going to be affected by a great deal of turmoil not only right here around us but all over the world."

"Doc are you telling me that all of the things that I'm seeing happening at Canon are part of this greater event that's going to happen all over the world?"

"In a word - yes, but don't be alarmed because there is still time for you to become part of a group that will not be subject to what's going to happen. Before I get too deeply into that, let me back up a bit and try to relate what I'm talking about on the whole to what you are discovering at Canon.

You are familiar with the first book of the Bible called Genesis are you not?"

"Yes sir, I know a little bit about it but I don't recall very much."

"What I want you to do is reach back into the recesses of your mind and recall the part where after God created the first couple he commanded them to tend His garden and be fruitful and multiply. Remember that in the garden where He placed them there were trees bearing fruit that were healthy for them to eat. Also in the garden there was a tree which He forbid them to eat from. That was the tree of the knowledge of good and evil. As it turned out because of the evil influence of Satan in the form of a serpent, both Adam and Eve did eat from the forbidden tree and committed the first sin. Think about it. What was the sin? It was the first transgression of God's law, His command. After that, from then and even now man has been transgressing His law daily with increasing boldness and recalcitrance.

What you see happening at Canon is simply an extension of the original transgression but it has been magnified many times over down through the years and has now culminated in Satan's last effort to destroy God's people beginning with a small segment of the human race."

"Sir what exactly does that mean?"

"You say you and Mimi have discovered a plot to develop a drug to destroy young people. Well this would be that segment of the population that the devil will begin with on route to eventually eliminating the whole human race. No doubt you have encountered some people that have given you cause to suspect that they are more than just carrying out their daily work functions."

"Wow, it's weird that you should mention it because that's one of the reasons why I was so excited about getting an opportunity to talk with you and with Midge. There is a group of upper level managers in the company who seem to have formed a conspiracy in producing this drug and one of them happens to be a man that I am temporarily reporting to right now. It was not too long ago that I was having lunch with him and he almost admitted that he was into devil worship. He didn't say it directly, but he went off into some kind of trance like meditation while speaking about his being driven by some higher power. At first I thought he was talking about my God, but it became clear as he went on that he definitely wasn't.

To add to my suspicions about his and some of the other managers devil worship I became friends with the secretary of the CEO of the company and she gave me a talisman that she found in a conference room after one of their late night meetings. I brought it with me but I left it in the car. Shall I go and get it - is it alright to bring it in here?"

"Yes please do. I would like to and I'm sure Midge would also like to examine it."

I got up quickly and went out to the car to get the piece. When I got there and didn't see it on the front seat where I was sitting my mind started racing thinking that suppose there was something about this thing that could make it disappear. For a brief moment I became afraid that I may have encountered something I really wasn't ready for and it was in my possession. Nevertheless I started looking around the car and felt such relief when I looked under the seat and there it was. I had wrapped it up in a big envelope and apparently it slipped down under the seat during the ride over. I grabbed it and ran back into the house.

"Here it is Doc."

I opened the package and handed it to him. Midge got up and came over to get a good look at it also. She examined it closely and said that it definitely was a symbol of devil worship and that it was used in their rituals. Doc commented that he had never seen one just like this piece but he had seen many similar ones. He then asked me if any of them knew I had it. I answered no, I'm pretty sure they didn't. Then he cautioned me about keeping it in my possession too long. He suggested I return it to whomever I received it from. He didn't elaborate on why and I didn't ask. Midge then started talking about the people I suspected of being in a cult. She said that I was to be careful if any of them approached me about attending any special meetings with them. When she said that I immediately thought about what Herb Crandall had invited me to and I told her. She warned me that if I go to that meeting I may be in for the shock of my life.

I asked her if there was anything that I could do to protect myself just in case I was being set up. Her immediate answer was yes - you can pray.

After Doc finished examining the talisman he placed it back in the envelope and advised me to get it back to its owner. Then he returned to talking about his sermon for Sunday.

"Ron, from the time the original couple committed the first sin until now there has been a deceiver loose on the earth who has duped mankind into believing that his way is the way to happiness. It didn't work then and it certainly can't work now. You must learn that the people whom you have come in contact with have made a commitment to the evil one and they will stop at nothing to carry out his evil schemes. This new drug you've discovered is perhaps the beginning of a plot to destroy the youth in our community but it is more than likely a test case to see just how effective it can be in a much larger scheme. You see the time is growing short for the deceiver to achieve his goal before a new world order is set to take over."

"A new world order - what does that mean?"

"Let me continue with my thesis and I will explain. Even after the first couple committed the original sin, God showed compassion and did not destroy them. Instead He allowed them to carry on with His directive and multiply. Through the years man did indeed multiply and increase in numbers and in strength gaining much wisdom from one generation to the next. But in each successive generation there was a faction that was influenced by the same devil who was present in the first garden. Always in that faction there would be leaders who would misdirect the people and goad them into believing things contrary to the truth. From Adam to Noah, from David to Daniel man would fall prey to the deceptive practices of the adversary. Although God sent prophets time after time to proclaim the truth, and He set down in writing commandments and statutes by which abundant living could be man's fortune, susceptibility to the "Big Lie" would drive him to forget the words of the prophets and gravitate toward self-destruction.

Even when God caused calamities, disasters and captivity to get their attention and remind them of His covenant with Abraham, the faithful father of nations after the great flood, they would not heed his warnings. As a last resort, God decided to clothe himself in flesh be born as a human and deliver His message about what eventually would become a new world order. In that human form the man we know of as Jesus the Christ came to redeem all mankind from sin. From the first advent of Jesus and His crucifixion and resurrection until the time of His second coming and glorious appearance, thousands of years will have elapsed.

But now comes the part that many have failed to understand and this is what I must get across to my people. In some of His last words to the disciples when asked about when shall He return He spoke to them privately about reading the signs of the time. He told them to watch out that no one deceives you.

For many will come in my name, claiming, 'I am the Christ,' and will deceive many. You will hear of wars and rumors of wars, but see to it that you are not alarmed. Such things must happen, but the end is still to come. Nation will rise against nation, and kingdom against kingdom. There will be famines and earthquakes in various places. All these are the beginning of birth pains. Then you will be handed over to be persecuted and put to death, and you will be hated by all nations because of me." (Mat 24:3-9 (NIV)

If you think about it look around you at what's happening right now. In the news you hear about all the turmoil going on in Europe the Middle-East and other countries, these are the wars and rumors of wars He was talking about. Earthquakes and tornadoes are increasing in size and devastation, diseases are returning we thought were licked and most of all man is destroying the land through which he is causing his own famine. If this is not the beginning of the signs of His imminent return then I have wasted much of my time studying the scriptures.

How all this relates to you and what's going on at Canon is simply this. That drug you've discovered is but a tool in the hands of those who continue to practice the evil that has been thrust upon all mankind from the beginning. Between you and Mimi you must find a way to expose the whole group who you suspect of being part of the cult. You must engage the proper authorities so they may intercept and thwart the movement before they are able to bring it to pass. If you feel you do not have the means to do so then allow me to invite my congregation to enter into a mass prayer and petition the real master to intervene. You cannot fight the devil by yourself and win. The higher power that you need to enable you is available but you must be ready to enter into covenant with Him and believe that He will fight your battle.

What I have given you here is but a brief overview of what I plan to present to my congregation over the next few weeks in more detail. I wish you would come for the whole series, because as the Lord gives me the words then I will deliver them to all that I can get to listen and hope that we can engage others to join with us in recognizing what was the real message that Jesus came to give us."

"Doc, all I can say is that after what you've told me here tonight, I have no intention of missing your sermon on Sunday. Mimi you've been awfully quiet throughout this whole evening are you okay?"

"Yes sure. I've just been listening and reflecting on the things that we've found out about Canon and I still find it hard to believe that it's really happening. I know what my father has been saying about the time growing short, because I've heard it so many times before, but to see real evidence of it happening so close to me is kind of scary. I'm not sure that we aren't placing ourselves in more danger than we ever thought about."

"Yeah Mimi, until now I hadn't thought about it that way either. But to put that in an even greater perspective, let me tell you something else that happened to me tonight just as I was leaving my building to come to you. There was a man in my building lobby who called me over to talk with him. He was a strange looking man who appeared to have an unnatural glow about him and I had never seen him before, but what was even more amazing about what he said was the fact that I hadn't walked out of the building more than a second when I turned around to get another look at him, he was gone. Now that was a little scary. Here's what he said, don't be alarmed at what you think you see in my appearance. Then he said I must listen to what he had to tell me because it would affect my future and those I care for. Next he said he had been sent to warn me about some events that will be taking place very soon and the outcome of those events will depend on the choices I make. Be diligent in your search for answers regarding the evil that is present in your workplace, but also be careful with whom you share your knowledge. Tonight you will hear words of wisdom from a man who is a true prophet of God and he will give you what you need to continue your search for the truth. Now what do you think about that?"

"You say he seemed to have a glow about him?" Doc asked.

"Yes he seemed like he was lit up but not from anything shinning on him."

"Ron, I believe you have been visited by an angel who just gave you some sage advice. As he has given you a warning do not fail to heed what he said and be very careful. Did he offer anything else to you?"

"Yes. Now that you mention it I do recall he also said I have something in my possession that was given to me as a blessing. I don't have any idea what he was talking about with that one. The only thing I could think of is an old clock that has been handed down through generations in my family and somehow I ended up with it. How could that old thing be a blessing it just barely works?"

"Ron please remember with God all things are possible and you never know just what he will use to bless you or even how he will use it. Just except the fact that it might be something which you will need in the very near future if that was part of what was told to you."

"Dad thanks for letting me bring this guy over tonight I hope he didn't overstep his welcome with his questions."

"On the contrary my dear I'm glad to have met him and I hope you invite him again. Mr. Powers, Ron it really was a pleasure meeting you and I will extend the invitation to you directly to come again, but I certainly hope to see you in church Sunday."

As we got up to get ready to leave because it was getting a little late the kids came in making a lot of noise. Midge had gone to get them but she went upstairs to get something and left them alone. Doc quieted them by saying they were not on the basketball court now and the noise was not necessary. As soon as he said that it triggered in my mind the announcement about Canon's involvement in sponsoring the youth basketball league in the city.

"Doc have you heard news about Canon getting involved in the sponsorship of a basketball youth league in the city?"

"Yes I believe I did hear something about that a little while back. Is that going on now?"

"I think the final plans have been made and the merger of the three corporate entities is in effect. It's very strange to me that Canon would be getting involved in something like that now unless it has something to do with test marketing the product we've been talking about."

"That's very interesting you should say that because it could be quite possible that you have hit the nail right on the head. You know this grandson here, as he pointed to the older taller boy, Joshua or Josh as we call him is quite a ball player in his youth league down in New Brunswick. He is a rising star and I would hate to see anything like that thing we were talking about somehow get into any of the beverages they consume at their games. Let's hope that it never happens but pray for divine intervention."

As we all said goodnight I told Midge I really appreciated her input on that talisman and I would get it back to its owner ASAP. She replied she was glad to have met me also and was happy to provide her input but she was also very serious about praying before I attend any meetings that I have been invited to by any of those people I suspect. I thanked her for the timely advice and said I would have to rely on Mimi to show me how to do that when the time came. Mimi looked at me and laughed then said I had better learn how to do it for myself if I wanted to survive what we may be facing soon.

We got in our separate cars and I watched Midge strap her youngsters in then get in herself and drive off. After Mimi helped Jerry in and got in herself, I turned around to thank them one last time and make one final wave to the Devereux's for their hospitality. But even as we got underway headed back to the city, I couldn't help thinking about all the things that Doc told me tonight about what is about to happen in perhaps the very near future. Could it be possible that Mimi and I were caught up in the middle of a major plot that could affect the whole world in just a matter of short time?

Chapter Nine
"Seeds"

All over the news Sunday morning reports were proclaiming war had broken out in Europe and the two major countries involved were Germany and Iran. Several other players aligned themselves with either side and the game board was now set for a battle of epic proportions. For many months now minor skirmishes had been occurring all centered on the welfare of Israel and its right to continue to exist as a country. Iran for years had been threatening to wipe them from the face of the earth and now they were preparing to carry out their threat. Germany, the primary defender of the European front was determined not to let this happen.

As I lay in bed listening to the radio, all the things that Doc said on Friday night started racing through my mind and I wondered if this was indeed the beginning of the terrible things he said were coming soon. In the overview he gave of his sermon which he was going to deliver over the next few weeks he said the world would begin to see wars and hear rumors of wars in the very near future. I heard his words but they didn't really sink in for me until I woke up this morning and started hearing these reports.

For some time now I had been hearing smatterings of these news reports talking about unrest in Europe and the Middle East, but I didn't pay much attention. It seemed to me that these squabbles were just the normal bickering and political positioning that was done on a daily basis. As the essence of today's reports started to really register, my concern grew. It was not for the plight of the foreign countries but I was focused on what the plot being hashed out at Canon Enterprises may have to do with what's happening over there.

I got up and even though it was early I called Mimi. After apologizing for the early call and waking her up, I asked if she heard the news. She replied I didn't wake her she was already up and yes she had heard it. Next she commented on how timely her father's words were and so much right on point. Then she asked if I was going to keep my promise and go to church with her and Jerry. I answered that after hearing the news this morning there was no way I was going to miss him preach. She told me what time I needed to meet her and then we hung up.

The more I thought about it, as I started to get ready to meet Mimi, there were a lot of things said on Friday that were beginning to make more sense to me now. Herb Crandall, Leonard Jablonski and the rest of that group were so deeply involved in the conspiracy that how I could have missed seeing it before was amazing. I guess it was because I just didn't want to believe it.

By 9:30 AM I was dressed and on my way to her place. By 10:00 we were all in the car and on our way to church. Unlike the Friday night traffic this Sunday morning ride was almost clear sailing as we crossed the bridge. The church actually wasn't too far from her father's house and we made good time getting there. As we pulled up in front of this large structure I was impressed but not surprised at the size of the church. In bold letters written across the building front were the words - Holy Trinity Church of God. Below that was a large blank neon cross hanging just above three wide ornate glass doors.

Mimi drove around to the back of the building and into a spacious parking lot with uniformed church security people directing traffic. She was recognized by one of them as the Pastor's daughter and was directed to a spot near the front entrance. We got out and joined with the throng of worshippers making their way inside. Once inside the glass doors, again I was impressed with the size of the foyer that led into the sanctuary. Mimi was greeted by a number of friendly hands and arms reaching out to embrace her and Jerry. After a brief hug she politely stepped back and introduced me. I was also extended the same warm welcome.

The formal service had not begun yet but the music coming from the pulpit area was a pleasant reminder for me of the days when I attended church back home. An usher guided us to seats about mid-way toward the front in the center section of the sanctuary. As I helped her with her coat and then removed my own I looked around at what appeared to be at least a thousand heads already there and people were still coming in. I knew he was a popular minister but I had no idea how large his following was.

We were only seated a short time before a man dressed in an elegant choir robe came in through a side entrance and stood in the center at the base of the pulpit. He paused for a moment then directed the congregation to stand. Next like at the beginning of a symphonic concert the musicians, seated at the base of the pulpit, opened up and suddenly from the rear of the room the most magnificent choral sound I had ever heard erupted like Mt. St. Helens as the seventy-seven voice choir proceeded down all four aisles to the stand behind the pulpit. The sound was so powerful it sent chills down my spine as they sang a rousing rendition of "Leaning on The Everlasting Arm". It had been a long time since I felt like that and I said to myself if this is just the beginning, then I may be in for something very special. I guess Mimi must have sensed my emotions for she looked at me and squeezed my hand.

After the choir settled in the stand and finished the song a minister came out and asked that we remain standing while he gave the invocation. It was all starting to come back to me now just how exhilarating it could be and I was embarrassed to have been in the city for as long as I had and not found a church to attend. I hadn't even tried looking.

The service moved through the program smoothly and reverently as the choir sang another song, announcements were made and a very intense pastoral prayer was offered which really set the stage for what was to be delivered next by Rev. Dr. Devereaux. Just before he came up to stand behind the sacred desk the choir performed a rendition of "Total Praise" that almost brought the house to its knees. From too many places in the house to count the joyous cries and shouts of praise emanated from the parishioners. He then took command of the service and in a booming baritone voice started speaking.

"Has God done anything for you this week worthy of your praise? Let me hear you praise Him."

The shouts of Hallelujah, praise God, praise Him, magnify Him, glorify Him resounded so loudly back at him it seemed that the very rafters of the building shook. A broad smile came across his face as he acknowledged the worshippers.

"Isn't it good to be in the House of the Lord one more time?"

"Yeeeeees, Yeees, Yes" the answer came without any hesitation.

"The Spirit of the Lord is here - I say the Spirit of the Lord is here - - I say the Spirit of the Lord is here" he said each time increasing the volume of his announcement. It didn't take too much after that to realize that the crowd was indeed ready to hear whatever he had to say.

As he stood with his arms raised and gesturing toward the ceiling in praise like a towering monument there was no doubt by anyone present that he was in charge of the service. Then after a short pause while looking out over his flock, he began to speak in a quiet voice that brought the crowd down to a mild whimper as he started his sermon.

"Good morning my brothers and sisters in the Lord, I greet you in the matchless name of Jesus the Christ. I don't know about you but I came to have church this morning and to deliver a message that has been given to me by Almighty God. Today I want to begin delivering a message that will be spread over the next four weeks which is so vital to your future that I pray you will be in attendance for each part until we're done. I'm sure you have been hearing in the news all of the things that are happening right now not only here at home but all around the world. It is not a coincidence that they are happening now and I want to prepare you for what else is going to happen very soon."

A silence came over the sanctuary as every eye was focused on him and every ear was attentive to what he was saying. I marveled at his mastery of controlling his audience and was enthralled at his smooth delivery.

"I invite you now to examine with me the scriptures as presented in several areas of your Bible beginning with John, Genesis, and Leviticus in this first segment of the series. I will announce to you when I am moving from one to the other so please stay with me. But first let us go before the Lord and ask his guidance.

Father God, exalted and eternal Lord, I come before you with a bowed head and a humbled heart to give you glory, honor and praise for all that you have already done in this your house, but more so for what you are about to do. I pray that you would anoint these lips for preaching, hide me behind the cross so that the people will see Jesus and give me strength to carry out your mission. I ask this blessing in the mighty and matchless name of my Lord and Savior Jesus Christ. Amen.

Please turn with me now to the book of St. John Chapter 1 verses 1-3

In the beginning was the Word, and the Word was with God,

and the Word was God.

2 *The same was in the beginning with God.*

[3] *All things were made by him; and without him was not*

anything made that was made.(KJV)

In order for us to truly understand where we're headed we must look first at where we've been. You see in the very beginning the Word, who became Jesus Christ, was at that time with God and He also was God. It was He who created everything. As the scripture says, there was nothing made that was made, without Him. He created our world but it was not the world that we read about in Genesis Chapter 1. The world He created was beautiful and filled with angels created by Him. It was not until one of His created angels, called Lucifer, decided in his arrogance that he would rise up to exalt himself above God. It was Lucifer who had been created as an angel, given the highest office in God's service and was the light bearer who decided to rebel. Lucifer was not content to be in His service but he wanted to rule even above His creator. A battle with God took place that resulted in Lucifer being cast out of Heaven along with one-third of the angels who were with him and banished to a world that became a wasteland. It is this wasteland that we read about in Genesis Chapter 1. After that encounter with Lucifer, God created a restored world in which He was not going to allow created angels to rule again but He was going to place in it beings who would have the essence of His character and be made in His own image. This was the world into which the original first couple was made and it was to be the perfect creation, for God saw it and said that it was good.

A beautiful garden was made and in it God created the first man Adam and the first woman Eve. But Lucifer who was now turned into Satan (the adversary) and the devil was allowed to remain in this world and he was also in the garden. So you see my brothers and my sisters the stage was set for the first test that man would have to take.

Please turn with me now to the book of Genesis Chapter 3 verses 1-5

Now the serpent was more crafty than any of the wild animals the Lord had made.

He said to the woman, 'Did God really say, You must not eat from any tree in the garden?' The woman said to the serpent, 'We may eat fruit from the trees in the garden but God did say, 'You must not eat fruit from the tree that is in the middle of the garden and you must not touch it, or you will die.''"You will not certainly die," the serpent said to the woman. [5] *"For God knows that when you eat from it your eyes will be opened, and you will be like God, knowing good and evil." (KJV)*

Recall with me now when God made man and woman in His own image he was creating something that was not only in His image, but this creation was a part of Him that was endowed with His character and a portion of His spirit. When he placed them in the Garden of Eden that He had prepared for them this was to be the ideal place for them to carry out His instructions. The fact that Satin in the form of the serpent was also in the garden deceiving the first couple, was truly the first test - and man failed exceedingly.

Hear me now brothers and sisters I am laying this foundation here because from this point on it was not just that the woman succumbed to the wiles of the devil, and persuaded her mate to do likewise but this was the beginning of the end for man as he was originally intended to be. When Adam disobeyed God and ate from the forbidden tree he along with Eve was expelled from the paradise that had been created for him and forced out into a world of hard labor and trials. But God was compassionate with the first couple and did not destroy them immediately, even though He had said eating from the forbidden tree was death, he gave them another chance. Although the sentence of death was not abolished, his life was prolonged and he was given a chance to try and become eligible again to receive the gift of eternal life which had been set up for him. What a God we serve!"

And the people said Amen.

"In the interest of time I want to fast forward now through several generations in which man was allowed to multiply as God intended but from that very first sin, man followed a pattern of continued sinning that would take him to the point where I want to culminate this series and tell you the truth of what is about to happen next. During this time in antiquity over a period of several generations man became a murderer (Cain slew Abel) a liar (Abraham to Abimilech), an abuser of family relations (Joseph and his brothers) even fallen angels assumed human form, seduced mortal women, and produced offspring of giants. Corruption grows among the descendants of Noah's three sons - Shem, Ham, and

Japheth - and culminates in a second great world apostasy at the Tower of Babel. Each man became tempted when, by his own evil desire, he is dragged away and enticed. Then, after desire has conceived, it gave birth to sin; and sin, when it is full-grown, gives birth to death. These were the things that man continued to do from beyond the original sin. But let us look now at God's response in which He laid down the conditions for receiving the gift of eternal life.

Turn with me now to the book of Leviticus Chapter 26 versus 3-13

3 *"'If you follow my decrees and are careful to obey my commands,*

4 *I will send you rain in its season, and the ground will yield its crops and the trees their fruit Your threshing will continue until grape harvest and the grape harvest will continue until planting, and you will eat all the food you want and live in safety in your land.*

6 *"'I will grant peace in the land, and you will lie down and no one will make you afraid. I will remove wild beasts from the land, and the sword will not pass through your country.*

7 *You will pursue your enemies, and they will fall by the sword before you.*

8 *Five of you will chase a hundred, and a hundred of you will chase ten thousand, and your enemies will fall by the sword before you.*

9 *"'I will look on you with favor and make you fruitful and increase your numbers, and I will keep my covenant with you.*

[10] You will still be eating last year's harvest when you will have to move it out to make room for the new.
[11] I will put my dwelling place[a] among you, and I will not abhor you.

[12] I will walk among you and be your God, and you will be my people.

[13] I am the Lord your God, who brought you out of Egypt so that you would no longer be slaves to the Egyptians; I broke the bars of your yoke and enabled you to walk with heads held high. (KJV)

Through all these generations God directed His prophets to speak to His people during hard times and mistake after mistake and finally even to the point of allowing them to experience hard bondage as slaves in Egypt for 400 years. But even then in His compassion, He brought them out of that period and told them in this book that this is what He would do for them if they listened and obeyed Him. Once again we didn't listen. So He had to tell them the other side of the story and this is what He said in verses 15-22.

But if you will not listen to me and carry out all these commands,

[15] and if you reject my decrees and abhor my laws and fail to carry out all my commands and so violate my covenant,

[16] then I will do this to you: I will bring on you sudden terror, wasting diseases and fever that will destroy your sight and sap your strength. You will plant seed in vain, because your enemies will eat it.

[17] I will set my face against you so that you will be defeated by your enemies; those who hate you will rule

over you, and you will flee even when no one is pursuing you.

[18] *"'If after all this you will not listen to me, I will punish you for your sins seven times over.*

[19] *I will break down your stubborn pride and make the sky above you like iron and the ground beneath you like bronze.*

[20] *Your strength will be spent in vain, because your soil will not yield its crops, nor will the trees of your land yield their fruit.*

[21] *"'If you remain hostile toward me and refuse to listen to me, I will multiply your afflictions seven times over, as your sins deserve.*

[22] *I will send wild animals against you, and they will rob you of your children, destroy your cattle and make you so few in number that your roads will be deserted.*

And even after all this He was still compassionate and provided a caveat by saying.

[40]*But if they will confess their sins and the sins of their ancestors-their unfaithfulness and their hostility toward me,*

[41] *which made me hostile toward them so that I sent them into the land of their enemies-then when their uncircumcised hearts are humbled and they pay for their sin,*

[42] *I will remember my covenant with Jacob and my covenant with Isaac and my covenant with Abraham, and I will remember the land.*

[43] *For the land will be deserted by them and will enjoy its Sabbaths while it lies desolate without them.*

They will pay for their sins because they rejected my laws and abhorred my decrees.

[44] Yet in spite of this, when they are in the land of their enemies, I will not reject them or abhor them so as to destroy them completely, breaking my covenant with them. I am the Lord their God.

[45] But for their sake I will remember the covenant with their ancestors whom I brought out of Egypt in the sight of the nations to be their God. I am the Lord.'"

From the time of the beginning until that period coming out of the bondage in Egypt, God never left His people and He promised that He never would. But in their desires to live according to their own dictates and not yield to His laws they grew in sin and rebellion and set up the conditions that we see here today. What is happening here right now in the world today is based on the premise that was established so many years ago during the time of our forefathers. We have received from them the corruption and mendacity that has been handed down through time to this present generation who has not yielded to obeying His laws but have continued in the disobedience of days of old.

My brothers and sisters now is the time for us to begin to understand that what we are experiencing now is the result of years of cumulative disobedience and shirking our collective responsibilities of true worship and praise of the one true God. When you look around at what is going on in your neighborhoods and in places not too far from you, you see that the overwhelming condition of sin is being conducted in a manner such that it has become acceptable as the right way to live. What used to be condemned as wrong has now become right and what used to be bad is now considered okay. The introduction of television and the computer has given mankind the means to convey his immorality in such a mass presentation that the wayward ways of sin have become acceptable as good all over the world.

Look around you brothers and sisters at what even some of you present here today have witnessed first-hand what I'm talking about. Within your own families you have seen the idolatry and greed motivation that have given over to the perverted behavior of even your own relatives. As it was alluded to in the book of Leviticus the time has come when He is not going to continue to abide by our lewd behaviors and perverted conduct calling wrong right, and right non-existent. It's time for us to wake up and see what is really going on and begin to conduct ourselves according to the commandments and statutes that He provided for us as a way to live and enjoy abundant life according to His ways. I know that you have come here to worship Him in spirit and in truth, but reflect now on what has been your understanding of what that really means. Have you done any introspection about your own acceptance of what you see even in your own neighborhood? Have you become one of those who allow the kind of lewd behavior on your street to continue and just turn your back or a deaf ear to it? Now is the time for you to stand up for the right way to live according to the mandate that God left us to follow in His Book.

As I close this portion of the series, I want you to be aware that this foundational sermon is just to establish the basis on which this world was created and to make sure that you understand that it is but a launching pad for where we are going from here. Do not be deceived any longer about what is happening in the world. I tell you that there is an evil presence here and it is real. It is driving many to commit sins and it has even entered some of your very households. But be comforted, although the time is growing short before the real culmination of the battle between good and evil takes place, you still have time to get on the right side of the war and be among those who will be sheltered when the time comes for needed protection from a Divine source.

I invite anyone who is present here this morning and has not received and accepted Jesus as his Lord and Savior to come forward and give me or the Deacons his hand and give God His heart. The time is growing very short before the opportunity will not be there. The choice is yours and He is waiting for you. Today He is your Savior tomorrow He will be your judge. Don't hesitate, come and let us help you to become counted as one of those who will be saved from the trials and tribulations that are coming shortly. Will you come?"

Slowly from out of the congregation one by one people got up and walked toward the front of the pulpit where Deacons and Deaconesses stood waiting with open arms to greet them. When the call was finished, I counted twelve who had answered. After the names were given and the announcement made to the rest of the congregation, Rev. Devereaux welcomed them and prayed for their salvation. The sanctuary was filled with the spirit and all the people welcomed the newcomers with praise.

At the conclusion of the service Mimi, Jerry and I set out to find Midge and her two kids. We found them in the foyer as the crowd was emptying out the sanctuary. The talk between the two sisters was about what they were going to do with the rest of the day. Midge said she was taking her children to a basketball game at the college that "Josh" wanted to see. She invited Jerry to come with them. Mimi thought about it for a minute then asked him if he wanted to go. Without any hesitation he said yes because both he and his cousin were big basketball fans and Josh was already playing in a junior league. The two sisters then discussed how they were going to get Jerry back home and it was settled. It was out of my hearing but somehow I had been volunteered to meet Midge after the game at a place on the Jersey side of the Lincoln Tunnel which was very popular and easy to find. This was in exchange for allowing Mimi to go home and prepare a good dinner for me. When I thought about the meal I had the last time I was at her place, being volunteered wasn't such a bad deal so I went along.

We separated, Midge took the kids to the game and Mimi and I headed back to the city. She dropped me off at my place and told me Midge would call me when she was ready. Also, thrown into the arrangement was the fact that I was going to get to drive the BMW. That sweetened the pot for me just a bit but it meant that I would have to go back to Mimi's apartment before dinner and be tempted by whatever she was preparing.

When I got home I turned on my TV to see what sports events were on. I found what appeared to be a good pro basketball game between the home town team and the first place team in the conference. Since I had what I thought would be a lot of time before having to go and pick up Jerry I fixed myself a light lunch and settled in to watch the game. Then an unusual thing started happening. It was not usual for a major sporting event like this to be interrupted, but it seemed like every ten or twelve minutes a report came on announcing an update on the escalating war over in Europe. The latest report saying that the clash between the two major combatants had reached the point where it was beginning to involve all of the immediate surrounding countries had attracted the attention of the US President. He was on now giving his position in the matter and stating that he would dispatch the US Secretary of State to the region to try and negotiate a peace settlement, as soon as possible.

Having just come from hearing Doc talk about all that is about to happen in this world, I couldn't help becoming uncomfortable as I continued to watch the game. The contestants on the basketball court battling each other for supremacy seemed like an inappropriately timed strange metaphor for what was actually happening in another court on the other side of the world. Although I hadn't heard how Doc was going to conclude his sermon series, my interest was really high on knowing just how it would end. Would his series end be a harbinger for how the end of the war would be?

My basketball game was just ending around 3:30 PM when my phone rang. It was Midge calling to say that their game was over and she would meet me at our rendezvous point in about an hour. I looked at my clock and determined I would have just enough time to go and get the car and be over there by that time. It also settled for me the question of whether I would have to fight the temptation of sampling whatever Mimi was cooking - there just wouldn't be enough time. So I resigned myself to the fact that I would just have to wait and build up an appetite.

Our rendezvous plan worked almost to perfection with both of us arriving at the meeting point within minutes of each other. I picked up Jerry exchanged goodbyes with Midge and her kids and we were on our way. During the ride back to the city Jerry was very excited about the college game and how he desired to play for them one day. He also ran on about how his slightly older cousin who was playing now for a team in his community was pretty good and he wanted to be like him too. I told him about the new co-sponsorship that Canon was doing to help the PAL with the youth league in the city. He asked about how he could get to play, and I really felt sorry to have to tell him that he would have to wait a couple of more years before he could. Undaunted by the news he said it would just give him more time to get better by playing with his cousin when he went to their house. He displayed a lot of patience for a youngster his age but he also revealed how close he was to his cousin.

When we arrived at his apartment building and I had put the car away, by the time we got upstairs Mimi was just about ready for us to eat. Jerry and I had just started another game on his basketball play set when the call came for us to come to the table. In a way, even though I was hungry, I regretted the call because I was determined to redeem myself from such an embarrassment the last time I played against him. All through dinner we had a fun conversation talking about all that we did today and how it would be a lot of fun to do it more often. I looked at Mimi and to see her laugh like that made me feel good knowing what she had gone through for the last few years after her husband died.

We finished dinner and I was allowed to go back and attempt to redeem myself on the basketball court while Mimi got on the telephone with her sister. We played for about two hours and unfortunately for me the result was almost the same as the first time. He commented with a sly grin that I just needed more practice and it sounded to me like he was the father and I was the child. When Mimi got off the phone, it was now around 7:30 PM, she came in and reminded Jerry that he still had some reading to do in preparation for school tomorrow so that ended our playtime. I left the room so he could begin his studies and Mimi and I went to the living room.

I settled one more time in that most comfortable sofa which once you sat down you didn't want to get up. Mimi then asked me what I thought about her father's sermon today and I told her that I wondered if he was looking into a crystal ball for his insight about the future. She replied that he didn't need one because he was an expert in Bible prophecy and all he was doing was telling it like it says in the book. In her experience growing up in New Orleans she said she never doubted his ability to see things happen in his mind before they actually happened in reality because she saw him do it too many times. Sometimes it was scary for her but he always assured her and her sister that if you have genuine faith and believe with all your heart that God is and He will reward those who diligently seek Him, then no matter what he saw, everything will turn out alright. And she said she couldn't remember a time for her when it didn't.

We continued talking and laughing for a while until Jerry came out and said he had finished his work and was going to go to bed. Mimi excused herself and went with him to say goodnight. Jerry said goodnight to me and again asked when I was coming back. Soon I told him, very soon. They both left the room. When Mimi returned she sat down beside me and said her son liked me very much and she was glad to see that because he needs an adult man in his life besides his grandfather. With that being said I took advantage of the opportunity and looked straight at her.

"I like him too and think he's a great kid but what about you what do you need?"

The question kind of caught her off guard and she stopped smiling when she looked back at me.

"Ron you know I like you very much and I would like to keep seeing you – not only for my son's welfare but for me as well. But I don't want to rush into something I will regret. I know it's been a few years since my husband passed, but when I lost him for a long time I felt like a single petal from a rose that was losing its beauty. The hurt that drove me to tears every night for months was getting the best of me. The loneliness I felt was driving me crazy. I even tried the bar scene for a short time with my girlfriend, but the guys I met just weren't for me, so that's when I threw myself into my studies and the job. I truly believe if I didn't have Jerry and my father in my life to keep me focused on living I may have done something tragic. You're the first one I've let my real feelings show with but I'm afraid of being left alone again. I couldn't take it."

She stopped and looked at me with tears welling up in her eyes and I melted.

"Mimi you are one beautiful lady and such a lovely person inside I can't imagine me ever causing you pain. I have to tell you I am falling in love with you and I want to be with you. To say I understand what you went through I would be lying because I've never had that happen to me, but I do know that if you let me in, I will never leave you. And besides I don't know anyone who can cook like you can."

She laughed as she punched me playfully and I had achieved my intention to lighten up the mood. I didn't want to push things too far at this moment because I realized she just wasn't ready yet, but I had made my point. We continued talking for a little while longer but the conversation had definitely taken a new direction. The door had been opened for a more intimate tone as we talked about us and where we might be going. Finally as the hour got late I said I needed to go. Then I kissed her long and hard. This time there was no turning away or resistance as she returned my embrace. When I released her I asked if she wanted me to stay the night. There was no quick no, but after a short pause, she looked at me and said not tonight but soon I think we can get to that. I smiled, got up and headed for the door. On my way out, I kissed her on the cheek and said I'll see you tomorrow.

#######

When I got to my office the next day there was a message on my phone from Herb Crandall wanting me to call him as soon as I got in. It sounded rather urgent so I wondered what could be going on. I quickly ran through my usual morning routine, settled into my chair and picked up the phone. I reached him on the first try.

"Mr. Crandall this is Ron Powers you called me?"

"Yes Ron how are you?"

"I'm fine thank you. Did you call me this morning?"

"No I actually called you on Friday late afternoon but I guess you had already gone for the day. I wanted to follow-up on that conversation we had about you changing positions and getting out of there. Remember I said that there was a meeting that I wanted you to attend so you could meet some people, some friends of mine. Well I've set the groundwork and they would like to have you come to a meeting this coming Friday night. Are you available?"

Before I answered I thought about what Midge told me. I paused a few seconds trying to think of whether to stall him until I had a chance to talk with her again, but then I realized that might not be such a good idea since I was still technically working for him and this could be a legitimate chance for me to get back to headquarters in a better position.

"Yes Mr. Crandall I will make myself available. What time is the meeting?"

"They usually begin around 7:00 PM. Why don't I take you to dinner before the meeting and then we can go there together?"

"Okay. That sounds fine to me. Will you come down here for me or do you want me to come up there?"

"Why don't you meet me in my office when you finish work, there are much better restaurants around here then down there? Just call me when you're headed up."

"Sounds like a plan to me. I'll talk to you on Friday."

"Oh Ron there's just one more thing. Have you been talking with a guy named Hernandez whose been interviewing some people down there?"

"As a matter of fact yes he has talked with me. Why do you ask?"

"I'm just curious about who he's talked with. I don't know what his role is at Canon. He didn't come through me, it seems like he was just planted here. One day he just showed up and was given an office. Even Jenkovitch doesn't know too much about him. He was given instructions by the board to just put this man on staff and provide him whatever he needs. What did he want to talk with you about?"

"He just wanted to know what I did and asked me about how things were going."

"Is that all he wanted to know?"

"Yeah, that's pretty much it."

"Okay Ron I'll see you on Friday."

When we hung up I knew then that the meeting on Friday was going to be about much more than work activities at Canon. As I pondered that thought, I realized I still had the talisman and now more than ever I wanted to get it back to Jennifer as quickly as I could. I wondered if somehow Herb Crandall knew that I had it. Unless Jennifer told him, I couldn't imagine how he would but so many strange things had been happening to me lately it would not be a surprise. I immediately got on the phone again and called her.

"Hello this is Jennifer may I help you?"

"Hi Jennifer this is Ron how you doing?"

"Hi Ron I'm just fine how are you?"

"Doing great thanks. Listen I want to get that article you let me borrow back to you, and I wanted to know when would be a good time?"

"Oh you know I really don't mind if you want to keep it. Mr. "J" hasn't said a word about missing it and I don't think I want to take it home - you know what I mean?"

"Yeah it scares you too huh?"

"In one word - yes. From all that I've seen after those meetings in that conference room I'm not sure just what strange powers that thing might have and I don't want anything weird happening to me or my family."

"Okay then what should we do with it?"

"Didn't you tell me you were taking it to someone who knows about those things?"

"Yes I did and she told me to get it back to whoever gave it to me. But if you don't want it, I think I have

another solution. Hey good talking with you again. I'll let you know where it finally ends up. But if you're boss does start asking you about it what will you tell him?"
"He doesn't know nor does anyone else know that I found it so if he asks I'll just say I don't know anything about it."

"Okay if you're comfortable with that I'll be in touch soon. Goodbye."

"Yeah that's fine – goodbye."

When I hung up with her I still had the strange feeling that having that trinket in my possession was not a good idea but I knew I wouldn't be able to reach Midge to discuss my new situation before late afternoon because she had classes. So I got it out of my briefcase and took it down to the security office where the lost and found storage area was and told them I need to store something there for the day. It was no problem and they took it off my hands. Thankfully I didn't have to explain to them what was in the package.

On the way down I overhead several people talking near the elevator about the war news that had been blaring through the airways over the weekend. It seemed like the whole world was beginning to unravel but now I had a better understanding of the reason for it. Doc's message on Sunday and his overview on Friday had really opened my eyes about a lot of things that I never considered before. I was still trying to put all the pieces together about how Tony's murder, the new drug, the youth target, Brent Woodley's disappearance and what's happening in Europe impacted each other.

Before going back to my office, I thought I'd stop by the labs and see if Mimi was busy. I really just wanted to see her. When I got there I looked through the door window as I usually did but I didn't see her. I saw Martin at one of the lab tables, but no Mimi. I started to go in but then decided I didn't want to interrupt his work and I knew he would ask a lot of questions about what happened over the weekend. He was still keeping the sample and I'm sure he was curious about when he would be able to turn it over to Marsha to complete the analysis. All during the conversation that Mimi and I had yesterday, it was funny that we never discussed any of the details on how she was going to get that analysis done.

Back in my office I checked my appointment book and was reminded that I was scheduled to meet with Tango Hernandez at 3:00. Since he had shown me his identification I was a little more comfortable about whose side he was on and I think we both are trying to discover what's really going on at Canon. When we last talked he said he was going to be meeting with Mr. Jenkovitch because there was something that Milton had he wanted to see. I wondered if he got to see what he wanted. From the first time that we met when he came to my office, I got the impression that he was the type of man who usually got what he wanted, but I also knew that if Mr. Jenkovitch had something that he really needed to hide, more than likely it would somehow come up missing.

In the time that I had between now and meeting with Tango, I turned my attention to what was going to happen to the kids once this product hit the market. Was there some kind of marketing plan that would get it into the drug stores who had signed up for sponsorship of the various youth leagues around the city and indeed around the country? I knew that over in Jersey, the league that Joshua, Midge's son, was playing in had a number of teams consisting of boys and girls between the ages of twelve to fourteen. I guess it was the same right here in the city but I was not familiar with any of them.

Somehow I had to find out just how close was the release date for the product. There was nothing that I know of or anyone who I could talk to who might have that information. The ones who were privy to it, certainly had to be part of the team that was involved in the conspiracy and they were not going to converse with anyone who was not a member of the gang. From the time that I had planted that seed in Mr. Jablonski's mind about how much I knew, every time I saw him since then he looked at me very strangely and got away from me as quickly as he could. Since he was so jittery, I surmised that the drug must be close to being production line ready or he wouldn't be so nervous.

I knew it was going to be very helpful when Mimi was able to complete her analysis of the sample that Martin found. But even then, regardless of what she came up with, how would we be able to stop the product from getting to market. I guess when Tony found out about what was going on he was getting ready to become a whistle blower and it got him killed. If only we could still find out where he hid the documents that he had uncovered. I'm sure that by now the apartment he lived in had been turned upside down by anyone and everyone who had an interest in what he knew so for me to try and go that route I believed would be useless.

From the time I first became involved in this mystery until now, I never thought about how much it all tied in to things that were happening now and were going to become more intense happenings in the near future. From that night being at a party having a good time to waking up the next morning and finding a note that set my whole life on a different course I'm now so thoroughly entrenched in this matter that even if I wanted to quit, I don't think I could. It's amazing to me the way that I've been drawn into this situation. It was as if some kind of destiny or fate had brought me into it. I need to talk to Midge sometime about that and see if there is something she could explain to me on the subject.

That night just before going to Doc's house for dinner, when the man in the lobby of my building told me I was going to experience the things he said I would, they all happened just as he said. Now I wondered why he came to me and was that message some kind of harbinger of things that were going to happen to me. Doc said he might have been some kind of angel and now I thought if he was, why was he coming to me at this time? When I reflect on all the things that seem to just draw me, and even the fact that I'm hearing all these things that Doc is telling me about the future, if someone had told me when I first got in town that this is what I'd be into within a few years I would have called them crazy.

In my reverie I got lost in the moment and failed to notice that the time was ticking away. Before I realized it was almost three O'clock and Mr. Hernandez was sure to be walking through my door any moment. Sure enough at exactly 3:05 he was standing in the doorway looking at me. I hesitated saying anything because I thought something was wrong. He usually just walked right in and sat down like it was his office, but this time he stopped. I wondered if he was really waiting for an invite to come in or was he playing some kind of mind game. After a few seconds and he didn't advance, I threw up my hands and said are you waiting for me to invite you in. He just laughed and sauntered in casually then sat down. I started the conversation.

"What was that all about? You usually just burst in and grab a seat."

"Well Ron I just hate being predictable so I thought I change up a little bit. Did I scare you?"

"No but you are a little weird you know that."

"Yeah some people say that but I function very well. Aren't you glad to see me?"

"Actually I am because there are some things I need to tell you and I hope you have something to tell me. For example did you get to meet with Mr. Jenkovitch and see what you were telling me you had to see?"

"Yes I did but I also know the document he showed me had been doctored up so that it was not what I expected. For him to do that he had to be in collusion with those high powered people in Washington we're tracking. I can tell you now the document I wanted to see is the original Request for Proposal (RFP) that was issued from the Human Services Department. What he showed me was from the right department alright, but it was not for the product that we were trying to tie to the incomplete paper I found in the lab. Whoever these guys are we're dealing with they are pretty sophisticated and have a tightly knit network. In any event I'm still watching him very closely. Now what do you have?"

"Okay. Remember I started telling you about the devil worship thing I think a lot of the high level managers around here are into. Well that talisman I told you I borrowed from Mr. Jenkovitch's secretary I took it to somebody who is really knowledgeable about those things and she told me it was definitely a trinket that would be used in those rituals. I suspected that even before she said so, but to hear it from an expert just confirms my suspicion about some type of diabolical conspiracy underway here. Now I can let you have it if you still want it.

"Sure thing, just get it to me."

On top of that just this morning, Herb Crandall invited me to attend a meeting this coming Friday in which he told me he wants me to meet some friends that could help me to advance on this job. I think what he's really up to is to get me into one of those occult sessions and make me one of them or make me disappear like Brent Woodley."

"Do you really think this whole conspiracy theory of yours is being driven by some devil worshippers?"

"Yes I do and if you want to hear something even stranger I think those scraps of paper you found in Lab 1 with the partial formula on it are the instructions for a drug that's going to harm every kid under the age of seventeen in our communities. One of the chemists who works in another lab has been able to get a sample of something that was kept in Lab 1. It's going to be analyzed by another chemist who works for Canon but not in that lab on Wednesday. Based on what she comes up with, I think we may have something really solid to give you so you can take some official action."

"That sounds great. Who's the chemist?"

"Why do you need to know that?"

"Still don't trust me huh? Okay if you want to keep that a secret that's fine. I don't need to know at this point but down the road if I do make it official as you say, I will need to know. You said the analysis will be done on Wednesday?"

"Yeah hopefully it can be completed by then and the results given to me. After I've had a chance to look at it and make some sense of what it all means, then I will invite you to look at it also."

"Okay, just one more thing. Are you planning to go to that meeting?"

"Yes I am but before I do I need to get some protection."

"Protection - Isn't that what I told you I'm here to do?"

"Yes you said that, but the kind of protection I need I don't think you can provide."

"Just what kind of protection is that?"

"I told you I suspect we're dealing with something that's not natural and in order to fight it we can't do it with natural weapons. It must be done with something stronger than that."

"Oh you're telling me you plan to take a spiritualist with you?" "No not exactly. What I plan to take with me isn't a human spiritualist but as it was told to me I should put on a whole fighting outfit. What I need is the Armor of God. On that Friday after we met I had dinner with a very popular preacher over in Jersey and some of things he opened my eyes to I was astounded at, but when I left there I had a whole different perspective on life. Between him and his daughter, who is the one I was referring to that knows about the occult, he told me about things happening now in this world that are not being driven by natural causes. He gave me this advice and told me I needed to learn quickly how to:

10 Finally, be strong in the Lord and in his mighty power.

11 Put on the full armor of God, so that you can take your stand against the devil's schemes.

12 For our struggle is not against flesh and blood, but against the rulers, against the authorities, against the powers of this dark world and against the spiritual forces of evil in the heavenly realms.

13 Therefore put on the full armor of God, so that when the day of evil comes, you may be able to stand your ground, and after you have done everything, to stand.

[14] Stand firm then, with the belt of truth buckled around your waist, with the breastplate of righteousness in place,

[15] and with your feet fitted with the readiness that comes from the gospel of peace. [16] In addition to all this, take up the shield of faith, with which you can extinguish all the flaming arrows of the evil one.

[17] Take the helmet of salvation and the sword of the Spirit, which is the word of God. (Ephesians 6:10-18, New International Version NIV)

So you see Tango I'm not going there empty handed but the protection I'm going to take will come from a Bible that has been blessed by that preacher."

"You sound like you really believe in that stuff. Well if it makes you feel safe then do what you think is best. But for me personally I would take my 9MM then I would feel safe. Okay I'll wait to hear from you on Wednesday and maybe you'll have some good news for me."

"Yeah okay - I hope so too. Let's see what's going to come from the analysis. I'll give you a call and let you know just as soon as I know and have had a chance to digest what's given to me."

Tango left my office at about four-thirty and I felt like I had just unloaded a burden on him that I had been carrying. It wasn't that I needed to tell him all that, but somehow it just seemed to flow out of me like I was being guided by some spirit I never knew existed inside of me. It was as if I had become a different person than the one I used to be. Could this all be because I had an encounter with the Reverend Doctor Devereaux and that I attended his church on Sunday. I don't know but the feeling I have now is something I've never experienced before.

Maybe one day it will all come to me just how I managed to live this long and not be exposed to some of the things he was telling me. The world as it is now is just waiting for something to happen that will make it better. From what he is saying the time is growing very near when that change for the better is going to happen. All the things I'm going through now are as I was thinking just a harbinger of what the angel in the lobby was saying. Maybe I've been chosen to do something mighty powerful but never knew it. Maybe there are some things I'm destined to do but have never been made aware of it until now.

Just as I was about to leave for the day and was in the process of putting my things away, a call came in from someone I would least expect to hear from. It was from someone who worked on the production line who I had interviewed when I was trying to find a way to improve the operation. She was calling to tell me that Maria Sanchez was being set up to be discharged by that Jablonski guy and she could really use my help. I don't know why she thought I could help her but I listened to the story and felt compelled to at least try and do something.

When I finished hearing the whole story it appears that Mr. Jablonski couldn't think of a way to reinstate Maria at a position comparable to the one he surreptitiously moved her out of so he was figuring a way to get her out of the company for good. From what this young lady was telling me he was fabricating some lies on her record that would make it seem like she had done some things while supervising the operation that were not in compliance with company policy but had never been exposed before now. It was one of those subjective things in which he as her immediate superior could make the judgment call. I knew this man had low scruples in fact almost non-existent, but I never thought he could stoop that low.

The problem for me now was to figure out just how I was going to be able to help her. I had no administrative clout that could intervene on her behalf and Jablonski was at a higher level than I was so what could I do. If I thought that Herb Crandall would help as the top man in personnel, the thought only lasted a second. He would probably help Leonard carry out his concocted scheme just to help him get rid of a problem. No, I couldn't turn to Crandall it had to be someone else who could possibly step in and thwart Leonard's proposed action. The only thing I could think to do was to approach the shop steward of the union and try and solicit his help, but with me being a manager he probably wouldn't even want to talk to me. After I got off the phone I sat there just thinking about the situation but no immediate solution came to mind.

Then I remembered that Mr. Jablonski had put himself in a position of having to attest to something that was a fabrication and he would have to prove it. Unless she actually did what he was claiming where was he going to get the needed proof from. I decided I was going to go down to his office and confront him. I was going to ask him why he was trying to ruin this young woman's career with the company. I suspected he would ask me just how I knew about anything he was doing with his people, so I prepared myself before meeting him by going down to the production area and talking to the people who knew Maria well and had worked for her. Based on what they could tell me I would have some sense about whether what he was proposing could possibly make a case for her dismissal. It was evident after just talking with a few people, that the workers loved Maria and were happy with her being their supervisor. I asked them if they would be willing to make a statement to management on her behalf saying exactly what they told me, if it should come down to that. There was no hesitation from any one of them; they all said certainly they would speak up for her.

Armed with this information I knew that if I have to make the shop steward listen to me then what I did should be enough to let him know I was trying to help her. Also now I felt like I had enough of a bargaining chip to at least go and meet with Mr. Jablonski and attempt to negotiate a win-win situation for everybody. What I was going to propose would be that he stop with his plan to get Maria terminated and I would back off pursuing him about the drug thing that I knew about. Of course I would also casually mention that I had spoken to some of the people on the line and I would make him aware of their support for her.

It seemed like a good plan to me and I was ready to go to his office and carry it out. There was only one thing that gave me pause to consider going. It was now about ten after five and I wasn't sure he would even be there. I knew from having seen him on more than one occasion leave the building at the stroke of five regardless of what the status of the work load was for any given day. How he had acceded to his position was a mystery to me, but I assumed it was because of the connection he had within that evil network. In any event I decided to at least go there and see if he was still around.

Once I got off the elevator on his floor I started walking toward his office when I noticed that there were few of the other employees left there. I thought this was a bit unusual because most of the other workers that I knew usually worked beyond the clock striking five. The closer I got to his office the more I was beginning to get the feeling that something wasn't right here. I could see light coming from his office so I got the feeling that he may still be in there, so I stepped up my pace. When I got within a few steps I noticed that there was something different about the light that was emanating from within. It wasn't like a normal incandescent lighting but it seemed like a glow that would come from a very powerful floodlight. I knew that this couldn't be the normal light for his office because none of any of our offices could have such lighting.

When I was almost at the opening of his doorway I could hear voices coming from inside. The voices sounded like they were mumbling something incoherent to me, almost as if they were speaking in a foreign language. It sounded to me like there must have been at least five or six of them but since I couldn't see them immediately I had to guess. Arriving at the entrance to his office I turned and looked in and had to step back right away. The shock at seeing what my eyes had a hard time processing had me reeling. I had never seen anything like that before and didn't know whether to turn around and run as fast as I could the other way or pick up one of the nearby phones and call security to come up here quick. Before I could make my own decision it was made for me and I froze in place.

Chapter Ten
"Crossroads"

From the time that the first announcements had been made about the war escalating in Europe until now about a week later, there has been speculation on what the American's role is going to be. The President sent his envoy over there to step in and try to negotiate a peace, but to no avail. His efforts were thwarted at every turn and his sense of accomplishing anything was growing thin. His report back to the President stated that this was a hopeless situation and very few options were available. The countries involved in the war had declared they were each fighting for a cause in which they both believed they were right. Their commitment is so strong that it moved them even to the point of citizens within their ranks volunteering to sacrifice themselves in suicide missions to carry out their belief in the cause.

The US President said he was not going to put boots on the ground because he felt this was not his war, but the cry from so many people in peripheral third world countries surrounding the major combatants, seeking help to abate the turmoil, placed an undue burden on his heart to get involved militarily. In his most recent closed press conference he deferred to his Secretary of Defense asking for an assessment of what price he would have to pay in terms of loss of soldiers if we were to get involved? The answer came back that the loss could not be justified by the need or the cost. Shortly after that statement he concluded the session by recommitting to stepped up diplomatic strategies, but he maintained his unwillingness to commit ground soldiers to the effort. Sandwiched between trying to honor the world wide acceptance of the US position as the world's peace maker and the growing concern by his own citizens about entering every skirmish outside of US borders, he was having great difficulty being at peace with his decision.

Matters became even more complicated when reports started coming in about a rising political star coming out of the German pool of politicos, who was taking the political arena by storm and was gathering a large following and momentum as the new advocate for peace. It is being said that this man is reminiscent of a powerful leader, from another era years ago, who had the same type of charisma and ambition. It is also being said that he seems to possess the same kind of indwelling spirit that the former leader had. To the people he appears as the answer to their prayers and the leader who will replace the need for any American intervention.

Unrecognized by the diplomatic envoy from the US, this man has suddenly emerged on the scene as one who does not need US approval because he has garnered the will of the German people and is vying for the support of the third world nations. It appears like no one wants to review the history of the former leader, who he emulates, and take into account what happened after that leader became so powerful he declared himself a dictator and started a new war. The rise to power of the ascending prospect is not without the support of the Vatican who sees him as the spiritual answer they have been waiting for. Having the world's dominant church backing and that of the political leaders has given him free access to all that both worlds have to offer.

At home in the US people are clamoring for an explanation from each local diocese regarding how the church has managed to involve itself in the warfare. Aside from the speech making and sidestepping by the local leaders, no satisfactory answers are being given and every effort is being made to avert the issue by telling the people they must keep faith and give this new leader some time to act.

Even though the war is raging thousands of miles away, the impact here is being felt throughout every community. From large corporations to small mom and pop businesses the atmosphere is filled with speculations that here is another military venture that even though the President says he's not going to be involved, somehow the confidence level in him keeping that promise is very low. Throughout American history whenever there has been a need to stimulate the economy, involvement in some type of military action has been the solution to the problem.

At Canon Enterprises like so many other larger corporations the concern was that their overseas operations would be affected. However, unlike many of them the top executives at Canon had a more sensitive issue to address. The new product that they were about to release to the world was just about ready for production and once tested in the domestic arena the next step was marketing to the global consumer. An untimely war was not in the plan but news has been circulated amongst the conspiracy gang at headquarters that at the gathering on this coming Friday night a new strategy will be made known to them on how to react.

Leonard Jablonski had received the news just like his cohorts but he was in need of more assurance than the others. He felt that since he was the one responsible for the actual production of the new drug, he wanted to know ahead of time just how his role would be affected with this new strategy. He called on Herb and Milton to help him summon the adversary for an advanced overview but they refused telling him it was not necessary because it would all be explained to him at the end of the week. They both reminded him about what happened at the last meeting when Milton appeared to take umbrage with Satan's instructions. Undaunted by the admonition Leonard was not to be denied. He was going to attempt to summon the leader on his own.

On that same day when I was on my way to his office to offer a proposition to settle the Maria Sanchez situation, I was right outside of his office when I heard voices and I noticed that the light coming from inside was unusually bright. It was so piercing that I thought there might be some kind of electrical problem. However, when I got to the doorway and looked inside what I saw was something uncanny. There were no visible bodies attached to the voices and there was Leonard high up against the wall of his office suspended in mid-air pleading for mercy to whatever was holding him. I could see the intense light coming from a spot right in the center of the room but there was nothing there that could have produced it. I looked all around the room but saw nothing. In the next minute I experienced an unusually concentrated rim of heat that paralyzed me in place. It seemed to be surrounding the spot where the light was but it revealed nothing.

I called out to Leonard and suddenly the mumbling voices ceased and I was thrown from the office into the hallway outside and the door slammed shut. It might have been seconds or several minutes I don't remember how long I lay there but when I came to I got up opened the door and re-entered. There he was lying on the floor next to his desk with shallow breathing. I ran down the hall and got some water from the cooler and went back to him. Then I picked his head up and forced him to drink. Slowly he responded and looked at me.

"Did you see anything?" he asked.

"I'm not sure what I saw. What happened here?"

"Nothing - nothing happened. What are you doing here?"

Once again he was alert and started talking as if really nothing did happen. Since he seemed okay I told him about my proposal. He was not receptive to the idea at all and told me that after Friday I wouldn't even be concerned about Maria Sanchez. Then he asked me to leave his office and leave him alone. I did. I was disappointed but there was nothing else I could do so I went home.

All the way home I couldn't get what I saw out of my mind. I knew Leonard was definitely one of them but the question in my mind was why would his own turn on him like that? My second question was about my sanity - did I really see what I think I saw or did I just imagine it? Once I was inside my apartment and started to undress I looked at the bruises on my arms where something very powerful had grabbed and tossed me out the door, then I knew it wasn't my imagination.

#######

With all the news centering on what was going on with the war, headline attention had been drawn away from the unsolved mystery about who killed Tony Oliver and the sudden disappearance of Brent Woodley. However, there were still two people who were more concerned with this mystery than the war. The Pocono sleuth, Mike Casio and the CPD ace detective Peter Callahan were hard at work attempting to solve it. Even though Sergeant Callahan had been chastised by his Captain because of the false arrest he made, he was still determined to resolve the crimes. In his continuing effort to put two and two together, as it were, he made one more call to detective Casio to compare notes on where they both were collectively.

When he reached him he was happy to hear that a positive identification had been made on the body in the Pocono Hospital morgue, from DNA samples they were able to get with the help of the victim's sister. Sergeant Callahan was glad to get this new update but he wanted to know why he hadn't been contacted. He was told that the information had been wired to him days ago. After hearing that he became greatly concerned about what else he may have missed. A few additional minutes were spent updating each other on where they were with the cases then they hung up. Sergeant Callahan immediately started searching through his files for any new records. The case file now had grown substantially and apparently he wasn't the only one placing documents there. Buried under several papers on the top he came across the notice about the confirmed identification and wondered who had received the information. He was upset but rather than run through the whole department trying to find out who put it there and didn't let him know, he just read the file and took into account that Brent Woodley was no longer a missing person.

His next step was to determine how Woodley turned up in the mountains in Pennsylvania. It was becoming clear from all of the other bits and pieces of information he had collected from various sources that it was Woodley who was the shooter in the Oliver case, but now he had to determine who eliminated him and why. The more he pondered the question the more the answer pointed back to someone in the Canon Enterprise hierarchy. As much as he wanted to go back and grill Leonard Jablonski some more, he was hesitant because of the mess that was created based on Jablonski's earlier testimony. However, his strong feelings that Jablonski knew more about the Woodley disappearance than he had revealed led him to go back to the plant unannounced anyway

At the receptionist desk when Callahan was announced to Jablonski that he was there to see him, Leonard, still somewhat unsettled from his recent encounter, was trying to figure out a way to avoid this interview. It was only through Callahan's persistence and telling him that he would only need a few minutes Leonard allowed him to come up to his office.

"Mr. Jablonski, thank you for seeing me on such short notice. I won't take up too much of your time since I only have a couple of questions and it shouldn't take long."

"Sergeant I think I already told you everything I know about who I believed was the driver of that getaway car. What else can I tell you?"

"Oh I'm sorry I should have told you first. I'm not here about that. There's something else I think you can help me with. You had an employee by the name of Brent Woodley working for you recently who has turned up missing. Isn't that right?"

When Leonard heard that, his tension level soared to a new height and the fear must have shown on his face. Although Callahan didn't comment on it, he certainly noticed.

"Yes he worked for me here but he has been missing for some time now and no one seems to know what happened to him. Why are you asking about him?"

"Well I've received a report that he has turned up in a morgue in Pennsylvania and I just wanted to ask if you knew why he might have been there. Was he on some type of company business?"

Leonard was now very uncomfortable and started to squirm in his seat. This reaction made Callahan push a little harder for information.

"No he didn't have that type of responsibility. I, I, I don't have any idea why he would have been there.

Maybe he just liked to go to Pennsylvania. I'm afraid I can't help you."

"Is there anyone else here who might know? What about some of your other managers?"

Leonard was very nervous and just wanted to get Callahan out of his office so he mentioned Herb Crandall as a possible other person.

"This Mr. Crandall does he also work here in the plant?"

"No, his office is at the headquarters in midtown."

"Okay thank you Mr. Jablonski that's all I need from you right now. I'll be going."

As soon as Callahan walked out, Leonard got on the phone and called Herb to explain to him what had just happened. He tried telling him he had no other choice but to give his name because he was sure he was becoming a suspect in the Woodley disappearance. Herb wasn't upset and told him to calm down he would handle the cop. Leonard felt relieved because he knew that Crandall was more adept at coming up with solutions to problems than he was.

When Callahan left the office he suspected Leonard would alert this Mr. Crandall and tell him that he would be calling so he didn't try to contact him immediately. He wanted to give him time to think about it and hope he would do something to incriminate himself that he could pick up on. He was right. By the time Sergeant Callahan paid a visit to Herb the next day, Crandall had already made contact with his henchmen advising him of the need for his services. Herb had not engaged Ivan since the Brent Woodley event and was a little skeptical about doing it because the target would be a member of the law enforcement community. However, based on what Leonard told him Callahan was getting too close to discovering the truth about the murder. In addition, Herb felt that Ivan was so proficient at what he does best, he was confident that Ivan could perform the service with a minimum amount of risk.

When Callahan came to visit Herb Crandall at his office he was greeted with a very friendly smile and cordially invited to sit down. Sergeant Callahan observed the smooth demeanor that Herb exhibited and was quickly put on guard that the man might be doing this to perhaps cover up something.

"Welcome Detective Callahan. I understand you are asking around about the disappearance of Brent Woodley one of our employees."

"Yes I was hoping that maybe someone from here could help me understand just why he was found dead so far away from home."

"And where would that be?"

"Oh I thought your Mr. Jablonski would have filled you in since he suggested that I contact you in the matter."

"Yes he did call me but I'm afraid he failed to mention that detail."

"Well your Mr. Woodley was found in a morgue in the Pocono Hospital in Pennsylvania. It seems that he was involved in a ski accident at the Camel Back Lodge. His body had been severely banged up which made recognition and identification prolonged for some time. But anyway the police up there were finally able to make an ID and it turned out to be Mr. Woodley. Now the question we have is what was he doing up there?"

"That's easy detective. I didn't know him well but I've been told by some people who did know him that he was an avid skier and visited that resort quite often. He must have just had a very bad day on the slopes. Accidents do happen there you know?"

"Yes I'm quite aware of that, but for the body to be as mangled as it was I suspect the accident wasn't just an accident. Do you know of any reason why someone would want to cause the demise of Mr. Woodley?"

Sergeant Callahan observed Herb very closely as he answered the question trying to see if there would be any glitch in his demeanor. However, for a man who was so skilled at lying, his armor produced not the slightest chink that the detective could recognize.

"Well as I said detective I didn't know the man very well but from as far as I know he didn't have any enemies around here or down at the plant where he actually worked. Perhaps you need to ask around up at the lodge. Maybe somebody there may have witnessed the accident."

"Perhaps you're right. We will check it out. Thank you for your time Mr. Crandall, I do appreciate it."

"Sure detective glad to be of help. If there's anything else I can assist you with feel free to call me."

"Oh before I leave there was one more thing I need to ask you. Do you belong to any group or organization that's connected with a cult? We've been getting reports lately that one's been discovered gaining a strong foothold in this community."

With that question thrown at him, Herb's heretofore impregnable armor showed a slight crack in the surface and he winced. Not missing a clue, Callahan picked up on the reaction and honed in on the response.

"Why are you even asking me a question like that? Not that I am, but if I am is there any crime associated with it?"

"No sir, I was just curious. Okay I'll be going now."

Sergeant Callahan had observed what he wanted to see with Mr. Crandall and it set his thinking off in a new direction. His commitment to ending this unsolved mystery was paying off and he was close to wrapping it up. On his way back to his office he stopped at the restaurant where the whole thing with Tony Oliver had occurred. He looked around the whole area again like he did when he was first assigned to the case. This time however, he was looking for something other than the details that had already been reported by the crime scene experts. This time he was looking for other worldly clues.

The people in the area were the same ones who always frequented the neighborhood and there wasn't anything different about the surroundings, but somehow Callahan had the feeling that he missed something before. As he got closer to the door of the restaurant he noticed that there were people outside smoking just as had been reported by the eyewitnesses he talked to before. But this time he observed one individual who didn't seem like the typical patron who would frequent that type of establishment. Peter wasn't one to jump to absurd conclusions but something inside of him was telling him to approach this person and casually engage him in light conversation.

Callahan didn't identify himself as a police officer at first, but as he talked with the person and the light banter back and forth began to reveal something very suspicious about the man, he felt the need to let him know who he was. When the man immediately backed off any further communication with the detective and started to walk away, Sergeant Callahan stopped him and asked for his identification. At first the man refused, but when Callahan opened his coat and exposed his armament the man complied with the request. It was Ivan and what had been said during the earlier conversation led Callahan to believe he may have been involved with the Tony incident. Once he had identified the man, Callahan called for a police vehicle to take Ivan down to the headquarters for further questioning.

#######

It was about 7:30 PM inside one of the well-equipped laboratories at the university and Marsha was well into doing an analysis on the sample that had been given to her by Martin. From everything that she was able to perform the results were becoming very complicated. Most of the elements in the sample were those which conformed to the standard scientific charts but there was one that had her completely baffled. It didn't react as expected to anything she tested it with and it didn't comply with any standard tests she ran. It was as if this one element was not from any known or previously identified source documents. It was neither a catalyst nor a retardant but it was just there in the sample and its function was unclear. She ran test after test and the same result came up every time. From what she could determine the sample being tested when combined with another acidic liquid such as orange juice or perhaps a sports drink would if introduced into the human digestive system begin to effect a reaction that could be detrimental to the stability of the nervous system.

After she ran the last test which had taken her several hours to complete, she couldn't wait to contact Ron and tell him what she found. She didn't want to use the telephone in the lab for fear of being overheard, since there were other students there running experiments, but when she attempted to leave she was confronted by one of the professors in charge and he wanted to know what she was working on. He had just come in and she didn't expect any of the teaching staff to be on site on this day. It was not usual for one to come in on a Wednesday night, that's why she chose the day to conduct the analysis. It seems that he had left something in there from his day's lecture and was there to retrieve it. He was just as surprised to see her there as she was to see him so the mutual shock registered in both.

"Hello Ms. Robinson how are you? Didn't expect to see you here this time of night. What are you working on?"

Marsha felt trapped and was for a minute at a loss for an explanation. However she had a quick wit and was undaunted by the challenge as she responded to his inquiry.

"Hello Dr. Pincher I'm fine thank you for asking. I didn't expect to see you here either what a coincidence. I was just completing a lab experiment that I've been curious about for some time."

"Oh really is it something I can help you with?"

"No I'm finished now, but thanks anyway."

Marsha gathered her things as quickly as she could, bid the professor goodnight and scampered out of there. He stood there watching her leave and was somewhat suspicious about her rush to depart. Then he looked around the lab for any possible illegal activity, but everything seemed to be in order so he retrieved what he came for and since all the other students were gone, he turned out the lights.

When Marsha got down to the street she breathed a sigh of relief and wondered whether that professor had any idea about what she may have been up to. She only thought about it for a minute and concluded that since she was sure she didn't leave anything behind that could incriminate her he would have nothing to go on if he did raise a question about her being there. Anyway, she had completed what Ron and Martin were counting on her to do, even if it didn't provide all the answers just as they expected it would.

Marsha knew she had to get home now as soon as she could because she had overstayed the time she had promised to be home to relieve the sitter. She wasn't worried about Jerry because he was in good hands, but she didn't want to make a habit out of not getting home when she said she would. In addition she was anxious to get there and get on the phone to update Ron on what she found.

As she entered her apartment Jerry met her and asked, as he did sometime when she came in later than usual, if she had been with Mr. Powers. She looked at him wondering if in his young mind he was trying to imply something or was he really genuinely interested in her developing something with a man he admired. She casually explained to him that she was not but she was at school doing her homework. She then put her arm around him and asked if he had done his. Satisfied that they both had done what they were supposed to do, she paid the sitter and said goodnight.

Jerry went to bed and Marsha called Ron.

"Hello this is Ron."

"Hope you hadn't gone to bed this is Mimi."

"No, no I was just sitting here watching television. How you doing?"

"Just great! I finished testing that sample you got from Lab 1. You won't believe what I found."

"At this point during this whole thing, I'm ready to believe anything. What did you find?"

"Well just as we suspected it is a drug designed to wreak havoc on the human nervous system. However, I wasn't able to determine whether it is aimed specifically at any age group and that may be because there is an ingredient in the mix that I was unable to identify. I have never seen anything like it and I wasn't able to cross-reference it with anything in our known elements database. How strange is that?"

"Yeah that is weird. So what now?"

"Until I can get a better handle on what element "X" is the only thing we can do is try to keep the integrity of the sample whole by refrigeration. I don't know what else to do. Maybe Martin will have an idea when I talk to him tomorrow and let him know what I found."

"Okay, but there's just one more thing. I told Tango Hernandez what we were up to and he wanted in on knowing about the sample. I promised him that after I had examined it I would let him look at it."

"You think that was a good idea. How do you know what he'll do with it?"

"I don't know, but I'd rather him have it than to see you get in any deeper trying to get answers through your school lab. It may not be safe for you. Anyway, I'm beginning to trust this guy after he came clean about who he really is and showed me his identification. Besides if he takes it, he has access to all the labs and scientific knowledge our government has. If they can't identify this element "X" then this country's really in trouble."

"Thanks for thinking about my welfare and my degree. You're right he may be able to find out something I wouldn't be able to using tools I don't have access to. How do you want to get it to him?"

"After work tomorrow let's arrange to meet him somewhere that won't expose any of us. Can you keep it okay until then?"

"Yes. I don't think one more day in the compact refrigerator I rented will hurt it, but I am concerned about keeping it in that state too long without knowing what it completely is."

"Okay then let me call you tomorrow after I've spoken to him and I'll fill you in on the plan details. Talk to you then. Goodnight."

"Sounds fine, I'll wait for your call. Goodnight."

After I hung up with Mimi I tried going to sleep but the vision I saw at Leonard's office kept popping into my mind. I knew he was deeply involved with the crew that was masterminding the scheme to mass-produce an evil product intended to inflict harm on a great number of suspected young people, but I just couldn't figure out why he was being victimized by his own. His hanging on the wall like that with no visible means of support was hard to believe but after all that I was being exposed to lately, it was just another oddball thing to happen. Finally, I was able to drift off to sleep, but I still didn't have any answers to my question.

The next morning as I arose to the sound of my favorite alarm clock, I sleepily did my shut off routine. This time though, before I actually got out of bed, I looked at the clock in a different way. I hearkened back to what the strange man in the lobby of my building said about something being in my possession that one-day was going to prove to be a blessing to me. Could it be this old alarm clock who members of my family told me many times before was blessed because of how it came to be in my family. I knew the story about my maternal ancestor Sulia and the history of her days as a slave in Virginia, but who and how the clock came to be blessed was still a mystery.

I only dwelled on it for another minute before the thoughts of what needed to be done today entered my mind. There were a lot of things that I needed to do especially after talking with Mimi last night about the sample and her discovery. It wasn't enough for her to have come up with the main ingredients in the sample, but to make the determination that confirmed for the most part its intended use, was significant.

I got up and rushed through my morning routine and hurried out the door to meet Alex. Again just like a fine clock work, he was there right on time and we sped downtown to the plant. Alex dropped me off and I entered the building noticing that there was a lot of commotion going on in the lobby. As I got closer to the center of it, I saw that Leonard Jablonski was talking to the police. There were four officers surrounding him and the worker crowd had surrounded them. From where I was standing I couldn't tell what was being said, but judging by Leonard's reaction he was being interrogated in a most unfriendly manner. It was strange to see him in this position because only yesterday I had seen him being treated so unkindly by another source.

At the end of their conversation the officers broke off their questioning and left the building. Leonard regained his composure and admonished the workers that had gathered. He chastised them for paying too much attention to his plight and not doing what they were supposed to be doing. Quickly they scattered and the lobby emptied out. I walked over to him and asked what that was all about. He turned to me and said in a harsh tone.

"How is it that every time I seem to have something go wrong for me, you turn up?"

I replied, "I don't know just lucky I guess."

He turned and walked away without addressing my question. I couldn't tell whether he was angrier at the police for questioning him in the manner they did right in front of his subordinates or that I was in the crowd. In any event when he walked away he blurted out over his shoulder that he couldn't wait until Friday came when he would see me at the meeting. This meeting he was referring to had to be the one Herb Crandall invited me to, but I wondered just how many other people knew about it.

When I got to my office, even though it was just a little after nine, who should be standing at my door but my favorite movie character - Mr. Moto.

"You're up early aren't you?" I said. "What's the matter you couldn't sleep?"

"Ron, it's much too early for your quips. I wanted to catch you early to follow up on what we talked about. Did you get to do what you told me you were going to do with that sample?"

"Yes. As a matter of fact I am glad you're here because what my chemist friend discovered is exactly what we suspected. This sample we found in Lab 1 is designed to hurt and do major harm to whomever ingests it. I still believe it is intended for adolescents but she couldn't confirm that part. The analysis that was done wasn't complete however, because there was something in the sample that couldn't be identified. This is where you come in. I am going to get the sample to you today and hope through your contacts you can come up with the missing portion of the analysis."

"What do you mean by missing portion? Your friend is a qualified chemist right?"

"That's correct but there's something in the sample that just didn't conform to any tests she was able to run."

"She, you said she - so it's a woman we're talking about."

"Yes it is. Does that matter?"

"Not at all I was just trying to guess who it might be since you wouldn't tell me. If she wasn't able to identify the missing piece what makes you think I will be successful?"

"Well for one thing, I believe you have access to more sophisticated labs than she does and for another you want to know the answer as badly as we do."

"Okay, we certainly agree on that part. How am I going to get this sample?"

"I told her that I wanted for all of us to meet somewhere that wouldn't expose any of us to prying eyes. Right now I'm not sure where that would be but let me think about it this morning and I'll get back to you no later than lunchtime. Are you going to be around then?"

"I'll be wherever you need me to be, but more than likely I'll be in my office. Just give me a call and we'll go from there.

"Yeah okay let's do that."

Tango left my office and I started thinking about where would be the best place for us to meet. There weren't a whole lot of places around the plant in which we could go to without someone recognizing one of us. Then the idea finally came to me. What better place for us to go than to the movie house that was only a few blocks away from the plant. When I called Mimi and told her the plan she thought it was a funny place to meet for what we had to do and she asked me if I was slyly trying to take her on a date. I assured her this was not a date but it was the only place I could think of where we could make the exchange and it would be dark enough so that we wouldn't be recognized. She agreed and we decided that at 7:00 O'clock we would arrive there individually and meet at the refreshment counter. This would give her time to go home and get the sample and still be back on time.

Right around lunchtime I contacted Tango and the plan was set in motion. Meanwhile, there were so many other things going on at the plant today I was having trouble keeping focused on the sample thing. The buzz around the plant that a new product was being rolled out on Monday was getting everybody excited. Even those who were not directly involved in any of the leg work done to make it, were extolling it as a breakthrough in new science. I marveled at how well the sales and marketing team had done their jobs in convincing people that this new drug was going to be a boon to mankind. If only I could have produced the results that Mimi had come up with and post it on the bulletin board, how excited would they be then? I wanted to holler out at the top of my lungs for the whole plant to hear that this product will kill people and we are going to make it happen, but I knew that would be a ludicrous thing to do because no one would believe me without some kind of proof.

The day couldn't go by quickly enough for me so that I would meet Mimi and Tango and make the exchange. With all the facilities he had at his disposal I was sincerely hoping that the results for a complete analysis wouldn't take too long. Then we would have the whole answer to who the target for the drug really is and we could notify the proper authorities and perhaps prevent the product launch. This all seemed like a good plan and I looked forward to seeing a speedy solution to the whole nightmare problem.

At the end of my business day I wrapped up my work and headed toward the Peacock Palace to have some dinner. I didn't want to go home because it probably would take me too long and I certainly didn't want to delay the rendezvous. When I arrived at the restaurant, it was kind of odd to see the place at night. I had never been there before at this time and somehow the atmosphere was different than that for the daytime crowd. There were quite a few people in there but none appeared to be the corporate types. The clientele now was that of the older more mature set who probably didn't live in the neighborhood but came to the place because there was a small band warming up and it seemed like the place had turned in to a jazz club.

I ordered my dinner and as the band started to play it was becoming an enjoyable evening. Oddly enough I thought about the remark Mimi made earlier about me slyly trying to take her on a date and it occurred to me that this would be an ideal place to do just that. I finished eating and the time was just about right for me to walk over to the movie house. When I got outside even the streets seemed to have changed over to a different setting. The hustle and bustle of the daytime activities had ceased and the semi quiet of the night was taking over. There weren't too many people walking around but a few cars did drive by sporadically.

At the theater I looked at my watch then bought a ticket and went inside. It was almost 7:00 right on the button but I didn't see either Mimi or Tango at the concession stand where we were supposed to meet. I expected that she might be a little late, but I was surprised that he wasn't there. That old feeling of something's not right began to surge up inside of me and I was doing everything I could to suppress it. Minutes went by and neither one of them showed. At a quarter after the hour I was beginning to wonder if our communications were not clear about the time so I decided to call Mimi at home to see if something had happened there. The phone rang several times and then the recording came on announcing there was no one available to take the call but leave a message. This really began to worry me and I didn't know how much longer I should wait here before going up there and see what happened. My concern for Tango was also mounting. It wasn't like him to not show without calling, especially when we both had looked forward to getting the sample in his hands.

Just as I was about to leave because the ushers were beginning to look strangely at me since I had not gone in to see the movie but was just hanging around the stand, in walked Tango in a hurried fashion. He almost sprinted over to me and quickly blurted out that we had to get out of there something was up. I didn't have a clue what he was talking about but he grabbed my arm with his powerful grip and started pulling me toward the door. I told him that my chemist friend had not shown up yet and I think we should wait for her. He responded by telling me there was no time for that because in a few minutes this place would be full of cops and if she was coming we would see her outside.

He was right. No sooner had we exited the theater minutes later several police cars and a SWAT unit showed up and quickly entered the theater. We moved across the street but kept close enough to see what was happening. I told Tango I didn't want to leave before I saw whether she was going to show up. He asked me how much longer I was going to wait and then pointed to an unmarked white box truck saying that was a standard bomb squad vehicle. By now it was almost forty-five minutes past the time we were scheduled to meet so I told him I guess she isn't coming. Then I asked him what this raid was all about and how he found out about it. He told me he had received an anonymous call before he left his office tipping him that it was going to happen but no details were left about why it was going to happen. After the tip he made a few calls of his own to try and gain more information about what was going on, but he was unsuccessful in getting any. He even used his shield to probe the police department but they wouldn't divulge any information, telling him it was a priority mission and a need to know only affair.

Now I was really worried about Mimi so I told Tango we needed to get up to her apartment and check on her. He readily agreed and said he had a car parked just around the corner. We quick stepped to his vehicle and headed across town. After I got in I noticed that he had a telephone in the car and I asked if I could call her. He punched in some kind of code to produce a dial tone and then told me now I could dial. The phone kept ringing and ringing for about two minutes with no answer, finally she picked up.

"Hello who is this?" came the agitated voice on the other side.

"Mimi this is Ron what's going on, where've you been?"

"Oh Ron, I'm glad you called I had an emergency with Jerry and had to take care of him. Where are you?"

"I'm on my way to your place. Is he alright?"

"Yes he's fine now but a little while I go I thought he was in big trouble. I'll explain when you get here. How soon will that be?"

"I'm riding with Tango and we're about fifteen minutes away."

"You think that's wise bringing him here? Are you sure about that?"

"I don't have any choice now we're almost there and we need to get the sample to him so he can start working on getting the rest of the analysis done. You can meet us in the lobby and give it to him."

"Yes I think that might be better. You may trust him, but I don't think I'm ready for that yet. Just have me buzzed when you get here and I'll come down. I really wish you could come up though Jerry would love to see you and it might help him feel better."

"No problem. I want to see him too and you can fill me in on what happened."

"Okay, see you soon."

"Yeah okay, bye."

"Goodbye."

"Sounds like she's not too happy to see me."

"No it's nothing like that she just had a medical emergency with her kid and is upset. She'll give you the sample."

A few minutes later we pulled up to her building and got out. Tango and I entered the lobby and I walked up to the desk and asked to page Mrs. Robinson. Of course "Mr. Moto" picked up on the name and said: "Now I know who the chemist is." I hadn't planned on introducing her that way but it was done so I had to move on. The receptionist spoke into the intercom and told Mimi she had visitors waiting. Mimi responded and told her she was coming down. Tango and I went and sat down in the waiting area and he commented saying he didn't know Canon chemists did this well. I ignored the comment and just looked toward the elevator for her.

The door opened and she came out with the thermos containing the sample in her hand. I introduced her to Tango and he said to me that they had already met. She acknowledged his statement then handed him the package telling him she also included in the bag all the notes she put together regarding what she found and her speculation on what she thought the product design was intended to do. He thanked her and said he would use all his resources available to come up with the missing pieces of the testing. He took the package and I said I would walk out with him. I turned to Mimi and whispered in her ear I would be right back.

Tango and I walked out and he offered to drive me home, but I said he needn't bother because I could get a cab later. Right now I wanted to go up and see how the kid is doing. He gave me an inquiring look but received no response. Then he said "Suit yourself," and left. I stood and watched him get in his car and drive away then returned inside. I told the desk I needed to speak with Mrs. Robinson again and the attendant politely accommodated me. Mimi answered the buzz and told the desk to allow me to come up.

Once on the floor I wasted no time in getting to the apartment thinking something may still be wrong. But now for the first time since I've been coming here I noticed the usually quiet floor was not so quiet tonight. I could hear coming from one of the apartments what sounded like a couple having a real disagreement. I tried to ignore it, but it was loud enough to get my attention so I stood outside their door and listened for a moment. Next I heard what probably was some dishes crashing then I knew it was time for me to move on before security would be coming to the rescue. I got to Mimi's door and rang the bell. She answered and invited me in.

"Hi, everything go alright with Mr. Hernandez?"

"Yeah, why are you so suspicious of him?"

"I don't know but something about him triggers an alert in my senses. Call it woman's intuition or whatever you want, but whenever I'm around him it flares up."

"Wow that's good to know. Maybe I should keep my guard up a little while longer. Anyway I'll deal with that later now, where's my buddy?"

"He's in bed but I don't think he's sleeping. You can go in."

I opened his bedroom door and quietly slipped in. He wasn't asleep but he wasn't fully awake either. The emergency room doctor had given him some type of antibiotic that was making him drowsy but he was fighting it not wanting to go to sleep. I looked at him and felt his head. It was a little warm but I don't think it was due to any fever.

"Hi champ I heard you had a little difficulty earlier this evening, what happened?"

He looked back at me with his eyes kind of teary and answered.

"I don't know but I felt really bad and my head was spinning. Then I felt real hot and couldn't breathe right that's when Mom called the emergency people and they took me to the hospital."

"Gees that was something. Did you eat anything that you haven't ever eaten before?"

"No but I took a sip of the tea that was in the little refrigerator Mom brought in. It was nasty so I left it there. Then a little while later I started feeling sick."

"You drank from that bottle in the little refrigerator?"

"Yes I thought it was just some new tea Mom was trying."

When I heard him say that I told him I would be right back and I went out to talk to Mimi.

"Did you know that Jerry took a taste of the sample?"

"What? Are you telling me he drank some of it?"

"Yes he just told me he thought it was some new tea you were trying. I'm glad he only tasted it. But now we know definitely just how sick it will make you."

"He didn't tell me anything about drinking that. Let me go in there."

"Wait. Please calm down before you do that. He didn't mean any harm and he's okay now. Why don't you wait until morning after you've had a good night's sleep, then talk to him?"

"Yes I guess you're right. But he scared me half to death. Okay, okay I'll wait. Is he sleeping now?"

"He wasn't a minute ago but I think he was on his way. Let me go back and check."

I quietly slipped back into the room and this time he was fast asleep so I went back out to her.

"Yes he's sleeping comfortably now. I bet he'll be back to normal in the morning. Are you alright?"

"Yes I guess I'm okay. I just need to go to sleep myself. Can you see yourself out?"

"Yeah sure, you get some sleep." I grabbed my coat and left.

On my way in to work the next day, Friday, as I sat in Alex's cab listening to the radio the song playing seemed strangely apropos for the time. It was "No Where to Run, No Where to Hide" a popular number by one of the premier girls groups of the past. It seemed to be talking directly to me about what was going on in my life and what challenges I was about to face. Since it was the day that I was scheduled to meet Herb Crandall for dinner and then be escorted to a late night meeting, I was already feeling apprehensive about the whole idea. It was too late to back out now without having some serious repercussions for my career at Canon, so I just had to think very strongly on what Mimi's sister told me about relying on the sword that is the Sword of the Spirit - the Bible she gave me.

I went through the day doing my daily functions without any new abnormal occurrences until about 3:30 PM when the call came in from Mr. Crandall reminding me about tonight. He told me to meet him in his office at 5:30 and we would head out. I was okay with that but I just had to keep my head together because of the accelerated activity going on around here. Things were beginning to speed up regarding the announcement that the new product was going to be released on Monday. I suspected that after the meeting tonight I would either be asked to move into a new position back at the headquarters where I would be once again under the direct eye of Herb and Milton, or that something was going to happen to me to make me not care anymore about anything. After the recent conversation I had with Jennifer about these meetings and seeing all the things I have I felt that my worst fears were about to be realized.

I kept saying to myself I wish I could reach Midge or her father and just talk with either of them one more time before tonight. Both had a way of reassuring and building confidence saying that nothing bad would happen to me as long as I put my trust in the power of the author and finisher of my faith as spelled out in the Bible she gave me. I knew Midge was unavailable because of her class schedule and I hesitated even attempting to call Doc because of his schedule so I continued to sit there trying to build up my strength on my own.

The hours past and it was almost time to go meet Mr. Crandall. I hadn't heard from Mimi today and I wondered if she was okay after the ordeal she went through last night with her son. On top of that I wondered about the bomb scare at the movie theater and whether it had anything to do with the fact that I was in there. Normally I wouldn't have considered these two things as having anything to do with me, but after witnessing what happened to Leonard Jablonski from his own people, I couldn't dismiss the thought that there really are some supernatural powers out there capable of making strange things happen to anyone they targeted.

I picked up the phone and called Mimi. She answered and after a brief conversation let me know both she and Jerry were fine but she couldn't talk right now because of a project she had to get finished before the end of business today. I quickly asked her whether she told Martin about Tango and she replied she had not yet, but she would once she finished her work. Not wanting to hold her up any longer, I reminded her that I was going to the meeting tonight I told her about. She admonished me to be very careful there and said she would pray for me. That's all I wanted to hear so I told her I would call her at home tonight then hung up.

After the call as I sat there reflecting once again on all the things that had happened over the last few months since the death of my colleague, so many things raced through my mind that it was difficult to keep them in some type of logical order. In me there was a strong sense that the time was growing very near when the trials and tribulations of the world that Doc spoke about in his sermon overview were on some type of accelerated schedule. Before that party which started my involvement in this whole sordid affair, I wondered if someone had not slipped the note into my pocket that night whether I would even be thinking the thoughts I am now. Would I even be in the middle of something that I don't truly understand?

Having grown up with just a basic background in religion and that was only because my mother used to force the kids to go to church, I was now thoroughly embarrassed at not knowing more about the things Doc and Midge were telling me about. Things like what was coming in the near future. After I left home and went to college I started associating with other students who like myself, chose a lifestyle that didn't include church attendance or any other type of Christian worship. Now, as was pointed out to me by Doc, it was God's grace that I made it through there and found the position I have. When I heard his words I realized that it was now time for me to find out what He has in store for me and what my purpose in life is.

In my reverie the time seemed to move more quickly than I was conscious of because when I finally looked up it was 5:00 O'clock. The normal orderly procedure for putting things away was abandoned as I just threw everything in a drawer. I quickly grabbed my hat, coat and briefcase and ran down to the elevator. Fortunately, when I got outside there was a cab pulling up to the building to discharge a passenger and I was able to get in. The driver was skillfully able to circumvent much of the Friday night getaway traffic as he got me to the headquarters building in enough time to have a few minutes to spare.

When I arrived at Mr. Crandall's' office his secretary said he was ready for me and for me to sit down because he would be coming right out. At first I was a little curious about why he didn't want me to come in, but then I saw someone come out whom I had never seen before. He was a rather strange looking older man who walked with a slight limp as he gave me a quick glance then proceeded down the hallway. Seconds later Mr. Crandall came out greeted me and shook my hand. He said for me to give him a minute while he closed up shop and got his coat then we could be on our way.

The restaurant he took me to I had never been before even when I worked in the building. It was within walking distance so I was surprised that I had never even heard of it before. It was called Shanghai Gardens, an Oriental style facility with many booths and a few tables surrounding a beautiful fountain in the center of the room. The walls and even the ceiling were decorated with what appeared to be several symbolic dragons and their human slayers and an assortment of other language symbols I couldn't identify. It wasn't creepy but I did get the feeling that each one of those figures represented something in their religion. We were guided to a booth and the waiter handed us a rather extensive menu.

We ordered both food and beverage simultaneously and waited. Herb seemed surprisingly nervous which made me uncomfortable. I asked him if anything was wrong and he immediately replied no, but I sensed something in his voice that wasn't genuine. We chatted a few minutes about some very mundane business activities and then he started to talk about the meeting we were going to. I got the sense that he was leading up to something that he was trying to prepare me for, but then the waiter came out with a food cart and started setting the plates down. Herb stopped.

No more was said as we ate. While we were eating though, soothing easy listening oriental music started playing softly through the PA system. It was very relaxing and everyone in the place seemed to enjoy it. During the whole meal Herb never said any more about what I thought he was leading up to, but when we finished eating he asked me if I was ready. The question seemed to have a double meaning that I couldn't quite fathom, but I answered in the affirmative anyway.

We left the restaurant, hailed a cab and he instructed the driver to take us to a place way over on the lower East Side. The building we pulled up in front of was an old walk up tenement that had a very dark exterior. It appeared very unlikely a place for any kind of business meeting but then I became aware of what was happening. We got out and he led me up a long steeply inclined set of steps to the front door. He rang the bell three times, which must have been some kind of code because someone answered over the intercom immediately. He uttered another code word and the door buzzed open. Inside the hallway on the first floor was dark, with a minimal amount of lighting on each side of the walls. The man who came to meet us was dressed in a dark, perhaps black business suit and he stepped back waiting for Herb to introduce me. Herd did so and we were instructed to follow him.

As we walked down the hall I tried to make out the pictures on the walls but it was difficult to see well. From all that I could tell they were pictures of some bi-gone heroes, perhaps out of the King Arthur days. We walked quietly to the back then turned and went down a long flight of stairs to a very large room that was illuminated only by candlelight. There were many people already in the room seated at several tables. It looked to me like a nightclub in the East Village on a Saturday night except there wasn't any music playing just light conversation. When Herb walked in with me, the conversation stopped and everyone turned around. He led me up to the front of the room where there was a long table that looked like it was set up as a dais but there were no chairs there. At the front of the room Herb turned me around to face the crowd and introduced me. The crowd responded in unison by saying welcome to the fold in an almost chanting fashion.

I was then led to a table right near the front that had two vacant chairs which must have been set up for the two of us. As I sat down, the other three people at the table who were all dressed in black greeted me and introduced themselves. They were all from Canon, but I had never seen any of them either at the headquarters or the plant. Not long after we were seated, then a tall heavy set man came forward and stood before the long table. He announced he was calling this special meeting to order and read some kind of doctrinal ordinance which the crowd repeated after him. The words were in some foreign language that I was unfamiliar with, but the one word said many times, I did recognize was Diablo and it sent a chill down my spine. When the chant was finished he started talking about a great new step forward in their assigned mission. Although I didn't know it at the time he was referring to the new drug that would be rolled out by Canon Enterprises on Monday.

After his short presentation, a group of women dressed in long black robes came in with serving trays carrying glasses and pitchers. Apparently this was to toast the achievement. A glass was given to everyone, including me, and we were instructed to stand and join in the toast spoken by the leader. Herb looked at me and nodded his approval for me to take it and drink. I hesitated at first but when I saw everyone else being served from the same pitcher I was, I assumed it couldn't be harmful. When the toast was done, the leader then invited Herb Crandall to the front to stand with me and make his announcement. Herb did so and told the crowd that I was going to be the newest executive manager in the fold. The crowd applauded and I felt a strange sensation like I was drifting on a cloud. I heard the words ending in promotion and it sounded great like I was being elevated to a new higher level at the office. For the moment the feeling was exhilarating, but then before I knew it, the cloud kept drifting higher and higher until it finally reached a height where the air was too thin and suddenly my eyes were wide open, but I wasn't there.

Chapter Eleven
"Decisions"

The sky was overcast and the cloudiness mirrored the mood of the people it covered. In Washington apprehension was the pervasive feeling of the day and it seemed that no one was immune to it. News of events continuing to escalate in Europe and reservations of the common people about when the US would become embroiled in the war was causing great concern. Throughout offices from the highest level in the Pentagon down to community conversations in local barbershops, talk centered on not if the US would get involved, but when. Even though the President had repeatedly denied any commitment to sending troops, the mounting pressure from several third world countries begging for support was beginning to have a dramatic effect on his reasoning.

Mounting sympathy for their plight was gaining support in the capitol city as well as in many cities across the nation. The need to recognize their sentiments and cater to the will of the people was beginning to make his adamancy fragile. As he was even now in the midst of his office consulting with his inner circle, the question was being revisited about the go or no go scenario and the cost versus the risk equation. In addition, the single point that kept coming up in these conversations was the appearance of this rising leader who everyone was talking about who was capturing the hearts of the political powers as well as those of the Vatican leaders.

It was only those who were not privy to the strength of either faction that were filing complaints and asking for help.

While the debate was being carried out in the Oval Office regarding world affairs, not far from there in other government offices another discussion was under way regarding matters closer to home. This discussion was addressing the discovery of a sample taken from a lab at Canon Enterprises which was now being analyzed by some highly competent chemists. Tango Hernandez had presented his superiors with the sample along with notes provided by Marsha, on the findings and posed the question to his superiors about a possible terrorist plot that may even involve some high level officials. He hesitated to mention any supernatural implications that were revealed to him by Ronald Powers because he wasn't ready to accept that conclusion yet.

Since Tango had returned to continue his investigation at Canon, his colleagues had pursued surveillance of the two high level officials in the Department of Human Services and found more suspicious activities being conducted, but they were not yet ready to make any arrests. Even the suspicious doctored R.F.P. that Tango brought in was not enough for them to move on because it lacked real proof. Although Tango was disappointed in what he perceived as a lack of progress he was thoroughly convinced that this new discovery would be enough to close the matter. In his mind, according to what he had been told by Marsha and Ron this would be just the proof they needed to solidify the evidence.

As the discussion continued and the details of Tango's terrorist hypothesis were examined, the meeting was interrupted when the door opened and one of the chemists barged in exclaiming the results of their testing. He was excited about their analysis and rather than waiting to be asked to divulge his findings he immediately handed some papers to the presiding officer and said: "Here read this." Right at the top of the paper were the words: "Deadly Potential". Following then was a long discourse on what was contained in the sample. Not only did their findings agree with Marsha Robinson's but they were also able to provide the missing information on element "X". Their analysis corroborated the CoMed/5 and U3/G main ingredient content but in addition revealed was an element which could only be produced from a rare plant found only in the bush country of Australia called **Snake vine** (*Tinospora smilacina*). They were also able to conclude that this deadly mixture when combined with an acidic drink such as orange juice or some other type of fruit juice could produce harmful if not deadly results in an adolescent or pre-adolescent population. They projected it would be most devastating to the 11 through 15 age group.

Harvey Hamlin's, the presiding CIA officer at the table, jaw dropped as he read the document to the rest of the group. Tango just sat back and reveled in his I told you so attitude, but said nothing.

"I can't believe what I've just been handed" Harvey said. "This is so incredulous my hands are shaking thinking that this is a product being produced by one of our own pharmaceutical companies. Mr. Hernandez you were absolutely right. Now we need to act."

Back in New York on the same day, or more accurately the same night Ron Powers had been drugged at the quasi business meeting he was invited to attend. While he sat there with his eyes wide open he was mesmerized and unable to move. He could hear all that was going on and his mind was extremely active in recording it but all he could do was watch. As the tall man at the center of the proceedings resumed his presentation he advised the gathering that in just a few moments he expected the appearance of the supreme leader - Satan, the devil who would allay their fears about the war in Europe. He would lay out for them the new strategy to complete the product test marketing in the US and how he would arrange to have it reach the foreign markets.

The exuberance of the attendees at first was exhibited by their mirth through raised voices of approval. Then through anticipation of the appearance of their worship idol a new aura was created in the room and the jovial mood became more serious. Suddenly the candles began to flicker and finally went out. In the darkness no one moved or even uttered a word while they all waited patiently. Seconds later just as quickly as the candles were snuffed out, they were relit and a new entity appeared in the room. Standing behind the long table in the center of the room was a figure that appeared to be half man and half ferocious animal. The eyes were blazing with an intense glow as if burning with flame, the hands had elongated fingers and they were pointing at the proposed new initiate. There was dead silence for a moment and then it spoke.

The voice was harsh and raspy but distinctively powerful as it commanded the tall man to bring the initiate to him. Ron Powers was removed from his seat and escorted to the front of the room to stand before the beast. Cognizant of all that was happening to him, Ron was like a two year old being led by adults and had no will to resist. Standing before the beast he cowered as it stood over him. The eyes of the beast seemed to penetrate deeply into his very soul and Ron wondered why his sword of protection was not working. As the beast started to mumble words he couldn't understand Ron watched as the tall man took his hand and raised it. The beast then instructed the tall man to cut Ron's finger so the blood ritual could be conducted. Before the act could be carried out, the beast felt something. It backed away from the table and pointed to something below the seat where Ron had been sitting.

Herb Crandall who was still seated at the table was commanded to bring forward the briefcase that was under Ron's chair. Herb went to pick it up, but quickly recoiled when he felt a charge run through his body as if an electrical current had shocked him. The beast saw this and raged at Herb telling him to try again. Then it chastised him for allowing what was inside the case to be brought into the room. Herb made another attempt to lift the case and take it to the beast, but the same result occurred. Shivering from the second shock, Herb asked for assistance from one of the other men at the table who eagerly rose to assist, but as soon as he touched the case he experienced the same result.

The beast enraged by the ineptitude of his subjects took it upon himself to get the briefcase. The thing appeared to float right through the long table as it approached Herb. Arriving at Herb's table it pushed him aside and bent down to retrieve the case. Suddenly a loud noise was heard as the alarm clock inside the case sounded at a decibel level that was irritating to the whole assembly.

Briiing, briiing briiing, the clock sounded and the spell was broken. Even from inside the briefcase, which had been left beside the bed, the alarm was loud enough to awaken him. Ron reached over and silenced it then lay back down staring at the ceiling of his own bedroom as the sunlight of a new day peered through his window. He was having an extremely hard time trying to remember how he got home or even when. The last thing he could remember vividly was standing in front of what appeared to be the devil as he was about to be subjected to some kind of blood ritual. Then he remembered that before he left for work yesterday something inside him said put the alarm clock inside his briefcase alongside the Bible and take it with him to the meeting. Could this have been the fulfillment of the prophecy that the man in the lobby told him about the clock? How many more of these strange things were going to happen to him he pondered?

He couldn't remember getting home, but since he was still in his clothes he knew he must have had help because he never would have gone to bed like that.

Staggering as he got to his feet he felt a little woozy as if he had a hangover, but he couldn't remember having anything to drink. Then it struck him. At the meeting he was given something to toast with and that must have been it. But then he thought why was I the only one to react like that when everyone drank from the same pitcher? It wasn't until much later that Ron learned all the members of the cult had been conditioned against the effects of the drug. Having more questions than answers he walked to the bathroom to get some relief.

Trying to put the pieces together of what happened last night he reviewed step by step from the time he went to meet Herb Crandall and they went to dinner to the time he arrived at the meeting. He remembered entering the dark building and going down into a huge room dimly lit by candlelight. He remembered also that Herb had announced he was being promoted to a new position and now he wondered if it was really true. From that point on things, except for the sudden entry of the beast, were not clear as if now he felt he had been dreaming. However, as he sat down to eat breakfast, his recollection of the alarm clock came to mind and he reveled at the possibility there really was some kind of blessing associated with it.

Most of the things that happened early last night he remembered, but was still stumped at the missing time span and now he needed to focus on what was to happen tomorrow. He knew he had to attend Rev. Devereaux's second installment in his sermon series and he was anxious to hear what it would cover. Since so many of the things he was witnessing now first-hand seemed to relate to things Doc had already told him in his series overview, he was eager to absorb all that he could. It was like he was playing catch up for all the time he lost in growing up ignorant of the truth.

It was only 9:30 AM so he, even as much as he wanted to, hesitated calling Mimi. But he wanted just as soon as possible to tell her all about last night and get her input. His attention was drawn away from that thought as he watched more news on television coming on about the happenings over in Europe. The more he listened to reports about the turmoil over there and then reflected on what was happening here at home, the more aware he became of how much evil was in the world no matter on which side of the big oceans you resided. He listened for a while longer then drifted off to sleep on his couch as the news just kept getting worse and his spirit was darkened.

When he woke up again it was 11:30 and he felt refreshed. Even though it had only been a couple of hours he had enjoyed a deep sleep during which his subconscious resolved some of the issues he was concerned about. He now recalled how he got home and was a little closer to filling in the gaps in time. It was Herb Crandall who had deposited him in his bed after bringing him home in a cab. However, the big missing piece for him now was how much of what he recalled really happened and how much of it was his dreaming after he got home. Now he was ready to call Mimi.

"Hello."

"Good morning Mimi this is Ron how you doin'?"

"Good morning Mr. Powers, I'm fine. I was just thinking about you. How did it go last night?"

"Well I'm not sure 'cause I'm having trouble remembering the whole night. The parts that I do remember are so weird none of it makes any sense. Listen rather than try to tell you everything over the phone what are you doing today?"

"I don't have anything special planned but I do need to run out and pick up a few things from the supermarket. Why, are you coming over?"

"Yes I'd really like to so I can sit down and tell you the whole story. What time are you going out?"

"What time is it now?"

"It's about eleven forty-five."

"Okay then why don't you plan on getting here around three O'clock. I should be finished and back by then."

"That sounds good, I'll see you then. How's my buddy?"

"He's just fine. You were right, he woke up the next morning and no one would have ever known he had that close call. He's staying with his cousin this weekend and I'll get him back tomorrow after church. You can see him then. Are you going to church with me?"

"You bet I am, after all that I've seen lately, I don't want to miss a single segment of "Doc's" series. I can't wait to get to part four and see what the end's going to be."

"You know you sound like some scripture out of the good book, have you been reading it?"

"No, haven't reached that point yet, but I'm sure starting to believe in what Doc said about it being a forecaster of future events. Well, I won't hold you up any longer, I'll see you at three. "

"Alright, see you then."

We hung up and I looked out the window. It was such a beautiful day, I decided to go walking just to get some fresh air and clear the cob webs from my brain. Whatever it was they put in that drink I was given it sure has a lasting effect. With the few hours I had before heading to Mimi's place it seemed like a good idea to stop by the local barbershop get a haircut and see what's being discussed. This was a place where all the solutions the world would ever need were available right there if any of the powers in charge would care to stop by and listen. I was directed to this shop by one of the tenants in my building who said that he had received some very useful tips just by coming in and listening.

As usual by the time I got in there the place was already crowded and standing room only was available. If I didn't have so much time to kill, I think I would have passed on waiting. Saturday was the particular day that most of the men and boys in the neighborhood would go in for a trim. Not only were the men getting haircuts but many came to find out what the number was that hit the previous day. Discussions around the chairs would run the gamut from sports events, to local politics, to world events and of course religious facts and myths. Today the topic, when I arrived, was who was Jesus and was he a pacifist or a warrior and was he coming back or not. Those who argued he was a warrior would bring up the temple event where He turned over the tables of the money changers and threw them out. Those who argued He was a pacifist quoted scripture saying his ideology was to turn the other cheek. These debates would go on for some time or until one or more of the participants got his trim and left, and then a new topic with another set of debaters would start. I hesitated to get involved in that discussion due to my lack of scriptural knowledge, but I always found it fascinating that the one who argued the loudest, I would find out later, was usually wrong about his statements.

On the subject of Jesus coming back to claim His position as King of Kings and Lord of Lords, there were more than enough naysayers in there who said ``that dude ain't comin' back nowhere." It was amazing that the barbers who did the cutting were usually silent in these debates and chose to not take one side or the other. I guess it was good diplomacy to keep all of their customers coming back, but I often wondered how they could not take a position on such an important subject. By the time it came for me to sit in the chair the conclusion, as far as it went before the loudest participant was ready to leave, was that this world was coming to an end soon and "there ain't nobody gonna stop that." He left and the discussion shifted to sports as new voices began to speak up. I sat there enjoying the bantering of some fairly sage characters and also the unruly discipline of others but it never got to the point of any serious confrontation.

When I left the shop, I reflected on what had been said about whether Jesus was coming back. In Doc's sermon series overview I remember him saying something about it, but at that point I was suffering from information overload and didn't process all he was revealing. Now the idea that my lack of Biblical knowledge didn't afford me the opportunity to participate in the debate made me want to attend Doc's whole lecture series even more. I tried to relate what the barbershop conclusions about the end of the world and Doc's perspective were but somehow there didn't seem to be any logical connection between the two. Maybe it was time for me to do as Mimi suggested, open the book and see for myself. By the time I got home it was almost time to go to her place so I grabbed a light lunch then took a shower.

#######

It was not usual for Detective Callahan to be working in his office on a Saturday, but today he was there anxiously trying to wrap up his conclusions on the Anthony Oliver murder case. After his intense interrogation of Ivan yesterday along with some of his colleagues, facts that had not been revealed before were now clear. The suspect's full name was Ivan Fiorini and he had enough prior arrests and convictions that if he had one more he would not be seeing the outside of prison walls for the rest of his life. This fact when presented to him loosened his tongue quite a bit and he became extremely cooperative in giving names of others involved. It didn't take too long before the name Herb Crandall came up and Peter Callahan sat back in his chair with a smile on his face. It was all coming together now. Brent Woodley did the shooting to kill Oliver and Ivan caused the accident to kill Woodley to keep him from exposing members of Canon and his occult group. By disfiguring Woodley it was hoped that the body would not be able to be identified. The only thing missing now was solid evidence on the connection with the occult group which the detective suspected as being terrorists. He continued to pump Ivan for details on that end, but strangely Ivan refused to divulge any more concerning that matter. It appeared that he was more afraid of what could happen to him by the thing that had the real power, than the wrath of any Herb Crandall or anyone else at Canon Enterprises.

As he wrote the finishing touches on his summary report for the Captain to review before submitting it to the next level of judiciary proceedings, there wasn't much he could put in there to address the terrorist piece. So he skipped over it by alluding to that segment as being part of a continuing open investigation. Satisfied that he had done his job, he put the file back in a secured drawer in the records room, packed up and went home to enjoy the rest of his weekend.

#######

When I arrived at Mimi's place that afternoon I ran into my old friend the doorman, Brad. He looked at me and we exchanged tongue in cheek pleasantries as he guided me into the lobby. I asked him if he had been on vacation since I hadn't seen him around lately and he just smiled and ignored my question. The desk receptionist called Mrs. Robinson and I was directed to the elevators. Once on the floor I paused as I had become accustomed to doing lately since I've been coming here. The sound of silence was back to its normal state so I kept moving toward her door.

"Hi, you're a little early aren't you?"

"Yeah, but I just couldn't wait to see you."

She smiled as she invited me in and told me to have a seat in the living room and she would be right there. On my way to my favorite seat on that comfortable sofa I had to admire the view. When you looked out the large window from here it was like you were standing on top of the world and it was at your command. How I wished that were the case. While I was still admiring the view she came in.

"Beautiful isn't it?

"Yes it is and you are fortunate to have it."

"Fortunate? I don't consider it fortunate when I think about all I had to go through to get it. The view, the car, the money - I would trade it all in to have what I lost back. But let's not get into that again, you know how I feel. Let's talk about you. What happened last night?"

"Mimi you won't believe what I saw. I don't remember all of it myself because at some point I must have blacked out. The next thing I remember is waking up in my own bed this morning and don't know how I got there."

"Were you drinking?"

"The only thing I had to drink was a glass of something they gave me to toast and celebrate the announcement of the new product. Whatever was in the drink, it only affected me and nobody else. It was really strange because the beverage was poured from one pitcher that everybody drank from. I saw a lot of our co-workers there besides Herb Crandall who brought me. In the crowd were Leonard Jablonski, Reggie Codey, your Lab 1 chemist, and even Milton Jenkovitch. Whatever we believed before about them being involved in some kind of conspiracy that meeting just proved we were right.

After dinner Herb took me to this old tenement building down on the Lower East Side and I remember going down a long dark flight of stairs into a room lit only by candlelight. There was a brief presentation by one of the guests and then I thought I heard Herb introducing me as the next executive manager for the company. I'm not sure about that part because then I was starting to feel the effects of the drink. Shortly after that I'm almost certain they went through some kind of ritual, because then I think I actually saw the devil appear. It spoke to me and then chastised Herb for bringing me there with the object I had. In my briefcase I had the Bible your sister gave me so I believe it was referring to that. Anyway after that I felt like I was floating on a cloud somewhere and then I woke up in my bed."

"Wow, sounds like you had quite a night. You say it spoke to you. What did it say?"

"At first it sounded like it was inviting me to join with them, and then it picked up on the contents of my briefcase and that was the end of my initiation. I don't think I was accepted as a member."

She laughed and said: "Aren't you glad of that?"

"You know what bothers me the most is that Herb Crandall actually believed that I would be interested in becoming one of them in order to get promoted. I'm surprised they let me go home unharmed after seeing what I did. At least I think I wasn't harmed other than that nasty drink they gave me that by the way brought on an awful headache this morning. It was like a hangover I haven't had in a long time."

"Do you feel anything other than a bad headache?"

"No. After I took some medication and laid back down for a while when I woke again I was fine. Why what do you think?"

"I don't know. We have to ask my sister about stuff like that. When you see her tomorrow tell her your story and listen to what she says. You feel okay now right? Would you like for me to fix you something to eat?"

"No, no I'm fine. As a matter of fact rather than you fix something why don't we go out and eat. That night when we were going to meet at the movies with Tango, rather than go all the way home I had dinner at the Peacock Palace. Do you know that the place changes over after working hours into a nice jazz nightclub? I ate there and it was great. Why don't I take you there? This time you can call it a date."

"Why Mr. Powers are you asking me out?"

"Yes I am and it's about time don't you think?"

"How can a girl refuse such an offer? It's still early though what time do they start the jazz show?"

"I don't know since it's a Saturday night, maybe they start earlier. Let me call down there and find out."

I called the restaurant and made reservations for 7:00 O'clock. They actually had two shows tonight one from 7 – 10 and the second one from 11 – 2. I thought we would be more comfortable with the first show since we had to get up early tomorrow. She agreed and we spent the next couple of hours watching a movie on television before she began getting dressed. By 6:30 she was ready and we left to go out.

We had a great time at dinner, enjoying the show and laughing and forgetting about our troubles. The food was good and the setting was romantic with just the right lighting. I looked at her and felt that whatever was developing between us was something genuine. There was no doubt in my mind that she was feeling the same way and that made it all the more an enjoyable evening. When the musicians announced they were playing their last number for this set, I almost wished that we could stay for the next one. However, as cozy as it was we both knew what we had to do tomorrow so we left.

When we got back to her place and parked the car in the garage. I looked at her and hesitated but then asked if I should come up. There was a long pause as we contemplated what I knew we were both thinking. Finally she said let's go. Once inside the apartment it almost felt like a repeat of the night when I brought her home from the party in my building. She was feeling good and so was I. We shed our coats and sat on the sofa for a few minutes reliving the night. At a pause in the conversation, with nothing more to say we looked at each other and then I kissed her and she responded. From there it was a short trip to the bedroom. And from there it was a shorter trip to a lasting paradise.

When I woke up the next morning it was 6:00 AM. I looked over at her and she was still fast asleep. I shook her gently and waited for her to open her eyes. When she did I told her I had to go home to change but would be back in time to go with her to church. She sleepily said okay and told me to take the car so I could get back soon. I did and drove home hoping there would be someplace to park around my building where I would not have to worry about the car still being there when I came back down. Fate favored me and I found one right in front of the building where some of the neighborhood idlers who I knew were already hanging out. I asked them to watch the car and for a few dollars I received a commitment.

I quickly went upstairs shaved and showered then sat down to a breakfast of toast and hot cereal. Not my usual Sunday morning feast but today was different. I wanted to get back to Mimi and then get over to the church to hear what Doc was going to say in the second installment of his sermon series. After I changed clothes I rushed back downstairs to check on the car. The gang that I had paid was no longer there but the car was – and just as I left it. I wondered how long had it been since they abandoned their post and did I just throw my money away. It didn't matter now because the transportation I needed was available and I was ready to go.

When I got back to Mimi's it was about 10:15 and when I had the desk call her she instructed them to tell me she was on the way down. She came down looking as radiant as I had ever seen her and I wondered if I had anything to do with that. It didn't matter because when she got in the car she asked me if I remembered how to get there and did I want to drive. The way she said it was so nonchalant as if last night never happened. I looked at her for a moment, a little puzzled but she didn't return my look. She just waited for my response. I said yes I think I remember and started to drive away. It seemed like there was some tension in the air but I couldn't understand why. We drove in silence until we reached the church. I wanted to ask her what was wrong, but I didn't hoping that after the service she might tell me.

Just like the last time the parking attendants directed us to a spot right near the front entrance and we got out and joined the others walking in. Also as before we were greeted by what seemed like the same people who saw us the last time and hugs were given all around. What was different this time was that one of the church ladies commented on me being with her again and I noticed the expression on Mimi's face when it was said. It was as if she was reacting to the comment like the woman had peeked into the bedroom last night and was inferring something. Mimi smiled a facetious smile and thanked the woman for her astute observation then took my hand and moved me into the sanctuary.

We were early just like the last time and the service had not yet officially started. Also like before the music interlude was coming from the group at the pulpit base.

The organist was very accomplished as were the other musicians accompanying him. Anyone entering the sanctuary had to be impressed with the skill set of these musicians as they displayed not only their artistic talents but also their dedication to the right rendering of each piece.

The service was again opened with the choir director entering the sanctuary and directing the congregation to stand as the choir prepared to march in. They came in singing a popular hymn of praise and the congregation joined in. After the choir was settled in the choir loft an associate minister gave the invocation. The rest of the service followed the order as was done at the last meeting. When it came time for Reverend Doctor Devereaux to enter and take command of the service, the mood of the congregation was more than ready to receive whatever message he had for them today.

His presence in the pulpit appeared holy and majestic and presented the image of someone who had been in touch with God. Even before he spoke his first words as he looked out over his people, the cries of hallelujah and praise God rang out. I looked around curiously to see whether the same number of people were here today as last week. There wasn't an empty seat in the house that I could spot. Then he began to speak.

"Good morning my brothers and sisters in the Lord. I greet you in His precious name once again and hope that you have had a blessed week. How many of you were here last week for the beginning of my sermon series?"

Almost every hand in the sanctuary went up.

"Hallelujah. I thank God for so many of you. For those who are coming now for the first time, I encourage you to get a copy of last week's tape and listen to it to hear the foundational message preached so you will be able to keep up with what's coming now and in the next few weeks. Amen?"

The crowd echoed Amen.

"Today we begin the second part of the series and I hope you've had a chance to reflect on what was said last week about the foundation of the world. As we examine the present and contemplate the future, it is always wise to study our history and look carefully at our past. But before I begin today's message let us turn to the Lord for His guidance.

Heavenly father, my lord and my God, once again we come into your presence and before your throne of grace to first say thank you one more time. Before we dare ask you for anything, we must acknowledge your goodness and your grace in allowing us to assemble here in your house one more time to give you praise. Thank you for waking us up this morning with the blood still flowing warm in our veins, thank you for providing all that we need in our time of need and most of all for directing our footsteps here so that we might hear a word from you and be blessed. Father we beseech you in the blessed name of your son Jesus that you would hide me behind the cross so that the people might see Him. Anoint these lips for preaching and strengthen me for the delivery of your message. I ask this blessing and guidance in the matchless name of Jesus the Christ. Amen.

Recall with me now brethren last week when we talked about how it all started. Remember when the Word first created this world it was filled with angels and all was well until the caretaker of the time, Lucifer decided he wanted to be like God. In fact he wanted to be God and rebelled from his role as the light bearer. He ultimately became Satin, the adversary, and the devil and was responsible for causing man to commit the first sin. From that point on down through the ages even to today man has chosen to disregard the instructions given to him while he sojourned in the paradise garden that had been provided for him today I want to look at the progression of sin and disobedience committed even by those who professed to love God. I'm sure you've read or heard the story about the Israelites who God designated as a chosen people to show the rest of the nations how to live by His standards. But because of their continued disobedience, even after the great flood, they were enslaved in Egypt for four hundred years before God sent help to free them. But even after their exodus to freedom they continued to rebel and as a consequence they wandered in the desert in search of the Promised Land for forty years.

Brothers and sisters read the end of Genesis and the Book of Exodus to understand that part of the story.

Even during this time of God's correction He didn't leave them or forsake them but provided all they would need in the wilderness and finally delivered them to the land that was prepared for them. Not without struggle, not without losing generations in the process but they finally reached the land that God had promised to give them. Keep in mind my brothers and sisters that it was God's love and compassion that was keeping them moving in a forward direction to carry out His plan for all mankind. Just look at where we are today and witness His love for He changes not. Had it not been for His compassion and patience the existence of mankind would have terminated after the great flood.

Now let us look briefly at all that happened in the days following their entry into the Promised Land. They were divinely helped in conquering lands that didn't belong to them, they were protected from dangers that were directed around them, they were allowed to increase in numbers and were blessed in more ways than they deserved. Even with all of that the people murmured against God and would not yield to His ways and follow His commands. Though He had laid down His laws in writing with the Ten Commandments, man still would not obey.

At this point I want to examine the role of three prominent men in the annals of Biblical history. Although there were many more during this period I've chosen to focus on these three because of their general familiarity to you. They each were chosen by God and loved God and were initially obedient to His word. But over the course of time each fell from grace because of their sin.

Please turn with me now to the book of First Samuel, Chapter 8 versus 1-22.

1. And it came to pass, when Samuel was old, that he made his sons judges over Israel. 2. Now the name of his firstborn was Joel, and the name of his second, Abiah:

they were judges in Beersheba. 3. And his sons walked not in his ways, but turned aside after lucre, and took bribes, and perverted judgment. 4. Then all the elders of Israel gathered themselves together, and came to Samuel unto Ramah, 5. and said unto him, Behold, thou art old, and thy sons walk not in thy ways: now make us a king to judge us like all the nations. 6. But the thing displeased Samuel, when they said, Give us a king to judge us. And Samuel prayed unto the Lord. 7. And the Lord said unto Samuel, Hearken unto the voice of the people in all that they say unto thee: for they have not rejected thee, but they have rejected me, that I should not reign over them. 8. According to all the works which they have done since the day that I brought them up out of Egypt even unto this day, wherewith they have forsaken me, and served other gods, so do they also unto thee. 9. Now therefore hearken unto their voice; howbeit yet protest solemnly unto them, and shew them the manner of the king that shall reign over them. 10. And Samuel told all the words of the Lord unto the people that asked of him a king. 11. And he said, this will be the manner of the king that shall reign over you; He will take your sons, and appoint them for himself, for his chariots. 12. And he will appoint him captains over thousands, and captains over fifties; and will set them to earn his ground, and to reap his harvest, and to make his instruments of war, and instruments of his chariots. 13. And he will take your daughters to be confectionaries, and to be cooks, and to be bakers. 14. And he will take your fields, and your vineyards, and your olive yards, even the best of them, and give them to his servants. 15. And he will take the tenth of your seed, and of your vineyards, and give to his officers, and to his servants. 16. And he will take your menservants, and maidservants, and your goodliest young men, and your asses, and put them to his work. 17. He will take the tenth of your sheep; and ye shall be his servants. 18. And ye shall cry out in that day because of your king which ye shall have chosen you; and the Lord will not hear you in that day. 19. Nevertheless the people refused to obey the voice of Samuel, and they said, Nay, but we will have a king over us. 20. That we also may be like all the nations, and that our king may judge us, and go out before us, and fight our battles. 21. And Samuel heard all the words of the people, and he rehearsed them in the ears of the Lord. 22. And the Lord said to Samuel, Hearken unto their voice, and make them a king. And Samuel said unto the men of Israel, Go ye every man unto his city.

So you see the people no longer wanted to be led by God, but clamored for a king to lead them. And Samuel, God's prophet of the time prayed to the Lord asking for help on how to deal with the people and God directed him to choose a king. But before the king's name was given to Samuel, God told him what having a king would be like and what the consequences would be. Even having been forewarned, the people still wanted a king and God directed Samuel to choose one. The man chosen to be the first king of Israel was Saul and he was God's choice. But over a period of time he too fell into disfavor because of his disobedience. Saul had been given many military victories in the settling of the Promised Land and was aided in all that he did. But despite the many military victories, Saul performed a ritual war sacrifice without the help of a priest effectively ignoring God. That was the first offense. Then later when Samuel sent him to fight the Amalekites, who were an enemy to the people, and instructed him, as God commanded, to destroy them completely and leave nothing alive, Saul decided to spare the ruler of the Amalekites and saved the best portion of their flocks hoping to present them as sacrifices to God. This was the second offense. God was not looking for his sacrifice but for his obedience. Then to cap his offenses against God, Saul consults with a medium prior to a battle with the Philistines, also an enemy of the people, and asks her to bring up Samuel who was dead so he could ask for his guidance. God had already said that this practice was forbidden. And so God had enough of Saul and his reign as king of Israel was doomed and he had to be replaced.

This brings us to the second character in the unfolding drama. David, the young shepherd boy replaced Saul. Now David was a favorite of God. For God said that he was a man after His own heart. But even David who had won God's approval also became disobedient. David's saving grace however was, even though he was complicit in a murder, committed adultery and numbered the people in a census when he was told not to, would always repent and beg God's forgiveness. His genuine sincerity in repentance gained God's favor and he was allowed to remain king for forty years even to the time of his death.

Following David in the line of kings was his son Solomon, who took over when David got old. Now

Solomon was given great wisdom and wealth by God after he prayed for help in leading the people. He led the nation for forty years just like his father. Solomon was the son of Bath Sheba who was the same woman David had committed adultery with. Like his father, Solomon started out with true devotion to God but in his maturing years turned away and did things that were disobedient. He did things like marrying pagan women and worshipping their gods, he oppressed his own people with high taxes and heavy burdens and finally his heart turned completely away from Jehovah, the one true God.

But even in spite of all this, from Saul to David to Solomon the line of kings continued just as it was in God's plan as told to Abraham in the beginning. Although unbeknownst to them each man though he had problems following God's instructions was being divinely directed toward a prophetic destiny. I tell you this brethren so that you can see from days of old even the leadership of nations was not always true followers of God. Under the misdirected leadership of Solomon things got to the point when his disobedience displeased God so much that he was told the nation of Israel would be divided and except for the promise God had made to his father David it would have been done during Solomon's days. Because of that promise the division of Israel did not occur until Solomon's son Rehoboam became king and then the nation did indeed become divided into the nations of Israel and Judah.

The division of the nation impacted the development of each faction for the next several hundred years. Even though the people who were still of one heritage, the twelve tribes of Israel, were now separated, they began developing along different paths. God had already revealed that the ultimate leader would come through the tribe of Judah. But to the Israelites through their kings, who turned them away from the one true God, they were not mindful of this revelation and the stage was being set for tragedy. We will get into this a little deeper in the next series segment but for now let's just leave it at that.

Now let us review what has happened in the world up to this point. Since the time of Adam's rejection of God's rules in the garden and the first couple committing the first sin, under the sway of Satin man continued in his disobedience even at the highest levels of government. The line of kings for both the nations of Israel and Judah took them through several generations of leaders some who were more willing to obey God than others. But the bottom line through it all, God's plan to make a way for man's redemption was being directed even if man was not aware, through the family of Judah the son of Jacob whose name was now changed to Israel.

I guess by now you're sitting there saying just what does all this have to do with me today. My brothers and sisters we are living in a time that is the culmination of all of man's past sins and the compounding of his continued disobedience to the laws that God set down for man to live by. It has been told through all of the generations that a repeat of the dictates that were set forth in the Books of Leviticus and Deuteronomy that if you live by these laws then you shall have peace and prosperity, but if you disobey them than the reverse of the blessings shall befall you. Man has not followed what was set forth in those books and he has not given himself to follow the laws. The time is fast approaching when there will no longer be a time for repentance but the call for action must happen now if we are to avert the disaster that is going to fall down on us.

I tell you the truth here today. You must believe that the time is coming soon and very soon when there will not be a place that you will be able to hide from the wrath of God. The time is coming when you shall no longer be able to disavow any knowledge of His laws. For he will set them in each heart and in each mind that His way is the only way to live if you want to have life and have it more abundantly.

The formula for living is very simple. If you live by His commandments and His statues then you shall have a good life, but if you do not then the reverse will be true. It has taken man many thousands of years to come to this point of realization, but the period of grace under which we have been living is quickly coming to an end and we shall no longer know the peace and comfort that we have known in the past. The devil is alive today and he is busy destroying all that he may devour. He comes to you in sheep's clothing and professes to be one who promises the good life for you but in reality what he will provide is misery and death to all who follow him.

You will see in the coming days something that will transpire through one of your major corporations. They are going to release a new drug into the community that will attempt to destroy all of your young people. This is the devil's method of getting the next generation out of the way so that he won't have to deal with the development of their young minds which are becoming superior to yours. He will not have to confront their new imaginations on how to live together. This is the future that could be if you teach them the right way to live. But you as their parents have not followed the right way to live your selves so therefore your teaching is flawed.

Time is not on your side any longer. For he who has not learned the way of the truth, at this point is subject to a rude awakening very soon. There are some who are sitting among you today, who still do not believe what is about to happen in this world. Even though you are beginning to see each and every day all of the strife torn nations across the oceans warring with each other, do not think for one minute that you are going to be immune to these wars. They will be coming to you just as they are over there. The leader that is being thrust upon the people there is the one who will make it possible for those armies to come across the waters and make war in your backyards. The rise of the one who they are calling the promised one, is none other than the son of disobedience the man of perdition.

You must recognize him now in all of his forms or it will soon be too late. Join with me now brethren. Come and give your heart to Jesus for he is the only one who can save you from what is going to be the most devastating time of your lives. The trials and tribulations that are about to be foisted on this world will be such that the world has never seen before. And as it has already been spelled out in the Book of Mathew that if Jesus does not return to stop the devastation, then there will be nothing left of the species called human or mankind to carry on.

The choice is yours. Just as in the very beginning, man has always been given the freedom to choose how he would live. Unfortunately too many of us and our forefathers have made the wrong choices and that's why we suffer today. Don't let another day go by in which you are putting off making the right decision. Don't let the time slip away from you and have regrets when it is too late.

Won't you come? Give the deacons your hand and give God your heart. You won't regret it and one day you will see that it will save your life. Come to Jesus now. Today He is your savior tomorrow He will be your judge. The doors of the church are open, let not your heart be troubled further when there can be new hope in your life. Won't you come?

As Doc closed his sermon and invitation all those who had listened to his warnings began to walk down the aisles. I sensed that there was something happening in the sanctuary that was affecting everybody. I could feel some type of presence in the house that was moving even me. I couldn't explain it but the feeling was so overwhelming that in my most inner self I had the urge to get up and join with those who were moving forward to take a deacon's hand. I looked at Mimi, she looked back at me and she must have sensed the struggle I was having in trying to make a decision for she squeezed my hand and nodded her head. The smile she gave made me realize that this was what she wanted also and that everything was alright. The next thing I knew I was making my way past the others in the row trying to get to the aisle.

As I walked down the aisle it seemed to me like I was taking the first step in that proverbial journey of a thousand miles. In my mind I knew that I should have done this a long time ago but even now all of the reasons why I didn't flashed before me. As a youngster, I was given the opportunity on many occasions to make this decision but I was never forced to. Though I was coerced to attend church when we got there and it came time for the welcome invitations to be extended my parents were not ones who would push me to make it. Now I don't know whether I wish they had or whether I am thankful that they didn't and allowed me to come to this point on my own. Maybe it was something that was also a part of my destiny that was being directed for me just as Doc said about the line of Judah.

After I went through the formality of providing answers to the questions posed by the deacons and then being received by Doc's smiling face, it was announced to the congregation who the new people were and how they were coming to join the church. Then I returned to my seat feeling a new sense of being. I don't know how to describe it, but it was a feeling that I had never had before. Mimi was smiling as I took my seat and her sister and the boys who were sitting behind us were too. Midge reached out and touched my shoulder and several of the congregants around us did also. It was a wonderful feeling.

When the service was over Mimi, Jerry, her sister and her kids met again in the lobby and just as before discussed what was to happen for the rest of the day. This time however, it was different; they all agreed that they wanted to celebrate my decision. In a way I felt like I was a kid again going to my birthday party. After a few minutes of back and forth with suggestions, it was decided that we would go to Midge's house and she would cook something special for me. She also said it would be good because she wanted to hear more about that meeting I attended. So it was, we piled into the two cars and were off to her house. When we got there I had to take a minute before I got out of the car as I looked at the house. I was a little stunned and surprised and had to gather myself because it seemed like I had been here before when I knew that I never have. But the feeling was so intense it was like I had already seen this place so vividly in a dream.

Chapter 12
"Look Back-Move Forward"

Just before the meeting on Friday ended, Harvey Hamlin went out to talk with his secretary. The findings that had just been presented to him by the Washington chemists had him so shaken he could hardly think straight. He told her to arrange a meeting with the FBI Director, the National Security Advisor, the US Attorney General and the Vice President as soon as she could make it happen. He further advised her to use as fuel for the urgency that this was a matter of a threat to the national security and should be given the highest priority. The thought that a major chemical company in his beloved United States was preparing to wreak havoc on the nation was more than he could stomach. She wrote down his exact instructions and told him she would start right away and get back to him. Harvey returned to the room where Tango Hernandez and the other CIA officials were waiting. He told them about his plan and advised each to gather all the data they had on the case and wait for his call because he was going to initiate some action against not only Canon Enterprises but also the two directors here in the city.

The group was anxious to know just how he planned to proceed, but he would only tell them that for right now he was going to host a meeting and get input from the right people. He had an action plan in mind but he didn't want to divulge his strategy until he had run it by them. Then he complimented Tango and the rest of his team on their dedication to finding all this out and he hoped that the plan he had in mind would be implemented in time to stop the drug from getting into the wrong hands. Tango thanked him and at the risk of being pushy he asked if he could know what the plan was. Harvey just responded by telling him to be patient a little longer and he would hear all about it when the meeting took place. Conceding that they weren't going to hear any more from their leader right now the group got up and dispersed to their own offices to wait for his call.

Tango was both excited and apprehensive at the same time about what was going to happen. Once he left the meeting room he thought about calling Ron to let him know what progress was being made but then he decided it would be better for him to wait until he heard the whole plan than to give out bits and pieces and not be able to answer the questions he was sure Ron was going to ask. And so he resigned himself to sit in his office and review everything that he had learned about the case while waiting to be paged. The rest of the day went by and he heard nothing from his leader so he left the office and went home thinking that nothing else was going to happen at least until Monday anyway.

#######

The beautiful weekend ended and Ron was having some trepidation about going into work today. He knew he had to face Herb Crandall sometime and he was sure that he was going to run into Leonard Jablonski at some point during the course of the day but he was unsure just how he was going to react. His first thought was to quickly get into his office and go over once again what he believed had happened at the Friday night meeting then prepare himself either for a call from Mr. Crandall or perhaps even a surprise visit from Leonard. Either way he knew he had to be ready for whatever they were going to confront him with. His idea of the future of this scenario regarding the introduction of the drug to the world beginning right here at home, was really beginning to lay heavy on his heart and he didn't know which way it was going to turn out. In any event he had to do something but the question was what? More and more he was feeling like he was caught between the proverbial rock and a hard place but his desire to crawl out from under both was driving him. He moved from one thought to another in his mind and rehashing the meeting was not getting him anywhere because there was too much of a time gap between when he arrived there and when he woke up the next morning.

Once in his office he had gotten by his first perceived hurdle, that of running into Jablonski. So he said to himself it must be a good sign for the rest of the day. However, it wasn't long before the phone rang and it was the dreaded call he feared.

"Hello, Ron Powers here."

"Hi Ron this is Herb Crandall, how are you?"

"Oh hi Mr. Crandall. I'm fine now but I guess I made somewhat of a fool out of myself on Friday. I don't even remember all that happened. Was I that bad?"

"No, no not at all you just seemed to take ill at the strangest time just before I was going to introduce you to the one that could do something special for you. Whatever you had at the Shanghai restaurant must not have agreed with you."

"Yes maybe you're right. But what exactly happened?"

"Well like I said we got into the meeting fine and the initial presentations were given then it was my turn to give mine when I noticed that you were not looking too well at the table so before I got up to talk I went over and asked if you were feeling alright. Before I could even finish asking you began to convulse and I thought you were going to pass out. The rest of the people at the table told me to take you out to the bathroom and place a wet cloth on your neck. What kind of remedy this was supposed to be I don't know but it seemed to work long enough for you to briefly recover and come back to the table.

It wasn't more than a few more minutes after you returned and I had just begun to deliver my speech before you became ill again. This time the consensus of the group was that you may be in need of some medical attention and I was asked to take you home. Although you appeared to be quite sick you wouldn't leave until you retrieved your briefcase and hung onto it while I took you up stairs. What was in it that was so important anyway? One of the other staffers would have brought it to you today."

"I'm really sorry and I still don't know what came over me. All I remember is waking up in bed Saturday morning with my clothes still on. As far as the briefcase goes, I just didn't want to leave it there. There was one thing that I seem to remember while I was at the meeting though. It seemed like I heard you saying something about me being promoted. Was I dreaming that or did I really hear it?"

"You really were having a bad bout of something. I know we had talked about that happening in the future but nothing was said that night. Are you okay now?"

"Yes. I guess I was just wishing for it. No matter, I'm fine now and ready to get back to work. "

"That's good I'm glad to hear it. I just wanted to check in with you and see what you remembered. I'll be in touch and we'll talk again about how we can get you into position for career advancement."

They hung up but when Herb Crandall mentioned he wanted to see what Ron remembered this triggered the thought for Ron that he was just probing to see whether there was any recollection of the night's events. Now more than ever he was convinced of the conspiracy that was underway at Canon. Having dealt with Mr. Crandall he was now ready to take on anything that Leonard Jablonski might have to say. He wasn't anxious to be the first one to initiate the confrontation but he knew that it would be better to get it over with sooner than later. So he decided to casually walk over to the area of Leonard's office and perhaps he might run into him without having to go into it.

His timing couldn't have been more perfect for as soon as he got near his office out he came headed for the elevator. With a slight look of surprise Leonard acknowledged him and started to speak.

"Well look what the dog brought in. I thought you'd be out taking a sick day. You looked pretty bad Friday but I see you managed to survive. I hope you're not contagious. Today is too big a day for me to have to deal with anything you have. What are you doing around here were you coming to see me again?"

"Funny you should ask that because actually I was. I just wanted to follow up on that conversation we had about Maria Sanchez and see how you resolved it."

"Well if you must know, I didn't have to resolve anything. Maria has resigned on her own volition. It seems that her mother has become seriously ill back in her home country, I believe she said the Dominican Republic and she was flying back there today to be with her. Isn't that strange?"

"Yeah I bet you thought it real strange. Did you have anything to do with making her mother sick?"

"Come now Mr. Powers your imagination is really going to be the death of you. The way you looked on Friday I thought it might be happening then."

It wasn't so much what he said as the way he said it that sent a chill down my spine as I watched him walk away looking back over his shoulder and smiling at me. Hearing what he said about Maria resigning abruptly and leaving the country made me wonder just how far reaching was the power of this cult and who could they affect when they needed to. I followed behind him down to production to see what was going on.

Today was the day that the new product was being rolled out. They had given it a name and I had to admit the marketing people had done a very creative job in applying a hook that was sure to get it some attention on the market shelves. The new drug was labeled "Candoo" and it was being marketed as an energy booster for the young adult population. It was especially aimed at those adolescents who were participating in sports. I got to the production area only to find where the product was being manufactured had been cordoned off with new walls that appeared to have been installed over night and only certain employees were being admitted inside. I went to the front entrance and showed my identification but was told that it was not cleared to get me in.

After being denied access to production I turned and headed for the labs. I wasn't sure what I was going to do when I got there but I knew I had to see if Marsha knew anything about what was going on. When I got there I stood outside the door and looked in as I usually did but it seemed like everyone in there was running around like it was a panic fire drill. I didn't know whether to wait and see what the hubbub was about or just barge in and ask. It didn't take long before my question was answered and Martin came running out into the hallway. He saw me and stopped for just a moment to hurriedly tell me that the chemists in his lab were trying to find a way to stop production of this deadly drug. The news of the product announcement along with the news that Marsha and Martin had revealed to them about the drug was causing a panic.

Even those who were fairly new employees knew that the reputation of the company for making excellent wonder drugs over many years would be at stake and possibly cost them their careers if what they were being told by Marsha and Martin is true. Feeling powerless to do anything about it, they had formed as a group to walk out if they couldn't stop production. There was division in the group however, because the senior chemists wouldn't believe the story and wanted to see for themselves. I continued to stand by the door hoping that Marsha who was right in the middle of things explaining that she was the one who had done an analysis on a sample taken from Lab 1 and she could corroborate the news. Not much work was being done in her lab as the group huddled around Marsha peppering her with questions and comments.

Finally when she turned briefly away from the group she saw me at the door and broke away long enough to come out.

"Can you believe what's happening in there?"

"Yes I see it. Where was Martin going in such a hurry?"

"He was going to try and get into production to see if he could reason with Jablonski."

"Reason with him? The man is being directed by something he can't control so reason is not something he's going to listen to. We need some high-powered help here. I'm going to go call Tango and see if he's been able to convince anybody in Washington to come to the rescue. What are you going to do?"

"There's not much I can do except continue to try and keep the peace inside there and hope that we can continue to work. Call me if you reach Tango and let me know what his status is."

"Okay I'll do that. See you later."

I left there and went back to my office. It was still early in the day but I knew from all the excitement that was in the air all around the building that this announcement and roll out was going to be something big. On every monitor in the hallways a product ad was being touted as the new wonder drug that would revolutionize the sports world for young adults. I couldn't help but wonder how this deception could be so pervasive and how all the people were buying into the hype. Again I had to give credit to the marketing department because they had done a magnificent job and had thus far duped a great many people into even allowing the product to get out the door. Somehow, just as it had been told to me by Doc it was painfully clear now that the deception being perpetrated on the nation was the work of none other than the master deceiver who is known for telling "The Big Lie."

#######

At police headquarters after the confession of Ivan Fiorini and his implication of some of the big wheels at Canon a task force had been formed to go down there and make arrests. However, when the Mayor got wind of what was about to happen he immediately stepped in and put a halt to the move. His first inclination was to gather more information on exactly what the police had that would allow them to do what he heard they were planning. Secondly because of who was involved and how much this major corporation had been an annual big contributor to the city's coffers he was not ready to be the one to cut off the funding. He called for a conference with the police department's top brass and he wanted to know all that they did. The meeting was scheduled for this afternoon in his office.

Two O'clock came and at the emergency meeting called by the Mayor, some of the city's top administrators in the legal department and a few of the city council members along with the Mayor sat around the big table in his conference room.

"Okay Jerry let's get this meeting underway. Will you please tell me what's to this rumor I've been hearing about you planning to arrest some of the top guys down there at Canon Enterprises. Have you lost your mind? They are perhaps our biggest revenue producers," the Mayor said.

Gerald O'Malley, the chief of police, knew he was on the spot but in light of all the evidence that had been collected by Detective Sergeant Peter Callahan and the taped confession of Ivan Fiorini he felt compelled to carry out what he believed would be the conclusion to a case that had been hanging around for some time without resolution. He prefaced his statement by clearing his throat for several minutes to allow himself time to gather his thoughts. The Mayor looked at him hard as if to say come on man get on with it and then he finally spoke.

"Mr. Mayor do you remember sometime ago there was a shooting of one of the managers from the Canon Enterprises location downtown that resulted in death?"

"Yes, yes certainly man go on."

"Since that murder my department has been diligently seeking the perpetrator without much success until recently. The case has been highlighted in the press ever since and we've been getting a lot of negative publicity for not finding and arresting someone. No arrests were made not because we had a lot to work with but because the killer fled the state and no one knew his whereabouts. Only recently through the persistence of our own Sergeant Callahan and the cooperation of another officer from Pennsylvania have we learned enough to pin down who the killer was. The killer was also a Canon employee but it goes deeper than that. After he killed the manager in the Peacock Palace restaurant he was also murdered in a vicious skiing incident up in the Pocono Mountains. He was killed to cover up something going on inside of Canon that we are just finding out about.

The murder of the manager, Anthony Oliver was committed to shut him up about what was happening at Canon. The second murder of, Brent Woodley, the one who shot and killed Oliver, was committed to cover up for the first one. Last week almost by accident we uncovered Woodley's murderer and he has confessed not only to that crime but has also revealed some things involving people at the highest levels inside Canon."

"This confessor's testimony which you're about to make the arrests based on, do you believe he's reliable?"

"He's a two time convicted felon and with the plea deal we offered him, he would be a fool to lie to us."

"I don't like it Jerry. No I don't like it one bit. This guy is as you say a two-time loser already and he's just trying to save his butt from permanent residency in our guesthouse. No I don't like it. Now I want you to call off your troops until I've had time to mull this over. I realize you and your people have been under the media scrutiny, I've shared some of that with you, but we're going to look even worse if this thing at Canon turns out to be different from what you're being told by someone who I can't put my trust in. I'll get back to you in the next few days and let you know my decision."

The chief just stared at the Mayor for a minute or two then looked around the room to see if he was going to get some support, but seeing none he was not inclined to disobey the command. He got up, as did the others in the room and they all departed with the status of business as usual continuing within the walls of Canon Enterprises.

All around the plant Canon employees were excited about what was happening. Except for the people who were directly involved in the production few knew just how deadly the product they were making could be. Even those who were working on the production line only had enough information to allow them to monitor the quality and to insure that the quantity that was expected to be shipped out by the end of the day was guaranteed. Those walking around in the halls, with the exception of the lab chemists, were paying much attention to the TV monitors as even the news media was touting the roll out of the new revolutionary drug.

As the day began to move by quickly I had not heard anything from Tango and I was becoming concerned about whether he was making any headway in getting help from the powers that be in his office. I tried calling him a few times but all I got was his answering machine.

Thinking he must be tied up sitting in his colleague's offices, I decided to allow perhaps another hour before trying him again. Meanwhile all I could do was continue my own work and hope that perhaps through some divine intervention, this deadly product would not leave this site.

In another part of the plant, Leonard Jablonski and some of the others in his group were laughing and joking about how they had against all odds brought the project they were entrusted with to fruition. To them it was a triumph and only the beginning of what they had been told by their ultimate leader would be a rewarding venture for all. From all that I could remember in that meeting I attended I marveled at how they could get excited knowing that what they were doing would be damaging to so many young people and destructive to future generations of this country. Could their greed be that egregious? Could their hearts be that cold and non-feeling? I guess the answer to the question only God really knows.

#######

In Washington the meeting that had been hastily called by the CIA Director was now underway. The only thing that had been changed was the location. At the insistence of the Vice-President the meeting was being held in his office conference room. Seated around the large conference table were the heads of the organizations that were responsible for the security of the nation. They included the National Security Advisor, the Attorney General, the FBI Director, the Secretary of Defense as well as the CIA Director, the Vice-President and Tango Hernandez. Prior to the VP calling the meeting to order the buzz around the table was centered on a great deal of hearsay even though they all had been given a brief on Friday stating the nature of the impromptu session.

"Gentlemen let this meeting come to order" the VP announced as he banged his gavel on the table. "The matter that has been brought to my attention is of an urgent nature and it is in the best interest of the nation that we address the issue immediately. You have all been given some detail in your brief but I'm going to ask Mr. Hamlin from the CIA department to elaborate on what has been provided. Mr. Hamlin would you tell us what's going on here?"

"Thank you Mr. Vice-President I would be glad to. Gentlemen what you have in your hands references something that I have not seen in all the years that I've been in office. Here we have right here in this country a major pharmaceutical company producing a product that is so potentially dangerous to the youth of this nation that I am still finding it hard to believe that it is actually happening. On Friday a team of some of our best scientific minds, chemists to be exact, brought the results of their analysis of a sample of the product to my office. What they discovered was a drug that is being produced by this company that could inflict severe respiratory damage, even deadly harm to individuals under the age of twenty. The sample was taken directly from one of the labs at Canon Enterprises in New York City recently and was flown here last week for their review. Barring the loss of some integrity of the sample due to the time lapse since its capture, there was still enough potency in it to cause major concern. Gentlemen we need to act quickly to thwart the distribution of this product and allow it to get into the hands of our youth."

"Mr. Hamlin may I ask how your office came about getting hold of the sample, I'm sure the chemists at Canon didn't volunteer it?" the Attorney General asked.

"Certainly, it is my understanding that the sample was obtained by a quality control manager and an in house chemist who was suspicious of the nature of the drug retrieving it."

"When you say retrieve it, just what do you mean exactly? Did they steal it, was it given to one of them? Just how did they retrieve it?"

"Mr. Attorney General given the nature of what's at stake here does it really matter how they obtained it?"

"Yes unfortunately for you it does Mr. Hamlin. The fact that Canon is one of the biggest pharmaceutical product producers in this country with a very large staff of legal scholars, it could very well have major implications on how the sample was retrieved. If it was obtained by some illegal means then the sample cannot be used to initiate any type of action against the company. What will have to happen to validate the sample is that a warrant must be issued to legally obtain it."

Tango sat there frozen with disbelief at what he was hearing. He could not bring himself to believe that these bastions of security of the nation were doing everything but dealing with maintaining it. He knew that while they sat their debating the legality of how a sample of a deadly product was obtained, the very product they were arguing over was about to be introduced into the marketplace and distributed to the people they were sworn to protect. Harvey Hamlin observed tango's obvious discomfort, but there was nothing either man could do.

Another twenty minutes was spent on debating the fact that the sample had been misappropriated and risk the legal entanglement that would ensue from initiating an action against Canon, or use the risk to national security as the basis for initiating some type of action was finally ended when the Attorney General prevailed. The meeting ended with a call being made to the New York State Attorney General to begin the legal procedure and obtain a search warrant to be served on Canon Enterprises in due course to appropriate the suspect sample.

Both Harvey and Tango left the meeting fuming at the final outcome and were outraged at how the government process worked when it came to what really was a matter of national security. Tango almost literally ran to a telephone to call Ron and let him know how the government had failed to do anything to stop what he was sure was happening right now.

"Canon Enterprises – this is Ron Powers."

"Ron this is Tango glad I caught you. Are you sitting down?"

"Yes why?"

"Because what I'm about to say will floor you."

"Man after all I've been seeing here lately, I don't think much else could surprise me, but go ahead try and shock me."

"Well I took the sample you gave me to the Bureau's chemical team and they ran their analysis. They concurred with your Ms. Robinson's findings and they were also able to identify that missing element that she couldn't. There was no doubt about it and they reported the dangers in their conclusions. When the report was given over to my supervisor he immediately called a high level conference with the powers that be here in D.C. It took the weekend to get them all together but the meeting was held just a little while ago. All was going along fine and I thought the outcome was going to be that my guys would fly up there on the next available flight and put an immediate halt to any further movement on that new drug. However, the next thing I know this legal wizard who has the title of Attorney General throws a very large wrench into the works and everything comes to a halt. I couldn't believe what I was hearing and neither could my boss but the bottom line at the end of the meeting was that nothing is going to be done for at least a few more days. I mean nothing from my office or anyone else's here. It is now up to your state Attorney General."

"Tango, I hear you but I don't have a clue about what you're saying. What do you mean it's up to the Attorney General here? What does he have to do with anything?"

"Well it's like this my friend, it seems the fact that you obtained the sample in a less then exemplary manner and not according to the proper confiscation procedures has caused some concern within the AG's thinking. He is more concerned with any possible legal repercussions from Canon if we barge in there and mess up their production schedule than he is about the safety of the youth of this country. His charge was that your AG must issue a warrant in order to make obtaining the sample legal. Therefore, the ball is now in his court and will probably sit there for the next few days."

"Tango I'm sitting down but still I feel light headed. You mean to tell me nothing is going to be done to stop this action here until a warrant gets prepared and served?"

"Bingo, you win the prize."

"I can't just sit here and do nothing. I've got to figure out a way to stop it."

"Ron don't do anything rash that you'll regret later. Give me a chance to look into some options. I'm going to explore some other possible avenues and hope I have success. I'll call you again just as soon as I have some good news to report. In the meantime, don't get yourself like Oliver, I'm not there to protect you."

"Thanks Tango I hear you but I'll be alright. I'll talk to you again soon I hope. Bye."

"Goodbye for now."

After hanging up with Tango I sat there in disbelief for another few minutes trying not to let what I heard really get to me. But there was no denying that the news had really upset me and I didn't have any idea what I could do but I just knew I had to do something. In all that was happening it seemed like there was no justification to what could be considered as the ultimate evil plot coming to fruition. I know that there were still many things that I didn't understand in all that Doc was teaching through his first two series sermons, but one thing kept going through my mind. Wasn't good supposed to triumph over evil and aren't the good people supposed to win? From all that I could see in this current scenario the appearance that evil was going to prevail really had to be the antithesis of the good versus evil hypothesis.

As the thoughts continued to spin around in my head about what to do, I got up and headed once again down to production. I wasn't sure what I was going to do once I got there but I figured I had to see just how far they had progressed in getting the product out the door. As I walked toward the elevator I could again hear the chorus of cheers coming from various sections in the office applauding the news reports streaming through the monitors that the announcement of the new wonder drug was taking the stock market by storm and Canon's stock was receiving a healthy boost. Since I too had a vested interest in Canon stock I was a little embarrassed in feeling some joy in thinking my investment was prospering, but the thought didn't last long when I considered the reason. When I got down to the loading docks and witnessed the third of three long trailers pulling away with full loads of the product, an intense feeling of helplessness came over me. To make matters even more disheartening, I looked through the window of the shipping office and could see standing there staring back at me with a wide mocking grin, Leonard Jablonski.

There was nothing else I could do at this point and it truly seemed like the good guys had lost. I considered going over to Marsha's lab and see how she was faring but I couldn't imagine she was doing any better in convincing her cohorts about the dangers in the product so I decided to call it a day and prepared to go home. I didn't want to talk to anybody, didn't even feel like tidying up my office as I usually did. I just wanted to get out of there and go home.

#######

As Reverend Devereaux sat in his study preparing the third segment of the four part series, the thoughts going through his mind reflected on something he had preached in his last sermon. Now that he too had heard the news being blasted almost every fifteen minutes over the airways about this new wonder drug coming out of Canon Enterprises, he marveled at how the prophecy that had been given to him was coming to pass. His recollection of the conversation that Mimi and I had with him regarding what we suspected going on at Canon had not been lost. After our conversation, he took it to the Lord in prayer and received His divine prophecy.

The more he heard in the reports how this wonder drug was going to help young people, the more he focused on what we had told him. So now even before the breaking news had come on the airways he had already alerted his flock that something harmful was going to come out of one of the major chemical corporations in the world that would be directed at the nation's youth. He was not going to harp on the accuracy of his prophecy but he was going to reemphasize to his people the need to be mindful of just how what had been accepted before as good was now turning toward evil. Even those who had been considered doing well for mankind were now subject to doing harm.

He knew what he wanted to say to get what he believed was God's message across, but he was unsure which scriptures would best provide a clear understanding. He looked up at the ceiling as if the answer was there and then he fell down on his knees and began to pray.

"Heavenly father, my Lord and my God be not far from me in this time of need. It is by your grace and your mercy that I have come this far by faith. I have been your faithful servant and have tried to deliver all that you have given me to guide your people. Now Lord give me the words I need to teach your people what they need to know. Give me the words that will lift them up and make them understand. Your words, not my words have carried me through times of distress before so I know that you hear me when I call. Hear me now O Lord for I am a willing servant and ready to deliver what you give me to say. I ask this guidance and the blessing in the majestic and precious name of Jesus the Christ. Amen!"

Slowly he got up from his kneeling position and sat at his desk and waited. It was his custom after offering the sacrifice of praise and being prayerful that he would just pause and wait for his answer. Knowing there was no set time for how long it would take for God to respond to his petition, he was prepared to just sit and wait however long it could take. Sometimes God would move in a hurry at other times it could take awhile. But this time he could hardly contain himself when suddenly a shiver ran through his body almost immediately after he got up. Never before had he received such a quick response to his prayers. The feeling was so overwhelming that he had to brace himself to contain the movement of the Holy Spirit as it ran through him.

The revelations coming through to him were so profound that he had to take a deep breath to relax himself as the thoughts began to fill his head. The scriptures were coming so rapidly it was difficult for him to keep up as they filled him. He tried to write them down on paper but they were coming too fast. Then he fumbled in his desk drawer to find the portable tape recorder he kept there. He got it out and quickly set it up to record his voice. The thoughts were still running rampantly in his brain so even his speech was hampered until he cried out for mercy. And then it happened like the speed of a 78 RPM record had been adjusted to run at 45 RPMs and he began receiving the messages at a rate he could handle.

It became clear now that the next segment in the series should deal with preparing for the Kingdom of God and the scriptures to use should come from several Bible passages. In his earlier sermons, Doc had already laid down the foundation by teaching on the origin of sin and how man had compounded his sinful ways through the centuries even at the highest levels of government. Now he was challenged to make the people understand that as the time grew closer when the second coming of Jesus would occur there was going to be severe trials and tribulations throughout the world. He reminded them of the wars that were taking place even right now in Europe were but a small harbinger of what was to come. He knew he had to warn them and instruct them on what to do, but before they could understand to do anything, he had to teach about the duality in prophecy to make it real. He must tell them about things that were prophesied to happen in one era were also referring to things that were going to also happen in yet another time to come. The time to come or as the Bible states, the latter days, is right now – the last days of the age.

To begin Doc was prompted to quote from the Book of Amos:

"Surely the Sovereign Lord does nothing without revealing his plans to his servants the prophets." (Amos 3:7 NIV)

"Brothers and sisters that quote may be found in the Book of Amos in the old testament. And so as God did with Moses on the mountain when He gave him His ten general laws and then inspired him to write the books of Leviticus and Deuteronomy in which he laid out specific instructions for the people let us look at how he used other prophets to also warn the people. In Leviticus and Deuteronomy it was spelled out for them in detail the consequences of choosing evil over good. Down through the ages the prophets were told about things that were going to happen even before they did.

Let us reflect for a moment on how that impacts us today. When we think about what we're experiencing now during these last and evil days, we must again go back to ancient times to look at the source. When the people, who had been chosen as the role model to show the world how to live according to God's plan, repeatedly ignored the prophets' warnings and disobeyed, they paid the penalty. See how Amos's instruction was brought to bear now by looking at an example of a prophet's warning. I want to use, as the example a name that I'm sure is familiar to most of you. The name is Elijah.

Now Elijah, as you know, was one of the most prominent prophets of the Old Testament and was used by God to warn Ahab, the king of Israel at that time. Elijah was charged to warn Ahab about the pending peril for the Nation of Israel if he did not turn from his idolatrous ways and encouraging the people to do wrong by doing the same. Ahab was not alone in his folly for he was married to a woman named Jezebel, I'm sure you've heard that name somewhere, who was even more idolatrous than her mate. Together they caused the nation of Israel to sin mightily against God. Now Elijah warned them that if they didn't repent and turn back to God, then there would be no more rain. Ahab ignored the warning continuously and so the rains ceased. For three years there was no rain and the drought continued so that the land became so dry that the grass was parched. All Israel was filled with fear. Then God told Elijah to return to Ahab.

When Elijah was brought before Ahab by Obadiah a man in charge of the king's palace who also happened to be a believer Ahab accused Elijah of being the troubler of Israel. Elijah responded telling the king that it was him who troubled Israel because of his worship of false gods and misleading the people. Then Elijah proposed a challenge to determine who the real God was and make it so the people of the nation could decide for themselves who they should worship.

Ahab then sent word throughout the land for all of his prophets and the people to assemble on Mount Carmel and take up the challenge. Elijah then went before the people and said: `How long will you waiver between two opinions? If the Lord is God, follow him; but if Baal is God, follow him'. But the people said nothing.

(1 King:18:21 NIV)

Then Elijah said to them "I am the only one of the Lord's prophet's left, but Baal has four hundred and fifty prophets. Get two bulls for us. Let them choose one for themselves, and let them cut it into pieces and put it on the wood but not set fire to it. I will prepare the other bull and put it on the wood but not set fire to it. Then you call on the name of your god, and I will call on the name of the Lord. The god who answers by fire – is God." (1 Kings 18: 22-24 NIV)

And so the challenge was underway and the prophets did as Elijah said. Then they called on the name of Baal from morning till noon.

"O Baal, answer us" they shouted. But there was no answer and they danced around the altar they made. At noon since there was no visible response, Elijah began to taunt them.

"Surely he is a god! Perhaps he is deep in thought, or busy, or traveling. Maybe he is sleeping and must be awakened." (1 Kings 18:27 NIV)

So they shouted louder, cut themselves until the blood flowed all around but with no results. Finally Elijah became impatient and called together all the people. Then he began his demonstration of the power of his God. He took twelve stones, one for each of the tribes of Israel and built an altar in the name of the Lord. Then he dug a trench around the altar, cut and prepared his bull for the offering, placed his wood on it and filled the trench with four buckets of water. He even doused the wood and the bull with water making sure that everything was soaking wet. Then when all was ready for the sacrifice Elijah prayed.

"O Lord, God of Abraham, Isaac and Israel, let it be known today that you are God in Israel and that I am your servant and have done all these things at your command. Answer me, O Lord answer me, so these people will know that you, O Lord, are God, and that you are turning their hearts back again." (1 Kings 18:36-37)

When he finished his prayer the fire of the Lord fell from heaven and burned up the sacrifice, the wood, the stones and the soil, and also licked up the water in the trench. What a mighty God we serve. All the prophets of Baal and the people saw this, fell to the ground and cried "The Lord - He is God! The Lord He is God!"

After this magnificent display of awesome power the people and even Ahab repented and turned back to God, but not for long. Shortly, thereafter Ahab and Jezebel returned to their wicked ways until once again Elijah was called by God to warn him a second time. But this time it was a warning of death, not only to him but to his wife also. And so it happened Syrians killed Ahab in battle and dogs devoured Jezebel by the wall of Jezreel.

As for the people from this time forward under the reigns of several kings in Israel, they vacillated, just as they had done during the days when judges governed the land, between worshipping God and continued idolatry. Even when Elijah was taken away by God, the prophet's mantle fell to Elisha, his protégé' to continue to provide warnings to the kings.

Finally, after so many repeated warnings and admonishments through the years the time came when God grew tired of Israel's idolatrous ways and sins against Him. Then around 722 B.C. Shalmaneser, the king of Assyria was allowed to invade the entire land, march against Samaria the capitol city lay siege and capture it. The Israelites were then deported to Assyria because they had angered the Lord so much that He removed them from His presence and gave them into the hands of plunderers.

From that time until about the middle of the twentieth century, in 1948 to be exact, the nation of Israel ceased to exist and the ten tribes that formed the nation were scattered and became known as the Lost Tribes of Israel. The other two remaining tribes from the twelve sons of Jacob remained in the land of Judah, which had separated from the one nation of Israel, presently exempted from the harsh punishment. Judah for the moment had escaped the wrath of God, but it would not be long before the folly of Israel would overtake that land also. But theirs is another story that we will cover in the next segment of this series.

You heard me say at the beginning of this sermon that the prophecies were dual in nature. Well let's talk about that for a moment. Now that you have heard how the nation of Israel came to be non-existent because of their continued reluctance to obey the dictates of God's laws, let's see what the duality means to us today. Even after His showing them favor in so many ways after delivering them from the land of their bondage in Egypt, they continued to rebel. He protected them from Pharaoh when their exodus was in peril, He provided food and water while they marched in the wilderness, in forty years their shoes didn't wear out and by day He went ahead of them in a pillar of cloud to guide them and by night a pillar of fire to give them light so they could travel by day or night. How much more could He have done to show them His love? Yet in all this they were still disobedient.

Now here is the duality. When Moses wrote the Books of Leviticus and Deuteronomy that we looked at in the last sermon, these instructions for living an abundant life were not just for that time long ago, but they were instructions for the end time that we are living in right now. The cause and effect relationships that were spelled out in those books represent principals that just as the laws of physics will never change so are they permanently established in our lives.

Although God sent many prophets to warn the people about the impending dangers for disobedience, their failure to grasp the significance of the warnings was to lead ultimately to their destruction as a people. It was not hard for them to accept the gifts that He provided, but it was hard for them to acknowledge that for every gift given there is an expected sacrifice that must be made. God didn't instruct them to feel He was to be ignored but they were to praise Him and worship Him and Him only. He told them early in their history "if my people, who are called by my name, will humble themselves and pray and seek my face and turn from their wicked ways, then will I hear from heaven and will heal their land." (2 Ch. 7:14 NIV)

The duality is this. Unless we change our ways we are headed for a repeat of yesterday's woes. But the corrective punishment will be so much greater this time because of our increased capacity to destroy whole nations with one blow, and so He will use what we have developed as His chastening rod.

Brothers and sisters what are we doing today? Have we learned any lessons from the past or have we just read this book as a history book and not a guide for right living. Just as the children of Israel failed to grasp what was being told to them by the prophets of old so are we continuing to ignore the teachings of those who have been called by God to deliver His message. Those who have been called to the ministry have an obligation to deliver the messages that they receive from God and deliver them without wavering in their content. Now is the time when all God's people need to understand that what happened in ancient times will also happen in the very near future if we do not heed the instructions given in Leviticus and Deuteronomy.

Just as Elijah spoke truth to power, so it is that truth must again be spoken to all those in power so that we will not repeat the same mistakes made by the kings of old and suffer the dire consequences of their actions. In today's scenario, the weapons that man has created that can cause mass destruction of such magnitude that not only would a nation cease to exist, but all of mankind would be obliterated from the earth. This is not a message of doom and gloom but a glimpse into the future according to what is already laid down in this book. The duality of the prophecies will again occur if we do not heed the warnings that have already been made abundantly clear.

It's not too late. Think about the message that I've given you today. Don't be part of the crowd that participates in the perpetuation of acts of disobedience. If you have not already accepted Jesus Christ as your savior and dedicated yourself to living according to His ways, then the time is now for you to step up and turn your life around. Don't be one of those who is waiting for proof of the impending crisis, because when it comes upon you by then it may be too late. Examine your ways, look deep within yourself and see what is keeping you from taking that next step of your future. Don't wait for the person next to you to step-up for their destiny is not the same as yours, what is waiting for them is not the same as what is waiting for you. To each man, woman and child God has given a special and unique assignment on his life, but you must act on what the Sprit is telling you, even right now.

Won't you come and give your hand to a deacon but give your heart to God. Won't you come? The doors of the church are open."

Reverend Devereaux spoke these last words into the tape recorder as he ended what he felt was God's message for the people in this segment. He turned off the recorder and leaned back in his chair feeling somewhat exhausted from the heavy input of the Holy Spirit into his psyche. He was feeling both elated at having been used once again as an agent of the Almighty, but he was also experiencing some depression as he absorbed what was being reaffirmed in him what he already suspected. He had read and studied the scriptures many times over from Genesis to Revelation, but never before had he felt such a strong feeling that what had been given to him tonight about the timing of things was so imminent.

Chapter 13
"Decisions"

It was now only a couple of weeks before the biggest holiday of the year would be celebrated. The Autumnal season had quietly relinquished its position in the Zodiac and the frost in the air attested to the change. People were scurrying around making last minute selections and changes to what they originally thought would be a good idea for a gift. All around the city and the suburbs the mood was generally a festive one except for those who were part of what had taken place recently at Canon Enterprises.

The dreaded new drug that Ronald Powers and Marsha Robinson had so desperately tried to prevent from hitting the market place had shipped and from all reports sales were skyrocketing. The feeble attempt by the Washington bureaucrats to implement a halting action had been delayed by legal protocols that were still being reviewed by the NY state Attorney General's office. Reverend Devereaux had delivered his third sermon in his provocative series about the Kingdom of God and attendance was booming. On the worldwide front the wars in Europe were still raging, but the rise to power of the man now being hailed as a possible savior and a peacemaker was gaining acceptance. And so it was there was much going on with the global state of affairs.

At Canon Enterprises, Milton Jenkovitch, Herbert Crandall, Leonard Jablonski and the rest of their cult were basking in the success of their mission and were just waiting to reap the promised rewards for their service. However, even though the stock reports displayed a significant increase in the value of Canon shares there was something that was about to affect it just waiting on the horizon.

All around the nation young aspiring athletes were buying into the advertisement hype about the new product's benefits. Some even latched onto the catchy jingle and were singing:

"If I want to do my best,
this will help me pass the test.
Lift it up and drink it down,
Candoo will make me sound.
Candoo – Candoo"

In addition, the fact that the price had been set to promote sales by the case was going over extremely well with organized youth leagues, especially the non-profits who were always leery of costs. With the end of year basketball tournaments underway and every player looking for a winning edge, it was hard for anyone with knowledge of the downside of Candoo to get their voice heard. Even the managers and coaches were completely taken in. But soon all that glitters is not gold for them was going to become more than just an adage.

#######

Tango Hernandez came back to the Canon plant with a dire mission assigned to him by his supervisor. His task was to get to whoever he needed to talk to in the NYAG's office and find out where the holdup was in serving the search warrant for the sample on Canon Enterprises. Right now, though, he was sitting in Ron Power's office commiserating with him over their mutual frustration at not being able to keep Candoo from launching.

"Ron I just sat there in disbelief listening to those men debating the legal ramifications of taking immediate action against this company when they knew full well what was at stake concerning these kids. Unbelievable, unbelievable I kept saying to myself while looking at my boss hoping he might have something to say that could impact their decisions. But there was nothing he could say or do at that point."

"Yeah Tango I hear you. When you called and told me what happened I couldn't believe it either. The main thing now is the fact that those kids out there are being exposed to this killer drug and they don't even know it and we're playing legal beagle games. It's not right no matter how you look at it. What's next for you?"

"Well I have an appointment first thing in the morning with a deputy Attorney General, maybe I can convince him about the urgency of this situation and have him get someone to walk through serving whatever papers need to be served on Canon immediately."

"Good luck with that. Let me know right away how you make out okay?"

"Yeah okay Ron, I'll do that."

Tango got up and left.

No more than ten minutes after Tango left and my face was turned to the computer behind me, I heard someone at my door clearing their throat. I turned around and there was Marsha standing in it.

"Well this is a pleasant surprise I'm usually coming down to your place. Come on in and have a sit down."

"I can't stay long I just came to warn you about something I just heard.

"That sounds ominous so it can't be good. What did you hear?"

"Remember that night when you and Martin got the sample out of Lab 1?"

"Sure why do you ask?"

"Because I've been told that some pictures were taken of you and Martin entering the Lab. Did you see or hear anything like pictures being taken?"

"You know now that you mention it, when we first got in there through the vent there was a bright flash, maybe even more than one. We looked around to see where it came from but found nothing, especially nothing that looked like a camera. Since we were in there awhile and it didn't happen again, we didn't think anything of it. So you're saying we got our pictures taken by some hidden camera in there."

"That's exactly what I'm saying. From what I'm told they have you in the act. You will probably be getting a call from that Mr. Crandall in Human Resources soon."

"Yeah I can hardly wait. Who did you get your information from?"

"I got it from Martin but he was told by one of the chemist's who works in Lab 1 who says he's on our side."

"He must be feeling the pangs of guilt."

"Maybe so, but we need all the help we can get, especially now. What are you going to do?"

"There's nothing I can do until I hear from Crandall and see what he wants to do with me. He will probably use this as his bargaining chip to get me off the case again. I really don't think he'll charge me with anything and get the police involved. It would draw too much attention to what's going on here. But with him you never know."

"You may be right, but anyway I have to get back. I'll talk to you later or tonight. Call me."

"Okay I will call you tonight."

When she left I had the feeling that any minute now I was going to hear from Herbert Crandall. One hour went by then two and nothing. The anticipation was beginning to make me uncomfortable thinking that he might be plotting something that I would be totally unprepared for. So I got up and walked into the halls not particularly headed anywhere but I just had to get out of my office.

The halls no longer reverberated on the monitors with the repetitive ads blasting the merits of Candoo like it was on roll out day, but even now there was still a smattering of gossip about how the product was doing among the employees. Somehow though word had also circulated about the downside of the drug and there were some mixed feelings about what was really going on within the company. I didn't stop to participate with any group discussing the subject but I did linger at the elevator long enough to overhear someone comment on the product's risks. It wasn't clear from what was said just how much they knew, but the fact that the drug was being talked about in a negative light gave me some sense of hope.

Then I decided to go down to the production area to see if possibly anything had changed there, but upon arrival as far as I could tell the drug was still being mass-produced without any obstructions. Just like that the hope I felt moments ago disappeared and the reality of despair returned. I walked by the production entrance knowing that I would not be admitted inside but I wanted to try and look in anyway. There was no longer a guard at the door but a combination key lock had been installed and only certain people were given the numbers. Seeing this I turned around and headed back to my office.

When I got there the first thing I noticed was the message light on my phone blinking which gave me the feeling that I had missed the dreaded call. However, when I checked my messages, none were from him. I didn't know how to feel at that point. Should I be happy that he didn't call or should I be apprehensive thinking about what he may be scheming to do. I decided to take the high road and said Que Sera, Sera and went on with my work.

By four O'clock I still hadn't heard from Crandall. Until then I had managed to block the fact from my mind as I focused on my tasks for the day, but when I looked up at the clock and the time registered, the feeling of concern returned. Now try as I might to block the thought that he was plotting something sinister, my resistance waned and it was getting the best of me. When the phone rang, I don't know why I jumped because I was expecting it, but I guess because I was so deeply engaged thinking about Crandall's next move, the timing of the ring surprised me.

"Hello this is Powers."

"Hello Mr. Powers this is Diane Benson, Mr. Crandall's secretary. He asked me to call and tell you he wants to see you at 9:30 tomorrow morning in his office. Are you available?"

I hesitated answering just for a moment thinking to myself what would happen if I said no. Actually, that thought lasted maybe only a second or two before my rational mind took over.

"Certainly Ms. Benson I can be there at that time."

"Thank you I will let him know. Goodbye."

For the rest of the work day, the little time that was left, I was really just going through the motions pretending to be productive when in actuality my mind had left the office right after I spoke to Ms. Benson. When the clock finally showed an appropriate time for me to leave I packed up my tools put them away and left.

On the way home I couldn't help but notice amidst the hustle and bustle of those who seemed to have the wherewithal to buy things and were rushing in and out of the stores, there was a larger than usual number of those who were just out there panhandling. Maybe it was just my imagination and maybe it was because of the holiday season, but it seemed like on every block there were at least two or three looking for a handout. I was keenly aware that the economy wasn't thriving but to witness first-hand the dichotomy between the proverbial haves and have-nots added to my feelings of depression and that even during this supposedly joyous season there was no universal happiness.

When I arrived at Mr. Crandall's office the next day I was greeted by his secretary who said he would be with me in just a moment. I was a few minutes early so I sat down in his waiting area and picked up a company magazine showing on the front-page trucks leaving the loading docks with the highly touted new product. I just shook my head and wondered how this was all going to turn out. It was only a few minutes more when Ms. Benson called me and told me to go in.

"Come in Powers. Take a seat, I'll be just one more minute."

I sat down in the chair right in front of him and waited for him to finish typing something on his computer.

"There that does it. Well Mr. Powers I see you've been very busy again. I had hoped when we talked the very first time and agreed that you would curtail your investigative urges that we had a deal. From the looks of these pictures that is not the case. What possessed you to do something like this?

He handed me a set of pictures showing Martin and me not only coming out of the vent but in various spots in Lab 1. There was nothing I could say. The camera had done its job and the pictures clearly showed both of us.

"Mr. Crandall what do you expect me to say? You have all the evidence. If you're looking for an explanation I can give you one easily. We went there to get a sample of the product that you know is not a health aid but a possible killer drug."

"There goes that wild imagination again. What makes you think Candoo is a killer drug?

"Because I had the sample we got from that lab analyzed and the findings said so."

"Nonsense. I don't know what you did to your sample but your analysis was wrong. Anyway I didn't call you here to debate your reasons for illegally entering that lab, but to give you an ultimatum if you want to continue in the employ of Canon Enterprises."

His words kind of caught me by surprise. I was expecting he was going to tell me I was being terminated and my career at Canon was over.

"I'm not going to make this a police matter, which I certainly should, but I still believe you have potential with this company and I'm going to give you one more chance to prove yourself. I've drawn up a contract between an employee advisory group of your peers who have the responsibility for helping workers like yourself to stay in line, and you. Of course I will be a part of the group. If you elect not to sign it, then you will leave me no alternative but to recommend your immediate suspension and ultimate termination. I don't want you to decide right now. Why don't you take the rest of the day off think about it and give me your decision tomorrow morning."

"Sir may I look at the contract?"

"Sure."

He handed it to me and I turned to the last page to see who were the signatories. As I suspected all of the names I recognized were a part of the cult group. But there was one name at the very end that gave me a start.

It read Satanicus T. Diabolus that gave me a chill. I then looked at the first page and it laid out what appeared to be an employee improvement plan that would be evaluated in stages. On the surface it didn't look like anything ominous but I'm sure that somewhere in the body I would find things that would not be in my favor. I handed it back to him and said I would consider it and let him know tomorrow.

"Fine. That's it. Sleep on it and I'm sure you'll thank me in the morning."

"Okay."

I got up to leave and was headed out the door, but before I did I turned around quickly and I could have sworn that for a moment I saw two people in the room. There was something standing behind Crandall but it disappeared. I knew then I had to get out of there.

I walked out of the building and hailed a cab. Not wanting to go home just yet I told the cabbie to take me to the park. Inside Central Park I knew there were several areas where I could sit on a bench and reflect and clear my head. He drove me to a nice area still in mid-town and I got out. With the cold weather set in, it was not hard to find an empty bench so I sat down and began to look around. As I sat there looking at all that nature has to offer the first snowflakes began falling and the chill on my face was exhilarating.

I looked at the trees that just a few months ago were full of green leaves that filled the air with a beautiful fragrance. Then they turned to a rich array of magnificent colors that drew the attention of artists from around the world. Now the leaves were gone and only the branches where they resided remained. Then I looked at the ground as the first signs of winter appeared and the accumulating snowflakes covered it with whiteness. I marveled at how smoothly the seasons changed and presented such a different spectacular view in each phase. It reminded me of a scriptural passage I read recently:

When I consider Your heavens, the work of Your fingers,
The moon and the stars, which You have ordained,
What is man that You are mindful of him,
And the son of man that You visit him?
For you have made him a little lower
than the angels.
And You have crowned him with glory and honor.
You have made him to have dominion over the works of Your hands,
You have put all things under his feet,
All sheep and oxen-
Even the beasts of the field,
The birds of the air,
And the fish of the sea,
That pass through the paths of the seas,
O Lord, our Lord,
How excellent is Your name in all the earth.

(Psalm 8:3-9 NKJV)

Then I said to myself surely there must be a God somewhere who in His infinite wisdom designed a plan that coordinates each movement and directs the program to run.

But the more I thought about it the more confused I became wondering just how a God who could produce all this beauty could allow such evil people to get away with the diabolical schemes they do. I never read it but I've heard it said that God's ways are past man's finding out but the mysteries we encounter now will all be resolved one day. This may be true but I was seeking answers to questions that needed to be resolved right now.

#######

Tango entered the state house around 9:00 AM and made his way to the Deputy Attorney General's office he had an appointment with. Upon arrival at his destination he was quickly announced and told he could be received right away. Apparently, someone from Washington had already alerted his host regarding the urgency of his visit.

"Please come in Mr. Hernandez and have a seat" the DAG said.

"Thank you I'm glad you could see me right away."

"Yes, I've been expecting you. A Mr. Hamlin from your Washington office called earlier and advised me regarding the nature of your visit so I've already set the wheels in motion."

"Excuse me sir but did you say you set the wheels in motion only today after his call?"

"Yes that's right, is there a problem?"

"I'm sorry but I don't understand. I was in a meeting just last week during which the USAG made a call to this office requesting the warrant to be served immediately. Why is it that the action is just now being taken?"

"Last week you say? I'm just getting back from a week of vacation but there was nothing on my desk or on my phone to alert me about that. I just pulled the file this morning when Mr. Hamlin called. I don't know what happened but I will find out."

"Yeah that's great. When you do find out where the breakdown was I'd like to know too."

"I'll see what I can do about that. But I hope you realize that even if an attempt to serve the warrant is made today, it may not be accepted."

"What do you mean accepted?"

"Well from what I read in the file the grounds for issuing the warrant are rather shaky. The sample that is in question was obtained illegally to begin with which makes the probable cause on which the warrant was generated open to question. I don't believe Canon's lawyers will, if there's nothing to hide, but if they elect to challenge the probable cause, then the warrant will be withdrawn and a hearing scheduled. That could take a few days or maybe weeks."

Tango sat there again with the same stunned look on his face he had at last week's meeting. Even though he worked in an organization that had constant interaction with the law, he was having a difficult time processing the judicial rhetoric he was being given right now. To him somehow the equation that represented a critical life situation was not balancing. On one side was the life and death factor and on the other the jurisprudence weight which was tipping the balance toward that side.

His consternation was caused by his failure to grasp how jurisprudence could outweigh the value of life.

"So what now we just wait and see what happens, is that it?"

"Yes Mr. Hernandez that's about it. I will know sometime this afternoon whether the warrant was served or if there was a problem. If you leave me your contact number, I will call you as soon as I know."

"Thank you I'll look forward to hearing from you but I must tell you I am very disappointed in how this whole warrant service is playing out."

"I understand your frustration and I will do all that I can to expedite the matter but right now there's nothing more I can do."

Tango realized he was at a standstill as far as what more he could do so he said goodbye to the DAG and left his office.

#######

By the time I got home the numbness in my hands and feet told me I sat in the park too long. I managed to fix a cup of hot coffee and drank it down quickly. The warmth of the liquid felt good inside but it wasn't having much of an effect on either my hands or my feet. So I shed my clothes and crawled into bed after placing an extra blanket over the sheets hoping my own body heat would restore my limbs.

As I lay there listening to the radio and staring at the ceiling my earlier reflections in the park returned to me. That haunting question of why God would allow evil to prevail just wouldn't go away. Although I enjoyed immensely Doc's sermons over the last few weeks he had only identified and explained the origin and perpetuation of sin, but at this point even he had not answered my question. Maybe it would happen in his last segment I don't know, but right now for me it was still a mystery.

While I was still pondering the question, suddenly the music program on the radio was interrupted for a newsbreak.

"We interrupt this program to bring you breaking news from Europe. From reliable sources over there we have learned that just a few minutes ago a document was signed by the major combatants in the area agreeing on a peace treaty that will put an end to the current warfare. It is our understanding this new covenant was negotiated by Andolinka Petravitch. Mr. Petravitch you may recall from earlier reports is the man who has been a rising star for the last few months. His status as the new leader and administrator of the peace has been confirmed by the United Nations. That's all we have at this point. More information on these new proceedings will be passed on to you as we receive them. We now return you to your regularly scheduled programming."

Laying there listening to this latest news, I began to wonder was this the answer to my question. Was the timing of this report intended to alert me to the fact that God was not just passively standing by, but finally intervening and using a man to do good in an evil situation? If this was truly the case it gave me hope that what was being done over there could very well be done over here also. With that idea in mind I moved my thinking to what might be happening with Tango's visit to the State House. I thought about calling him, but right now my body was not ready to do anything but take a nap and get warm.

#######

Tango left the State House as disappointed as he had ever been while working on a case. The frustration level he was at far exceeded anything he could remember experiencing over his long career. He knew that he had no control over what was happening but he wanted to do something to help the cause anyway. His first inkling was to go back to the Canon plant and see if he could use his authority to demand access into the production area. He thought that perhaps if he could get in there he could cause some type of disruption that would at least halt production for a little while. It was not a great plan, in fact it wasn't a plan at all, but it was something.

When he arrived at the plant he didn't bother to stop by his office but went straight to his intended destination. At the production entrance door he encountered the new lock. Looking at the number of possible combinations that could be programmed into this type of lock, he knew wild guessing was out of the question if he wanted to get in via that method. His next option was to go directly to Leonard Jablonski's office and use his authority to try and intimidate him. To his dismay however, upon arriving at the office Leonard was not in it.

Tango asked his secretary where he was and she replied he had gone uptown to the headquarters and probably would not be back today. So far Tango's day was not going anywhere near the way he had planned for it to go and his frustration level was still on the rise. He then asked her if there was any way he could be reached because it was regarding an urgent matter. She answered only that he was meeting with the CEO and it was unlikely he would accept any calls. Tango's next question to her was who had the combination to the lock on the production entrance door. She hesitated for a moment then looked at him and answered - she didn't know. He looked back at her suspiciously, but what else could he do? So with that he was out of options for the moment and he left.

His next move was to go to the labs and talk to Marsha or Martin hoping they may have had some success with halting production. When he got there to his surprise the room was empty. There wasn't a single person in there. He thought it very strange so he went to the two adjacent labs to check. Again nothing - there was no one there either. He couldn't believe all the chemists were gone. Where could they all be? As he was about to leave the area, he met one of them coming from the opposite direction so he stopped him.

"Excuse me are you from one of these labs?"

"Yes - who are you?"

Tango started to show him his real ID but then thought better of it.

"I'm on special assignment here from Washington. Hernandez is my name."

"Oh you're the Mr. Hernandez everyone's talking about. I've heard of you."

"Good, then can you tell me where all your colleagues are?"

"I guess you haven't heard. There's a big meeting going on right now in the auditorium concerning our latest product release. I just came back to check on an experiment I have running. I'll be returning there in a few minutes."

"Can I get in that meeting?"

"I don't' know. Do you have lab clearance?"

"Who's running the meeting?"

"Edwin Kissinger, the Vice President of Consumer Products. Why? Do you know him?"

"Maybe. But I think he'll let me in."

The chemist continued on to his lab and Tango headed toward the auditorium.

Before going in he opened the door partially, stood outside and listened for a minute trying to get a sense of what was going on. There was no one guarding the door so walking in was not going to be a problem. Right now Mr. Kissinger was speaking and he was telling the group about all the rumors that were flying around about Candoo.

"Many of you here today have been hearing various comments about our new product Candoo. Let me assure you that none of the negative sayings have any basis in truth. Do not let your thinking be swayed by what you hear either inside or outside of this plant. I have invited Mr. Petory Sheoliter from our Board of Directors to come and speak to you just to emphasize the importance of your continuing to work together to produce this revolutionary product for the world. Don't allow dissension among you to mar the possibilities for significant company growth as a result of this new product's sales. Having said that let me bring on our esteemed board member."

When he finished talking Tango eased his way into the back of the room and sat down. He looked around to see if he could locate Marsha and Martin. It didn't take long before he spotted them sitting together right near the front. Mr. Sheoliter from the board got up to speak, but before he opened his mouth he performed a rather strange gesture. He stretched out his arms opened them wide and waved them over the room as if he were a Pope blessing his flock. Suddenly, Tango felt a sensation like something had touched him, but he wasn't sitting close to anyone. When he looked around the room he noticed the look on the faces of the audience had become as a group mesmerized by the speaker. He focused in on Marsha and Martin and they had been overtaken by the spell also. Then he listened to the words coming from the speaker.

Everything he heard he knew was a lie, but he felt compelled to accept it as truth. Inside he wanted to jump up and scream loudly protesting the speaker's words but he was constrained by a force he couldn't resist. He struggled mightily to overcome the force, but it was too strong so he just sat back and listened.

After about a half hour presentation the board member concluded his remarks and once again waved his arms over the crowd. Tango felt the force leaving him and his constraint was released, but now his impetus to challenge the speaker's veracity was all but gone. As soon as he could muster his strength he stood on his feet and quickly exited the room. Outside in the hallway he took a deep breath and felt his wrist for a pulse. Everything seemed to be normal, but he knew something had happened to him. Slowly he left the area and went to his office to try and assess what had just happened. Once inside he recalled something that Ron told him some time ago about supernatural demonic forces being at work here. Until now he had dismissed the idea as just Ron's overactive imagination. Now he wasn't so sure about that. Too many strange occurrences were happening almost simultaneously involving the plant not to give some credence to Ron's notions. Tango was beginning to accept it but even when he did his question was how do I confront it and win?

#######

Ron woke up from his nap about 1:30 PM and felt warm and refreshed. With all that had happened lately he was surprised that he was able to enter into a deep REM sleep and awaken with such a feeling of calm and repose. He was certainly aware that his problems had not gone away and there was a dilemma he had to face in the morning, but through it all he felt something inside of him that was giving him strength.

He got up and looked out his window at the newly fallen snow. How pristine and pure the grounds looked were the first thoughts that came to mind. But he knew in just a matter of hours the dirt of the world would overtake the purity and what started out as a thing of beauty would become something to be abhorred. How strange it was that he would think of this comparison. It reminded him of the first sermon he heard from Doc about the beginning of creation and how what started out to be a thing of beauty had been corrupted by evil. Then his thoughts turned to the beginning of Canon Enterprises could there be a fair comparison here also? Even though he had not been employed there for very long, from all that he read and heard about the company it had the reputation of producing some of the finest health products that had become staples in medicine cabinets throughout the world. When did the change come that introduced the evil element into their operations? The answer to that question he would probably never know but what he was sure of it did happen.

After his encounter with Herb Crandall Ron had a decision to make. Was he going to compromise his sense of right and wrong to keep his job or was he going to continue to expose the deadly product that was already in the hands of those who would become willing or unknowing parties to the evil plot. Why he was even hesitating about making the decision was also causing him some discomfort. He actually liked working for the company and had enjoyed it up until his first exposure to what was really going on behind the overt scenes. But was his employment worth the internal pain that he would cause himself if he continued to defy his moral convictions. Right now he needed a friend and a confidant he could bare his soul to and he knew whom he had to turn to.

He started getting ready for the trip to his office all the while hoping that the person he needed to see would be available. When he was ready he called Alex. Within fifteen minutes Alex was waiting for him outside. As usual the trip downtown covered the same route he was accustomed to traveling almost daily. But somehow this time something seemed to be different. Maybe it was because there was an overcast sky or maybe it was because he was witnessing what appeared to be more homeless people than ever before huddling together to escape the bite of the cold. He felt compassion for them, but then he laughed to himself thinking about the possibility that he may be joining them soon if Herb Crandall has his way.

Alex pulled up in front of the plant and Ron got out. He walked inside and displayed his badge to the lobby receptionist as he made his way to the elevators. There were very few people moving around on the first level and he thought that was unusual for this time of day. However, he didn't think long on it but kept his mind focused on whom he wanted to see and where he wanted to go. The only thing he was silently hoping for was that he wouldn't run into the one person he really didn't want to see right now. As it turned out he was spared that encounter and was able to get to the lab floor.

Coming out of the elevator he saw a number of chemists he recognized from previous meetings. They all seemed to be heading in the direction of Lab 1. He knew they all couldn't possibly be assigned to work in there, especially after all the controversy Marsha and Martin had raised about the work going on in there. When he reached Marsha's lab door he peered inside before entering as he usually did. She was in there but appeared to be engaged in a rather animated discussion with one of the other chemists. It wasn't hard to tell that the other chemist was disagreeing with her about whatever it was they were discussing. After a few more minutes Marsha disengaged and headed for the door.

When she rushed out she almost knocked Ron down as she pushed hard opening the door. It was easy to see she was so aggravated that whoever was on the other side of the door couldn't really have mattered much at that point. When she felt the resistance of the door as she pushed and then looked to see what caused it she saw Ron. Surprised for a moment her blank stare looking at him wasn't revealing what she was thinking one way or the other. Quickly, she excused herself and turned to walk away without saying anything more. Ron hurried after her and grabbed her arm as he turned her around.

"Well hello to you too."

She stopped then took a deep breath and exhaled before she spoke.

"Ron, I'm so sorry but now is not a good time to talk to me."

"Why, what's the matter?"

"I'm just getting so frustrated with what's going on around here I can' t take it anymore."

"Come on I can see you're upset let's go down to the cafeteria and get some coffee.

Maybe that will calm you down a bit and you can tell me what happened in there to set you off like this."

She agreed and we went. Once there I picked up two coffees while she found a place to sit down.

"Okay now what's happening?"

"Do you know about the meeting this morning?"

"No I just came to work a few minutes ago. What meeting you talking about?"

"Well this morning Mr. Kissinger, the Consumer Products VP, held a meeting to talk about Candoo. He started off telling everybody that the negative things being said about the product were false then he brought in this person from the Board of Directors to speak to only the chemists. You know who Kissinger is don't you?"

"Yeah I know who he is but I don't really know him. So what about him?"

"Well this Mr. Sheoliter or something like that from the board managed to convince everybody in the room, even me for the time being, that the Candoo product was the greatest thing since the discovery of fire. I can't explain how he did it, but while he was speaking, I was hearing his lies but they sounded so much like the truth that I found myself agreeing with him. It wasn't until after I returned to my lab that I realized I had been hypnotized or something and all the other chemists had been brought under the same spell. But the difference between me and the others, is that when I came back, I recovered my senses and realized I'd been had - they didn't. Did you see me arguing with that fool Roger in the lab"

"Yes I saw you and him talking rather excitedly."

"Excitedly – he made me so angry I was about to punch him because he was so hooked on what that board guy said he wanted to go down to Lab 1 and help them discover an accelerant to speed up the production of the product. And he wasn't the only chemist to want to do it. Can you believe that?"

"At this point I'm ready to believe anything. Before you go back in there and do something you may be sorry for later why don't we both call it quits for today and get out of here. Do you have school tonight?"

"No - and even if I did I think I would have to miss class today. Why do you ask?"

"You need to vent and I need to talk to you about something that happened to me today so why don't we get together and have a misery party."

This brought a smile to her face and then a giggle, as she seemed to relax.

"Yeah okay what do you have in mind?"

"Why don't I order some Chinese take-out and bring it over to your place and we can have a chop stick feast. How about what we had before does that sound good?"

"Yes that's fine and make sure you bring Jerry's favorite soy sauce. He'll be glad to see you again. What time are you coming?"

"How about 6:30 is that okay?"

"That's fine I'll see you then but I can't leave here now. I must go back in the lab and see if I can talk some sense into anybody still in there. Don't worry about me I'm okay now - I'll be fine. You go ahead and leave if you want to."

"I am going back home, but before I do that I want to stop by Tango's office and see how he made out today. I'll see you later."

We separated. She went back to her lab and I headed toward Tango's office. On the way I kept thinking about what Marsha said happened during the meeting. The way she described it was like the guy from the board had cast a spell over the whole room. I thought to myself could that be possible. Then I reflected on what had happened to me at the meeting I went to with Herb Crandall and I concluded that it certainly was and is possible.

When I arrived at Tango's office I found him sitting in his chair staring out the window. He didn't even seem to notice that I was standing in his doorway so I cleared my throat expecting him to at least acknowledge my existence. For several minutes I just stood there and observed him. He wasn't moving at all, just staring out the window. For a short time it appeared like he wasn't even breathing. I moved closer to him and touched his shoulder hoping to get some kind of reaction. He didn't jump or anything but slowly turned around and looked at me with a kind of blank stare. Not knowing what was wrong I started to shake him and calling out his name. He responded and the life in his eyes returned.

"Ron, Ron how long have you been here?" he said.

"I just got here and found you looking like a zombie. What's wrong?"

"I don't know but ever since I went to this science meeting earlier I've been feeling this weird sensation like I'm not in control of me anymore. It feels like something has taken over my senses but I can't imagine what it could be. Have you ever had that happen to you?"

"As a matter of fact yes it has. Sometime later I'll tell you all about it but right now let's talk about you. Tell me about the meeting - was it the same one that Marsha was in and some guy from the Board of Directors was speaking?"

"Yes I did see her there and that other chemist what's his name – Martin, he was there too. How did you know?"

"I just left Marsha and she told me some weird things were happening in there."

"Weird is right. I don't know what that guy did but he seemed to cast a spell over everyone in there. He had all the people believing everything he said. When I came out of there I felt like I had been hypnotized or something because I was wrestling with the truth that I know and the lies that he told and you know what?"

"What?"

"His lies were sounding believable. I'm still trying to get myself together and shake the cobwebs off my brain. Anyway, I do have some good news to tell you."

"That would be good to hear for a change. What is it?"

"I have a message on my telephone from the DAG I met with this morning telling me that the sample we were trying to get has been secured and is right now on its way to Washington to be analyzed. Maybe when the

D.C. powers see a sample legally obtained showing the same results that we found then we'll get some action to stop this. I should know something by the end of the day."

"That is good news - best I've heard today. Are you sure you're okay? I was about to leave and go back home because I've had quite a day myself."

"Yeah I'm fine now. There are some things I still need to do here and I will wait for that important phone call. I will let you know tomorrow what happened in Washington."

"Sounds great. I'll talk to you then."

I left Tango's office going home feeling a little better that at least one thing seemed to be going our way. The fact that a new sample had been sent to Washington to be analyzed should provide us with the action we need to get production of Candoo halted.

One thing was still bothering me. Both Tango and Marsha gave the same account of what happened at the meeting as far as a spell being cast over the audience. I began to wonder just how high up was the conspiracy. Was the whole Board of Directors part of the plot?

That night when I got to Marsha's place I went through the usual routine getting in. Once inside the apartment I unloaded the Chinese food and she started to set the table. Jerry was glad to see me and wanted to get me involved in another round of toy basketball massacre at my expense. However, mom intervened and reminded him that he had exams coming up next week and he needed to study. Disgruntled but obedient he went back to his room to wait until called for dinner. I looked at her and she looked back as if to say – what's more important his school work or you wanting to return to childhood playing games. I quickly yielded and went and sat down on the couch until she was ready.

"Jerry come on and eat." she hollered.

He came running out of his room and sat at the table. I got up and also took a seat at the table. The chair at the head still remained unoccupied as we each sat on either side. I had not earned the right yet to assume that position and I was okay with it. I knew that she was moving closer to me, but until such time that she pointed me in that direction, I was not going to push it.

"Are you going to say the blessing?" Jerry asked.

I looked at him still feeling somewhat embarrassed but I managed to stumble through what I thought was an adequate blessing. It was nothing that would have approached her father's words but it sufficed and they seemed to accept it as we dug into the plates.

After dinner and Jerry had gone back to finish his studies Mimi and I sat on the couch and began to rehash the day's events. She started out finishing her story about what happened at the meeting called specifically for the chemists. The man from the board who came in to speak to them had to be one of that cult we knew was operating inside Canon. What he did to cast a spell over the whole room was uncanny but effective. She went on to say that even she was brought under the spell for a time and everything that he was saying seemed to be the truth.

I told her that when I met with Tango he related the same experience. He was at the meeting and said he felt the same trauma. It wasn't until after he got back to his office that he was able to recover from what he felt was a hypnotic suggestion. We are at the point now where I think the ruler of darkness that has influenced this whole group is gearing up to enforce a final battle with those who would oppose him and he is not ready or willing to yield to anybody who might stand in his way. Believe me I think we are in for a serious battle that is escalating and I don't think we alone have the means to stop him.

She agreed but said that her father had the answer and he would be speaking on the final outcome of this whole situation in his next and final sermon in his series. While we were just beginning to get engaged in our recollection of today's events, Jerry came out and told his mother that he had finished studying and he felt he was ready to take his exams. She got up from the couch embraced him and told him that was great but now he should go to bed. Jerry heard her words but looked at me wondering if I was going to intervene and possibly ask to let him stay up a little longer so we could play his basketball game. I recognized his visceral plea but thought better than to comply with it, so I said nothing. Mimi started to escort him to his bedroom to put him in bed, but before they left I told him I would come over Saturday and we could play all day. His whole demeanor changed and a broad smile came over his face.

When she came out she said that he told her to tell me goodnight and was hoping that I could go with him to the basketball game on Friday night that his cousin was playing in. I told Mimi I wouldn't miss it and I would be happy to take him if she wasn't able to go. She told me she was planning on it and it would be a nice Friday night activity for all of us.

Then we got back to discussing events at Canon. I finished telling her about Tango's experience and how it related to what happened to her. It seems that we are collectively experiencing and entering into a climatic situation at Canon where not only has the product been delivered to the world but the effect that is intended to render the youth population null and void has been initiated. I said to her that Tango told me the sample that we were seeking to get from Canon had been yielded and the scientists in Washington were right now in possession of it and doing the analysis. My thoughts were that once they came up with the same conclusion that had been surfaced when you did your analysis, then the proper legal orders would be issued to force Canon to cease and desist from any further production of Candoo.

She was glad to hear that, but she also felt there might be something else at work here which might preclude that from happening. I questioned her about what she was saying and she explained it to me.

"My father has said many times that we are in a period right now where the "Ruler of this world" meaning Satan is aware that the coming Kingdom of God is about to happen and he has only a short time to complete his mission of destroying all of God's children, including us."

I wasn't quite ready to hear what she was saying and I asked her did she really believe that. She replied that she certainly believed it and if we are observant we would agree that when we look at all that's happening at Canon and also around the world how can we not believe it. When I thought about it, I had to agree with her.

When we finished talking about what happened today at her meeting then I told her about what happened to me with Herb Crandall. She didn't seem surprised and told me she felt that somehow I was part of the opposition that God was using to thwart the plans of this evil group at Canon. I felt kind of funny when she said that because I thought I would be the last person He would choose to use for anything like that. She explained to me that if I continue to read and study my Bible I would find that He has used the most unlikely people to carry out His work and that I would be no exception. I thought about it for a minute and from what I had read so far, I had to agree with her. But why would I be chosen was something I was not yet ready to accept.

We talked for a good while longer and as the night progressed the conversation turned from what was happening at Canon and indeed the world we started to focus on what was happening with us. I told her that I was really falling in love with her and that I wanted to be with her on a permanent basis. She told me she felt very strongly about me, but was still ambivalent about making any permanent commitment. She confided in me that one thing she had to consider was her financial circumstance. She went on to say that if she were to remarry before Jerry turns eighteen, under the settlement agreement, she would lose the remaining portion of it and that would jeopardize his secure future.

I had never thought about that and when she laid it out for me, how could I blame her for being reluctant to become too deeply involved with me. I knew she felt for me as much as I felt for her, but now I also realized just what might be holding her back too. When she finished talking, I told her I understood how she felt and that I would always be there for her whether we could make it legal or not. She thanked me for being so understanding and leaned over and kissed me. I responded and held her tightly as I kissed her back. We both knew there was a mutual understanding about where the relationship was going, but right now our physical emotions needed to be satisfied and there was no stopping. She got up and went to check on Jerry then returned and we went into her bedroom.

Even though we had been together before, each time I was with her was like a brand new experience. As she disrobed I watched as she tantalized me with her deliberate almost stripper like motions. The glow on her face was as stimulating as was viewing the revealing of her beautiful body when she shed her garments piece by piece. Whether her show was done to escalate my desire to have her on a permanent basis, I don't know, but when she finally came to bed that was the last thing on my mind. It was a beautiful night and everything that was bothering us before melted away with the culmination of our love's consummation.

The morning came and fortunately I woke up very early and was able to dress and leave. I didn't want to have Jerry wake up and find me still there with his mother. The time wasn't right for that scenario.

Although I had spent a very pleasant night and felt more relaxed than I had in a long time, now I knew I had to face the decision I was supposed to let Mr. Crandall know I had made. In my apartment I went through my normal morning routine getting ready for work, but there was something bothering me that I had not considered before. What if I tell Crandall, I won't sign his contract? Am I really ready to lose my employment and have to start looking all over again for a new job? The thought of having to start the job seeking process all over again was not very appealing to me, since it took me quite awhile to find this one. So I decided to accept his offer and sign the contract and continue in my employ at Canon. I finished showering, eating breakfast dressed and went down to meet Alex as I usually did.

The day seemed to be colder than it had been the last few days and I wondered whether this was some kind of omen that I should be mindful of. I tossed it aside and got in the cab.

"Good mornin' my brutha, how you be?" Alex said in his morning greeting.

"I'm fine my brother how are you?"

"Much betta this mornin'. Did good yestidy and made decent money for a change. Maybe my fate turnin' `round bout now an I'm gonna live betta."

"Alex you're going to be fine. You just keep working the way you do and everything is going to turn out all right for you. You mark my words, you will be fine."

"Hope you right my bruther. Hope you right."

We pulled up in front of the Mid-town office and I got out and went inside as usual. On my way up to Herb

Crandall's office I started having second thoughts about what I had decided earlier. I needed a little more time to firm up my thinking. Since I was early for our 9:30 meeting I thought I would go and visit my old office and see whether any changes had been made in my absence. When I got there I found the key still opened the door and nothing seemed to have been bothered since the time I left it. This was encouraging in a way because it told me that no action against me had been initiated.

I spent a few minutes sitting at my old desk and reviewing the things that occurred since I assumed possession of it. Overall I had a good career going and until I became involved in the murder mystery and the consequential revelation of the drug plot, I believe I was on the right track to moving up the proverbial corporate ladder. Now this could all be coming to an abrupt end if I make the wrong decision. On the other hand as I thought more about it, something seemed to be entering my thoughts and guiding me to a different viewpoint. The thoughts coming into my mind now were prompting me to consider how I was being manipulated into making a rash decision.

I can't say that I knew what was moving me in this direction, but it felt like another mind was overlapping mine and telling me what to do. When the time came for me to go and meet Mr. Crandall, I had a new feeling of confidence in telling him I would not accept his proposal and I wouldn't sign his contract. Moreover I was prepared now to place him in a position to have to defend even offering me the type of contract he was.

"Hi Diane is he ready for me?"

"Hello Mr. Powers I think so but let me check."

She buzzed him on the intercom and told him I was here.

"Okay Mr. Powers you can go in."

I took a deep breath and boldly walked through the door. Herb Crandall was seated in his big executive chair looking at me as I walked in and he must have noticed something different about me because he asked.

"There's something different about you did you get a haircut or shave differently?"

"No, I'm just feeling more energized than I have in a long time."

"Well okay let's get on with it. We both know why you're here so no sense in prolonging this meeting. I trust you've had a chance to think about what I told you yesterday and are prepared to sign the contract."

"Not exactly Mr. Crandall. There are some things I want to talk about first. Would you mind showing me that contract again I'd like to look at it more closely?"

"Nothing has changed in it since yesterday. What are you looking for?"

"Oh I just think before I sign something as important as this I ought to know exactly what's in it. Wouldn't you agree?"

"Sure, sure. Okay here it is but let's not delay too long."

I took the document and just as I suspected there were some statements in there that referred to things that had absolutely nothing to do with my employment at Canon. There were words in there talking about my soul, my commitment to serve someone, a name I didn't even understand and regarding my worship responsibilities. When I asked about these things he began to stumble in providing an explanation and the previously unflappable Mr. Crandall started to look uncomfortable. He got so nervous that he finally got up from his chair walked around the desk and snatched the paper from my hand.

"It's obvious Mr. Powers that you are not ready to sign this document so why don't we just forget it and talk about the alternatives. As I told you yesterday not signing this behavior improvement strategy plan will ultimately result in your being separated from the company. You are aware of that are you not?"

"Yes I understood what you said but now let me make you aware of something. If I am terminated I will engage an outside attorney to review the terms on which my separation, as you call it, was based. I'm sure he would like to look at that contract you just presented me."

Immediately, his tone and demeanor changed.

"Let's not be hasty. Obviously you have given this some thought and I respect that. However, there's another way we can resolve this issue."

With that statement he leaned back in his chair smiled at me and started to twirl the signet ring on his right hand. It was strange how he was no longer talking but just staring at me and continuing to twirl the ring. Quickly the temperature in the room started dropping. It was like all the heat had been turned off and the windows thrown wide open. I stared at him and he seemed to be enjoying it because it wasn't affecting him.

First my hands started to get numb, just like when I was outside in the park. Then my feet reacted the same. Soon I was sitting there unable to move but conscious of everything that was going on.

The more he twirled his ring, the colder it got in the room. Then I looked behind him and the same figure that I thought I saw before was standing there. As my body became more frigid I felt the beat of my heart slowing down and the circulation to my lower extremities becoming retarded. I tried to move and get up to run out of there but none of my limbs were responding to the thoughts I was sending out. Finally, when I could no longer bear the cold, my eyes closed.

Chapter 14
"Horizon"

From Maine to Florida, New York to California and states in between Candoo was sweeping the nation like an out of control pandemic. Athletic groups catering to the adolescent population, especially in basketball, were purchasing the product at a record pace and Canon Enterprises was enjoying the financial benefits. Whether they competed in the inner city or in the suburbs young players craved the heavily advertised product.

Those who were knowledgeable about the devastating potential of the drug were desperately seeking a means to refute the claims of the advertisers and pleading for help from the Federal government to intervene in stopping its further production. The renowned scientists in Washington who had been given the task of analyzing the new sample obtained legally from Canon Enterprises had completed their review and were astonished at their new findings. When they compared the results of the latest examination with that of their previous findings, the deadly potential discovered in the first sample was no longer present.

A key element present in the first sample was clearly missing from the second and that immediately prompted a question regarding what caused the change. While the scientists were aware that the integrity of the first sample had been compromised somewhat by the amount of time lost prior to their receiving it, there was no denying the presence of the CoMed 5 element in it.

Now that factor was completely unobservable in the current sample and there was nothing dangerous or potentially dangerous in it. The results were submitted to Mr. Hamlin at the CIA.

When Harvey Hamlin received the report he was puzzled. Either the original sample was a hoax or the chemists at Canon Enterprises had doctored the second sample in order to prevent discovery of its deadly potential revealed by one of his top agents. In either case his only option was to get hold of Tango Hernandez and discuss the new situation.

"Hello Tango Hernandez speaking."

"Tango this is Harvey I'm glad I caught you. I just received the test results from the scientists working on the new sample submitted. You're not going to believe what they found."

"Please tell me they concur with what we said about the first sample."

"Sorry can't do that. As a matter of fact they verified that the second sample was clean.

There was nothing wrong with it except that it may be a little high on the sugar content.

Now my question to you is what happened?"

"Sir I'm pretty sure I know what happened. It's clear that the legal sample from Canon was doctored up when they gave it to us. What we need to do is go down to one of the distributors selling the product and buy some right off the shelf. This way we'll know which sample to believe."

"Good idea. I'll have one of the agents here find out who's selling it and get some. How are things going up there?"

"Well I was hoping to get some help through a positive report from the scientists so we could move on getting this place shut down or at least restrained from producing any more of that Candoo crap. But I guess now that's not going to happen, at least not for a while until we let them go at it again with a sample off the streets. Other than that, even though a lot of weird things are going on around here there's nothing I can do about it. Please let me know how the street sample analysis turns out."

"I will do that. I just hope that high priced brain trust is not going to make me jump through hoops getting them to do another analysis on the same product."

"Yeah me too. It's critical that they give it one more shot so we can know exactly what these kids are getting."

"I agree. I'll do my best here. Keep on plugging up there and see what you can come up with to stop this madness."

"Will do sir - goodbye."

The purchase was made from a local distributor right in the heart of the city. When the agent arrived at the Federal Building with a case of Candoo he was directed to go straight to the lab where the team of scientists had been alerted to expect him. The fight to get the chemists to take another look at the product was not as daunting a task as Harvey Hamil had envisioned. It seems that since he was so adamant about his suspicions it peeked their curiosity.

The package was delivered and they immediately went into action testing the new batch. However, what they found different about this new sample was the fact that there were written instructions inside the box stating that to get the maximum effect of the product it should be mixed with a fruit drink such as apple or orange juice. In their previous analysis they had not been made aware that this was a recommended use of the drug. Since new parameters were being introduced this elevated their interest level even more.

Procedures for testing that had already been established for the prior samples were tweaked to account for the introduction of the new element. After the first run which lasted about one hour the results were significantly different from previous findings. Excited about the new discovery all four of the highly motivated chemists were now eager to begin the second run. Carefully insuring that the conditions under which the second run would be made were those strictly adhering to the first, they initiated the procedure.

Another hour passed and the second run was ready for analysis. And again the results, although slightly different from the first but within the allowable margin of error, revealed that with the addition of the fruit juice factor the product was now a potentially deadly drug. Milan Patel, the lead chemist was on the telephone minutes later calling Harvey Hamlin to make a verbal report and advise him that the written report would be in his hands by late afternoon. He went on to warn him that the team's latest findings concur with the original claim that the drug is dangerous but under certain conditions. He cautioned Harvey to read the written report carefully because of the ramifications of another ingredient outside of the specific product involved.

Harvey was elated to hear the news about the current findings correlation to the original sample but he was also hesitant about making an unmitigated indictment against Canon until he had read the full report. Inside he was having mixed emotions about the whole thing. It was difficult for him to accept the fact that a company for years had been previously a leading edge pharmaceutical producer could sink to such a low point that it would allow a product such as Candoo to be manufactured by them. What could have caused the change?

#######

Back at Canon Enterprises headquarters as Ron Powers sat in a chair in Herbert Crandall's office feeling his life slowly slipping away from him due to a frigid temperature condition, the office door suddenly opened and Diane Benson burst in exclaiming that she had been calling on the intercom without success and Mr. Jenkovitch was on the phone needing to speak to Crandall right away. The spell was immediately broken and the glaze that had come over Ron's eyes abated and he looked around the room. There was no cold air, not even a hint of a breeze. Somehow a powerful illusion had been created by which he was duped into believing that he was succumbing to sub-zero temperature and he was freezing to death. It didn't take him long to recover after the realization and he jumped up from the chair and bolted out of the room almost knocking the secretary down.

Running wildly down the hallway he wasn't sure just where he was going. All he knew was that he had to get as far away from Crandall as he could, immediately. After reaching some distance between him and Crandall's office he slowed down and caught his breath. Still feeling somewhat lightheaded he sat down in a chair in a vacant office and tried to gather himself. The thoughts running through his mind were frightening. He envisioned what had just happened to him could happen to anyone who came in contact with the presence that he saw standing behind Herbert. Although he couldn't make out exactly what it was, he felt that it was powerful enough to create in him the illusion that would have killed him had not a minor miracle occurred.

When he had gained enough strength and composure to get up and walk calmly again he headed toward the street. Getting back to the plant now became his primary goal. He had to get to Tango and let him know about this latest incident and his encounter with Herbert Crandall. If this would not be enough to convince him there was in fact an evil spirit associated with not only Crandall but with several others in the cult, then he was going to invite Tango to go and meet with Crandall one on one himself. Once outside in the cold air Ron's presence of mind was again intact. Inside the plant it appeared like nothing had changed but he had the feeling that somehow there was something very different going on. He quickly made his way up to Tango's office only to find him staring out the window again like he found him the last time. However, this time when Ron stepped in the room Tango turned around and looked straight at him.

"Ron, I was just thinking about you. I guess I summoned you up."

"Man, don't say things like that I had enough of that conjuring mumbo, jumbo stuff for one day."

"What are you talking about?"

"I just left Herb Crandall's office and believe me he had me thinking I was freezing to death right there in the office, through some kind of spell he and this thing that was in there with him placed on me. It may sound crazy but it's true. We have got to stop production of Candoo and get these people locked up somewhere. Have you heard from your people?"

"Yes. I got a call earlier from Harvey. He said that the sample we got from Canon was completely clean. I told him I suspected it had been doctored just for us and we needed to get some from one of our local retailers selling it. He agreed and was going to do it.

I'm expecting his call any minute now. Since I know that arrangements were being made to get a sample directly from some local vendors distributing the product, if it turns out like I expect it will after the scientists examine that batch, then I think we're home free in getting some type of immediate directive to stop production if not shut the whole place down."

"That would be great. How long do you think it's going to take?"

"I don't know. It all depends on what the latest findings turn up."

Tango and I sat there talking for about another hour really just passing time waiting for the phone call he was expecting. Into about the third hour the telephone finally rang and it was Harvey Hamil from the Washington office.

"Tango - Harvey here. I think we got'em. From the report that was just handed to me it looks like that Candoo by itself is not so bad but once combined with a fruit drink then it becomes potentially deadly. Even if we can't bring Canon down based on these latest findings I believe we can at least get production halted until a real investigation can take place about the whole operation. I've already wired a copy of this report to the New York Attorney General's office and asked him to move quickly on getting the halting action started."

"Boss that's the best news I've heard today. Ron Powers, you know the man who got this whole thing started, is sitting here with me and I'm sure he would love to hear what you're telling me. Do you mind if I put you on speaker and you can repeat what you just told me?"

"Sure no problem."

When I heard the news it felt like a huge weight had been lifted off my shoulders and a deep sense of relief came over me. Although I still had some reservations about the whole thing being finished, I felt this was the closest we've ever been to making it happen. I congratulated Tango and thanked him for his diligence and perseverance, but he in turn thanked me because I was the one who really got it going. I stayed there a few minutes longer as we discussed the murder resolution and what we thought would happen at Canon, and then I left and headed home.

Things were indeed beginning to look like they were going our way finally and I couldn't wait to get there and call Mimi to tell her the good news. There were many things that had happened which she didn't know about but I knew this was a school night for her so my call would have to wait. I walked in my door and noticed a note had been slipped under it that read you are invited to another party in the building. This time however, it was to be the highlight of the year because it was going to be a holiday bash to end the year. Since it was to be held on Saturday I felt like this would be a good time to inquire of my host whether it would be okay for me to bring an additional guest.

I was thinking it would be nice to have Mimi and her sister join me at the party after the tournament game on Friday night. This was a game in which Midge's son's team was expected to conclude their season by winning the final game and the championship of that league. Saturday's party would be a nice celebration for the adults and after church on Sunday then we would celebrate with the kids. It seemed like a good idea and I was going to add this to my list of things to tell her.

Around 9:00 O'clock I figured she should be home by now and had a chance to feed Jerry and monitor his schoolwork so I called her.

"Hello."

"Hi - this is Ron how you doin'?"

"Oh I guess I'm okay just a little tired. How are you doing?"

"Where would you like for me to begin, it's been one of those days?"

"Did something bad happen? I know you were scheduled to meet with that Crandall person."

"Well let's just say it turned out okay but for a while I didn't think I was going to get out of that meeting alive."

"What do you mean alive?"

"It was both scary and yet illuminating. While I was in there supposedly to accept his proposal for keeping my job, when I decided to look at the contract he was offering me more closely I saw some things in there that made no sense so I told him I wouldn't sign it. Then he became very angry and withdrawn looked at me very hard and started twirling a ring on his finger. After a few minutes of watching him do that the room started getting colder and colder. But it was very odd because strangely it was like he wasn't being affected by the temperature drop; only me. After several minutes I could hardly breathe and I felt like my lights were going out permanently. I still can't explain what was happening but then I think I also saw another presence in the room standing behind him also staring at me.

It got so cold in there I was about to pass out. Fortunately, his secretary opened the door suddenly to give him an important message and it was like the spell had been broken because the room was no longer cold. I realized then that the room temperature had not actually dropped but I was under the illusion that it had, even to the point of freezing to death. When it dawned on me what was happening, I jumped up and got out of there as fast as I could."

"My God! Are you sure you're alright now?"

"Yeah I'm fine now but that shook me up pretty good. And that's how my day started. But after all that it turned out pretty good when I had a chance to talk to Tango. He informed about some things that happened in Washington and now I do have some good news to report."

"Well that's a turn around. What's the good news? Please tell me our troubles are ending and those evil people are all going to disappear."

"I don't think I can take it that far, but at least according to Tango a case of Candoo was purchased from a local distributor and then sent to the same chemists who analyzed our sample. This time the results were completely different than when they finished their last analysis. This time they came to the same conclusion that we've been trying to tell the world about that drug. Tango also said that the results of their report were being wired to the NY District Attorney's office to request some immediate action be taken to halt production temporarily and possibly permanently."

"Hallelujah Jesus - it's about time."

"Wait there's more. What they found is that Candoo when combined with fruit juices can be potentially deadly. Just like you said at the start."

"You know Ron since so many kids playing in basketball leagues everywhere are now getting into that stuff I'm wondering if my nephew's team has done it. And by the way Jerry has been pestering me about reminding you that you made him a promise to go to the tournament game on Friday."

"Well you can tell him I'm definitely going and I'll be there right on time to pick you guys up. I think you said the game starts at 7:30 PM right? "

"Yes, but we should try to get there at least a half hour earlier. Remember its Friday and the traffic is going to be a problem."

"Okay then I'll get to your place by 5:00 and if you're ready we can leave right away. But getting back to what you said about so many youth basketball teams buying into the Candoo hype, do you think Josh's team is doing it? Maybe you ought to call your sister and warn her. I hope it's not too late.

"Yes you're right. I'll call her right after we hang up."

"We ought to hang up now and let you call her. All I really wanted to tell you anyway was what happened with me in Crandall's office but more importantly I wanted you know the good news about possibly stopping Canon from making any more of that Candoo stuff."

"Thanks for that information and you're right I should call her now. Will I see you tomorrow?"

"I hope so. Maybe we can get together for lunch. I'll be back at the plant, at least until I hear more from Crandall about my future."

"Okay call me around noon and let me know what the plan is."

"Right! Talk to you then. Bye."

We hung up and I'm sure she called her sister. After she brought up the possibility that the use of Candoo could be affecting someone I knew this really started to bother me even more. It was one thing to know that there were many young people out there who were possibly using the drink, but to know someone close to you could be involved, was a different story.

When I got to my office at the plant the next day I found there was a new buzz of excitement permeating the place. It seems that the police had come back again to talk with Leonard Jablonski and it was causing quite a stir. From what I could tell according to the bits and pieces I could make out eavesdropping on some of the elevator talk, rumor had it Mr. Jablonski under pressure confessed to knowing about the plot to get rid of Anthony Oliver and implicated himself in the scheme to carry out his demise. The Mayor, who previously had been reluctant to allow the police chief to move in on anyone at Canon lately had been convinced that there were some strange things going on there, so he was now on board with the action.

Peter Callahan, the ace detective handling the case, wasted no time after receiving his chief's approval in going after Jablonski. He singled him out first, even though he was aware that there were several others involved, because he recalled from their previous encounter he was perhaps the one most likely to yield critical information when confronted. The last time they talked Leonard got very nervous and anxious to dismiss Callahan. But now armed with a new sense of urgency to completely close out this whole Canon mystery, Callahan was intent on getting all that he could out of Jablonski and then pursue the others.

I continued on to my office keeping in mind that things were finally looking like they were really coming to some positive conclusion. If Jablonski, as expected gave up the others when taken into custody, then that could mean a cease and desist order from the DA's office may not even be necessary to shut down production. If the major team managers were absent then that would mean enough spokes in the wheel would be missing to slow down, if not stop production. This was all contingent on what would happen with Leonard and from all that I had seen from the powers backing him, there was no guarantee that the outcome would be as we expected.

Feeling confident that if Herb Crandall was aware of what was going on down here, and I believed that his spies here would have called him, then he wasn't going to be calling me any time soon, so I went about my daily routine as usual. My feelings of mixed emotions regarding where we actually were in the case and where we might possibly be at the conclusion of the interrogation of Jablonski kept me from fully concentrating on my work but I managed to complete some tasks that had been left in limbo since my visit with Crandall.

Along about 11:00 AM I took a break and went down to the cafeteria hoping to hear some kind of update via the gossip network about the disposition of Jablonski, but no one in there or even on my way was talking about it anymore. After finishing my coffee I decided to stroll by his office just to be inquisitive and see whether his secretary might be in a talkative mood. When I arrived there his office was empty and so was the secretary's desk. This started me to wonder whether she was possibly involved in the conspiracy.

I didn't hang around but went back to my office to continue working. It was not long before a call came in from Tango telling about what I was already trying to get. He had been contacted by Callahan because of his position with the CIA and informed that Jablonski had indeed rolled over on the whole cult organization inside Canon and their scheme to eliminate Oliver and subsequently Brent Woodley. Leonard was trying to bargain his way into a deal to receive clemency and lessen the punishment for his involvement in the conspiracy. Tango went on to say that Callahan was now in the process of getting arrest warrants for all of them.

According to Tango it seems that Leonard Jablonski had not only identified all the Canon employees involved in the plot, but he also produced a copy of the original RFP that was sent only to Canon Enterprises. In addition, to increase the value of his bargaining chips he decoded the acronym P.T.D.T.Y. and revealed that it was a "Project to Destroy the Youth" which was the first step in his idol's master plan. And finally after Detective Callahan kept pressuring him by asking: "Is there anything else?" Leonard broke down and produced the chemical formula for mixing CoMed 5, U3/G and the other elements for making Candoo. His disregard for or lapse of memory regarding his last encounter with the adversary was to be his ultimate downfall.

Two days after his interview with Callahan the body of Leonard Jablonski was discovered in the bedroom of his West Side luxury Condo. The cause of death baffled the coroner and his staff of forensic experts. The autopsy determined that the actual cause of death was the result of an electrocution, but from where the body was found in bed the source of the power supply could not be determined. And so it was Detective Callahan's star witness was no longer available, but his testimony was on record.

After hearing that, twelve o'clock couldn't come soon enough because I was eager to share the information with Marsha. When it did I skipped calling her and almost ran down to her lab. Inside the lab I saw her and Martin talking to a group of the other chemists in an apparently rather heated discussion. I hesitated walking right in the middle of whatever was going on there but fortunately another of their colleagues was about to go in so I asked him to let Marsha know that I was outside. He agreed, walked in and delivered the message without regard for the discussion. To me it seemed like he was accustomed to hearing this conversation from that group.

When Marsha got the message she broke off from the group and came to the hallway.

"What was that all about?" I asked.

"Just the same old argument. You won't believe how stubborn some of these old supposedly wizened owls can be. They just refuse to believe anything negative about Candoo. They suspect that Martin and I are jeopardizing, for some unknown reason, their year-end bonuses because of what we contend about Candoo, one of our best selling products. I can't wait until that report you told me about becomes a matter of public information. Then maybe their bonuses won't be so important when they learn about what the drug could do to possibly their own kids or grandkids."

"Yeah it is hard to believe at this point. But if you're ready to go to lunch I have some more good news to share with you. Can you go now?"

"Sure give me a minute to wrap up some things in there and I'll be right out."

Marsha went back inside talked to Martin for a minute ignoring the rest of the group and then came back out.

Since it was really cold outside we went to lunch in the cafeteria. We both agreed it was not the best option for a good meal, but in light of the weather it was acceptable. When I told her about the additional good news I was about to give her, she said I must have a touch of Jesus spreading the Gospel. I laughed so hard everyone around us in the room turned to see what the cause of the hilarity was. Embarrassed, I quickly regained my composure and told her how far off the mark she was with that comparison. She laughed also.

One thing was clear for both of us, it appeared like the end was near for the conspiracy and we had the upper hand. After reviewing the impending possible scenarios we agreed that the most important thing that should happen soon would be the halting of Candoo production. We continued to eat and talk about the future of the case and then the conversation turned to tomorrow's basketball tournament final. Then she mentioned that she had heard this morning there was a Nor-Easter snow storm coming out of the Mid-West possibly headed this way that could impact the decision to get the game in. I had not heard a weather report the whole day so it was coming as a surprise to me but I asked when was the last time she heard it. She responded saying not since this morning, but it was something we needed to pay attention to.

After lunch we separated and returned to our respective workstations. Since hearing about the possible snowstorm heading our way I thought about how things could be affected regarding the order to stop Candoo production. If the weather prediction turns out to be as serious as Marsha felt it might, then offices will be closed early as a precaution and the order to cease and desist would be held up. Even worse, round up of the cult offenders would be delayed. This could be a serious turn of events, not only for the players participating in the tournament but for all the family, students, friends, vendors and anyone else associated with the big game who was anticipating a big crowd.

In the cab ride home the radio confirmed, more than once, what Marsha said about the storm. It was definitely heading this way and with each subsequent report the severity was increasing. By the time I arrived at my apartment, the last report had the expected accumulation to be between one and a half to two feet of pure snow. Looking out my window the current conditions already seemed just right for some type of major weather event.

As I got out, paid the driver and started to head upstairs I noticed the strange man I had seen now on a few occasions once again standing in the lobby. This time he was standing by the tall Christmas tree seemingly admiring the decorations. When he spotted me again just like before he motioned for me to come to him. The last time we talked his eerie prediction happened exactly as he said it would so I was a bit leery in approaching him to hear what he had to say. His appearance had not changed and I believe he was wearing the same clothing.

When I got close to him he smiled a broad smile showing perfectly aligned white teeth and then spoke quietly.

"Do you yet not believe?"

Somewhat surprised by the question I wasn't sure just how to answer him so I hesitated then I blurted out a weak response.

"You know I think this is the third time you've spoken to me and yet I don't even know your name. Who are you?"

"My name is not important. Only the messages I bring to you are. I say again - do you yet not believe?"

When he repeated his question the second time with a little more urgency in requiring an answer, I felt strangely compelled to reply with my own question.

"Do I believe what?"

The broad smile disappeared and a serious look replaced it.

"From all that you have seen and witnessed have you yet not understood what is happening to you and all around you?"

I had to admit over the last few weeks I had seen and experienced a lot of things, but had no idea why they were all happening to me, so I answered.

"Yes I've seen and experienced some strange things but tell me why are they happening to me."

"You have been chosen to bare witness to a soon coming event and you are the one chosen to proclaim the revelation. Until such time as it will occur you will have a hedge of protection mounted around you to shield you from any hurt, harm or danger. Do you believe my words?"

At this saying I was stunned but managed to meekly answer "Yes I do."

"Then it will be well with you."

He finished speaking turned and walked away. This time I tried to stay focused and see where he would go. But just like before the minute he walked through the front door – he vanished. I didn't know whether it was a real encounter or whether I was hallucinating but when he left I felt an inner peace and calm like never before.

Friday morning came and I woke up extra early, even before my loud alarm went off. I jumped out of bed and ran to the window to see if the prediction was coming true. Sure enough it was beginning to snow and the flakes were very broad and steady. Then I turned on the news to get the latest weather update. As I suspected, the weather crews were confirming this event to be one of the worst in many years. Announcements were already scrawling across the TV screen about school closings, airports shutdown, non-essential government offices closing and several others closing. I strained my eyes to see if there was any reference to Canon Enterprises being one of them, but was not surprised when there was none. I had never known in the time that I was in their employ about the company closing for any reason - thus far.

Going on the assumption that the company was going to be open for business, I prepared myself to leave the apartment a little earlier. Traffic was likely to be at a snail's pace so I called Alex and asked him if he could pick me up a half-hour early. He had already anticipated my call and said he would be there on time, if he could. Knowing him that meant, barring some major catastrophe, he would be there just as I asked.

Even though the snow was starting to come down heavier surprisingly Alex was able to get me to the plant in almost the same amount of time as on a normal day. I could tell as soon as I entered the building many people were heeding the weather advisory and staying home. Security officers instead of the regular receptionist were now manning the reception desk in the lobby. I cleared their screening check and made my way to the elevators.

In a way I was glad it was snowing hard because I thought maybe enough production workers wouldn't show up to run the operation so a natural shut down would be imminent. After I settled in, had my coffee and checked telephone messages I tooka walk down to the production area just to see if my wish was being granted. Not so! The workers were trickling but steadily coming in. Production was going to continue. I wondered how many of them knew about the product they were making.

On the way back to my office I stopped by the labs to see if Marsha came in. Not only was she not there, but also the lab was completely empty. Perhaps none of the projects going on in there were so important as to risk coming to work in a snow storm, unlike that of the Candoo production workers. It was curious to me that the work on a product where the workers should be least concerned about would draw more dedicated effort than research and development work on products more beneficial to man. Then I thought maybe the difference wasn't so much a matter of dedication as it was a financial issue. If the production workers didn't work, they would not get paid. Not so with the chemists. This idea prompted my next thought. In a country where the dichotomy between the "haves" and the "have not-s" was growing wider, the question of how do the "have not-s" become part of the "haves" group may never get answered, was real. Maybe in the world to come, the inequity will be resolved.

Back in my office I saw the message light on my phone blinking so I retrieved the one message. It was from Marsha saying that Jerry's school was closed so she was staying home today with him. She went on to say that she had heard from her sister and the tournament final game was being rescheduled to Monday night. I suspected that might happen so hearing the confirmation was no surprise. I started to call her back when an announcement came blaring over the hall public address system. Apparently the powers in charge decided that the latest weather report was severe enough to warrant dismissing all employees early and closing the building. I was told later this was not a first, but the senior staff member relaying the information said the last time was over fifteen years ago and the reason for that was the company did not want to be responsible for people getting stranded in their building over night.

By noon a blizzard was raging outside. Most of the workers who had dared to come in to work were already gone or in the process of exiting. I sat in my office just a little while longer contemplating whether to risk taking a cab and getting stuck in traffic somewhere or trudging the few blocks to the subway and hope the trains were running. The subway idea prevailed and I started my trek. As I was laboring to walk through the mounting snow it occurred to me that rather than go home now might be a good time to honor my promise to Jerry. I ducked into a local pharmacy to call Mimi and see whether it would be alright to come over now. No more than ten steps into the establishment on a shelf right near the door was a sign promoting Candoo in a two for one sale. It took all I had to control my urge to rip down the sign and turn over the shelving. Fortunately, my better judgment kicked in and I walked by the display.

Mimi answered on the third ring and was happy to hear my suggestion. She said Jerry would love to have my company and it would give her a chance to catch up on some schoolwork. It was settled, luckily, the train needed to get to her place could be boarded at the same station where I would catch my own train. I left the store going in the opposite direction of the display avoiding having to look at it again.

Finally getting to the station I observed that quite a few others had the same idea as me about skipping the taxi option. Even for this time of day, given the weather condition, more than the usual number of riders was scurrying to run down to the tracks. I squeezed in among them and we waited in hope that the train we needed was indeed coming. There were no announcements over the public address system about anything. That didn't give me and I'm sure all the others a good feeling about our fate.

About fifteen minutes passed and we could hear rumbling of the subway in the near distance. Following shortly thereafter the train headlight could be seen making its way slowly toward the platform. A collective sigh of relief could be heard from the crowd acknowledging the wait was over. The train stopped and the pushing and shoving began. I managed to wedge myself between two combatants vying for the same space at the same time. Next came the battle for a seat. Since I was only going a few stops, I elected not to engage in the contest. Standing holding on to the hanger straps I braced as the car began to move. Slowly at first but then picked up some speed as we distanced ourselves from the station.

Another fifteen minutes and four platforms later the train halted at my stop. I got off and ascended the steps to daylight. The snow was still coming down hard and the walk was even more laborious than before. Although her building was only five city blocks from the subway entrance it seemed like a mile run given the challenging weather condition. When I arrived there my legs were crying out for relief and I had to sit down in the lobby for a few minutes before I even went up to the desk. There was only one person on the desk not the usual crew. There were a few men outside shoveling the snow but I did not see Bruce anywhere. At the desk the announcement was made that I wished to see Mrs. Robinson and the response was given to allow me to go upstairs.

Once at her apartment door I hesitated a moment as I usually did to listen to sound or lack thereof of noise coming from the other apartments. The sound of silence prevailed as it normally did and I proceeded to ring her bell.

"Just a minute" she hollered out.

Moments later she answered the door looking as radiant as ever dressed in a casual outfit that even though lose fitting could not hide her physical gifts. Jerry bolted from his room right after and grabbed my hand before I could even get my coat off. Mimi interceded quickly and advised him to at least let me get inside the house. He released his grip and I shed my outer garment. Mimi took it hung it up and then after a brief greeting conversation with her I was pulled into the playroom. Jerry had everything already setup for another round of playtime basketball so I was once again challenged to upset his winning record.

We played for at least two hours straight while Mimi completed her school assignments and was taking a nap when the phone rang. It was Reverend Deveraux, her father, checking on his girls to see whether they and his grandchildren were okay. She answered the phone and assured him that she was fine and that she also had company to help her if needed. He inquired who it might be and was happy to hear that it was I. Apparently I had passed his screen test and was being accepted into his good graces.

Surprisingly he asked to speak with me for a moment. I broke off my encounter with Jerry's game skills and went to the phone.

"Hello sir how are you" I said.

"I'm fine Ron and glad to know that you are looking after my daughter and her young man."

"I'm happy to do it and as far as looking after Jerry he is consistently whipping my butt – excuse me sir - playing that basketball game you gave him."

"Don't feel badly I've only beaten him a couple of times since I gave it to him some time ago. It takes practice and he does that regularly. Listen there is something I want to talk to you about."

"Yes sir I'm listening."

"First I hope you will be coming to the service on Sunday to hear the last segment in my series."

"I'm planning to come provided we can get there."

"I think by then the roads should be cleared up, so I'll be looking forward to seeing you and my family. That's not only why I wanted to talk you. As you know I have been praying about what's happening in this world and preaching about something that is ultimately going to happen in the near future. A few nights ago I had a dream that was not very clear but somehow I could see that it involved you. Your image, as I remember it, was plain enough. It was just the surrounding events that were not very clear. But the important thing was the message I received stating that you are to be a key player in the upcoming event. I don't want to alarm you in any way, but I do want you to know that if you haven't already received some kind of warning, be it through dreams or some other vehicle, know that you will."

When he said that my recollection of what the man in the lobby said was beginning to scare me. Even though "Doc" said not to be alarmed, it was hard not to knowing that the man in the lobby had already made a prediction that came true and now "Doc" telling me I'm going to be involved in some kind of Biblical event.

"Sir, it's kind of weird you should say that because just yesterday that strange man I told you about, who I had seen two or three times before in my building, told me that I was going to see exactly what you're telling me."

"Did he give you any details on what's going to happen to you?

"No he just said that I had been chosen for something and that I was going to make some kind of announcement that will affect the nation."

"Son, my dream was right. You are the one. Don't say anything to Mimi about this but prepare yourself for things to begin to happen to you that you have never experienced before.

I thought to myself, that's an understatement. Things have already been happening to me that never did before.

"What should I do?"

"Nothing! It will happen to you according to God's will so don't do anything. Just wait on Him and you will know when the time comes what and how to do it."

"Sir that's not very comforting but I will do as you say. Thank you for telling me. I hope to see and talk more with you on Sunday."

"As do I. Please put my grandson on so I can say a few words to him."

"Sure thing, I'll get him."

I put the phone down and went and got Jerry. After that conversation with "Doc", needless to say my concentration on beating Jerry at his game was faulty. I wanted so much to share his message with Mimi but was mindful of what he said about not doing so. Somehow though she seemed to sense when I came out of the playroom that her father had given me some kind of upsetting news. She didn't press me for an explanation but told me that if I needed to discuss anything he said with her she would be there. I looked at her compassionately but said nothing.

It was beginning to get late and the snow was still coming down. I was not prepared to stay overnight, but looking outside the window, even though it was a beautiful view of the snow covered city, I couldn't imagine that the trains were even running anymore much less any taxi's. She had already invited me to sleep on the couch and Jerry was delighted to hear it. I agreed. She prepared dinner and after eating we all sat around the table talking about everything.

The subject that came up almost immediately was the tournament game having to be replayed. It was obvious how much Jerry idolized his cousin and his basketball skills. To him he was more like his big brother rather than a cousin. Mimi thought very highly of him also because not only was he good athletically but he was also a good student and this was what was more important to her for his influence on her son. We made plans on how we would get to the game on Monday hoping that everything would be back to normal by then. As usual the food was enjoyable as was the conversation.

After dinner we watched a general audience movie and time again passed quickly before it was time for the young man to go to bed. She allowed him a little extra time because tomorrow was Saturday but when the clock showed 10:30 PM she told him it was time. He reluctantly agreed said goodnight to me and went off to bed. When she returned there was a serious look on her face as she sat down beside me.

"You are going to church with us Sunday aren't you?"

"Yes I was planning on it why do you ask?"

"Because I know this is the culmination of my father's sermon series and I believe he's going to shake some people up."

"How do you mean shake 'em up?"

"For the last few days whenever I talk with him he starts talking about how he needs to make clear to his people about the Kingdom of God and what it really means. I've never seen him like this before. It's like something is about to happen either to him or this world or both."

"You seem apprehensive are you?"

"I don't know what to be apprehensive about. I just have these feelings that something is about to happen and it is going to be something big. I realize we've been through a lot in the last few weeks and maybe that's why I feel this way. I hope the business with the murder and Candoo and all that stuff is about to be ended but somehow I think there's more to be concerned about than just that."

"Yeah, I think I know what you mean. It hasn't been easy for you or me but I believe we are near the end whatever that may be. So let's enjoy the ride and see what happens."

"Well I'm getting sleepy myself so I think I'll turn in. Too bad I can't invite you in this time but I don't think it would be a good idea since he knows you're still here and he may just wake up and explore tonight. Will you be okay on the couch? I have extra blankets if you need one."

"I agree, I don't think he's quite ready to see us in bed together. Yes I'll be fine this is a very comfortable couch."

Saturday morning came and I woke up before anyone else in the house. Not having anything to change into or even take care of my usual hygiene I decided it was better if I just left. I didn't want to wake her or Jerry up so I left a note telling her I would call later. The time I spent here I always enjoyed and wanted very much to make it a permanent arrangement, but as she had explained to me this was not to be any time soon so I just accepted things as they were.

When I got outside in the early morning hour it was still dark but you could see signs in the moonlight of an overcast sky. It was bitter cold and my legs were still aching from the over exertion yesterday. The streets were relatively clean and I hoped that a cab might come along soon so I wouldn't have to repeat the walk to the subway. In this area, except for the current weather condition, cabs were usually easy to flag down. As I started walking slowly toward the station a cab was coming from the opposite direction so I waved my hands furiously hoping to attract his attention. He saw me and acknowledged my signal and started to turn around.

I was relieved after getting in and feeling the warmth of the heater. The ride uptown was slow as the driver was being extremely cautious about some of the streets, especially as we got closer to my place. Just as I thought before, attention to clean up in my area was not as meticulous as that of the East Side posh neighborhood. Finally arriving at my building I paid the driver got out and went inside. Before I went to the elevator however, I looked around again to see if the strange man was anywhere around. Not this time! I guess he delivered his message and that was all he had to say.

Once inside my apartment I went straight to the bathroom and started running the water to take a hot bath. Of all the things that tenants living here could complain about, the provision of heat and hot water was not one of them. Thankfully, there was always a sufficient supply of both. In my rush to get the tub ready I failed to see the note that had been shoved under the door. It wasn't until I came out that I saw it and picked it up. It was an announcement saying that the year-end bash scheduled for tonight was cancelled due to the weather. Even though I was looking forward to it, given the cancellation of the tournament game and the severe weather from yesterday, I was not surprised. In a way it was a good thing because now it would give me a chance to relax and give my aching legs a chance to recover. So after taking my hot bath and aside from the short conversation I had with Mimi in the early afternoon, I spent the rest of the day reflecting on all that happened during the week and looking forward to hearing what "Doc" was going to preach about tomorrow.

Chapter 15
"Dual Prophecy"

The trip to church on Sunday morning was uneventful as most of the streets had been completely plowed and returned to normal road conditions. Traffic was still lighter than usual I guess because most regular people were electing to just spend the rest of the weekend recuperating from having to negotiate the storm. However, this was not so with the faithful because when we arrived in a relatively short time and pulled into the parking lot, the number of cars vying for a parking spot was no less than it would have been without the storm. This was a good sign that no matter what the obstacles were in getting to church the sanctuary was going to be filled with the normal count of believers. Now that via word of mouth the sermon series message was getting out, there was even an increase in the number of those who were coming for the first time to hear the finale.

We walked inside and spotted Midge and her kids coming in from the opposite entrance so we met and as a group entered the sanctuary and were fortunate to get seats all together. As I looked around, my assessment of the packed house idea was confirmed as the number of vacant seats went to zero quickly. We were seated only a short time before the pulpit musicians came in and got set up to begin the praise and worship portion of the service. They started playing and a few minutes later a choral ensemble that I had not seen before came in and joined in singing hymns of praise. The congregation was invited to also join in and soon the temple resounded with spiritual reverence. While the praise and worship continued, in walked the choir director elegantly robed and took his place in the center of the pulpit. At his direction, the praise and worship hymns concluded, but then the thundering sound of the full choir erupted from the rear of the church as they marched in singing "Leaning On the Everlasting Arm." Filling all four aisles as they marched in not only was the sound beautiful enough to delight the ears of the most critical listener, but the magnificence of the procession was as stately as any royal coronation.

At the end of the procession, the large choir filled the loft to capacity and the director signaled the end of the song. An assistant Minister then stood and delivered the invocation. Powerfully and reverently his strong voice petitioned the presence of the Lord to the service. Following this, the order of service continued in following the normal Baptist tradition.

When the time came for the sermon to be delivered and the choir sang its last song, the preacher, who was already seated on the platform stepped forward and took his place behind the sacred desk. A towering figure with a booming voice, Reverend Devereaux began to speak. Gently at first then each subsequent sentence rose to a greater power level.

"Praise the Lord Saints. Praise the Lord. I greet you this morning and stand before you once again humbled by the awesome responsibility that has been placed on me to Sheppard this flock. In these troubling times we need a Savior. One who is able to deliver us from evil, stand before us to quiet the storm and pick us up when we fall. We need a Savior. One who is available every hour of every day and will not leave us or forsake us. We need a Savior. One who is our water when we thirst, our food when we hunger and our healing medicine when we hurt. We need a Savior. Well, saints I'm here to tell you that we have one and his name is Jesus. He's our rock, our strong tower and a mighty fortress that will not break under pressure. We need a Savior who we can call on anytime, even right now. But before we ask for anything we need to go before Him with prayer and thanksgiving. Pray with me now saints.

Heavenly Father, eternal and merciful God how good and how pleasant it is to be in your house once more. We come before you this morning thanking you for waking us up and guiding us to this place that we may worship you in spirit and in truth. We thank you for the blessings you have already provided for us both individually and collectively and pray that you will continue to watch over this flock as we move forward into the future. We don't know what tomorrow will bring or what the future has in store, but we do know who controls both. And so we walk by faith and not by sight following where you lead. Guide us O Lord and keep us on that narrow path that leads to salvation. It is in the mighty and matchless name of Jesus, the risen Christ that we pray now let every heart say – Amen.

For those of you who are visiting with us for the first time and some of you who may have missed part of the series I invite you to get a copy of the tapes and listen carefully to the messages. While I am going to briefly review this morning how we got to where we are today, much of the detail you need to know will not be covered so I encourage you to get the tapes to get a clear understanding.

I believe all of you are familiar with the phrase - 'In the beginning God created the heavens and the earth and the earth was without form and void'. This phrase is used in the first sentence of the first Chapter of Genesis at the very beginning of your Bible. Although you may be familiar with these words, I dare say that most do not understand the true meaning. For you see the phrase actually refers to the recreation of the earth.

Before this event, angels under the leadership of a powerful and highly positioned angel in the Heavenly realm, called Lucifer originally inhabited it. But Lucifer not content with his position rebelled against God and was defeated. It was then that the earth became the formless void that the phrase refers to.

God was still intent on creating beings that would fill the earth and eventually become part of His family so he created man in His own image filled with the essence of His character. Man was then placed in an idyllic situation called the Garden of Eden and was given all that he would need to live a joyful life. However, he was also given an opportunity to be tested to see whether he would obey God's instructions. I don't have to tell you this part you know the story, man along with his female companion elected to use his gift of free will to make choices and failed the test miserably. Not by his own administrations but under the guile of the evil one who formerly was called Lucifer, but now called Satan and the Devil, man was deceived. Satan was also in the Garden, disguised as a serpent, and enticed the couple to disobey God.

This act of disobedience was the beginning that established man's fate that he is to realize in the here and now or what the Bible refers to as the latter days. From that time of the original sin of disobedience, man has continued to disobey and violate God's commandments through the ages. Even though many profits, priests and Sheppard's were sent to guide him along the right path, man rejected them all. God even used His prophet Moses to set His instructions down in writing on how to live, in the form of the Ten Commandments, which for us may be found in the Book of Exodus - Chapter 20, versus 1 -17. Saints, these were not ten suggestions on how to live, but they were God's commandments. In addition to the Commandments, God gave Moses more detailed instructions for the people on right living and how to be blessed abundantly. These words were spelled out in the Books of Leviticus and Deuteronomy, Chapters 26 and 28 respectively. But this time as an incentive to follow the right path, in those same chapters admonishment was given in the form of curses if man chose not to follow His instructions.

The choice was then and still is man's to follow and be blessed or disobey and be cursed. If you are paying attention and look around today you can attest to all that is happening around the world, because man continues to ignore the warnings. However, let me not jump too far ahead in my message before I lay down what happened in between the time that Moses led the people out of bondage in Egypt and directed them toward a Promised Land that God had set aside for them and the first experience of God's wrath. The Promised Land was an area God had reserved for the people, the Israelites, whom He had chosen to be a model for the world to follow.

But even they disobeyed Him from the time that He brought them out of bondage in Egypt through the years they wandered in the wilderness trying to get to that Promised Land. They continued to provoke and anger God until something had to be done. In one of my earlier messages I revealed to you that much of prophecy in the Bible is dual in nature. What this means is the things prophesied back then and actually happened are going to happen again. But before God carries out His promise of retribution, being the righteous God that He is warnings are given. In the Book of Amos - Chapter 3, verse 7 it reads "Surely the Lord GOD will do nothing, but he revealeth his secret unto his servants the prophets." (KJV)

The trek through the wilderness, a journey that should have taken months, took forty years. The Israelites oscillated between pure Yahweh (God) worship and sacrilege. But finally, by His grace, they were allowed under the leadership of Joshua, the man who succeeded Moses after his death, to enter the Promised Land. Although possession of the territory came at a heavy price because the Israelites had to battle several ethnic groups who already lived there, this land was God's promise to them and so they prevailed.

And so they entered the land around 1400 BC and over the next 600 years established the Israelite Kingdom. Eventually Jerusalem in the region of Judah became the centerpiece of the Jewish nation. Remember this because Jerusalem was to become then and even now the focus of what was and is about to take place. At the beginning of this period the people were governed by a series of judges. Gideon, Samson, Jephthah and Deborah are some of their names that you may recognize. And yes, ladies a woman was among the early judges. But the people still were not happy being led by them, even though they were chosen by God, so they cried out for a king to lead them. Now as I said before God always sends a warning, so through Samuel, a prophet of God, a king by the name of Saul was chosen, but even though Saul was God's early choice Samuel was instructed to warn the people about choosing a king to rule over them.

Saul ruled for about 40 years before he too disobeyed God and fell out of favor. David succeeded him. Now I'm sure you're familiar with the story about David and Goliath and how he became king so I won't go into it, but you may not be aware of how significant his accession to the throne was in terms of the future of his lineage. David found favor in the eyes of God and he was blessed when he became king. He was not perfect for he too committed some sinful acts, but God loved his contrite spirit and his pure heart.

After another 40 years under David's tumultuous but successful reign, the kingship passed on to Solomon his son. Please stay with me folks because I'm going somewhere with this, but right now it's important for you to understand that the line of kings through this bloodline would lead to the birth of our Lord and Savior Jesus Christ. Again let me not digress too far from the key point of this message. Under Solomon's reign the first temple in Jerusalem was built. This was the centerpiece of early worship and Solomon in his early years also found favor with God. However, as he grew older and was influenced by his many wives, he began to turn away from God and like Saul fell out of favor. So much so that the once united kingdom of Israel became divided into two nations - Israel and Judah, during the reign of his son Rehoboam. It was only because of God's promise to David that the kingdom remained intact during Solomon's reign.

The nation of Israel then became home for ten of the twelve tribes that formerly made up the United Kingdom. The two remaining tribes were Judah and Benjamin. Out of this separation the term Jew came into being. Both nations moved forward through periods of devotion and disobedience over several years governed by a series of kings who ruled with absolute authority.

Although Judah managed to produce some kings who did right in the eyes of God, Israel produced none. From the time the United Kingdom separated around 931 B.C. until the fall of Samaria, the capital of Israel around 722 B.C, God continued to send His messengers to warn the people, but the results remained the same.

After the fall of Samaria at the hands of the Assyrians under a ruthless conqueror named Sargon II, the ten tribes were first captured and then scattered among other nations just as they had been warned. They became known as the lost tribes of Israel. But brothers and sisters they weren't lost, God knew where they were scattered. This is an important point because of what is to happen later in the prophetic accounting.

Now that Israel was defeated the focus turns to Jerusalem. The remaining tribes now called Jews were keenly aware of what happened to Samaria and more so they knew the reason why. But, just as the Israelites ignored God's warnings, the Jews following in their footsteps continued their disobedient ways. Just as Samaria had been sent prophets to warn them, so too were messengers sent to Judah. The fact that Jerusalem in Judah was where Solomon's temple had been constructed and dedicated to God, this became an even greater source of provocation for Him when pagan sacrifices and rituals were conducted right in His house. How long could this continue? Well the answer came soon.

Before I continue, I need to give you the source documents, the text, for what has been covered so far. I encourage you to read these books in their entirety so you will have a good understanding of the details that I just don't have time to cover in this message. The Biblical accounts I refer to may be found in the books of First and Second Samuel and First and Second Kings in the Old Testament. Now I want to turn your attention to the Books of Daniel and Revelation as we move toward drawing this message to its conclusion.

We are talking about Jerusalem now and the attitude and practices of the Jews. Just like the warnings given to the Israelites through many prophets, so too were the Jews given Major Prophets like Daniel. In his book he is instructed by God to warn about the impending crises that will happen to Judah and Jerusalem in that period, but the book was not only a warning for that time, but also a warning for us in what was called the latter days - which my friends is right now.

Because the Jews, just like their northern neighbors continued in their sins of disobedience, Jerusalem fell to the Babylonians in 586 B.C. under king Nebuchadnezzar and Daniel was captured and deported to Babylon. However, while exiled there Daniel found favor with God because he would not violate his belief and trust in the one true God. Daniel, along with three of his Hebrew friends, you know their names, they were Shadrach, Meshach and Abednego were recognized by the king as having attributes that others did not so they were elevated to high positions in the king's administration. God had gifted Daniel, just like Joseph in earlier times, with the ability to be able to interpret dreams. When the time came and the king needed to have a dream of his interpreted Daniel answered the call.

What he told the king was a revelation not only for the time then but is a message for the time called now. His message told of four kingdoms that would come to pass including and succeeding Nebuchadnezzar's. The dream was interpreted using a statue of a king made up of various metals representing different kingdoms. Daniel said this to the king:

[31] "Your Majesty looked, and there before you stood a large statue—an enormous, dazzling statue, awesome in appearance. [32] The head of the statue was made of pure gold, its chest and arms of silver, its belly and thighs of bronze, [33] its legs of iron, its feet partly of iron and partly of baked clay.
[34] While you were watching, a rock was cut out, but not by human hands. It struck the statue on its feet of iron and clay and smashed them [35] Then the iron, the clay, the bronze, the silver and the gold were all broken to pieces and became like chaff on a threshing floor in the summer. The wind swept them away without leaving a trace. But the rock that struck the statue became a huge mountain and filled the whole earth.
[36] "This was the dream, and now we will interpret it to the king.
[37] Your Majesty, you are the king of kings. The God of heaven has given you dominion and power and might and glory; [38] in your hands he has placed all mankind and the beasts of the field and the birds in the sky. Wherever they live, he has made you ruler over them all. You are that head of gold. [39] "After you, another kingdom will arise, inferior to yours. Next, a third kingdom, one of bronze, will rule over the whole earth.
[40] Finally, there will be a fourth kingdom, strong as iron-for iron breaks and smashes everything—and as iron breaks things to pieces, so it will crush and break all the others. [41] Just as you saw that the feet and toes were partly of baked clay and partly of iron, so this will be a divided kingdom; yet it will have

some of the strength of iron in it, even as you saw iron mixed with clay. [42] As the toes were partly iron and partly clay, so this kingdom will be partly strong and partly brittle. [43] And just as you saw the iron mixed with baked clay, so the people will be a mixture and will not remain united, any more than iron mixes with clay. [44] "In the time of those kings, the God of heaven will set up a kingdom that will never be destroyed, nor will it be left to another people. It will crush all those kingdoms and bring them to an end, but it will itself endure forever. [45] This is the meaning of the vision of the rock cut out of a mountain, but not by human hands—a rock that broke the iron, the bronze, the clay, the silver and the gold to pieces. "The great God has shown the king what will take place in the future. The dream is true and its interpretation n is trustworthy (Daniel 2:29-45 - New International Version -NIV)

Daniel's interpretation of the four kingdoms is what I want to talk about here because we are witnessing right now the resurgence of the fourth kingdom that will lead to the establishment of the fifth and final kingdom. The first kingdom that Daniel saw was the Babylonians that ended in 539 B.C. when they were defeated by the Medo-Persians. The second kingdom, the Persians ended in 330 B.C when the Greeks conquered them. The third kingdom, under the rule of Alexander the Great ended around 146 B.C. when the Greek peninsula was annexed by the rising empire of Rome. This fourth kingdom, Rome is the one we need to focus on because this is the one that will lead to the establishment of the fifth and final kingdom.

Now the rise of the fourth kingdom, which became known as the Roman Empire was referred to in Daniel's dream interpretation, as the legs of the statue, which like the empire was separated into two parts. Over a period of about twelve centuries, the Roman Empire grew from a fledgling city-state at the start to the most dominant military and political power of the time. This had all been revealed to Daniel in dreams long before it actually happened. Here was just another example of God sending a messenger to warn the people. Rome continued to grow in power until the late 5th century A.D. or about the year 476 when due to declining morals and values, political corruption and most of all idolatry it finally fell.

After the fall of the Roman Empire or the fourth kingdom, Daniel Chapters 2 and 7 and Revelation 13 and 17 tell us that there will be ten revivals or resurrections of that kingdom. Now both Daniel and the apostle John, the author of Revelation, speak of the kingdoms as beasts. Daniel saw them as four beasts while John integrated them into one beast. This was because Daniel was looking forward and John was looking backward in history. At the writing of Revelation, the four kingdoms had already been combined into the one empire and so he referred to it as the beast. Daniel's fourth beast had ten horns while John's beast had seven heads and ten horns. The seven heads referred to are the last seven resurrections and the ten horns of John's beast refer to ten kings who will arise during the last resurrection.

The first three revivals would be at the hands of Non-Christian or gentile nations. Keep in mind that this period is after the advent of Jesus Christ and the start of the Christian era. These nations were called Vandals, Herulis and Ostrogoths. The names are not important for you to remember, but what is important is that they were noted in Daniel's story as the three horns that were uprooted.

I was considering the horns, and there was another horn, a little one, coming up among them, before whom three of the first horns were plucked out by the roots, And there, in this horn, were eyes like the eyes of a man, and a mouth speaking pompous words.

(Dan. 7:8 NKJV)

The little horn refers to the rise of the Catholic religious order under the first Pope. From this point on the next seven resurrections would still be connected in some way to the Catholic religion and the association gave rise to the term the Holy Roman Empire. As I said earlier in the book of Revelation John refers to his beast as having seven heads and ten horns. One head had received a deadly wound but was healed. This head refers to the fall or death of the Roman Empire in 476, but the healing came when the emperor Justinian restored the empire in 554. This was the first resurrection.

Please stay with me church we're coming to the end.

The second resurrection came when Charles, also known as Charlemagne, the leader of a barbaric tribe mostly of Germanic origin called the Franks, came to embrace Catholicism. As the man who became emperor of the Holy Roman Empire through his crowning by Pope Leo, Charles felt that he had a duty to spread the Christian faith using whatever means necessary. This was not God's plan but his own.

The next resurrection, the third, came under the leadership of a ruthless warrior named Otto the Great who was anointed as a German king in 936 A.D. He became the first of a long line of German emperors who would dominate the European political arena. In 962 the Pope bestowed the imperial crown upon him and for the next 800 years German kings would call themselves Roman emperors of the German nation.

Resurrection number four took place when in the 15th century Frederick V of Habsburg, Germany was crowned by the pope as a new Holy Roman Emperor. This title, under the heading of the Habsburg Dynasty, endured through his family until the dynasty ended in 1806 when the rise of the Protestant Reformation in opposition to the Roman Church weakened the dynasty considerably and paved the way for the next resurrection. This one would come not from within Germany or even Italy, but France.

The fifth resurrection came when a new general by the name of Napoleon Bonaparte rose to power in the early nineteenth century. Napoleon who has been credited for being a military genius, even to this day, crushed finally what remained of the Hapsburg Empire and set out to accomplish his vision of restoring the Roman Empire. Napoleon crowned himself in 1804 the new Roman Emperor establishing a new leader of the quasi Roman Empire.

Now Napoleon had his problems with the Catholic Church because he did not want to share his power. He also differed with the church because of its political power and capacity to influence kings all through the previous resurrections. However, Napoleon was able to overcome the volatile relationship by creating and getting the church to sign the concordat of 1801, which was an agreement that established the parameters of church and state.

Napoleon continued to rise in power with the endorsement of the Roman Church until it is said that at his political height he ruled 70 million subjects across the European continent. However, his ambition to rule the world was just a harbinger of another power hungry figure that was to follow him and it led to his and his empire's downfall. After launching a disastrous militarily campaign against Russia in 1812 he was thoroughly humiliated and lost over half a million troops. Shortly after that he engaged in another military campaign at the famous battle of Waterloo in which he was totally defeated and that ended his reign and that of the fifth resurrection.

The sixth resurrection would come at the hands of a duo of men rising to power from Italy and Germany. In 1914, the First World War broke out which transformed the face of Europe. When it ended four years later major problems remained. Out of the political and economic turmoil two new strongmen would arise with new dreams of uniting Europe and expanding beyond its borders. Their names were Benito Mussolini in Italy and Adolf Hitler in Germany. Both of these men signed agreements with the Roman Church that gave a legitimate face to their fascist beliefs. Also both men embraced the desire to restore the Roman Empire and formed an alliance creating what was called the Rome-Berlin Axis. Hitler bragged that the new German Empire would not only be restored but it would rival the prior Holy Roman Empire.

From 1939 until 1945, under the leadership of these two powerful men who some say were demon possessed, the Second World War raged involving countries in over five continents including the United States. At the conclusion of this "War to end all Wars" as it has been referred to the accepted belief was that there would never be another war of that magnitude. However, this being only the sixth resurrection, there was still according to Daniel's and the Apostle John's revelations one more that had to come. Even though several countries on the European continent had been almost totally destroyed, as we look around today and marvel at how quickly the countries, especially the German nation have recovered, it's not hard to see that what has been prophesied is in the process of coming to realization.

According to scripture, in Revelation Chapter 17:8 (NKJV) the angel was talking to John and it says:

"The beast that you saw was, and is not, and will ascend out of the bottomless pit and go to perdition. And those who dwell on the earth will marvel, whose names are not written in the Book of Life from the foundation of the world when they see the beast that was, and is not, and yet is."

Let's examine the language in this scripture and see what it really means. Having looked at our review of the resurrections we have seen how an empire could once exist, then disappear, then reappear in a somewhat different form. In the scripture the beast, symbolic of an empire "was, and is not, and yet is" is telling us that the

Roman Empire, which does not now exist, will be restored yet again in the near future. It was, meaning it existed in the past; it currently "is not," meaning it doesn't exist right now, and "yet is" means it is developing.

As for the seventh resurrection we need but look at the formation of new alliances of European nations to see how it will develop. European unification coming via the city of Rome and involving the Vatican as the religious foundation and backing is fostering the new resurgence. It is but a matter of time before we will see it in its final form fulfilling the prophecy of the seven resurrections.

Brothers and sisters I'm telling you that right now the seventh resurrection is underway. We see and hear the reports almost daily of the wars raging in Europe but be mindful of what is the under developing structure. We also hear of a new leader emerging - consider who this might really be. We must be observant of the signs that are being presented to us. As I told you earlier in my message, God always sends messages and messengers to warn us about impending actions. So we must take heed and be forewarned regarding the signs if there is any possibility of thwarting His future discipline. Before I close let me draw your attention to one more scripture so that we may all have a clearer picture of the signs and what is about to happen.

In Matthew Chapter 24 Jesus told His disciples about specific signs to watch out for before the end will come. Until now man did not have the means to totally destroy the whole world and wipe out every man on the planet so some of these signs were clearly meant for the future. But now with the creation of the atom bomb and other nuclear devices we have the capability. Let's look at the signs and see where we are today.

Jesus said there would be wars and rumors of wars. Well check that one off. Wars are raging right now that we hear about almost daily. He said there would be drought and famine. Well check that one off too. When we look at some of the third world countries and even right here at home we can already see evidence of that. He said there would be earthquakes. We can also see that happening now with earthquakes and other natural disasters occurring more frequently in all parts of the world. He said there would be pestilence. Who among you has not heard of the AIDs epidemic? Is this not pestilence? Check that one off too. He said nation would rise against nation. Well we already see that happening - check that one off. He said many would come in my name - well this emerging leader we've been hearing about over there, as well as some others, seems to fit that description to me so let's check that one off too. Finally He said that the gospel of the kingdom would be preached to all nations and then the end would come. Until now that was virtually impossible because the technology to reach the entire world was not there. But now it is so should we not place a check there also?

And so as you can see all that is necessary for the end to come is already lining up to bring about that glorious day when He shall reappear. Brethren, I truly believe that the time has come when He is no longer willing to be patient with our disobedience. The wrath of His anger is about to be carried out. But let us also be mindful that God is a merciful but discerning God who will relent immediately if man in a totally collective effort will turn from his evil ways and seek His face. It's not too late. Remember that even in the time of Jonah when God sent him to the city of Nineveh to preach and instruct the people about their indiscretions, they listened to his teachings and repented. And so God relented from the immediate destruction of Assyria. If He did it for them, He will do it for us too.

There will be no escape from the wrath to come if man continues down the path of destruction. Please hear me now I cannot emphasize enough the importance of genuine repentance and acceptance of the teachings of Jesus about the coming Kingdom of God. I don't think the references that have been made previously about that Kingdom have been made clear to you. So now I want to clarify what it all means.

As I have referred to in the Books of Daniel and Revelation it was given to the profits Daniel and John to see in the distant future what was going to happen to man if he continued to disobey. What is going on in the world right now is the final resurrection of the Roman Empire, or the revival of the fourth kingdom. It is also to be referred to as the Holy Roman Empire because of the religious leader who is also right now emerging as a leader in the European area. This leader will lead the world to the brink of destruction.

There is going to come a time of utter chaos in the world because of people following the leadership of this religious leader who is the Anti-Christ. No man shall be spared the wrath of God when he at the command of this, world dominating, figure takes upon himself the mark of the beast on his hand or on his forehead. It will be irreversible and everlasting. The time is drawing very near when all this is going to come to pass for the Lord has spoken it and so it shall be done

On the day of the Great Tribulation when God will separate His people from the rest, like the wheat from the chaff, in a moment, in the twinkling of an eye, those who have obeyed the voice of God and those who have been called according to his purpose shall be spared and taken to a place of safety. It will be a time of great destruction to the world and all that is in it. The sun will cease to shine and the moon will no longer give off its light.

In the Book of Revelation the things that are spelled out in the Chapters we talked about are real and will be carried out by the angels that have been given the task of making it happen. There is a future in the final outcome for those who are willing to repent and be part of the saints who will be glorified with spiritual bodies and become part of the Heavenly Host who will return to the earth to serve under the tutelage of Christ himself during the Millennium.

My brothers and sisters this message has not been given to scare you but to awaken you to what is about to happen in this world soon. It's not a message of gloom and doom as so many of today's skeptics refer to it, but it is a message of hope and a directive on how you can achieve eternal life. Consider your life right now. If you have not accepted Jesus Christ as your Lord and Savior, I invite you to come and take the hand of a deacon or deaconess. Confess your need to be saved and join the throng of those who lives will be changed at His coming. The doors of the church are now open.

Won't you come? The time is growing short when the choice will not be available anymore. Today He will be your Savior, tomorrow He will be your judge. Come, don't let this opportunity pass you by. Come!

After the formal service ended and the benediction given the congregation was so inspired by the message that the sanctuary was slow in emptying. Mimi and I along with Midge also remained seated longer than we usually would just reflecting on what "Doc" said about the near future. The kids, not fully cognizant of what it all meant, were getting impatient to go but even they sensed something big had just happened. Finally, we all got up and began to exit.

As we stood in the lobby trying to decide what to do now, the idea came up that Josh was going to be playing in the biggest game of his young life on tomorrow night so we wanted to do something that would help him get prepared. The question was what could that be? After listening to the adults toss around several possibilities, it was Jerry who came up with the perfect solution. Not too far from where Midge lived in a nearby town was an amusement arcade that had a series of basketball hoops set up in a row. Jerry had been there before while visiting with his cousin so he knew all about it. What was great about the idea was that it would give Jerry a chance to compete against his idol while providing *Josh a* chance to perfect his jump shot. The sister who also was big on basketball would tag along and compete against both the boys. In addition to the site being an ideal place for the kids, there was a nice quick serve food emporium there that would give the adults a chance to eat and talk. The kids would join us to eat when they finished playing.

We ordered meals from the concessionaires then found a table in a corner of the courtyard away from the main crowd large enough to accommodate all of us. Soon after we sat down and started to dig in, Midge started talking.

"Mimi did you notice how intense dad was in today's delivery? I can't remember ever seeing him like that giving a sermon. I'm worried about him."

"Yes sister I did notice. It was as if he was talking about something going to happen tomorrow. You think he knows something he didn't say?"

"I don't know but I just have a strange feeling even though he was talking about future events that something is looming just over the horizon for us. Maybe it's just me but I can't shake the feeling ever since he preached."

"Well sis whatever is going to happen is going to happen so as dad used to say let's enjoy today for tomorrow will take care of itself."

I listened to both of them and got caught up in the sense of foreboding because I too sensed an unusual tone of urgency in the preacher's message. But as Mimi said let's enjoy today and help Josh get ready for tomorrow's game.

After about another twenty minutes the kids came and found us in the courtyard. Tired and famished Josh wanted to order something from each vendor. Midge quickly halted that idea and advised making another choice. Josh settled on the large hamburger plate with all the trimmings and of course Jerry wanted the same. Carolyn decided she wanted something different so she chose an oriental meal. They got their food and returned to the table where each of them made the meals quickly disappear.

When Joshua was finished eating I asked him about the team's readiness for tomorrow's game. His answer was so astute I was a little surprised at such wisdom coming from one so young. He looked straight at me and said:

"The coach has shown us how to play the game and what we can expect from the other team, so now it's up to us to do what he said do. But no matter the outcome he told us to go and have fun. I think we're ready for anything."

I applauded him for his attitude and clearly understood why Jerry looked up to him. Midge's smile at his answer also told me a lot about how she was raising him. It was now about four O'clock and we left the arcade.

Outside we said our goodbyes and talked about meeting again after the game. Mimi dropped me off at my place and she continued on home. Inside my building lobby I looked around again for the strange man, now almost as a conditioned reflex action. He was not there so I went upstairs and let myself in the apartment. Not long after taking off my coat and settling in I heard a report on the news about the latest occurrence in war-ravaged Europe. But this time the report was not about the war. It was talking about some outbreak of reactions by their young soccer players to a sports drink. When I heard that news it immediately got my attention so I sat down to hear the whole story. Unfortunately, the reporter had little more information than it was a serious outbreak affecting large groups of young people in several countries. He never did divulge the name of the drink so I went to bed wondering - could it be Candoo?

#######

In Washington the next day as lawmakers were preparing to vacate the city for their annual holiday break, some who were privy to breaking news about the outbreak reaction affecting youth in Europe and the Middle East were concerned enough to delay exiting until they knew more about it. Reports were now coming in at a high and secretive level that the source of the problem could be attributed to a sport drink made in the U.S.

Tango Hernandez, who had returned to the capital to oversee the round up of those high level executives involved in the Candoo conspiracy was one of those receiving the latest reports. While he was excited that the criminal element embedded in the workings of a revered government agency were being apprehended here at home, he was saddened by the fact that the drug had reached foreign shores and possibly could be the cause of something that was sure to present a new challenge to international diplomatic relations. Assured that the arrests and processing was under control, he turned his full attention to learning all he could about whether the drug really was Candoo.

When confirmation came via the latest electronic media that Candoo was in fact the cause of the outbreak, Tango called Ron in New York.

"Hello, this is Ron Powers."

"Ron - Tango here, how are you?"

"Hi Tango - I'm fine where are you?"

"I'm back in D.C. riding herd on the Health Service people roundup."

"Yeah I heard that was happening. How's it going?"

"That's going well but there's a new problem surfacing quickly."

"Oh yeah, what's that?"

"I don't know if you heard the news yet but Candoo has reached Europe and the Middle East and is wreaking havoc on young people, particularly those involved in soccer."

"I did hear something briefly on the news last night about that but no one said it was definitely Candoo."

"Well as of a report that I received just a little while ago it has been confirmed. The reporters last night probably didn't know yet."

"So what happens now?"

"I'm not sure but I'll be meeting with my boss and the rest of the team soon and I'll know more. I will keep you updated. What's happening with the round up there?"

"The police started moving in around here last week but I don't think they're finished. I don't know what happened at the headquarters. When I find out I'll call you."

"Okay looks like we both have some information to get. I'll talk to you soon."

"Yeah okay - bye."

After hanging up with Tango I started thinking about who I could call at headquarters to find out what's happening there. Moments later Jennifer's name popped into my mind. I had not spoken to her in some time and I wasn't sure whether she was even still there especially after all that happened, but it couldn't hurt to try her number. On the third ring she answered.

"Jennifer speaking may I help you?"

"Hi Jennifer this is Ron Powers remember me?"

"Hi. Of course I remember you are you still around?"

"Yeah for now, but I don't know how much longer. Listen I just wanted to find out what's going on up there since all the scandal news broke. What do you know?"

"For the last few days the police have been all over this place. They even tried to arrest Mr. Jenkovitch on Friday, but somehow he got out of it. When they went to get Herbert Crandall no one could find him and he hasn't been seen since. I don't know what's going to happen now. Mr. Jenkovitch is very nervous but he's not doing or saying anything to anybody."

"They can't find Crandall huh? I'm not surprised. Have you heard anything about the plant shutting down?"

"No. I've heard nothing. Is it supposed to?"

"Well not completely, but one product line should shut down right away if I can make it happen."

"Is that the Candoo line?"

"Yes, you know about it right?"

"I've heard some things about it."

"Well thanks for the update – watch your back up there."

"You know I will. You be careful too. Goodbye."

"Bye."

Now it was time to walk around the plant and find out who was missing. I left my office and headed straight to production. Once there I was shocked to see the formerly protected entrance door wide open and nobody guarding the line. There were a few workers in there but they were just standing around or sitting doing nothing. The line was down so I went over to one of them and asked what was going on. The reply was that they were waiting for new orders on what to do since Jablonski left.

I can't say that I felt sorry for them because I was too happy to know that Candoo was dead or at least very ill. But I did feel badly that they may be out of work soon just before the big holiday. My foremost and primary question had been answered, but somehow I had the feeling that the force behind this whole nightmare was not giving up. There had to be something more to follow. I left production and went to find Marsha in the labs. When I got there it was like a deserted island. The only two people in there were she and Martin.

I opened the lab door and walked in. It didn't take long before they hurriedly told me, before I even asked, that the other chemists were down in Lab 1 huddling together trying to come up with ways to protect themselves from being included in the police roundup.

Even those who had been sympathetic to the development of the new product and even volunteered to help devise methods to increase production, were now scrambling to put distance between them. It seems that all of the monetary glitter of what they expected would be a large windfall in their pockets for the big holiday, was now a liability should they be implicated in any association with creating the monster. Ironic as it was those same chemists who argued with Mimi and Martin about the merits of Candoo were now asking for help in developing some type of antidote and begging for bailout support should they be called as witnesses.

It entered my mind to go down there and see exactly how they were handling the division, but Marsha discouraged me from doing so by saying I could get myself in more trouble than it would be worth because of who was involved. Apparently some of the most trusted and senior chemists in the company had been duped into believing the lie about Candoo. So I backed off and decided to go back to my office and see whether Tango had called with any new information on the situation overseas. When I got there no messages were on the phone, but I did notice that someone had placed a note on my desk.

Quickly, I opened and read it. It was a warning from an “anonymous observer” that the time had come when I would be removed from the planet because of my interference in something that I had no idea how big it was. It was not signed and there was no specific information regarding just how soon I was to be removed so I couldn’t really become too concerned about it. But since someone had taken the time to come to my office and carefully place it where it wouldn't be missed, I did have to acknowledge that an observer was watching out for my negative welfare. I set the note aside and didn't give it any further thought. But strangely enough as soon as I did that, the phone rang.

"Hello - Ron Powers here."

"So you think you've won don't you?" came the response on the other end. It was clearly the voice of Herb Crandall and from the tone it seemed that he was in some distress.

"Believe me Powers you have not yet seen the magnitude of the evil that is going to come over you in the next few days and there is nothing you can do to stop it. You have angered powers that you have no idea how strong they are. I tried to convert you and bring you into the fold that would protect you, but you refused and now you must pay the price. Goodbye - I will not be seeing you again in this world."

His last statement was so eerie it did get to me because it sounded so imminent. But when he hung up I thought about what the strange man in my building had already told me about my being protected so I dismissed the feeling and went back to doing my work.

I stayed at my desk through the lunch hour and didn't hear from Marsha so I assumed she was doing the same trying to deal with the situation there with her colleagues. Around 4:30 she called and wanted to talk about the plans for getting to the game tonight. We worked out the details and I started to wrap up my work tasks for the day. I was not sure just what tomorrow was going to present in terms of new challenges but for today I had had enough to think about. At exactly 5:00 O'clock I put everything away as I usually did and headed for the street to get a cab.

In the ride home it was a little weird because this was the same driver I had ridden with a little while back who was so interested in what was going on at Canon that I suspected he might have been a plant for one of the company's board members trying to get an assessment regarding employee morale. He asked again about what we made there and how the company was doing. I started to give him the standard elevator talk reply but in the middle of one of my sentences he looked at me in his rearview mirror and asked directly about Candoo. I sensed that he knew more than what he was letting on and was probing for more than just a standard reply, so I asked him what he had heard about it.

He said that he heard it was a dangerous drug and it shouldn't be on the market. I looked at his face in the mirror and asked him where he got that from. He declined to give any information regarding his sources but he asked me point blank whether the information was correct. I didn't want to corroborate his information at this point especially since the company's official position regarding the product had not been made public so I adroitly danced around providing a direct answer. The answer I gave was like a woman's old fashion hoop skirt - it covered everything but touched on nothing. Even though I'm sure he didn't receive what he was looking for he seemed to be satisfied with my response and continued to drive silently.

As we got closer to my place and the street lighting got progressively worse, I wondered just how many others in the general public were asking the same question that the driver had posed to me. I wondered if the news about what was happening overseas had reached right down to the grass roots population and those that were involved in any kind of sports activities as coaches or supervisors were becoming aware of the potential danger associated with Candoo. It was a challenging thought and I wondered about tonight's game and whether the coaches had heard the news.

When I got upstairs and looked at the clock I realized I didn't have a whole lot of time to change and get ready to meet Mimi if I planned to be on time. I quickly shed my suit and searched for what I considered to be appropriate arena clothing. Fortunately, I had recently bought a heavy athletic warm-up suit that was perfect for the occasion. I changed put on my heavy winter overcoat and headed out the door.

There was no time to try and get hold of Alex so I took the brief walk to the dreaded subway station. As I descended the stairs and again witnessed the usual transit station activity it crossed my mind about what's going to happen to these people when what "Doc" says is going to happen, happens. Will they have any opportunity to seek salvation and how will they receive word about the chance? Of course I had no answer to the question but the next time I talk to the preacher I intended to ask him.

After the few station stops between my neighborhood and Mimi's I once again ascended the stairs to the street and walked quickly to her building. It was still cold and I wondered whether there was going to be adequate warmth inside the gym where the game was to be played. If there was one thing I hated at any sporting event it was to be uncomfortable trying to enjoy the game. I was not familiar with the High School that was hosting the event, but from what I had heard from Midge it was fairly new and had all of the state of the art equipment. With that in mind I set aside my trepidation about being cold inside the gym.

I walked in the lobby and followed the usual routine of announcing myself to the desk person and having her page Mrs. Robinson. It was not long before the reply came back from her that I was to go outside and wait and she would pick me up in just a few minutes. So I went back out and faced the cold. Minutes later I saw the car coming from the garage area and pulling up in front of me. She rolled down the window and asked if I wanted to drive. Being that I had no idea where the school was I declined saying that in the interest of time she had better do the driving.

When I got inside the car Jerry was already very excited and starting talking rapidly about how his cousin was going to destroy those Regal Cadillac's, which was the other team named after their sponsor a dealership in the area. I listened to him rant for a minute but then cautioned him about placing all of the responsibility on one player's shoulders. I reminded him that it was a team sport and all of them had to play together to get good results. He quickly acknowledged my sports wisdom, but then reasserted his belief that his cousin was the star player. Realizing that I was not going to win that battle I backed off and just said I hoped it was going to be a good game.

Mimi wasn't exactly sure where the school was either even though she had a fairly good idea about the location so after we got into the area it was just a matter of time before we were able to find it. We got there relatively early but cars were already starting to enter the parking lot. Even though this was a youth basketball tournament the publicity that it had been given by the media, prompted by the league's wealthy sponsors, you would have thought that this was a professional outing. We pulled into the lot and found a spot to park almost right away. The crowd that was amassing indicated a wide cross section of patrons coming to see the kids perform. I could see that there were obviously parents coming out to support their kids but also there were people from the neighborhood, representatives from the sponsoring organizations, scouts from colleges around the area and more so just people who enjoyed watching basketball at any level.

We went inside and after I paid the modest admission fee for all of us and also contributed to a box that was seeking donations to help support the league, I was gratified when we entered the gym to find the room temperature nice and cozy. I quickly removed my overcoat and took Mimi's and Jerry's over to an area where they were checking garments. Midge was correct in telling me about the school for it was easy to see that the architect and builders had not missed any creature comfort amenities for the school. I don't know what kind of budget was set aside for this high school, but whatever it cost, the Board of Education certainly got their money's worth from the investment.

As the crowd continued to pour in, the gym began to fill up quickly. I'm glad we came early because we were able to get seats fairly close to the courtside. For a youth basketball game I was really impressed at how organized the event was so far. There were even cheerleaders for both teams made up of volunteers from the high school's large cheer team. They had divided themselves up in equal numbers to support the younger kids. In addition, the high school band had volunteered to play the National Anthem. Jerry could hardly contain himself anticipating the start of the game and before long his enthusiasm began to infect me. Now I was ready to get started also.

Since we arrived early, Mimi called her sister who had gotten tied up with some of her school obligations and was going to be a little late getting there, and told her we would try to save her and her companion seats. The seats were the bench type so clearly it was not going *to* be easy to hold space since people were beginning to arrive in bunches. Luckily Mimi spotted Midge coming in the door, shortly after we were seated, and stood up to try and get her attention. Waving her arms vigorously she was able to attract her sister and her companion, who I had never seen before, and they started toward our location. Curious I asked Mimi who was the guy she was with. Mimi laughed and asked me whether I was being protective of her sister. I answered no, not yet but I still wanted to know who he was. She replied that the man was her ex-husband and the father of her kids.

He was tall and athletically built so I could see where Josh got his basketball genes from. When they arrived at our seats and Mimi introduced me to him we shook hands and I could feel the strength in his large hands. Midge also mentioned that he was a former college and semi-pro basketball player who never missed any of his son's games. He was the one responsible for the early skills training that Josh received in all sports. I was impressed and wondered to myself why after looking at them seemingly get along so well, what happened to the marriage. I planned to ask Mimi later, but right now things were beginning to get underway with the game.

At 7:15 right on the mark the lights dimmed for a couple of seconds and then came back up. Standing in the middle of the court was the school's principal with mike in hand ready to provide the opening ceremonies. He gave a brief speech about the school and how happy he was that the league selected his school to host this tournament. After his remarks he then called to the floor the president of the league along with some of his associates. The president then provided his commercial about how they were about helping the kids to become the best they could be both on the court and in life. It was a nice opening for such a big game for the kids and it really sold the program to parents and other supporters. I felt confident that after his remarks the donation box was going to gather more funds than it did when we entered.

After the league president spoke he turned the mike over to the announcer for the game who was to introduce the teams. The lights went down again as a spotlight focused on one end of the court and the announcer began to announce the players for the Cadillac's who were assigned the visiting team role. As each player was introduced and the crowd applauded wildly, it was hard to believe that this was just, not even a semi-pro game, but a youth basketball game. When he finished with the players for the Cadillac's the spotlight switched to the other end of the court and the players for the Right-Aid Raiders, the designated home team, trotted in as they were introduced. I was so impressed at how organized this whole presentation was I knew that soon I had to get involved in some way with helping the program to continue to help these kids.

At almost exactly 7:30 PM both starting teams assembled on the floor ready for the tip-off. Josh was a starter at the small forward position and I marveled at how calm he seemed to be. I also marveled at how tall at this young age some of the players were on both sides. Even though the Raiders were generally somewhat smaller I could see no fear on any of their faces regarding the Cadillac's.

The referee stood at center court and positioned both jumpers readying them for the toss. The ball was then thrown up in the air and the game was underway. As expected, the Cadillac's controlled the tip and the ball went to their back court players. Quickly the ball was placed in the hands of their point guard as he directed traffic in the opening series. As he crossed the center court line the ball was passed around deftly and it became obvious right away that these youngsters had been well coached. They moved the ball around smoothly in a weave pattern for a few minutes and then the shooting guard broke toward the basket and received a bullet pass from the point guard right on target as he cut. The move was quick and precise as the guard was able to get under the basket and score a simple layup.

Undaunted by the excellent execution on the opening play, the Raiders point guard brought the ball up the court from that end and started their play series. Just like the Cadillac's, it was also obvious that they were well coached and their skill set was not to be taken lightly by any opponent. It was also obvious after just a few minutes of play how each of these teams came to be the league's representatives of the best teams. The scoring went back and forth by each team throughout the first quarter and at the end the score was tied at 15 points each.

The second quarter started with the Raiders having the ball and the intensity of play appeared to increase after the break. Each team was playing with a high level of controlled enthusiasm and mistakes on both sides were few. Josh was having a particularly good game having scored six of his team's first fifteen points and captured three rebounds. As the game progressed the coaches for both teams were bellowing out instructions and encouraging their players to keep their heads in the game. Their intent was for them not to lose concentration on what they had been taught.

It was an exciting game and I can't remember any game I had ever been to that was much more thrilling than to watch these young players compete. I could see without looking directly at him, but through the corner of my eye, that Nathan, Josh's father was bubbling over with pride and satisfaction. I believe he was just as into the game as the coaches for he was directing play from the stands. The game continued with the score see-sawing back and forth until late in the second quarter when the Cadillac's went on a run and were able to garner a six point lead. As the final minutes ticked off in the half the buzzer sounded and the score on the board read 36 to 30 in favor of the Cadillac's. Mildly disappointed, Nate got up and invited me to go with him out to the concession stand to get something for the ladies. Apparently, he wanted to talk to me. After asking the ladies what they would like, we both got up excused ourselves and left the gym.

When we reached the food concession he turned to me and said:

"I've heard a lot about you from Midge and Mimi. How long have you been dating?"

I was a little surprised at the question coming so directly since we just met but it was clear he was leading up to something so I answered him.

"We've been going out now a few months why do you ask?"

"Do you plan to marry her?"

"Yeah I really would like to. You sound like her father – why all the questions?"

"Man, don't get me wrong I just wanted to see if you had the same run in with her father that I did. You know that I'm her former husband and those are my kids don't you?"

"Yeah I've been told."

"Well I just wanted to let you know the reason why we're not together anymore."

I couldn't have planned finding this out any better than the way it was working. Now I was all ready to hear his explanation, but I casually offered him a way out.

"You certainly don't have to explain anything to me" I said, but he continued on anyway.

"I guess I still love her. She's a beautiful lady inside and out, but I just couldn't get with that religious thing with her father. I'm not now and I guess I never have been into all that. She wanted me to go to church with her every Sunday and I did at first but it just wasn't me. Besides Sunday morning is when I go out and play hoops with the guys. After a while it just got to the point where I wanted to play the game more than going with her so she gave up trying to convince me otherwise and then she quit the marriage. I'm still not into all that church stuff but I really need her back. So I guess I'm just asking you how you're handling it?"

I didn't know what to say to him because he sounded much like I was just a short time ago. It wasn't until I got hooked on "Doc's" messages that I came around to a new way of thinking. I wanted to say that to him just how I was affected when I realized what Reverend Deveraux was really talking about and began to read for myself what the Bible said about it. Maybe now was the beginning of the time when what the strange man in my building was referring to when he said I had to spread the Word. I don't know but I got this feeling and was almost compelled to say something that would try and get Nate back in church to hear more of what "Doc" had to say.

Just as I started to address the idea with him our turn to order came up at the stand and that conversation ended. I did however, manage to say to him that we needed to talk more about it so we exchanged contact information and promised to get together again at another time and that was it. When we returned to our seats it was obvious that the ladies had been talking about us because their conversation changed abruptly as we arrived. I didn't say anything and neither did he but we both knew what was happening.

The teams came out to start the second half and play began. Both teams seemed to be more energized than at the start of the game and I attributed this to rousing pep talks by both coaches during the intermission. Josh quickly contributed by scoring a basket within the first few seconds and his individual energy *level seemed to* surpass his other team members. Jerry was very excited by this and stood up and cheered loudly as well as Nate. The ladies were trying to restrain their emotions but I could tell Midge was just as excited as Nate when they looked at each other smiling as they beamed with pride.

The scoring deficit that was present at the conclusion of the first half was erased and the score was again tied as they came up to the mid-point of the third quarter. Both teams were exhibiting a great deal of enthusiasm as they continued to compete at a very high level. However, I knew from experience that even though they were very young, running up and down the court at the pace they were going was going to take its toll at some point. What I could not have imagined though was the fact that there were some other factors that were about to come into play.

After a brief time out called by the Cadillac's coach, both teams resumed play. The intensity was still there but then something strange began to happen. During a drive to the basket one of the Cadillac players, without being touched, suddenly dropped the ball grabbed his stomach and fell to the floor. The silence in the crowed was deafening as everyone there sympathetically fell to the floor with the young man. Trainers and coaches for the team came out immediately to attend to the young man. With their assistance, after a minute or so, he was able to gingerly walk off the floor and play resumed.

It wasn't more than another minute or two later two players from the Raiders went down with apparently the same ailment. Moments after that another Cadillac's player had fallen and now almost the whole starting team was disabled to some degree. The remaining bench players entered the game but the sense permeating the crowd was that there was something very wrong going on here. Midge, Nate, Mimi and I were very concerned but when I looked at Mimi I knew what we were both thinking.

Not long after the first outbreak it was just a matter of time before the situation struck very close to home. Josh who was picking up more of the responsibility and playing even harder because now the substitute players were playing, had the ball and was driving to the basket when just as the first casualty did, he went down in a heap. It was hard to restrain Nate from running onto the floor accompanied by Midge but Mimi and I had to do it. The thoughts running through each of our minds could not have been hard to read by anyone aware of what was going on in youth sports. I looked at Mimi squeezed her hand and whispered I hope this is not what we think it is.

Chapter 16
"Redemption Tomorrow"

[9] After this manner therefore pray ye: Our Father which art in heaven, Hallowed be thy name.
*[10] **Thy kingdom come, Thy will be done in earth, as it is in heaven.***
[11] Give us this day our daily bread.
[12] And forgive us our debts, as we forgive our debtors.
[13] And lead us not into temptation, but deliver us from evil: For thine is the kingdom, and the power, and the glory, forever. Amen. (Matthew 6:9-13 KJV)

From the time that I first arrived in this city until now my life has been filled with a myriad of interesting things. But over the last several months both real and supernatural experiences have been foisted upon me in such a manner I still find it hard to believe. If someone had said to me at the start that these things would happen, I seriously would have looked at them wondering if they were in possession of a sound mind. In recent months occurrences have seemingly been orchestrated by some master arranger to provide me with maximum exposure to the syncopated rhythms of life.

When I think back and reflect on the times when growing up as a boy in the rural setting of a state that not too long ago had been one of the centers of a conglomerate of segregated states, many things come to mind about my rearing. I used to hear stories from adults who had the single intention of just scaring the daylights out of kids. Some of them were so intense that I would go to bed thinking that the whole world must be filled with nothing but evil people. At the time, it never occurred to me that the people telling the stories were the real evil ones. I came from a very loving home replete with the usual squabbles that families go through, but the one thing that I remember most coming from my mother was that as long as I believed that I could do something in life, then with the help of God, I could do it.

Somehow after she passed and left me at a fairly young age, that encouragement was not reinforced by my father and eventually dissipated. I didn't know at the time, and it wasn't until much later that I learned my father was struggling himself trying to understand why God took his beloved wife away so soon. After she departed we became somewhat estranged living in the same house. He threw himself into working harder at a number of different jobs and I just threw myself at whatever seemed to be good for me at the time.

Both of us drifted away from the church without her guidance and influence and I can't say that I was very disappointed then. Going to church for me was a chore I had to do because she insisted upon it. I guess he felt the same way too. The things that I do remember growing up in the church to that point were in Sunday school I didn't understand all the things my school teacher was trying to convey and I was completely turned off. Things like being born again, a kingdom was coming, Jesus was my savior - just didn't resonate with me. When I attempted to talk to some friends my age about it, they were just as confused as I was so the blind leading and following the blind was an appropriate expression for where we were.

Fortunately, I liked public school and was able to maintain slightly above average grades right up through high school. Blessed also with a gift of football talent I was able to get a scholarship to one of the local colleges where during my tenure there I excelled in mastering the art of getting in the middle of everything I had no business doing. My inquisitive nature would always lead me into areas which I didn't have enough good sense to stay out of. However, as the saying goes God looks out for fools and babies, I surmise that since I was no longer a baby I must have been the other. Looking back now and having been re-educated by Reverend Devereaux I am aware that there must have been then and even now something or someone that was protecting me from all the things I should have fallen prey to.

All during the years that I was growing up and before I left to go north and discover the big city, I never encountered a situation where the presence of evil permeated a whole environment. I knew about the occult and cult groups, though I had never been actually exposed to one, so to say now that it was new to me would be distorting the truth. When I came to Canon and after that memorable party launched my investigation into what was really going on here, my hands on experience with both was accelerated to the nth degree. Now as I look at where I am with regard to my childhood I wonder whether I am in the middle of another situation because this is where I'm supposed to be and that that someone who has always protected me is going to continue to do so.

#######

At Canon Enterprises today it appeared as if things were beginning to fall in place regarding the end of Candoo and the evil empire. The production line was down, the chemists who developed the product were running scared fearing for their very existence and the purveyors of gross evil were being rounded up - what a wonderful day this was. There was no way that I could have known that the day's positive outlook would suddenly turn deadly by evening. When I left work for the day and headed to Mimi's to pick her and Jerry up go to the basketball game, I was feeling quite good. Except for the cold, I was enjoying the feeling of having overcome something I had been working on for months. Isn't it strange though, how things can turn around so quickly in life with just a matter of a few hours elapsing in between the exalted highs and the devastating low's?

The tournament basketball game tonight in Jersey was supposed to be one of the crowning achievements in the life of a young rising star in the Devereaux family. Everyone was expecting to celebrate not only an anticipated victory on the court, but also a possible reunion of Midge and Nate. Since I have been with Mimi for some time now and become close friends with "Doc" I feel like one of the family. So what happened this night was as devastating to me as it was to the blood bonded family.

When the players began tumbling to the floor one after the other from no apparent hits or brushes from their opponents it was clear to everyone present that something very mysterious was at work here. Mimi and I looked at each other with a sense of trepidation suspecting that what we were seeing is the result of what we've been hearing about in the news. The crowd was in awe at what they were witnessing and the officials were at a loss as to what possibly could be the cause. Coaches and trainers for both teams were attending to their players but it was now determined that their skills were insufficient to address the emergency. So the 911 call was made.

In a matter of minutes ambulances began arriving and carting the youngsters off to area hospitals. Since the demand was higher than for normal emergency calls assistance was radioed for from surrounding towns. As we watched the succession of emergency vehicles arrive and then leave with what just a short time ago were healthy young individuals it was difficult to maintain composure. For Nate and Midge it would have been a futile effort made by anyone attempting to restrain them when they saw their first born child being carted away. Nate had her by the arm hurriedly exiting the gym chasing after the para-medics as they placed him in the ambulance. Their attempt for both of them to board the vehicle was rejected and only Midge was allowed to get in. Instructions were given for Nate to either follow the ambulance or come immediately to University Hospital.

Mimi and I with Carolyn and Jerry in tow went out to the parking lot and met Nate frantically trying to remember where he parked the car. I grabbed his arm and tried to calm him down by saying we were parked near here and he should ride with us. We all scrambled to get in Mimi's car wasting no time en route to the hospital. When we got there the emergency room was filled to capacity and getting to speak to the attendant who was swamped with other parents who had arrived before us trying to get the same information we were was futile. "Where's my child? - - Where is my child?" This was the question on every parent's lips.

The attendant was doing the best she could to try and coordinate admissions data with the deluge of questions being thrown at her by the onslaught of parents. Finally a doctor from the trauma center who seemed to be accustomed to handling mass admissions corralled the parent group by speaking through a loudspeaker and was able to bring some order to the chaos. His calm demeanor was reassuring and most of the parents responded to his instructions. However, there were still some who outrageously demanded to know immediately what was happening and had to be restrained by the hospital security. When the turn finally came for Nate to speak to the attendant he was told that his boy had been admitted but he was just like the others right now in intensive care and being administered to. There was no other information available at this time. He was cautioned to be patient and take a seat in the waiting area and more information would be given as soon as it became available.

At this point Midge who had already given her insurance information to the attendant prior to Joshua being admitted was beside herself with shock and the tears came gushing down her cheeks when she found Nate grabbed and held on to him. He tried to console her but was having a hard time processing what was happening to his son himself. Mimi and I sat with them not knowing what to say that could bring any comfort in a situation that we really didn't know what the extent of the problem might be. Mimi whispered in my ear that we should get hold of the Raider's coach and find out whether he had indeed served Candoo to his team. I quickly agreed and after telling Nate I was going to find the coach and get some information but I would be back as soon as I could, I went out. He was too distraught to say anything other than okay so I got up grabbed Mimi by the arm and we left the area.

After we searched the whole emergency waiting area and didn't see him we found out from another parent that the coach had gone to one of the other hospitals with some of the kids. He wasn't sure just which hospital he went to but thought that it was the University Medical Center just a short distance from here. Now I had to decide whether to leave Nate and Midge here without transportation or go and find coach and get the information we needed. Mimi and I decided the critical issue right now was finding out whether Candoo was the cause and in order to do that we had to speak to the coach. I volunteered to run back to where Nate was and tell him what we were doing. Mimi agreed and said for me to meet her at the car.

When I got back to Nate and Midge she had regained her composure somewhat and asked me whether I thought this could have anything to do with what she had been hearing on the news. I wasn't really surprised at her astute observation but I wanted to try and spare her further anguish so I guardedly answered that I wasn't sure but Mimi and I were on the way to find out. She looked at me intently and asked that I get back to her right away. I assured her I would and left the hospital.

Mimi and I arrived at the Medical Center in what I suspect would be record time as a result of my exceeding all speed limits and maybe even carefully ignoring a traffic light or two. Once inside in the emergency waiting area we found the Raider's coach, Jacob Neilly, or coach Jake as he was referred to by his kids, sitting with I believe were some of the parents of the youngsters who had been brought there. He was trying to console them making an effort to explain what he believed happened. We quickly approached the group and interceded rudely questioning him on whether the kids had been given Candoo at half-time. He got up from the group and looked at us strangely asking why that question. With a tone of anger in her voice Mimi asked again did he give them any Candoo? Feeling somewhat legally threatened he cautiously answered yes but it was right out of the bottles they had purchased from the supermarket. He also quickly added that they followed the instructions provided with the package. Mimi pushed again for more detail and he told her that each boy was given two cups of the drink that had been mixed with a popular brand of orange juice. She then informed him all about Candoo and advised him he should accompany us back to the school to retrieve what was left of the product and take a bottle to the hospital's lab.

After listening to what she told him he anxiously joined with us in getting back to the high school. When we got there the gym had been emptied but several administrators and the police were still there trying to assess what happened. Coach approached the principal told him the story and asked to be let back into the gym boy's locker room where the drinks were. The principal quickly walked with us to the locker room and allowed the coach to retrieve the remaining drinks and take the rest of the bottles. Again we wasted no time in getting back to University Hospital where Mimi met with the medical staff and informed them about what she had and told them that she was a chemist who knew something about this product. The same doctor who was successful in calming the crowd when we were there before was called and he met and consulted with Mimi while I stayed in the waiting room. Several minutes later, Mimi came out from wherever he took her and explained that she had given instructions on what they had and what tests they needed to run to determine how to treat the kids.

I don't know at that point whether I felt better that she was able to advise them or whether I was just so angry that this happened at all. There was nothing more we could do here so we went looking for Midge and Nate. We found them in the coffee shop near the waiting room where they had gone to get something to eat. We went inside and Mimi sat down with them while I went to the counter to get us some coffee. When I got back to the table the conversation was very animated about how this could have happened. Midge was grilling Mimi with questions seeking answers on how Candoo was able to pass FDA inspections and get into the stores. Both Mimi and I felt pressured to answer her but no matter what we offered it was not enough to console her and Nate. After several attempts at trying to answer her logically, we finally were able to get onto something she would accept. The influence of demonic forces present in the whole matter resonated with her. This she understood.

After the subject regarding negative forces being at work was raised there was silence at the table for several minutes. Midge had stopped talking and started staring off into space. I ended the silence by asking her where her father was. She broke her trance and slowly responded saying daddy was out of town in Washington, DC but would get here as soon as he could. Reverend Devereaux apparently had been summoned by the Foreign Relations Committee to help deal with the mounting accusations of U.S. treachery raised by several countries. His expertise in the field of end time prophetic events was thought to be relevant in this situation at this time. I wondered if the powers in Washington were finally waking up to what's really happening in the world now.

We sat in the coffee shop for another half hour when a nurse came in and announced that parents or guardians of the admitted youth would be permitted to visit for a short time. Nate and Midge got up quickly along with a few others and headed for the elevators. The intensive care unit was only on the third floor, but the elevator could not move fast enough to get Nate and Midge there. When the door opened on the floor the dim lighting in the hallway and the hushed voices of the nurses and attendants could not have been a more somber setting in preparation for what the couple was about to see.

#######

In Washington at this time many lawmakers aborted their plans to exit the city for the holiday break. The escalating tension caused by veiled threats and innuendos from some countries responding to the spreading idea that the U.S. was flooding their markets with a drug that was tantamount to initiating chemical warfare, had to be addressed. In offices at the highest levels discussions centered on what this product was and how could it have been exported without some FDA oversight. Finger pointing and counter punching was running rampant throughout offices representing both sides of the political aisle. Wherever Herb Crandall was his indwelled demonic spirit must have been reveling at the knowledge of the chaos surfacing in his target realm.

Also going on at this time was the Foreign Relations Committee meeting attended by the U.S. Vice-President, the CIA Director, several senior senators and other high ranking officials. The primary question on the floor was how did this happen. This was the meeting that Reverend Devereaux had been invited to provide his insight on things unexplainable via normal reasoning. Tango Hernandez was also present. The committee chairman had the floor and was attempting to inform his members and guests about what he knew of the international relations debacle.

"Gentlemen thank you for coming with such short notice to this hastily called session. Let me assure you that this committee had no prior knowledge regarding this Candoo product but we are actively investigating its history from creation to export. The oversight or lack thereof by the FDA is under scrutiny as I speak and I expect to have a full report by this time tomorrow. However, I have been informed by reliable sources that the FDA may have been infiltrated by some mysterious agents who are the source of the problem. When I say mysterious I implore you to keep an open mind when I introduce our guest who will speak on the subject. Gentlemen let me introduce to some and present to others Reverend Doctor Devereaux from New Jersey a distinguished scholar on the matter that we have before us. Reverend Devereaux please come forward."

The preacher got up from his seat and went to the podium.

"Mr. Chairman thank you for inviting me here to address this august and esteemed body. I like so many of you have been troubled by the news reports regarding a certain product created and produced here in this country that has so negatively affected the lives of young people in other parts of the world. It is difficult for me to accept the findings from one of our own government agencies that reveals an atrocity created and foisted upon the people of this country, as well as those in other parts of the world, by a company whose reputation has been for years an exemplary model for all corporations. However, as reluctant as I may be the facts are undeniable. I'm confident that by now all of you have been made aware of the reports charging the Canon Enterprises pharmaceutical company with creating and marketing the product called Candoo.

Candoo, as you may already know has the potential to be a devastating and possibly deadly drug when ingested by young people under the age of twenty-one. Hard to believe? Yes by all means. My reason for being here is not to tell you what you already know, but to examine with you the underlying motive behind the product's creation and to look at the intentions of the force driving the motivation. What I am about to say may offend some of you, but then truth telling is always capable of offending somebody.

Now all of you know that I'm a preacher, but I'm not going to sermonize or try to convince you to join my church today. What I am going to talk about is something that is happening right now in this world that you certainly need to be aware of. I don't know how many of you read the Bible but whether you believe in it or not the answers to what's happening in our world right now are in that book.

I said I'm not going to preach and I'm not, but I do need to draw your attention to just a couple of scriptures to help me make my point about world affairs, the Canon Corporation and some of our government agencies. There is a book in the Bible called Ephesians in which the Apostle Paul has written a letter to the people of a land called Ephesus which is now western Turkey. In that letter he talks about fighting a war that as it was then we are even now all involved in. Let me just quote a few lines from that letter.

[12] For we wrestle not against flesh and blood, but against principalities, against powers, against the rulers of the darkness of this world, against spiritual wickedness in high places.

Ephesians 6:12 King James Version (KJV)

What he was talking about is dealing with forces that are influenced by demonic spirits. Those same spirits did not go away when Paul died nor did they disappear when the age changed. I'm here to tell you that they are very present today. Now I realize many of you are thinking right now that I'm a religious fanatic or some sought of doom and gloom preacher, but let me draw your attention to what is happening in the world around you even as I speak. Before I do that let me continue with the second scripture I want to quote to finish my point. This passage is from the Book of Revelation which I'm confidant all of you have heard of if not read.

This great dragon—the ancient serpent called the devil, or Satan, the one deceiving the whole world - was thrown down to the earth with all his angels. (Rev. 12:9)

Now let us look at the facts. We know that there has been a serious breach in the protocols that have governed our country and its industries for centuries. We also know that until recently the types of atrocities, such as the development of a product like Candoo, was unheard of. Further we accept that the agencies put in place to monitor any deviant activities have been heretofore successful in their oversight. Then let us ask ourselves how what should not have been able to happen, happened. The answer my friends goes right back to the scripture from Revelations and that is – Satan, the great dragon, through his lackeys, has deceived the whole world and pulled the wool right over the eyes of the people who have been entrusted with seeing the wrong that they have allowed to be conducted right before them. Further the scripture dealing with spiritual wickedness in high places is referring to those who have acceded to high positions, in our corporations and even in our government, that are under the influence of Satan himself.

You may balk at the use of the term dragon in this current day and age and want to associate it with mythological tales of yesterday, but the reference as given in this book paints a vivid picture of a beast called Satan and the devil that may be seen as a true dragon of today. There will be times in the very near future when you will even ask yourself how you could have missed all of the signs that were being shown to you by the actions of those associates closest to you. Again it will be because of the deceptive practices of that master deceiver. Do not be alarmed at what I'm telling you now because even though these scripture were written a long time ago they represent prophecy that has fulfillment in our lifetime as its destiny.

Now my friends regarding what's happening in the Middle East and Europe, through the artful skills of our most experienced ambassadors we will be able to pacify the furor being raised by the most zealous foreign accusers. However, the problem goes deeper than what has been caused by their reaction to the product called Candoo. This is just the tip of the iceberg when it comes down to what is going to happen in the world soon.

Let me conclude my remarks by saying I have been made aware that the men and women who are responsible for creating and delivering this evil drink Candoo to the general public, are being rounded up and placed in legal custody. But for each one of them that is apprehended I offer that there is a willing and able replacement ready to step in and continue the mission of the devil. There is only one way that we will be able to thwart the wiles of Satan and possibly curtail what has been prophesied to occur soon. The answers gentlemen are provided right here in this book. You who make the laws and determine how the people shall be governed according to them, should if you haven't already done so familiarize yourselves with God's laws as spelled out here and then initiate your decisions based on what you find.

That's all I have to give you today and I hope you will take seriously what I've said. If it sounded like I was preaching to you blame it on my head and not my heart. I came here to sincerely provide insight on what I know about prophecy and what I see happening around the world today and how they are interrelated. What you do with the information is up to you but realize the decisions you make in response to the foreign accusers will affect the whole world. I caution you as the world's greatest military power to not be hasty in your responses but be wise in your actions. I will now receive any questions you may have but I must leave shortly to attend to an urgent family matter that I have back in New Jersey."

The preacher stood at the podium and waited for them, but there was silence in the room for several minutes. The expression on the faces of most attendees was one of bewilderment and on the remaining ones that of confusion. No questions were raised nor were there any hands motioning to be recognized. Dr. Devereaux was puzzled at the response and wondered whether he had frightened the illustrious body with his comments. So he asked a question of them.

"Have you understood what I was trying to tell you or did I totally confuse all of you?"

A burst of laughter rippled through the room loosening up the tension and finally a hand went up and was recognized.

"Reverend Devereaux I'm Senator Williams from Vermont. I don't think it's a matter of this body not understanding what you told us, but I believe my colleagues and I are just frozen by the enormity of the challenge that you have placed on us to make the right decision on how we respond to this international fiasco. If what you say is true, and I believe it is, then however we decide to respond may lead to bringing their war home to us in some form or fashion. What do you suggest we do?"

"Senator thank you for your comment and your question, but I am not a diplomat nor an elected official so I don't feel I am in a position to advise or suggest to you a course of action on the matter. What I will do with confidence is again point you to this book that I carry with me everywhere and tell you that this is my sword – called the Sword of the Spirit and say that whenever I have an important decision to make I let it be my guide. Open it, read it and then open your hearts to understand and receive its wisdom. Then you shall know collectively how to answer your own question. Gentlemen if there are no other questions, then I must leave you and head for the airport."

Reverend Devereaux left the room and was provided with a police escort in getting to the airport to catch his flight. Tango Hernandez who had been sitting in the room beside his director had listened intently to the preacher's remarks and finally concluded he had to now believe in all the things Ron Powers had been telling him were indeed true. He left the meeting thinking that whatever the outcome was going to be with the arrests of those at Canon and the Human Services organizations and perhaps other groups that he had yet to identify their complicity in the conspiracy, his ability to control it was not within his power. So he returned to his Washington office and placed a call to Mr. Powers.

#######

After identifying themselves as Joshua's parents and getting the room number from the nurses at the desk in ICU, Nate and Midge rushed to see their son. At the entrance to the room even in the subdued lighting they could see him along with two others in the large room connected to machines that were monitoring their very existence. The sounds of the equipment tracking their life signs sounded like a macabre symphony with rhythms that were steady but foreboding. Midge stopped at the doorway momentarily trying to prepare her mind for what seemed like the nexus to a horrific nightmare. Nate pausing with her was still having trouble accepting what his eyes were reporting to his brain.

Joshua was breathing through the ventilator in a steady pattern but his eyes were open as he stared blankly at the ceiling. His companions in the room were in the same condition and each of them appeared to have experienced the same trauma. The tears in Midge's eyes could no longer be contained as they burst forth and ran down her cheeks. Nate trying to maintain a manly composure wrapped his arms around her tightly but eventually he lost it also and let lose his own tears. The sight of their son lying there with only the technical service of these machines allowing him to cling to life was more than any normal parent could imagine as what even in their wildest nightmares would happen to their child.

Cautiously they both approached the bed not really knowing what they should do to offer comfort to their child. They knew that there was nothing medically they could offer nor was there any magical spell that she could conjure up to reverse this condition even with all her knowledge of the workings of the occult. So after just looking at him and sobbing for a minute she grabbed his hand and began to speak.

"Josh I believe you can hear me. This is mom and your father is here too. Wherever you are right now, I want you to find a way to return to us. We love you very much and pray for your safe return. I know you are a fighter and this is the fight of your life. Don't give up."

When she finished she looked at him to see whether there was any sign of change in his expression. There was none. He continued to stare at the ceiling with the blank expression and his machine assisted breathing continued at the regulated pace. The heart monitor continued its steady beeping and the tubes that ran through his body at certain points continued to administer the prescribed medication. Through teary eyes the couple looked at each other each one hoping for something from the other that would answer the question of what should we do now.

While they were pondering a nurse appeared at the door and whispered that the time for their visit needed to end. Midge grabbed Josh's hand one more time and squeezed gently before letting go and slowly walked out of the room beside Nate. At the doorway they both stopped and turned to look at the image of their son one more time.

Still seated in the waiting room Mimi and I anxiously waited for Midge and Nate to come back down so we could find out what was happening. When they did return we heard the sad report of what Josh was going through. Perhaps in another language I'm unfamiliar with there may be words that could adequately express the grief I felt at that moment, but right then as I searched my brain in my language nothing came to mind so I just hung my head and said nothing. Mimi reached out and embraced her sister as they both shed tears. While they hugged clinging to each other, I overheard her whisper "Where's daddy?" It was as if the two adult ladies had both returned to the days in their youth when if something went wrong they would just go to their father and he would miraculously make everything alright. Nate and I stood by helplessly watching the sisters but there was nothing either one of us could say or do to make things better.

The time was now 10:15 PM and we were all aware that "Doc" was coming but who knew when. There was no way to get an update on where he was or how soon he might arrive so we continued to huddle holding onto one another with the hope that our shared emotions might be comforting. The hands on the clock seemed to be frozen in place as we waited. Not only were we anticipating "Doc's" arrival, but as we sat there I believe each of us was hoping that at any moment a doctor, a nurse, an aide or some medical professional would walk in the room and announce some good news to all the waiting parents.

Around 11:30 as we sat alternately nodding off and waking up the anticipated moment arrived and "Doc" walked into the room. I don't remember who spotted him first but it was not long before all of us surrounded him. He looked a bit tired and drawn and later I understood that his initially scheduled flight had been held up for some time due to some weather conditions. Had it been someone other than him I think the combination of stressful situations would have pushed them over the edge. But since I had gotten to know him over the last few months I learned that he was truly a man of faith and nothing seemed to upset him.

After greeting all of us he turned especially back to Midge and said: "How's my grandson?" She tried as best she could to answer him but was too emotionally charged. He then turned to Nate expecting a reply. Whatever the relationship had been between them before tonight it was set aside and Nate gave the preacher all the details. When Nate finished "Doc" went over to the reception desk and asked where the chapel was. He returned gathered us together and led the way there. In a way it was strange, especially for me, because in all the time our group had been at the hospital none of us even asked where the chapel was and yet within a short time of his arrival we were all assembled in God's sanctuary.

The chapel was not very large, but made comfortable with soft lighting and cushioned pews in front of an altar beneath an elevated cross. "Doc" escorted us to the altar had us join hands and kneel as he began to pray.

"Heavenly Father, Almighty God, we come before you with bowed heads and humble hearts. Into your presence we come thanking you for all you have already done in our lives. Thank you for the blessings you've provided, thank you for the very air that we breathe and thank you for the privilege of being able to call upon you in times of need. As Jesus said in the Holy writ if we just call on you and ask anything in His name it shall be done. Well Lord we need you right now and I'm sending up this petition asking in the blessed name of Jesus that you hear this prayer.

These last and evil days, as the time draws near when you shall return your son Jesus to this world to right the wrongs, establish justice according to your righteousness, bind up the powers of darkness and instill truth in the heart of every man, we are seeing the doers of evil deeds inflict severe hurt on those who are innocent. We need you now Lord because there are several young men lying in this hospital right now who need your healing power. These young men who have fallen victim to the wiles of the one whom you have banished from your realm, need your mercy.

In times like these we stretch our hands to thee for we know there is no power greater that can heal and restore health and wholesomeness like you. We pray that you would dispatch your angel with healing hands that have been dipped in the blood of Jesus to touch all those who are in need. Touch and heal not only those here in this hospital, but those everywhere on this planet who likewise have fallen victim to the devil's deceit. And then Lord we pray you would open our eyes and help us to see Jesus. Open our eyes that we may see how to follow Him. Grant us your loving peace and make all dissension cease. Help us to daily make our faith increase as we learn to praise you and never cease.

Give us vision to see and realize it is you that has given us the hills and mountains; you that has given us the level planes. It is you that has given us our food and clothing; given us shelter from the storm and the rain. But even with all that you have provided we continue to war and hurt one another. O Lord on this day we pray that you would hasten the time when all shall be corrected and no longer will we call wrong - right and evil – good.

Father God listen to my cry, have mercy on these young men and heal them right now as we ask this blessing in the mighty and matchless name of Jesus the risen Christ. Amen."

When the preacher finished praying he got up and walked out with the rest of the group following close behind. Once outside the chapel he turned to Midge and said: "Now let's go see my grandson." He placed his arm around her and together they approached the elevators. Nate stayed behind with Mimi and me because we weren't sure whether or not all of us would be permitted to go up at the same time. Then he thought about it and said: "Let's try it and see what happens." We all agreed and caught the next elevator headed to the third floor. On the floor when we got off we didn't see Midge or "Doc", neither was there anyone at the reception desk so we moved on toward Josh's room.

Once we got there "Doc" and Midge were already at Josh's bedside. We stopped just inside the doorway but even from where we were we could see his condition appeared to be just as Nate described it earlier. The machine's monitoring lights were visible and we could hear the beeps on all three as they almost in synch continued their rhythmically steady pace. It was difficult to hear what the preacher was saying but looking at what was being done there was no need for conjecture. He placed his right hand on Josh's forehead closed his unseeing eyes and then held Midge's right hand with his left as she placed her other hand in Josh's. It looked like a master electrician completing an electrical power relay that made the loop an entirely closed circuit. As we stood there watching, although we couldn't hear it, we could feel the intensity of his prayer as if shock waves were emanating from his body.

But suddenly right in the middle of his supplication all the machines stopped working, the lights in the room went out and darkness hovered like a thick blanket. It was only a few seconds before the lights came back on, the machines restarted and normalcy seemed to have been restored. But things were far from normal. There was a distinct difference in the room. In the center right between "Doc" and Midge and where we were standing a light green mist started coming up through the floor. At first it appeared like a colored fog but as it continued to rise it began to congeal and form some kind of grotesque figure. Even though it was slightly more than translucent we could make out hands and arms a torso, legs and a head that was anything but human. On the end of the hands were long nails that looked more like claws and legs and feet that were severely deformed.

Once it reached its full height it moved quickly to where Josh was lying and reached out and grabbed "Doc" and Midge enveloping them in the mist. They both started choking as if there was no air inside the fog. Nate and I seeing what was happening started toward the thing to lend "Doc" a hand but after taking no more than two steps forward we were both repelled backward with a powerful force. When we tried again to move forward we ran into what seemed like an impenetrable wall that kept us in place. We could see everything but were helpless to do anything. As the fog thickened we could hear the pair gasping for air.

Suddenly from the other side of the room a great white light formed near the ceiling like a huge bubble and began floating toward the thing. Inside the bubble we could see the figure of a man clothed in an all-white robe like garment. We could see the eyes as they blazed like a raging fire and then we heard a voice coming from within that sounded like thunder as it resounded toward the thing. "How is it you are not afraid to put forth your hand to destroy the Lord's anointed?" it said. Then it engaged the thing head on and immediately "Doc" and Midge were thrown to the floor as the battle began. The room started shaking like a mighty earthquake or major volcano erupting and the tables and machines were tossed about like crumbs in front of a fan. The beds were moving around also but not turned over as the two entities fought a cosmic battle for supremacy. The brightness of the light bubble intensified so much that all we could picture was the light and we dared not look at it too long. All we could hear was the sound of thunder roaring as if the storm of the century was right here in this room.

It may have been minutes or it may have lasted an hour, I really don't remember, but when it ended the light dissipated and the thing was gone. "Doc" and Midge appeared to be fine and everything in the room looked like nothing had ever happened. The beds were back in place, all the equipment was where it was before and operating properly and the lighting was also just as it was. "Doc" and Midge appeared to be fine as Nate and I along with Mimi were finally able to go over to them. "Doc" just looked at us calmly and went back to laying hands on Josh. At that point I felt such a compelling urge to leave the room and go to the chapel it was as if something was calling me that I couldn't ignore so I excused myself and went.

Inside the chapel as I was drawn to the altar and began to genuflect I heard a voice speaking to me that seemed like it was coming from the cross.

"Ronald Powers hear my words and record all that I say for you will need to know them in the near future. What you have just witnessed is the beginning of what Reverend Devereaux has been preaching about. However what you saw was not the true beast but just one of his minions sent to do his bidding. The real battle that is yet to take place will commence at the return of Jesus and then all the world will bear witness to the final destruction of the true beast. The figure you saw in the light was the archangel Michael who is God's warrior.

The seven seals in the Book of Revelation that you have heard about are now being opened and the four horsemen spoken of in the first four seals are preparing to ride. As it has been told to you these have been named the four horsemen of the Apocalypse because of their influence on the end times. See now with your spiritual eyes as I show you what must take place over the next few years."

With that I looked up and on the wall behind the cross as if a movie projector had been turned on I could see the vision as he described it. I saw a large scroll and - as the first seal opened the first horse, a white horse, ridden by a man holding a bow and given a crown came riding out as a conqueror bent on conquest. His role is to create religious deception because when Jesus does come He will also be riding a white horse but He will be armed with a sword and wearing many crowns. Through this deception the laws of society will break down and lawlessness will abound. Violence will be rampant and terror will confront all the people.

Then the second seal opened and another horse came out. This one was a fiery red one and its rider was given power to take peace from the earth. The horse was the color of blood and I saw nation rising against nation as men became bent on destroying each other. Wars abound and rage ensues until massive armies assemble confront each other and unleash mass destruction.

Next the third seal opened and a black horse came out. Its rider was holding a pair of scales in his hand. This seal represents an imbalance in the cost of goods and services and an extreme scarcity of food and other bare necessities for life. Following major warfare scarcity of food and famine due to the disruption of the agricultural process is always the result.

The fourth seal was then opened and a sickly looking pale horse came out. Its rider was named Death and Hades (the grave) followed close behind him. This seal represented wide spread disease epidemics and pandemics again as the result of war and other violent conditions. This seal also represented earthquakes and other natural disasters that would contribute to the spread of pestilence.

The fifth seal representing religious persecution opened. This seal was for all those who were slain because of the word of God and the testimony they maintained. The vision showed that there would be a time, a period of great tribulation when the persecution of Christians and the church of God and all those who keep the Commandments would begin.

Then the sixth seal opened and I saw a great earthquake, the sun turned black like sackcloth made of goat hair, the moon turned blood red, and the stars in the sky fell to earth like figs dropping to the ground during a wind storm. Even the sky receded like a scroll rolling up and every mountain and island was moved from its place. With the opening of this seal a transition occurs from the Great Tribulation to a period of intensified punishments on all who remain unrepentant against the Creator.

Before the seventh seal opened the vision stopped and the wall went blank. I shuddered thinking that it may be withheld from me because it was too terrifying, but moments later while I was still focused the vision returned and the seventh seal opened. This was the final seal and when it was broken the entire scroll lay open. My vision had been interrupted because the opening of this seal represented a silence in heaven for the space of about half-hour. All creation was in awe by what was about to happen. The great and awesome "Day of the

Lord" the event angels have been anticipating for thousands of years had arrived.

At the opening of this seal I saw seven angels given seven trumpets and each one prepared to sound. The first angel sounded and hail and fire mixed with blood was thrown to the earth. Then a third of earth's trees were burned up along with all the green grass. Then the second angel sounded and something like a great burning mountain was thrown into the sea and a third of the sea turned to blood. One third of the creatures in the sea died and one third of the ships were destroyed. Then the third angel sounded and a great star burning like a torch fell from heaven on a third of the rivers and on the springs of water. I saw on the star a name that read "Wormwood" and a third of the waters became wormwood. After that the fourth trumpet sounded and a third of the sun, the moon and the stars was struck and a third of the day and the night ceased to shine. Then the fifth angel sounded and out of a bottomless pit up came locusts who were given power to torment all who did not have the seal of God on their foreheads. Those bitten would not die, even as they tried to, but they would be tormented for five months. Next the sixth angel sounded and I heard a voice saying:" Release the four angels which are bound at the great river Euphrates." And so the four angels who had been prepared for this very hour, day, month and year were released to kill a third of all mankind. Finally the seventh angel sounded and I heard loud voices coming from heaven saying; "The kingdoms of this world have become the kingdoms of our Lord and of His Christ and He shall reign forever and ever."

Then the wall went blank again and I heard the voice that summoned me before say:

What you have just seen are things which must come to pass if mankind does not change his ways. As a witness you are now being called upon to tell the world. In the past it was told to you that this day would be coming and for such a time as now you have been prepared. Set all that you have seen and heard down in a book and tell it to all that you may encounter. To aide you in your task a new blessing has been set-aside for you. Inside the clock that was handed down to you as an inheritance is a map folded up and taped to the bottom. This clock that belonged to your maternal ancestor Sulia, who was the slave consort of a master who loved her, was meant for you. The map will direct you to a tree behind the house of Marilyn Devereaux, Marsha's sister. Sulia lived in the house many years ago and a portion of her spirit is with you that is why you seemed to know the place. At the base of the tree you will find an arrow pointing to a spot where you should dig. Below the ground at that spot is hidden a steel box that contains thirty $20 gold pieces that were given to Sulia by her master. Tell Marilyn the story, she will understand then find the box and share the treasure with her. Use your portion to publish and distribute the book to the world. Go now and fulfill your destiny."

When the voice finished, my head was spinning from all that I had just heard and seen earlier. I got up reeling at first as though I had been drinking, but managed to steady myself turn around and head for the exit. As if I had not been through enough for the day when I looked at the doorway there was my old friend, the strange man standing there. He beckoned me to him as he usually did, but by now I was no longer apprehensive. When I got close he presented me with a small box and said: "You have been asking me my name and now I will tell you. I am Gabriel and I am here for you always. Although you will not see me again, my spirit is with you. In this box is a vial containing the antidote to "Candoo". Give it to the one who will soon be called Doctor Robinson. She will know what to do with it."

After he handed the box to me he turned around and walked, no he didn't walk he seemed to glide away and I stood there watching him. He was still in plain sight until he reached the end of the corridor and turned right. This time I didn't chase after him to see where he would go because I knew that when I got there he would be gone. With the box in hand and real hope now in my heart and my mind I started walking slowly down the hall.

As I walked the images I had seen would be forever etched in my brain. After witnessing the most awesome display of supernatural power I have ever seen in my life, I pondered whether this was truly the beginning of the end. I reached the end of the hall thinking about what was said to me about having been prepared for a task and there was more for me to do in this life before it would be over. Then the words echoed over again in my mind about what the preacher had said in his sermon series. As I reminisced I could hear just outside the first of several loud claps of thunder followed immediately by the downpour of rain as it smashed against the building.

For six thousand years man has walked this earth breaking God's laws and disobeying the commandments given him as prime instructions for abundant life. Even though the prophets, messengers, disciples and ultimately a Savior were sent to shed light on the prime-evil darkness, man has succumbed to the persuasive powers of the one who created sin from the beginning. Over the thousands of years man has pushed steadily toward the brink of self-destruction and now that the capability has been achieved and the weapons for total annihilation are a reality, the time is at hand when an intervention is needed.

From the time that God created man in his own image and placed him in a garden paradise that was intended for him to thrive and rule, he fell short of His glory. The increasing irreverence has created a condition that unless remedied and corrected will result in the end of God's creation. Man by his own destructive instruments will cease to exist, but God in His infinite wisdom has a master plan.

The demonstration I saw tonight has opened my eyes and I must try to open the eyes of all whom I meet. The time left is relatively short before the world we see now will cease to be as it is. In the vision that I saw in the chapel when the seventh seal opened it said that the kingdoms of this world have become the kingdoms of Our Lord and His Christ. Now it is finally clear to me what that really meant. The heavens above are not the place where El Shaddai (God Almighty) will correct the evils let loose and run amuck on this world. No, not in the heavens but as it is revealed in the Book Of Revelation this world, our world, will be changed and out of all the other creations in the Solar System of this Galaxy, God has chosen to make this earth His

- **KINGDOM PLANET**

Then I opened the exit door and stepped out into the rain.

www.ingramcontent.com/pod-product-compliance
Lightning Source LLC
Chambersburg PA
CBHW070611310726
48982CB00001B/47

* 9 7 8 1 9 3 5 0 7 9 0 3 3 *